The Crimson Bloom

Book Three of the Georgia Gold Series

Denise Weimer

The Crimson Bloom

Book Three of the Georgia Gold Series

Denise Weimer

Canterbury House Publishing

www. canterburyhousepublishing. com
Vilas, North Carolina

Canterbury House Publishing

www. canterburyhousepublishing. com

Copyright © 2014 Denise Weimer
All rights reserved under International and Pan-American Copyright Conventions.

Book Design by Tracy Arendt
Cover Art by John Kollock

Library of Congress Cataloging-in-Publication Data

Weimer, Denise.
The crimson bloom : third novel of the Georgia gold series / by Denise
Weimer.
    pages cm. -- (The Georgia gold series; bk. 3)
  ISBN 978-0-9881897-4-4 (print) -- ISBN 978-0-9881897-7-5 (e-book) 1.
Female friendship--Fiction. 2. Families--Georgia--Fiction. 3. United
States--History--Civil War, 1861-1865--Fiction. I. Title.
  PS3623.E4323C75 2014
  813'.6--dc23

2013044922

First Edition: April 2014

AUTHOR'S NOTE:
This is a work of fiction. Names characters, places and incidents are either the
product of the author's imagination or are used fictitiously, and any resemblance
to actual persons living or dead, business establishments, events, or locales is
entirely coincidental.

For information about permission to reproduce selections from this book write to:
Permissions
Canterbury House Publishing, Ltd.
225 Ira Harmon Rd.
Vilas, NC 28692

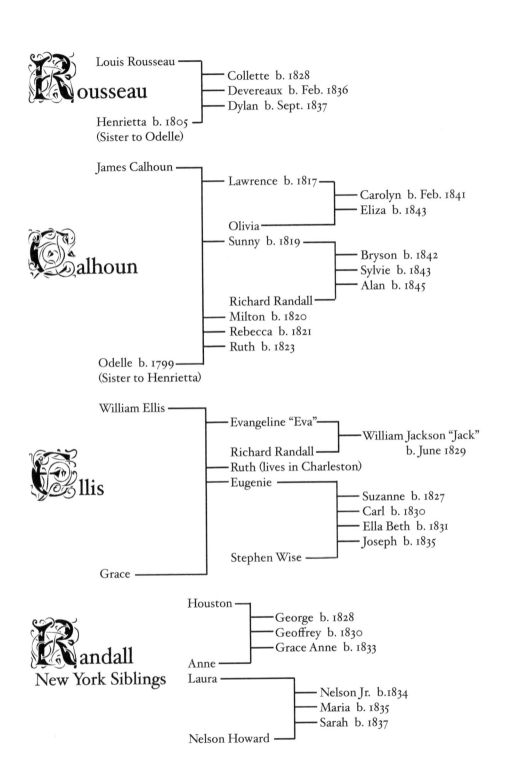

Rousseau

Louis Rousseau ─┐
├─ Collette b. 1828
├─ Devereaux b. Feb. 1836
├─ Dylan b. Sept. 1837

Henrietta b. 1805 ─┘
(Sister to Odelle)

Calhoun

James Calhoun ─┐
├─ Lawrence b. 1817 ─┐
│ ├─ Carolyn b. Feb. 1841
│ └─ Eliza b. 1843
│ Olivia ─┘
├─ Sunny b. 1819 ─┐
│ ├─ Bryson b. 1842
│ ├─ Sylvie b. 1843
│ └─ Alan b. 1845
│ Richard Randall ─┘
├─ Milton b. 1820
├─ Rebecca b. 1821
└─ Ruth b. 1823

Odelle b. 1799 ─┘
(Sister to Henrietta)

Ellis

William Ellis ─┐
├─ Evangeline "Eva" ─┐
│ ├─ William Jackson "Jack"
│ │   b. June 1829
│ Richard Randall ─┘
├─ Ruth (lives in Charleston)
├─ Eugenie ─┐
│ ├─ Suzanne b. 1827
│ ├─ Carl b. 1830
│ ├─ Ella Beth b. 1831
│ └─ Joseph b. 1835
│ Stephen Wise ─┘
Grace ─┘

Randall
New York Siblings

Houston ─┐
├─ George b. 1828
├─ Geoffrey b. 1830
└─ Grace Anne b. 1833

Anne ─┘
Laura ─┐
├─ Nelson Jr. b.1834
├─ Maria b. 1835
└─ Sarah b. 1837

Nelson Howard ─┘

FOREWORD

My personal trip back to Habersham County of the mid-1800s started with a private tour of a summer home of that period, perfectly preserved in every detail, and with the letters and diaries of that family. To the gentleman who offered this glimpse into his ancestors' lives – and who also lent me my initial stack of books and the skill of his historical editing – I owe boundless thanks. Thank you, Mr. John Kollock.

Mr. Kollock's cover artwork for Book Three of The Georgia Gold Series depicts an aerial view of Factor's Row and the Savannah River in Savannah, Georgia, during the Civil War years.

Most of the places, people and events in *The Crimson Bloom* actually existed – apart from the main characters, of course. I sought to drop my characters into a very realistic time and place. You met Mahala, Jack, Carolyn, Dev and Dylan in Book One, *Sautee Shadows*, set during the Georgia Gold Rush and the Cherokee Removal. You followed them as their stories united in love, friendship and competition – but as the nation splintered – in *The Gray Divide*. Now, I hope you enjoy their exciting journey in *The Crimson Bloom*. Their saga will conclude in the final novel of The Georgia Gold Series, *Bright as Gold*.

CHAPTER ONE

April 10, 1862
Chatham County, Georgia

On a Friday morning, Dylan Rousseau stood outside his parsonage in the faint light of dawn. He directed his gaze toward the cold, clear sky arching above his parish. There was not a cloud in sight. And yet, the distant booming that he had first noticed yesterday from the direction of the city of Savannah, and that had prevented all but the most fitful of sleep last night, persisted. His breath puffed in the frosty air as he expelled it in a painful sigh. It could only mean one thing. Fort Pulaski was under bombardment.

He turned on his heel and re-entered his small home, the place that had been his retreat from the world. Here, among an elderly, peace-loving congregation, he had hidden for the past several years. Hidden from so many things, and for far too long. He could no longer hide from himself, or from the sin that stained even a minister's well-meaning heart.

Dylan packed a few personal effects into his cloth duffel: under-things, plain shirts, an extra pair of shoes. He wouldn't need much where he was headed. In search of his Bible, he strode into his study. There, the book lay beside his brother's most recent letter, which for the hundredth time had begged Dylan to serve as chaplain to the Oglethorpe Light Infantry of the 8th Georgia Regiment in the South's struggle for independence from the North. Between sickness among the troops and the battle last year at Manassas, Devereaux's men needed fresh recruits. Action was expected any day. A group of volunteers was set to leave next week. Would Dylan be among them?

Dylan groaned. There was every logical reason for him to refuse, starting with the fact that his faith did not dovetail with fighting for a cause that protected the institution of slavery. When he'd gone to Princeton Seminary, he'd walked away from the empire his family had built on that evil practice. As the eldest, it was Dev who would inherit The Marshes, the Rousseau rice plantation. Also unlike Dev, who was a graduate of Virginia Military Institute and now captain of a unit which had already distinguished itself in battle, Dylan was not a soldier. He had no military training. He didn't even like to hunt. Dev's letter had described the lean rations, the ruined farmland. He'd painted a picture sure to be at odds with everything Dylan had ever known. But he'd asked for his brother's help, in person during his last visit in February, and again in this letter. And that was something Devereaux never did. There had been something honest and raw in his plea. And now, with the family in Savannah in danger, Dylan could no longer ignore it. As he locked up his house, he trusted whatever he left behind would be sent to his parents' town residence in Savannah, but if not, it was of little import. With one last look at the white-washed Presbyterian church he'd overseen, Dylan turned his mount away.

Dressed in the clothes of the low country gentleman as which he'd been raised, Dylan tried to reassure himself as his horse took the familiar road to Savannah. Military experts considered Fort Pulaski to be invincible. Surrounded by the Savannah River and swampy marshes, its brick walls were seven and a half feet thick and backed by massive masonry piers. The nearest firm land for erecting batteries was on Tybee Island, over a mile away. Firing above 700 yards, smoothbore guns and mortars would never breach Confederate-held walls. Doubtless the foolish Yankee commander had merely been under pressure for some action when he undertook the pointless bombardment.

Another reason for fear niggled in his chest ... something more sinister than deprivation and combat, or again being in the shadow of his charismatic older brother. It was the thought of once again seeing Dev's wife, Carolyn.

Memories of the weeks following their last meeting assailed him with gut-wrenching nausea. He'd spent hours pouring out his guilt to the Lord. Finally, he'd believed God had forgiven his covetousness. But when he faced her mere hours from now, would he be able to look upon her as a sister-in-law, or would the sight of her sweet face and petite form once again prove his undoing?

She was why he had to go, even more than the questions civilians now raised about a young man out of uniform or the spiritual needs in the army. It should no longer matter that Dev had stolen what he'd wanted. Carolyn had married Devereaux, not Dylan. Dev's relationship with Carolyn had been rocky at first, it was true, but in recent months as it became clear the two were making progress towards a real union, Dylan's jealousy had crawled out of the hole in his soul like an ugly, greedy serpent. Making things right with Dev was the only way he knew to make amends. If he didn't try, his internal landscape would be stripped barer than Virginia's.

When he reached Oglethorpe Square it was around noon. Still immaculate, the beautiful town house's gate opened onto the sandy street. Dylan's small, dark-haired mother came running out to meet him.

"Oh, Dylan, what's going on? Do you know what's going on?"

He swung a leg off his stallion and gave the reins to the groom. Trying to be patient, he replied, "I know no more than you, Mother. Probably less, as I've just arrived in town." Dylan tugged his duffel out of his saddle bag and slung it over his back.

As a loud "boom" rattled the windows of the house, Henrietta moved as if to dodge an incoming shell. Dylan smiled and took her arm. "Come inside, Mother."

"Do you think you could ride out and see what's happening?" she persisted as she allowed him to lead her up the steps.

"You know Pulaski is above ten miles away, and the Yankees command both shores of the river all the way up to Venus Point. It will take a little while for news to trickle in."

"Yes, yes, we've been waiting and waiting. The bombardment shouldn't be going on this long! Oh, my nerves are like glass. One more boom, and I fear they will shatter."

"Calm yourself, Mother. Haven't you been the one who has always told *me* Pulaski will never fall?" Dylan put his arm around her as he escorted her inside and closed the door.

"Yes, but Dylan, we had to admit it was possible when the Yankees cut off all supplies and communication to our poor boys out there. We knew they had enough food to last until late summer. I guess we were hoping some miracle could occur," she said, wringing her hands. "But this we didn't expect: they say the Yankees are using *rifled guns*! Rifled guns! What if they prove capable of breaching the fort?"

Dylan patted her hand. "In a little while, I'll saddle a fresh mount and take it to the newspaper office. Where's Father?"

"I'm here, Son," boomed Louis, emerging from his study. Dylan guessed he might have been hiding there from his wife's hysterics. "Did you come because you thought I needed some help handling these Rousseau women?" The portly man grinned at his own mirth.

"I know you can handle things, but I admit I was worried. So I came on early."

"Early?" questioned a soft voice from the stairway.

Dev turned to see Carolyn on the landing. She was as beautiful as ever, and just as unaware of it. She had never fully gotten past the image of herself as a plump, awkward youth, even though every woman in Savannah now envied her quiet poise, her petite but lithe figure, and her brilliant marriage into one of the wealthiest rice dynasties along the coast. His heart stopped, then started again. There was a rush of gratefulness that he could now look her in the eye. If she had realized how close he'd come during his last visit to revealing his feelings for her, she'd never give any indication now. She was, after all, well-practiced in treating him as a friend, then a brother … ever since the day he'd come to her rescue at Madame Granet's dancing school. He had once thought she might feel more for him. But that was a long time ago, and quite possibly a product of wishful thinking.

"Yes. Early." Dylan glanced at his mother. He hadn't wanted to tell them of his enlistment the minute he walked in the door. Maybe he could at least get them to the parlor. "Can we sit down?"

"Of course, dear." Henrietta took his arm and looked up at him with concern. Louis and Carolyn followed them into the adjoining room, where they all settled onto chairs.

"What is it, Dylan?" Carolyn asked.

Dylan rested a hand on each knee. His voice was soft but unhesitating. "I'm joining up."

"What?" Henrietta cried.

"Son, the men in the fort are cut off. There's nothing you can do to help them, if that's what you're thinking," Louis put in.

"No, Father, that's not what I'm thinking. Nor do I intend to join the coastal militia. Devereaux informed me a set of fresh recruits for the 8th will be leaving in a few days. I aim to be with them."

"Are you sure, Dylan?" Carolyn asked, trying to suppress her pleasure. For a long time now she'd wanted to see him working among the enlisted men. And Dylan guessed a large part of that was her desire for reconciliation between him and Dev.

"Quite sure."

"What … changed your mind?"

He turned to look at her. The regret and yearning were still there, yes, but they no longer pierced him through like an arrow. It was bearable. "Dev's request just wouldn't let me go," he said simply. In response, she smiled a slow, grateful smile. He smiled back.

"This is good, Son," Louis declared. "We fear to have you in danger, but this decision – you can be proud of it."

"But he needs a uniform!" Henrietta declared. "And right away!"

Dylan shook his head, not wanting to add to her anxiety, but Henrietta cut in, "You can't go join the Rebel Army looking like *that*. They'll hang you for a spy!"

Louis laughed. "She has a point."

Carolyn said, "Didn't we have some material left over from making Dev's uniform?" She put her hand on Henrietta's arm. "And you made two of them. Between us maybe we put aside enough fabric for a whole suit."

12

After a brief lunch, the women and their maids set up in the parlor. Measuring tapes flew and scissors snipped while Dylan and Louis read the newspaper, Dylan often standing for fitting purposes. Henrietta was pinning the lining of the jacket around his chest when suddenly the cannonade ceased. Louis put down his paper, Carolyn her needle. Henrietta stared at him. They waited in silence, but the bombardment did not resume.

Finally, Carolyn whispered, "Is it over?"

"Did they give up?" Louis wondered aloud.

"What will we do if the Yankees have won?" Henrietta cried.

Dylan wasn't sure why they all seemed to be expecting *him* to answer. But to his own surprise, he did. "If they have, I think you would be safer at Forests of Green."

"My thoughts exactly." Louis laid his paper on the end table.

His voice sounded loud in the stillness and Henrietta started, shifting to face him. "But Louis, I thought we had talked about the three of us going down to Brightwell. After all, it's the logical choice to be with my sister and Carolyn's parents."

With Federal gunboats patrolling both Ossabaw and Warsaw Sounds Louis had decided that putting in a rice crop on Harveys Island was imprudent, to say the least. At the end of the year previous he had sent their carriages, horses and valuables to Forests of Green, the family's upland farm in the foothills near Clarkesville, and the majority of the field hands to Brightwell, Carolyn's Calhoun family plantation, in Liberty County. Louis had expressed the desire to soon follow and provide whatever aid he could to Carolyn's father, Lawrence. Carolyn's father's health had finally stabilized following an extended bout with scarlet fever, though her grandfather had passed away the year previous. But with the added slaves to feed, the honorable thing to do would be to lend a hand at Brightwell.

"We talked about it, yes, but that was before the Yankee horde succeeded in knocking down our front door!"

"But Louis, Brightwell must be productive if we expect the field hands we sent there to eat!"

"I know that, my dear. And I still will go. This whole situation is dratted inconvenient, but the truth is, I'd feel a lot better with you ladies far from the coast. We never know when and where the Yankees might land."

"Clarkesville?" Henrietta asked faintly.

"Yes. I don't like it, but it's for the best."

"But for how long?" Henrietta demanded, looking close to tears. "We cannot accept an indefinite separation."

"I will rejoin you in Habersham County as soon as most of the crop is in," Louis answered. "And I'd like to send written instructions with you to my foreman at Forests of Green. Our government has urged us to plant more subsistence crops, less cotton and rice, and that's exactly what I'd like him to do – put in more corn, more wheat. More vegetables. We must grow what we need to survive."

Dylan saw his mother's lip tremble as she unpinned the lining on his chest. He caught her hand and pressed it. "Father's words may sound ominous," he softened his tone, "but he only means to take every precaution to assure your safety and comfort. Everything will be all right."

"Will it?" She blinked back tears. "It feels to me like everything is falling down around our ears. You going into the army. Fort Pulaski under attack – probably surrendered. And being sent away from my husband."

"Do you need to go lie down, my dear?" Louis inquired.

She pulled back from Dylan and shook her head. "No – no, I have to make this uniform. I'll have my son go off to Virginia looking like a gentleman and a soldier, and no less."

Louis smiled proudly at her. In the moments that mattered, his wife was capable of rising above anxiety's control.

As Henrietta dabbed her eyes with Dylan's handkerchief, Carolyn ventured a question. "If we are unsafe at Brightwell, what of my mother? And my grandmother? Should they not accompany us to the mountains?"

"An excellent idea, Carolyn," Louis agreed. "I'll recommend that to them. You are a married lady, so you may of course choose where you wish to stay. It is my strong hope, however, that even if they decline, you would still accompany your mother-in-law to Forests of Green."

"Of course I will. Forests of Green is home now."

Dylan knew Carolyn loved the peaceful upland farm more than any other place on earth, partly because her closest friend, Mahala Franklin, helped her grandmother run a hotel in the nearby town of Clarkesville. But getting there entailed two to three days of travel, and that raised another concern. "The more people in your party, the safer your travels will be," Dylan suggested. "What of asking the Randalls if they might also be bound inland?"

His mother's face lit up. Her niece, Sunny, was the widow of Richard Randall, whose son from his first marriage, Jack, now ran the Randall and Ellis shipping firm as a private blockade-running operation. While Henrietta and many others thought less of Jack for not enlisting or at least aligning his firm with the Confederacy, she did have a soft spot for Sunny and her daughter, Sylvie. "An excellent idea! I shall invite them to tea tomorrow."

Dylan wondered why Carolyn looked faintly displeased.

Later that evening, he rode out in search of news. What he learned confirmed their worst fears. The northern scarp of Pulaski had been destroyed, the inside of the fort laid bare to the enemy. With projectiles threatening the magazine, twenty-five-year-old Confederate Colonel Olmstead had been forced to make a difficult decision – perhaps not difficult where logic was concerned, but because he would know well what the people of Savannah expected. Yet, to their great chagrin, he had lowered the Stars and Bars and raised a white sheet. Tonight the militia surrendered. Tomorrow the Stars and Stripes would again fly over Cockspur Island.

It was early May, time for Mahala Franklin to begin thinking of ending her visit in the beautiful Sautee Valley. Even though her home was now a county away in Clarkesville with her white grandmother, the spring visits Martha Franklin had first permitted to the adoptive farm family from whom she had taken Mahala as a youth remained an integral part of Mahala's life. She loved spending time with Ben and Nancy Emmitt and their grown sons who now had farms of their own, including the youngest, Jacob, who farmed the land Mahala's father had left to her in his will. She had nothing but good memories of the time before she had been Mahala Franklin, proper heiress of the owner of The Franklin Hotel. When she had merely been Mahala Emmitt, a half-Cherokee orphan whose mother had died in childbirth and whose father had been mysteriously murdered for his gold, now missing. Mahala had even heard that the threat of coastal invasion had brought many Savannah residents to the mountains, her best friend Carolyn Calhoun Rousseau among them. She was eager to see Carolyn again. But something held her back. It was a change she sensed in her Cherokee grandfather.

Henry Cornsilk, who now lived with Jacob on Mahala's land adjoining the Emmitt farm, had always loved to recount the days of his youth and spin the yarns of his people. But this spring, even in the midst of doing so, his mind wandered. In the middle of a conversation, he would suddenly gaze absently at dogwoods or azaleas in bloom, or at the chinked log walls of his cabin. Mahala wondered if in his mind's eye he might be seeing his wife Sally and daughter Kawani, and maybe even the sons who now lived in the West. She didn't like it when he left her that way. She didn't like the way he left the land that had once comforted and connected him.

In an effort to maintain contact, she spent long hours at his side, either while she did chores or simply sitting, perhaps holding his tough, wrinkled hand. She asked many questions, hoping that giving the answers would keep his mind sharp.

One evening as they sat on a bench outside the cabin watching the moon rise, she inquired, "Have you heard about the pikes Mr. Edwin Williams is making for the Confederacy, Grandfather?"

"No, tell me, my dear."

"Well, he's gotten a contract with Governor Brown to manufacture a bunch of them in his blacksmith shop and deliver them to troops on the coast, I think in case of a cavalry charge. Apparently there's a shortage of arms."

"Pikes." Henry laughed quietly.

"Yes. I'm sure the Yankees will be in terror of *that*."

Henry guffawed gently, then abruptly changed the subject as he was now wont to do. "That boy," he said. "He does not do so well, does he?"

He couldn't be speaking of Jack Randall, of whom she had just been thinking, considering how much the soldiers in Savannah must need him to run in guns on his ships. She and Jack had been competitors for years, ever since the charismatic entrepreneur had purchased The Palace Hotel and opened it to the coastal wealthy who summered in Habersham County. But only since Jack had turned his family's shipping firm into Georgia's premiere blockade running enterprise had their barbed flirtations become a much more transparent correspondence. As usual, her mind was frequently on Jack. She quickly shifted her mental focus. "Clay?" Mahala questioned. "What makes you say that?"

"You do not tell me of him. Has he stopped writing you?"

"It's been a while…"

"And his last letter, did you read it to me?"

"Well … I don't think so," she hedged.

"It was not good?"

Mahala laughed and jostled Henry's arm. "How do you know everything?" she asked in loving exasperation. He merely smiled calmly. She would try to keep her answer as simple as possible, to avoid him probing into the further splintering of the Cherokee Nation and becoming upset. She said, "You're right. There were more desertions. Some of his fellow soldiers really disappointed him."

"I'm sorry. He's a good boy. You still care for him, Mahala?"

Mahala's face softened as she considered her long history with Clay, longer than her history with Jack, in fact. They had met as children in the store Clay Fraser's adoptive parents owned. Growing up, she had taught him to read and write in their native language. She'd looked on him as an older brother, but he had always wanted more. Eventually her refusal of his marriage proposal had driven him west, where he now served among what was left of Drew's Confederate Cherokees. "I do have a tender spot for him."

"And the man – Jack?"

Mahala smirked. "I think it's a tough spot where he's concerned."

Henry chuckled. Then he told her, "Do not settle for less than the best, Mahala. They may both have their strengths, but you must find what is best for *you*. Do not grow impatient. The best is worth waiting for."

"Until I'm gnarled and silver-haired?"

"No, my Mahala," Henry said affectionately, turning her chin toward him and patting it gently. "You will be as your mother would have been – still looking like thirty summers at fifty. But I do so wish I had more to leave to you."

"Leave me? Where are you going?"

"Pawsh, child. We both know I am old. You are the only thing keeping me here. I have thought often about your father's gold. I never felt settled about it. Lately I have wondered if perhaps he buried it."

"But where, *Ududu*?" Mahala asked, trying to push away the alarm that had risen in her at Henry's words. "And how could we ever know? It could be in any of a hundred places, even if that were the case."

Henry nodded slowly. He sighed. "Ah, that's true. You should keep your eyes and ears open, though, Mahala. Old secrets have a way of telling themselves years later."

"All right, *Ududu*," she said, mainly to appease him. Over the past couple of years she had decided the mystery of her father's gold – more than $5,000 worth, according to the receipts left in his strongbox – and his murder – would never be solved. She had investigated herself as much as she could, ruling out the man who'd owned the land where Michael had mined most of his gold before buying the property on which they now sat. Rex Clarke had been a drunk and a womanizer who'd almost forced his lecherous designs on Mahala, an attempt that had exiled the lawyer from Clarkesville, but he was not a murderer. The testimony of the sister of the woman with whom Rex had spent that fateful night in 1838 had clarified that. It was commonly believed now that Michael's killer had been a drifter angry at Michael's refusal to take on a gold mining partner.

Mahala kissed the leathery, familiar cheek as her grandfather rose to go into bed. He squeezed her hand and gave her a special smile.

"Remember the time I first saw you?" Henry asked, patting her cheek. "You were scared of me."

"Because you were wrapped in a bear skin and straight from hiding in the mountains!"

"Yes, that was in the days following the Cherokee round-up. But I came back for you."

"You've been here ever since," Mahala said gratefully.

"I loved you from the moment I saw those amazing blue eyes peeking at me from behind your mother's skirt. I love you now, more than ever, Mahala. I always will." He smoothed back a strand of Mahala's black hair.

"I know, Grandfather. I love you, too."

After he went inside, Mahala sat back down. She remained a moment, trying to shake the heavy feeling in her heart. The form of her adoptive brother Jacob appeared in the doorway.

"Shall I walk you home, Mahala?"

She picked up her bonnet. "No, I'll be fine. Plenty of light tonight."

Jacob frowned. "Enough for roving vagabonds to spot a pretty girl alone on the road."

"Oh, Jacob."

"At least let me walk you to the property line."

"All right, then."

As they set out the cool damp of spring and the smell of freshly turned earth filled the air. Mahala could hear the gurgling of Sautee Creek. But she sensed Jacob did not share her appreciation of the surroundings tonight.

"Sam 'n' Seth were talkin' about rumors that Sumner Smith might be getting up a regiment in these parts," he said.

"Oh, Jacob, they don't think to go, do they?"

He lifted one broad shoulder. "Nobody thought we'd still be fighting this long," was all he said. It was true. When the war with the Yankees had started in 1861, many people had prophesied that it would be a short war. The newly formed Confederate States had licked the Union soldiers at the Battle of First Manassas in Virginia that summer, but the Yankees had kept coming back. And back. They had so many more men.

"But they have young families – farms!" Mahala protested of her other brothers. "What would the wives do come harvest time?"

"Same as all the other wives, I guess. Harvest it themselves. Hire help if they could."

"You say that so coldly!" Mahala cried.

"It ain't cold, Mahala. I'm thinking of all the men dyin' while I'm not doing my part."

"*All* of you? Go off together?"

"Maybe. I'd be awful sorry about leavin' your land lie, Mahala, but you have plenty in your account to pay for help this fall. You'd come out o.k. – maybe not quite so good, but not in the hole, either. We need to talk about Henry. I think Ma would take him in. I think he'd be happier there than at the hotel, much as he loves you. He just gets kinda confused these days."

Mahala nodded and wiped a stray tear from the corner of one eye.

Jacob touched her arm. "Hey, I'm not saying it's for sure. Don't cry. I just thought I should let you know we're considering it – enlisting. We'll talk again."

"Yes. We'll talk again."

She walked the rest of the way alone, her eyes on the light Nancy had left burning for her. If only the road of life was that simple. But then it was, Henry would say. It didn't feel that simple right now.

Inside the two-story, clapboard-covered log house, her adoptive parents were fast asleep. They didn't even stir at the creak her foot made on the stairs. Mahala went to bed but slept fitfully, unexplained heaviness still on her chest.

The next morning she slept late and had just come down to breakfast when the door burst open. Jacob rushed into the room where the three of them were gathered over eggs and biscuits with gravy. Their conversation came to an abrupt halt at the sight of his face. Under his rumpled dark hair, it looked as white as a sheet.

"Henry – he's dead!" he blurted. "He died in his sleep."

Then Jacob covered his face and sobbed.

Carolyn surveyed the kitchen garden at Forests of Green with a swell of satisfaction. The planting was done. As Louis had directed, they had sown more of each vegetable than the year before. The neat red furrows before her were now germinating beans, tomatoes, squash, cucumbers, radishes and pumpkins. She shook out the last of the water in her can and – with a glance at the orchards and the expanded corn field spreading out to the woods – went back to the well to draw up more water.

She found she loved this type of work – the way the hours passed and the satisfaction of accomplishment at the end of the day. Staying busy also kept her from missing Mahala's company quite so much. Carolyn had never been in Habersham when her closest friend wasn't around.

She had just gotten the bucket up when she heard the rattle of carriage wheels. Her initial suspicion of who might be coming made her stiffen. She was right. It was Cousin Sylvie Randall – again.

Splashing water on her bodice in her haste, Carolyn refilled her watering can and lugged it with a fast, lopsided hobble back to the garden – and out of view of the front drive. She watered very, very slowly. Maybe Henrietta would do the honors today and leave her be. After all, Sylvie came practically every day now. And Carolyn didn't mean to be ungracious … she just didn't think she could abide the girl's litany of complaints this morning.

"Whatever does one *do* in these parts?" Sylvie had asked her first day in Habersham.

"One generally enjoys the peace and quiet," Carolyn had replied. "We spend a lot of time outdoors. When we want to go somewhere, there are numerous excursions to choose from to the mountains and waterfalls."

"Sweat and aching muscles? No, thanks. Don't you have parties?"

"We used to, when the men were around. It's not the same without them."

"How about a benefit?" Sylvie had suggested with sparkling eyes. "A tableaux or a bazaar?"

Everyone had agreed it was a nice idea, but no one had volunteered to hostess and organize it. That was probably due to the fact that most locals viewed Sylvie Randall as spoiled and selfish. Jack's integrity in business had won him many friends in the area, but even his good reputation couldn't cover his young half-sister's insensitivity during a time when most people were undergoing great hardship. And even many who had liked Jack as a hotel owner weren't so fond of him as a blockade runner. Not when their own local boys were shipping off to the killing fields by the hundreds. In fact, Sylvie's latest endeavors centered upon Charles Phillips' regiment, which in March had been camped on a hill outside Clarkesville and trained in the bean pasture just north of the Soquee River bridge. From there they'd been mustered into service at Camp McDonald in Big Shanty, Georgia. Since these boys were probably getting homesick and would soon be in need of supplies, Sylvie was convinced that a benefit for them was just the thing, and she was still looking for recruits to help her carry it off. Carolyn couldn't help thinking she'd rather just donate the money.

The next moment Henrietta came out the side door flapping a white piece of paper and calling Carolyn's name. Oh, dear. "You must come in! You'll never guess what Miss Randall has brought us! A letter from Dylan!"

Carolyn's interest rose, but she protested, "I'm not dressed for company."

"Oh, who cares? Come on. I can't wait another minute. We're going to read it aloud."

Carolyn obliged. Her anxious mother-in-law shooed her into the parlor, where Cousin Sylvie sat in a pink and white striped dress, nibbling a scone.

"Oh, my," the lovely blonde girl murmured in a tone of muted shock upon sight of Carolyn's untidy hair and clay-stained skirt. "You look like a native."

"Hopefully I shall learn to survive like one," Carolyn replied, wanting to add that they hadn't a blockade runner heading up their family, but rather two brothers in the army whose father was unable to produce rice under the looming guns of Yankee steamers. She held her tongue, though, remembering that this month Sylvie's younger brothers were being ushered into the army as part of the Savannah Cadets. She would soon enough experience her share of worry, too.

"Sit down, sit down," Henrietta urged.

Carolyn was surprised that she was going to share Dylan's letter with Sylvie present. What if it contained private thoughts? But Carolyn, too, was curious about what he had written – anxious most of all for news of her husband's safety – so she again remained silent.

"All right, let's see here," Henrietta began. "He arrived safely to Meadow Bridges, Virginia, near the Chickahominy River. They were drilled in proper use and care of their weapons and on army procedures while waiting for the 8th to come up the Peninsula. The 8th had been fighting near Yorktown, he says. 'Apparently it was a long and hard siege,'" Henrietta read, "'for when I finally saw the OLI I was in shock. No longer the dapper youths of Savannah, these were gaunt, battle-hardened men, covered in mud and soaked to the skin. I found Devereaux well but very sober. He told me they had driven back the Yankees in the Battle of Dam #1 but then to hold their front line they had been forced to squat for eighteen sordid days in two-and-a-half-foot deep trenches fifteen or so inches high with water. Any man who so much as raised his head was instantly picked off by Union sharpshooters in the trees of the swamp facing them. The Oglethorpes were cautious and did not fare so bad on this score, but several men of other companies lost fingers and lives. Hamilton Branch did get shot in the hand while bringing in supplies. He's been furloughed home.

"'When at last they were allowed to pull out they had to march all night through the rain on roads churned to a muddy quagmire. Belatedly I asked myself again if this was the type of life I could handle. Already I wish for a wider brim on my hat, for the cold spring rains run down my neck, and I have to keep reminding myself there is no umbrella at hand and no shelter to take!'"

Henrietta paused and laughed. She said to Sylvie, "Dylan was always my sensible child, so aware of the finer qualities of life. Dev is a man's man, but Dylan – such a gentleman."

Carolyn stared at her incredulously, but her mother-in-law went on.

"Let's see. They saw action soon enough, as the Federals were in pursuit. There was a skirmish, and they lost their knapsacks. Oh, dear, Dylan was flustered by that. I must send him a box of supplies straight off – scissors and emery paper and so forth–"

21

"Is Devereaux all right?" Carolyn clasped her hands prayer style in her lap, focused on Henrietta's eyes and waited.

Henrietta fidgeted in her seat, perturbed. "Yes. Dylan says here 'I had a new admiration for my brother, so calm and cool under fire, so quick to make decisions – whereas my hand shook so hard I dropped my powder, and my rammer rattled so that I could hardly get it in my gun. So I guess I have killed my first man. I didn't aim at anyone in particular. But I hope if I shot anyone he was prepared to meet his Maker. It is this sort of issue that keeps me awake at night.'" Henrietta paused and murmured to herself, "Poor Dylan. Sensitive soul. You won't find a more humane man ..."

"Where are they now?" Carolyn inquired.

"He says they're falling back toward Richmond, that he will write again once they camp."

Carolyn sighed. "Hopefully Dev will, too. I spend most of my life now waiting on news."

"Oh, that reminds me." Sylvie turned to face Carolyn. "I have news of your friend, Mahala Franklin."

"You do?"

"Yes. Her grandmother said there's been a delay in her return to town. It seems her grandfather passed away."

"Oh, no! Mr. Cornsilk! He meant the world to her."

Sylvie nodded. "He was the Indian, wasn't he?" she asked with thinly veiled fascination – and not altogether of the healthy variety.

"Yes," Carolyn responded rather stiffly. "How was it you came to learn this news, Sylvie?"

"Oh, I called upon them – the Franklins."

"You did?"

"Yes. Nothing else to do. I figured I might as well get to know her ... you know, in case Mother's wrong about Jack and he does decide to pop the question one day."

Carolyn's brows went up. "And would you be approving of that?"

"Well, that was what I was trying to figure out."

"When she returns to town, Mahala will of course observe a time of bereavement. She may not feel up to visitors." *Especially of the nosy and judgmental variety.*

Sylvie shrugged. "Of course." Her smile was not reflected in her eyes.

Henrietta didn't help. "Sometimes company keeps one's mind off the grief," she put in, obviously not speaking from experience, Carolyn thought. "And how could a girl like Mahala fail to be honored by a visit from Miss Randall?"

"I know Mahala," Carolyn insisted.

Henrietta frowned at her. She folded Dylan's letter and directed her attentions towards Sylvie. "What do you think of your cousin Dylan, Miss Randall? I know you haven't seen him much with that country church of his, but you did get to visit that day in Savannah – briefly – when you came to tea. Is he not handsome and well-spoken?"

Sylvie smiled. "Yes, he was, Aunt Henrietta. I admired him very much."

"I have it on good authority he would not be averse to receiving correspondence from you, should you feel so inclined."

"Really?" Sylvie seemed to consider this news with interest.

"Yes, indeed. It's our duty, my dear, to keep up the spirits of our men," Henrietta encouraged her, patting Sylvie's silk-clad knee.

Carolyn could hardly hold in her consternation until the girl's carriage rattled back down the drive. Then she turned to her mother-in-law.

"On whose authority do you have it?" she questioned.

"What do you mean?"

"On whose authority that Dylan would like to hear from Sylvie Randall?"

"On mine, of course." Henrietta smirked. "Dylan is too much of a gentleman not to write her back. It hasn't been such a bad thing having one of my sons married to one of my great nieces, hm? Why not two?"

"Why are you so intent on setting them up?" Carolyn's chin went up as she placed her hands on her hips and confronted Henrietta.

"You forget your place, Carolyn," Henrietta snapped. She brushed past and closed the door behind them. "Why should *you* have any opinion on who Dylan might take to wife? You made your choice, remember."

Heat rose to Carolyn's face as indignation overcame censure. "Now that's not fair. No one could love Devereaux more than I, or be more devoted. I just don't think Sylvie is Dylan's type."

"Well, that's up to him, now, isn't it? And if I want to encourage him where your cousin is concerned, that's a mother's prerogative. He could do worse. And access to the Randall fortune just might come in handy after the war."

As Henrietta turned and went up the stairs, Carolyn inwardly groaned. Oh, this tangle of Clarkesville-Savannah family relationships had grown increasingly confusing, ever since the moment she set eyes on the handsome sons of the much younger sister of her grandmother Odelle. And it might just all end in a big mess.

t seemed hard to believe he was gone. Especially once Mahala returned to town. Surely Henry was just home in the cabin with Jacob on her Sautee land, she thought. How could everything just go on the same without him?

But the reality of her memories would always intrude. She had sat by her grandfather's body, prepared for burial by Nancy. She had stood by the open earth next to her parents' graves while the preacher from Nacoochee said the final words. She'd cried in the night, feeling the support structure of her world had shattered.

It had been some comfort that Henry's passing had been peaceful and painless, and that he was now with "the One God," as he had liked to say. But still Mahala found it hard to feel anything but longing to hear his stories and rest in his arms one last time, surrounded by the most perfect unconditional love she'd known on earth. It was hard to want to do anything, much less act pleasant about it.

Martha seemed to understand this, and she had not pressed Mahala to do any chores, giving her plenty of time to grieve. But Mahala soon found that focusing too much on her loss only made the chasm in her heart yawn wider. She took up her normal duties. The activity distracted her during the day and made her fall asleep faster at night.

She visited Carolyn soon after her own return to Clarkesville, but about that same time Carolyn's mother and grandmother were arriving from the coast. Everything was in a flutter at Forests of Green, and the ladies were so polished and grand that Mahala felt awkward and vulnerable under their cool gazes. Odelle and Olivia were polite on the surface, but Mahala thought they were studying her simple dress and red-rimmed eyes and dismissing her as a needy peasant who had attached herself to Carolyn for whatever benefits relationship might provide. Under normal circumstances, she might not have thought that, and even if she had, would not have let it ruffle her. But right now her emotional armor was sagging … not only because of Henry's death, but because all three of her adopted brothers had enlisted with the First Georgia Partisan Rangers, Company C. The men left in late May for Loudon, Tennessee, to join the Department of East Tennessee.

During their initial visit after Mahala's return to town, Carolyn pulled her aside to warn her that she might receive a visit from Jack's sister Sylvie. Not a day later the prediction proved true. Martha turned the girl away with the excuse of Mahala's bereavement, but the following afternoon Sylvie was back. Mahala was cleaning upstairs and heard a youthful voice asking after her. She went to the landing and peeked down. There stood the dark-haired young woman in a dress so sumptuous it made Mahala's eyes bug out. What did the girl wear to balls? She held a fancy little box in her hands.

"She's *cleaning*, but I'll check and see if she is able to come down," Leon told Sylvie in a tone that suggested Sylvie should not want to mingle with a filthy maid. It was the tone Mahala's father's cousin, who helped them manage the hotel, had always used when speaking of her. The enmity with which Leon looked on Mahala ever since Martha had brought her to live in Clarkesville as a young girl had never completely disappeared. While his father Thomas owned one of two dry goods stores in town, Leon had grown up with older brothers to fill the needs there. Thus, he'd insinuated himself into the good graces of Martha's husband before his death. The way he saw it, Mahala's presence – made even more unworthy by her mixed blood – had waylaid his plans for future inheritance.

Angry, Mahala bit her lip.

"*Cleaning?*" Sylvie squeaked.

"Yes. Just a moment, Miss Randall."

Mahala dashed back into the guest room as Leon mounted the stairs. She would receive Sylvie to spite Leon, that's what she'd do, and despite her own reclusive inclinations. She leaned into the mirror, fixing her hair and biting her lips. Then she untied her apron.

Leon arrived at the door and announced, "Miss Sylvie Randall is here to see you. Shall I tell her you're busy?"

"No, Leon, I shall go down," Mahala said with the air of a princess. She tossed her apron at his bony chest as she sailed past him, ignoring his disgusted snort. Mahala braced herself for scrutiny and descended the stairs.

Sylvie looked amused at her regal entrance. The girl's eyes took in every inch of Mahala's plain cotton dress. Then she smirked and held out the box. "Lovely to see you again, Miss Franklin. Here, I brought you a gift."

"Oh?" Mahala was taken aback. "What is it?"

"Chocolates. From France. I figured if you wouldn't see me today, I'd leave them to sweeten you up for next time." Sylvie looked mischievous.

Mahala only hesitated a second before seizing the box. Absurd as the gesture was, in truth she could use chocolate right now. "Thank you," she said. She led the way to the parlor and opened the door. "Come in."

As Sylvie entered, Mahala saw Leon on the landing rolling his eyes. Argh, but it was hard not to hate that sourpuss. She followed her distinguished guest in and shut the door behind them with enough finality to fall just short of a slam.

Sylvie jumped, then turned and smiled. "That cousin of yours looks like he needs a good drink of Madeira."

Unexpectedly, Mahala giggled. "Castor oil," she suggested, making Sylvie laugh. Mahala quickly sobered and invited Jack's sister to sit down. She decided to come right to the point. "Why did you want to visit me, Miss Randall? Your mother left no doubt as to her feelings about me when we last met."

"Oh. Mother." Sylvie waved airily. "I make up my own mind about things. It's boring here, and at least you're interesting. I need someone to pass the time with."

Mahala's brows rose in surprise. She folded her hands over the box of chocolates. "I'm afraid you might not find me as entertaining as usual right now, Miss Randall."

"Ah, yes, your grandfather. My condolences. Try a chocolate."

Again Mahala was astonished. Sylvie Randall actually thought a box of Parisian confections an anecdote to the grief of personal loss? Well, maybe before she got mad she ought to consider that the girl might actually be trying to help. Unsure as before which Sylvie was – naive or impossibly cold and selfish – Mahala opened the box and scanned the decorated candies.

"The ones with light brown drizzle are coffee flavored."

Mahala held out the box to her guest. Sylvie took one, then so did Mahala. Mahala had never tasted anything so good – well, except for the chocolate mousse Jack had given her when she was sixteen. For half a second she actually did forget herself.

"See? These make everything better," Sylvie stated with a kittenish smile. "Jack brought them for me on his last trip – and the material for this dress. Like it?" She smoothed the silk organza with a gentle hand.

"It's beautiful." She thought as she put the chocolates aside that she would never dare to even touch the muted blue plaid fabric. Her work-roughened hands would probably pick the fabric!

"My brother is the most dashing man in Georgia. Some people may criticize him for not running arms, but as far as I'm concerned they can just choke on the coffee – and the meat – and the spices – they stuff their faces with that they wouldn't even have if not for him!" Sylvie's eyes cut to Mahala. "What do *you* think of Jack's dealing only in civilian cargoes?"

As if I would dare criticize him after that diatribe! Mahala blinked and sat back, weighing her answer. "I think Jack is a man of sensitive conscience, and he will do as it dictates. He follows principles he holds very dear. He does not need to answer to his critics – only to that Higher Power we are all accountable to."

A slow smile spread over Sylvie's face. "My thoughts exactly. Jack's different. He marches to his own drum. I guess that's why I love him so much. He doesn't like to be reeled in, you know. He likes to come and go at his own whim and be accountable to none. All the ladies are fascinated by that independence – that elusiveness – and they think they can tame it. Ridiculous. He'll never change."

Mahala knew Sylvie was testing, maybe even warning, her. She decided forthrightness was the best response. "I can certainly see what you mean," she said. "But Sylvie, your brother has given me no reason to expect a commitment, if that's what you are thinking."

"Most girls would take a stream of letters as *something*. Don't you?"

Mahala shrugged, glad the younger woman could not tell how fast her heart was beating. She said in what she hoped was a casual tone, "I care about Jack, yes, but he's already shown me that even friendship with him is temperamental at best."

"But he loves you, Miss Franklin. Oh, he does. Don't look so shocked."

"Did he tell you that?" Mahala asked, wishing she didn't sound so breathless. Jack's sister must not receive the impression that she was a love-sick fortune-hunter.

"No. But he didn't have to. I know Jack. All anyone has to do is speak your name and he looks like someone just crashed a symbol next to him." Sylvie paused, laughed, pretending she had no idea the effect her words were having on Mahala. "So I thought … we should spend some time together. I can't stay now. Mother thinks I'm out strolling. But I'll come back tomorrow afternoon. And the next. Say, the same time each day. That way we can get to know each other despite Mother."

Sylvie rose and started for the door. Flustered, Mahala followed her and let her out. She was speechless at the way the girl had just dropped a virtual cannonball and then invited herself back. "You are not – returning home soon, then?" she ventured at the door.

"Not right away. Jack was right to send us inland again. The city panicked at the appearance of Yankees. The governor sent troops to the coast – and slaves to dig fortifications. A lot of the businesses moved inland, too. No one can enter or leave without a pass. Mother says we'll wait a while to make sure the Yankees stay put."

"That sounds wise," Mahala agreed. Everyone knew how badly the Union wanted control of the major seaports of the South, including Savannah. The net of their blockade kept tightening and tightening.

"Oh, from now on, I'll come at tea time. That way you can be prepared to entertain."

Mahala took a tiny step back. Another assumption. So like her brother! "I'm sorry, Miss Randall, but I must be honest with you," she replied. "I'm often too busy to observe the niceties to which you are accustomed. I am not able to sit down to tea every day. I don't mean to be rude, but while I would welcome you for afternoon visits, you'll have to follow me around while I do my chores."

Sylvie looked taken aback. Then she laughed. "No wonder Jack likes you. You're not afraid of him one bit, are you? Nor of me. Very well. But don't expect me to help."

Mahala nodded. "But you might not want to wear a silk gown."

The next afternoon, Sylvie arrived wearing a sensible cotton dress. The girl stood in the corner of a guest room with her nose rucked up while Mahala stripped the linens from the bed.

"That wheezy, consumptive-looking man we passed on the stairs," Sylvie said. "He didn't stay in here, did he?"

"He did indeed."

"Ugh! How do you *stand* it? Must you wave that sheet around so carelessly?"

"Mr. Lowell is really very nice – and very rich, though he may not look like it. He's one of our best customers," Mahala said, folding the sheet. "And I don't think he's consumptive. He has severe allergies."

Still, Sylvie went to the window, turned the lock with her lace-trimmed handkerchief, and tugged open the glass. She sucked in a draught of fresh air while Mahala smothered a smile.

"Why don't you hire more help?" Sylvie wanted to know. "You work like a slave!"

"I probably work even harder than Maddie," Mahala agreed, referring to her grandmother's cook. "But we can't afford to hire more help." Which was exactly the reason Martha gave for hanging onto Maddie, even though Maddie had made it clear she would not leave even if she were paid. She loved her kitchen and her customers, and she especially loved Mahala.

"Then your only way out is to marry Jack," Sylvie said as though she had found the lost piece of a mental puzzle.

"Out?" Mahala echoed. "I'm not looking for a way out, Sylvie. Even if I married a wealthy man, I would never just leave my grandmother hanging. And when it comes to what I'm looking for in a man, money's not the deciding factor. Like any woman, I need love and companionship.

If Jack is not the one who can offer me that, I'll keep looking for someone who can."

The fact that Mahala spoke as though she was not desperate seemed to strike a chord in Sylvie. "I never meant to imply Jack was not loving," she said, coming slowly up to the bed and gingerly clasping the edge of the clean sheet Mahala was spreading. Holding it between a thumb and forefinger, she managed to help make the bed without touching the mattress. "He's very affectionate. Very good to us. Just independent."

"Of course." Independent was an understatement. Jack had pushed her away for years, and somehow she'd always known that was because of his childhood. She tried not to act too interested so Sylvie would continue.

"You should have known him when he was a child. I didn't, of course. He was fourteen when I was born. Even still, I remember him being great fun. Always swinging me around in the air and never too stiff to play my little games. He adored me, you know. He didn't always care for Mother, though."

"Oh?" Mahala prompted gently, pretending she knew nothing on that score. Self-assured Sunny, slave owner and socialite, as Southern as they came, had been a hard pill for the boy Jack to swallow, coming quickly in the wake of his own mother's death. According to Jack, Eva Randall had been quiet, tender and self-sacrificing.

"He thought she was trying to replace *his* mother. On their first meeting he rolled a hoop into a painting she was making. Years later he found out the painting was of *him*. And then Mother says he was always playing tricks ..."

"I can't imagine," Mahala murmured, smoothing the sheets.

"Yes, he still likes to keep people guessing, doesn't he? It took him a long time to get along with Mother. Really not until after our father died. Jack wanted to go back north, to be with Father's family. That was where he was raised, after all, in New York. He never quite fit in down here. He didn't really have friends, growing up. That's why I'm pretty sure before he died Father must have asked Jack to take care of us. Otherwise, knowing how Jack feels about slavery and the Union and all, he probably would have left."

Mahala straightened and impulsively reached for Jack's sister's hand. She met her gaze. "Sylvie, you must know how Jack loves you and the rest of his family down here. You should have heard him when he first described you to me."

"Really?" Sylvie asked, suddenly vulnerable. Sylvie knew Mahala was giving her an offering. At their first meeting, Sylvie had made it painfully clear that Jack had never spoken to her of Mahala, reinforcing

Mahala's belief that Jack and his family felt she would never be good enough for him.

"Yes. He told me how beautiful you were, and how spirited. His eyes fairly sparkled when he spoke of you." An image of those green eyes, sharp and unbidden, rose with painful clarity in Mahala's mind. "He is so proud of you. You should never doubt that he would do anything for you. Willingly."

Sylvie bit her lip and looked away. "Of course he would. He's my brother. Now, can we leave this awful room?"

With Sylvie following her around the rest of the afternoon, and the rest of the week, Mahala listened to stories of the young Jack. Once Sylvie had warmed to Mahala, it became clear that Sylvie's half brother was one of her favorite topics. She still looked at him with stars in her eyes. What Mahala learned created an endearing and even somewhat vulnerable picture. In that week, she came to know more about the man who had captured her unwilling fascination than she had in the years before from Jack himself. And she even began to like Sylvie a little.

That Saturday, when Sylvie came to call and announced that she and Sunny were returning to Savannah, having decided the Yankees were successfully being held from the city, Mahala was surprised to feel disappointment.

"But don't worry," the girl said encouragingly. "I've decided I approve of you. Jack likes you, Carolyn likes you, and I like you, too. You need some polishing, but that's nothing I couldn't take care of. I shall be your advocate. And Jack *always* listens to what I say."

Mahala smiled at the petite but determined young lady in front of her. Sylvie leaned forward to give Mahala a kiss on the cheek. Mahala gently hugged her, afraid to muss the perfect curls and elaborately rouched gown.

"Thank you for keeping me company – and for your help."

"Oh, it's nothing. Nothing compared to how I can help you in the future," Sylvie winked at her.

Mahala suppressed a grin. Just maybe she would.

But as Jack's sister breezed from the hotel, Mahala's heart fell. Now she was left alone with her grief, the loneliness all that much more intense.

June 22, 1862
Off the South Carolina coast

In the failing light Jack stood on *Evangeline*'s deck with a spy glass in hand, its lens trained on the Union warships at the entrance to Charleston harbor. To the naked eye they were mere specks on the horizon, but with the aid of the magnifying instrument he could make out the two masts on the steamers and the fluttering American flags.

"We know of at least four gunboats on duty in the immediate vicinity," he said to his pilot, Lawrence Birch. "*Flag, Keystone State, James Adger* and *Seneca*. We may be big, but I think we can outrun any of them if need be."

"Time to put that anthracite coal to the test. The men in the engine room will be ready."

Jack nodded and glanced around, trusting *Evangeline*'s low profile, dull color and minimized masts and spars – pulled down on their hinges upon sighting land – would also help the ship blend with the horizon. "In the darkest part of the night we'll make our dash for land well to eastward. Then we'll feel our way up Maffit's Channel keeping land close aboard and passing inside Rattlesnake Shoals, just as Robert Lawson advised."

"I sure hope his information was good," Lawrence said of Jack's friend from Importing and Exporting Company of South Carolina. One could say the older man had become Jack's blockade running mentor.

"According to him, it's the only channel the blockade runners use now," Jack replied, snapping the spyglass down to size.

In December of last year, Charleston's main shipping lane had been obstructed when the Yankees had sunk sixteen old whaling ships laden with stone – and thus known as the "Stone Fleet." This plan was only a stalling tactic for the North – they knew the strong tides would eventually render the sunken ships ineffective. In fact, some even said that the pressure from the whalers actually served to deepen the harbor channel as the sediment was sucked from beneath the ships back into the sea. But it bought the Yankees a little more time to buy and build more steamers.

In January, a second "Stone Fleet" had been sunk in Maffit's Channel, but Lawson had assured them that by running the course he described a whole string of steamers had avoided both the obstructions and the patrolling Yankee ships.

"Nervous?" Birch asked.

Jack nodded. He didn't have to expound or justify, for both men were all too aware that this trip was not like the others. Not only was it their first time running into Charleston since Savannah had become too closely guarded, but this time instead of an exclusively civilian cargo they were standing atop 112,000 pounds gunpowder, 10,000 small arms, a half million percussion caps, and twenty tons of lead – a floating arsenal intended for the Georgia Militia. Briefly Jack wished they had a British crew. If set upon they might raise the Union Jack and present English papers. And British crewmen when seized were released after testifying at prize trials for the captured cargo, whereas Southern sailors were shipped off to military prison.

Why had he decided to take such a risk? The corner of Jack's mouth turned down slightly as he again reminded himself of the reasons. *Profit.* War supplies were beginning to logjam in the Bahamas. Confederate agents were desperate for even one-half cargo space on reliable sailing vessels. *Necessity.* He felt angry as he recalled the trap the suspicious officials in Savannah had tried to set for him his last visit home. They had long suspected he'd used his family's ships to help escaping slaves on their way to freedom. Good thing he had thought to look into the real identity of the man named Nathaniel who had asked for his help ... *ex*-slave as it turned out, repaying a debt to the local authorities. Carolyn Rousseau had also gone out of her way, even risking her husband's wrath, to warn him. He owed her one. He intended to repay the debt very soon. She had also written him that he would be watched by the authorities. Jack wouldn't put it past the odious Augustus Blinkwell and those policemen in his pocket to trump up charges, or incite a mob riot, when next he showed his face in Savannah. Blinkwell had hated him since Jack had turned down his insultingly ludicrous offer to take over Randall and Ellis in the name of the Confederate Navy.

The correspondence from both Carolyn and Sylvie had also disclosed that the firm's reputation was growing shaky. Rumors of his Northern sympathies – even suggestions of espionage – were being bandied about. In response, Sylvie's tone had been saucy and imperious: "They can say what they will, Jack. They're all just jealous." But his heart had wrenched as she had written of the deprivations of the local soldiers ... his half-brothers. She wouldn't have told him about that if she didn't hope he would read her silent plea and help them. And then, the final straw ... a brief note from his cousin Ella Beth, who once had set her cap for him, timidly revealing the grief and anxiety his continued maverick course was bringing to their aging Ellis grandparents. So there at the bottom of it all, at the bedrock of his motivation, was again the strongest force of all: *love.* He would never let those under his protection suffer on his account, not when he had the power to do otherwise.

Because of these things, love chief among them, Jack had arranged a meeting with Louis Heyliger, Confederate War Department agent in Nassau. Heyliger had been more than happy to receive him and had in turn introduced him to his broker, Henry Adderly. Adderly oversaw cargo transfers, arranged for dock space and storage facilities and provided coal and provisions for ships, both military and private, carrying Confederate goods.

No, this was not the time for questioning. He had cast his lot and must follow up the move with decisive action. Hesitation at this juncture could cost them everything. But he did believe in being prepared for emergencies. In his quarters he bound official papers inside the folded Confederate flag Lawson had once given him, tied the parcel with twine and weighted it with a flat rock.

While the ship lay like a ghost on the face of the sea, he went to his cabin for a few hours' sleep, having a crew member wake him around three. As he dressed, his mind felt calm and sharp.

Half an hour later, with Jack at the helm, *Evangeline*'s engine shuddered, and a vibration moved through the ship. In the tropical coastal darkness they steamed ahead, aiming for the opening near land left by the northernmost gunboat. Jack's adrenaline flowed and his heart pumped as he prayed for stealth. The night was black and still, unlike a few days prior when tempests had rocked the port. Dark covered them like a cloak, for the Yankee ships gave no sign they detected *Evangeline*.

Jack breathed a bit easier as they navigated Maffit's Channel, with the reassuring bulk of Sullivan's Island on their right. Still, progress was slow as they passed along the side of the shoals, sounding for depth in an attempt to avoid obstructions.

"Show the red light only," Jack directed as they approached Fort Moultrie.

The signal light was lit. Moments later an answering red pinpoint showed from the fort on the island. The men gave each other thumbs up gestures and grinned in relief. But their joy was short-lived. They had just passed the fort when *Evangeline* stalled like a plug in a drain, though steam still passed through her funnel.

"Sand bar!" the muffled cry came. "Sand bar!"

"Reverse the wheel," Jack directed, the command repeated in low, swift tones across the deck.

There was a churning, but the ship did not dislodge.

From up ahead on the opposite bank of the combined Ashley and Cooper Rivers, a flare of light broke the darkness of the night sky. A whine of a sound shrilled toward them, and the water five hundred yards distant sprayed in all directions. *Sumter was firing on them!*

"Show the red light again!" Jack called to the sailors close at hand.

The signal was relit, and the ship rocked as the chief engineer moved the giant paddle wheel back and forth in an attempt to free them from land. As much as Jack admired the new twin screw steamers for their ability to execute rapid turns, he was heartily grateful for his side wheel right now. And he was heartily grateful when Sumter ceased fire and returned their signal.

But the exchange had attracted the notice of a Union steamer, which approached up the Main Ship Channel. She threw a shell in their direction. It landed far short.

"Sir, I don't think they can reach us," said Jack's first officer, appearing at his elbow. "The battery landward is preparing their guns. They have four, plus a rifled cannon, so the Yankees won't come in too close."

At that moment the rifled gun from Moultrie side exploded, the shot passing three hundred yards over the Union gunboat.

"I agree," Jack said. "They're also within range of Sumter. They don't pose a threat, not if we can break free quickly enough."

As he spoke a huge surge from the engine room caused them to rock almost off their feet. *Evangeline* was emancipated. There was cheering from fore to aft, and the sailors on deck broke lustily into "The Bonnie Blue Flag," no longer concerned about the Yankees hearing, in fact wanting them to hear.

We are a band of brothers,
And native to the soil,
Fighting for the property
We gained by honest toil.
And when our rights were threatened
The cry rose near and far:
'Hurrah for the Bonnie Blue Flag
That bears a single star!'

Jack had no doubt the tune carried back to the Yankee ears on the nearby vessel. But they were home free, casually moderating their fires now, passing by Sumter's friendly guns into the harbor. Leaving the helmsman to navigate the harbor buoys, Jack stepped into his stateroom and slipped the folds of the flag from the twine. He carried the silken bundle to a young sailor on watch amidship.

"Might as well raise the standard, sailor," he instructed.

"Aye, aye, Captain," the boy replied with a grin.

The faint gray of a June dawn revealed the outcropping of Castle Pinckney and beyond it, the twinkling lights of Charleston's battery and wharf. They steamed into port with the Stars and Bars floating triumphantly at *Evangeline's* helm.

A couple of days later, Jack awoke as the train steamed into the station at Savannah. Despite having shed his coat and cravat, he was covered with fine, sticky sweat. The humidity was intense, and the open windows had let in dust and cinders. He must look a sight. He sat up and distastefully shook out his linen jacket.

Andrew Willis, his clerk who had joined him in Charleston, smiled. He had perfectly even teeth. The man was fully dressed, his bow tie fluffed, and appeared as natty as ever.

"Do you never get rumpled?" Jack asked him irritably.

"Why, I'm sure I do, Sir," Andrew replied, apologetic.

Not enough sleep, Jack thought. *I've not had a decent night since I left the Bahamas.*

As the passengers disembarked, Jack carefully retied his cravat, finger combed his hair, and donned his hat. Thus restored to respectability, he climbed down the steps onto the busy platform. He wasted no time in getting to the rear of the train, Andrew trailing behind, leaving a wide berth for Jack's dark mood. Here several box cars carried the Randall and Ellis shipment. A Confederate guard leaning on his musket in the first of their cars peeked his head out of the cattle door.

"Everything o.k.?" Jack asked.

"Yes, Sir. No problem at all."

"Good. The detachment of soldiers should be here soon with the wagons. You did wire ahead, Willis?"

"Of course, Sir," Andrew said.

Jack looked around. His face grew even less pleasant. Instead of the anticipated escort, he saw a large, middle-aged man in policeman's clothing pushing his way through the crowd. When Jack realized the officer's intent to approach him, he was not surprised. The man wore a surly grin that bore anything but good will.

"Jack Randall?"

"Yes."

"Officer Charles Blake, Savannah police. You've been gone quite a while. We were beginning to think you'd not be returning to town," said the man, removing a cigar from a paper and searching in his pocket for a match. Jack had little doubt this was the very man who'd arranged the trap for him when he was last in Savannah.

Andrew looked alarmed.

"Since when do my comings and goings concern the Savannah police?"

"Since suspicions of treason were raised from reliable quarters."

"Treason?" Jack barked.

"That's right. Why don't you come along with me? I'd like to ask you a few questions down at headquarters."

"I don't think so. I just risked my ship, my life, and the lives of nearly a hundred crewmen running guns and ammunition into Charleston harbor. Arms for the Confederacy – to be delivered today to Brigadier General Hugh Mercer to aid in the defense of Savannah." Jack fumbled in his own pocket and brought out a fat wad of papers. He unfolded them and shoved them into the impudent policeman's face. "Here. See for yourself. Letters and manifests that document the entire exchange. Look all you like. Take special note of Heyliger's signature there on the top. But I'm not going anywhere. And I suggest you not get between Governor Brown and the transfer of these supplies to his local militia."

Blake frowned, rifling through the papers, clearly incensed at Jack's tone and at having his moment of revenge thwarted. But what could he do? There were the signatures. Important signatures. "Let me see in that car," he demanded, shoving the papers back at Jack.

The soldier stood aside as, cigar clamped between thick lips, the portly man pulled his frame up onto the train.

"Excuse me, Sir, but I have to ask that you not smoke in this car," the young soldier said.

"What?"

"I will hold your cigar for you, Sir."

Blake looked mutinous, but with a glare he gave the young man the cigar. Jack waited while the policeman opened crates under the guard's watchful eye. Andrew looked like he'd swallowed a frog, thought Jack. He gave his clerk a reassuring look, then turned with a smile as a chain of quartermaster's wagons rumbled up to the station. Ah. At last. A sergeant jumped down from the lead vehicle and introduced himself. Officer Blake poked his red face out of the box car.

"Well, Sir, is it all right with you if these gentlemen take these munitions to the men who need them?" Jack asked baitingly.

"It's a good thing you've seen the light," Blake huffed, jumping to the ground. "And not a moment too soon. Not a moment too soon," he repeated, wagging a finger.

Back held stiff, he started to walk away, but the guard on the train called, "Excuse me, Sir – your cigar?" He dangled it rather distastefully from two fingers.

"Bah!" Blake growled, waving a dismissive hand in the air behind him.

"Toss it down," Jack said.

When the cigar hit the ground, Jack extinguished it beneath his heel with a feeling of satisfaction. *One more fire put out.* Now, to transfer the civilian goods to the Randall warehouse, and he would be free to seek out the company of those who made this all worthwhile.

June 28, 1862
Henrico County, Virginia

The rumble of artillery sparring forever in his ears, Devereaux Rousseau approached the group of Oglethorpes gathered in the hot summer sun. The men looked up eagerly. They had been in position here near the Price House and Garnett's Farm, just west of the New Bridge Road, for most of the month. And they had listened to the sounds of battle and watched the powder rise to the north, on the other bank of the Chickahominy River, for the past two days.

As Dev came to stand before Company B, the soldiers rose and saluted.

"Any word, Captain?" asked Hank Watson. Typically Hank was the group's comic relief, but today his expression was grave.

"Major General Jones feels the enemy before us is preparing to retreat," Dev answered. "He believes the time may be ideal for us to strike. He's been unable to locate General John Magruder, so he's sent a staff officer directly to General Lee to request permission for an assault. We have but to wait for the reply."

"Yes, Sir," was the respectful answer. They all knew Dev was generous in sharing information with them, and to press him with more questions would be unacceptable.

But as Dev made for a cluster of shade trees nearby, he heard their murmurings.

"Not many of us here south of the river. Yesterday when the 1st and the 9th went out they said there were still a lot of Yanks along Nine Mile Road. If they try for Richmond, can we hold them?"

"Sure we can. How long do we have to sit around and wait? I say put the 8th in the action, and they'll get results."

Dylan followed Dev over to a big oak tree and sank down beside him – close, but not too close. Here, in a moment away from military formality, they could share an exchange as brothers. But a brief but tell-tale scratch at the nape of Dylan's neck reminded both men that Dylan, like so many of the soldiers, had become host to an embarrassing and frustrating invader. Lice.

The tiny insects had plagued the regiment since their miserable accommodations on the peninsula. The officers were not exempt, though so far Dev had managed to stay nit-free.

"Everyone's restless," Dylan said, quite unnecessarily. "They're about to go crazy just sitting around listening to the racket." He unplugged his canteen and took a swallow.

Dev did likewise, removing his hat and swiping his brow. He brushed his wavy dark hair off his forehead. It was a fair day, but the combination of sun and wool was a bit toasty. "Yep, I know," he said. He was glad – a little surprised – that Dylan had sought him out. Since arriving, his brother had seemed content to relate to him merely as an enlisted man to his officer, even while he was obviously establishing relationships with the other privates and NCOs. This had puzzled him, and frankly, had hurt a bit, too. Now Dev asked, "So, how you feeling about another battle?"

Dylan shrugged, but his mouth twitched. "It's inevitable, isn't it? I mean, so far I've not been in a major engagement, but it's bound to happen sooner or later. And maybe this will be it, the great, decisive battle for Richmond." They all knew that safeguarding the Confederacy's capital was paramount.

"Maybe." Dev's voice betrayed his doubt, though he never would have let on as much to anyone else. The longer he'd been in the army, the more frays he'd been in, the more elusive that "great, decisive battle" became. He was beginning to believe they were enmeshed in a chain of bloody debacles that would stretch on forever. But maybe, just maybe, Lee would change all that. It had actually been a stroke of good luck when slow-to-fight Johnston had been wounded in the Battle of Seven Pines at the end of last month, providing Confederate President Jeff Davis with the perfect opportunity to move Lee from a desk to active command. Now the Yankees under McClellan were attempting to shift their supply line from the York River to the James, and Lee was out not to stop them but to destroy them. The game was on.

"I like the outlook of the men much better now, on the eve of battle, than in camp. The lures of gambling and carousing in Richmond were hard to compete with," Dylan remarked.

"Do you regret coming?" Dev asked. "Maybe I shouldn't have pushed you so. I didn't know William Dunlap of D was to be appointed regimental chaplain."

"Oh, no – no," Dylan answered. "It was not you, but God, who made the decision for me." Dylan pointed quickly skyward. "*He* would not give me any rest until I came. And I'm fine just serving as chaplain to Company B. I like it better that way, actually. I can build friendships with the men. They see that I mean what I say."

"You do as you preach, huh?" Dev commented.

"Yeah – most of the time," Dylan answered with a strange reluctance.

They sat silently a minute, both looking out into the field and at the glinting metal teepees of stacked arms. Finally Dev asked the question he had been struggling with. "Dylan, are you angry with me?"

Dylan's face turned toward him. One of those unusual red heads not normally covered with freckles, long exposure to the sun had finally brought out a rash of the brown dots, along with a brownish-red tan. Still, his strong jaw and intense brown eyes made him a handsome man. "Angry at you?" he asked. "Why would I be?"

"I don't know. You tell me. I thought it might be because I pressed you to join up, but if it's not that …" Dev allowed his voice to trail away. He knew all too well that in the past he'd instigated competition between them by always trying to be better at everything than his younger brother. That attitude had culminated in his machinations to gain Carolyn's heart even though Dylan had been courting her. The harshness of life during war had finally shown the rivalry between them for the petty selfishness it was, at least on Dev's part. There was a lot of damage to undo. He added, "I just don't want there to be anything between us – anything I can fix, I mean."

"There's nothing you should be concerned about. You should just concentrate on being captain."

"But being your brother is more important," Dev admitted. It felt like he had just dropped a boulder into a still pond. Dylan listened without saying a word. He sensed he was on the edge of something big. He tiptoed up to it, not quite sure what to say – what his brother needed. "And I know I didn't always do the best job of that."

Dylan nodded his head. "It's o.k., Dev. People change. Our tussles as boys were a long time ago."

"I just want you to know … I love you." Embarrassed, Dev stood up. He chanced a quick glance at the younger man on the ground. Dylan was still nodding, his elbows braced on his knees with his face tilted down, but Dev could tell that he was choked up, unable to answer, his eyes filled with tears. "O.k. then." Dev started to walk away.

He had gone about ten steps when Dylan called out in a quavery voice: "Hey, Captain."

Dev turned.

"The same to you." Dylan saluted his brother.

Dev smiled. A surprising sense of rightness filled him – his conscience, Dylan would probably say. He put on his hat and raised his hand to his own forehead before turning away.

Coming toward him he saw Edward Magruder, one star on his collar marking him as the regimental major. Slender, young – only a year older than Dev – with a mustache, goatee and piercing eyes, Magruder was accounted one of the handsomest men in the 8th. He had come to Virginia as the captain of the Rome Light Guards, Company A. It was said his lovely wife Florence had marched at the head of the column with him upon the company's departure from the city, a pistol and a dagger in her belt. Dev could not picture Carolyn doing that. But Carolyn, his wife, had done something just as noteworthy, maybe more so, though not as public. He would never forget how she'd gone to Frances Bartow to successfully plead for his chance to go to Virginia even though initially the married men were being left behind. It had been a turning point in their relationship. Her selfless gesture had made Dev realize how priceless she really was.

Dev smiled to himself and snapped off a smart salute. As he had expected, Magruder brought orders being relayed down the chain of command.

"Form up your men, Captain Rousseau. General Toombs has ordered General Anderson to advance with the 7th and 8th Georgia, and promised his support in the action. Companies A, B and K will be deployed as skirmishers." He paused to smile briefly. "I have no doubt our men will again show what they are made of."

"Yes, Sir," Dev replied. He listened quietly as Magruder relayed further details, but his mind kept going back to the mention of General Robert Toombs, politician from their home state. Toombs was known to have a scorn for West Point-trained officers and military red tape. He couldn't help wondering if Lee had sanctioned this attack. But attack they would, for "Tige" Anderson was colonel of their brigade, and his orders were not questioned. He was trusted and loved by all his men.

The sun was behind them by the time the 7th and 8th were formed up. They marched into a field of ripening wheat which shone in the evening light, waving and breaking under the pressure of advancing ranks. Dev walked out in front, sword drawn at his side. He glanced back and with a sickening feeling in his gut saw the faces of the men he knew under the new regimental battle flag – red with a blue St. Andrew's cross and the thirteen stars of the Confederacy – carried by Lieutenant Montgomery. There was Dylan's bright hair. How scared he must be. Dev experienced a sharp regret. Right now he wished his younger brother anywhere but on this field that would soon be covered with wounded and dead.

God protect him.

"Ready, Company B," he called. "Forward at the double quick!"

Beside them Company A, the Rome boys, did likewise, fanning out into a skirmish line that covered the whole front of the advancing regiment. They pressed across the field toward the Union breastworks manned by two regiments. Already the Yanks were opening up with a blast of musket fire. Already Georgia men were falling. One of them was John Krenson, wounded in the pine thicket at Manassas and still bearing the medical discharge papers he had chosen to ignore in his pocket.

They swept on through a skirt of woods and a thicket, past a swampy area, and uphill through a pine woods. The combined infantry and artillery power was galling. They broke and temporarily fell back. Dev and the other officers urged the men forward again. Again the wall of lead was too much. Colonel Lucius Lamar took a place at the front, waving his sword. He was struck down but continued to urge them on from where he lay.

"Come on, Oglethorpes!" Devereaux cried, running out ahead.

He forgot to be afraid. He could see the powder-grimed faces of the enemy. Bullets whizzed by him, and dirt and leaves flew in the air from the artillery explosions. But just a few more yards! They would have those breastworks, and the line of blue would crumble.

Then a deafening explosion occurred just off his right side, and he knew no more.

When Dev came to an indistinguishable amount of time later, a sharp pain between his neck and his shoulders caused him to sit up with a yell.

In the dim twilight, an orderly with a blood-stained apron and a pair of tweezers drew back from potential attack. "Sorry, Cap'n. I've got to get that piece of shell out."

"Is that what happened?" Dev pressed a hand to his aching head and leaned back on a bedroll. Apparently he was at a makeshift dressing station. Other men, not seriously wounded, were also being treated around him. He guessed the crucial cases were being taken into Richmond. "How did I get off the field? What happened in the battle?"

"Your brother dragged you off, most of the way himself, though some of your men helped him. They retreated right after the shell hit you. Had to run all the way back through that wicked bullet storm."

"He did?" Dev queried, frowning in disbelief at the images the orderly's words created in his mind. "Where is he–?" He cut off, for the orderly had resumed his probing.

"The regiment reformed, but nothing else is gonna happen tonight, they say. He'll be along."

Dev gritted his teeth and held as still as possible until he felt the sliver of metal slide nastily from his skin. He let out his breath as the orderly swabbed the wound and pressed a bandage to the spot.

"Hold this."

Dev obliged, thinking of his own filthy hands and casting an even less confident look at the nurse's. He noticed a blood-soaked frock coat lying to one side.

"That mine?" he asked incredulously.

"Yes, Sir."

"All that blood came from this little cut?"

"When your brother brought you in you were bleeding from both ears, not just the cut. Everything feel all right now?"

"If by all right you mean the worst headache I've ever had in my life, sure." Dev grimaced. "My eyes feel like they're swollen to twice their normal size. But I can see. I'm alive."

"Then you're doing great. Lie here and rest a while, Captain."

Dev started to rise. "I need to get back to my company."

The orderly gave him a slight push and he fell flat, his equilibrium shot. "Rest, or who knows, you might end up keeling over dead into the latrine later. You had quite a concussion."

"Just for a while." Dev's eyes fluttered shut, but he forced them open again.

"I'm watching you. Try to leave again, Sir, and I'll have them take you into Richmond."

Dev didn't say anything, but he thought the medics must love bossing officers around and getting away with it. He closed his eyes. That provided small relief. He lay listening to the moans of the wounded and the distant movement of armies and thanked God he had survived another battle.

Eventually, feeling a touch on his arm, he opened his eyes again. Dylan crouched beside him, his skin smeared and streaked, his tousled hair filthy, but a beatific smile breaking over his face.

"You all right?"

"Thanks to you," Dev said. "Guess I'll have to recommend you for a promotion."

"You might not be so grateful when you discover I gave you my lice."

They both laughed, but Dev stopped quickly at the pain. "Think my head's going to explode," he mumbled.

Dylan grew serious. "You don't know how close you came to just that, Dev. That's exactly what happened to the man next to you. I saw you go down, and it felt like the world just stopped. I couldn't get over to you fast enough. I thought – I thought …" He paused, gulping down emotion. "Can you see o.k.? Can you hear?"

"I see and hear a blubbering kid brother who just dragged me 150 yards through raining lead," Dev said. "What am I gonna do? *I'm* supposed to be the brave one. Now everybody's going to know you were just holding out on us."

"No, Dev. The way you jumped up there right in front … I could never do that. But neither would I think for a second of leaving you at the mercy of the enemy. Lieutenant Colonel Towers surrendered, you know, with about fifteen or twenty of his men."

"He did?" Dev asked incredulously. "What else?"

"Colonel Lamar was wounded–"

"I saw."

"–and left on the field."

"Too bad he didn't have a brother here to save him, huh?"

Dylan modestly ignored the comment. He continued. "And Major Magruder looks about like you, all swathed in bandages. He was hit in the shoulder, too. A bullet shot away part of his nose, but he wouldn't leave the field."

So much for good looks, Dev thought. "What about our men?"

"We lost a few. But they're o.k. They will be heartened to hear you'll be fine, too."

"They won't hear it. They'll see it." Dev glanced around and grabbed his soiled coat. "Help me up. We've got to go while that man over there has his back turned. Quick."

With the assistance of Dylan, who grinned without comment at his normally fearless brother's sneaky evasion of an orderly, Dev loped dizzily out of the hospital area.

"You're not going to tell Carolyn," Dev said as they made their way through the deepening twilight.

"You're right. *You* are. She'd faint from thinking the worst the moment she laid eyes on a letter from me."

"She'll worry needlessly."

"For heaven's sake, man, have you learned nothing yet about the harm of keeping things from each other? She needs to know."

Dev regarded him with consternation, remembering how angry he'd been when he'd learned months after it happened that Carolyn had lost their baby. He knew Dylan was right. "Fine then," he sighed. "I'll tell her. I guess you've got one up on me."

Dylan smiled wryly, almost sadly. "I'd say that depends on how you look at it."

CHAPTER THREE

Late June, 1862
Clarkesville, Georgia

he sky was a mix of sun and clouds, but Mahala opted to hang out the sheets at midmorning anyway, hoping the heat would do quick work before a possible late afternoon thunder shower. They got a lot of those in June.

Her heart felt as heavy as those foreboding clouds. She considered the cause, disgusted with what she found inside. She was like a jealous little girl, she thought – jealous of Carolyn, of the doting company her mother and grandmother provided, of the loving letters she received from her husband. Jealous of anyone who received the desires of their heart while she was left out in the cold.

I'm happy for her. I am, Mahala told herself. *I just want that sort of closeness, too.* And was that wrong? What twenty-four-year-old woman wouldn't? By society's standard she was hard on the heels of middle age! A woman of her maturity needed family about her, preferably her own. Martha did all she could, but it just wasn't enough. Having no natural parents alive, and with the passing of her grandfather, Mahala felt more keenly than ever the need for love – a man's love.

Her own need made her impatient with herself, impatient with life. She didn't like feeling vulnerable.

Mahala shook out a wet sheet and folded it over the clothes line, slipping a wooden pin down over both corners. Then she did another. Sighing, she bent for a third. As she straightened, her eyes fell on a pair of long, slim boots. She stood up, following the vision upwards.

"Hello there!"

Mahala nearly dropped the sheet. Her heart raced madly as she focused on the face smiling at her in the blinding sunlight.

"Jack!" she cried. It didn't seem possible.

He grinned back at her. "Hello, Mahala."

"Is it really you?"

"No, I was killed on the high seas, and you now are beholding my ghost, come to haunt you in the middle of the day while you're hanging out laundry."

It was really him. "I – I'm just so shocked!"

"Do you need to pinch me?" he asked. Then a sly gleam came into his green eyes. "Or better yet, why don't you hug me?"

Before she could protest, he swooped one arm around her, the one he had been holding out for her to pinch. She stepped forward awkwardly, clasping the wet bundle in one arm and putting the other around his neck. With a whisper of the wavy brown locks that curled at his neck, the side of his face brushed hers. He smelled incredibly good. She stepped back, tucking a strand of hair behind her ear in an embarrassed gesture.

"It's good to see you," she said. She prayed he could not tell *how* good. "What – what brings you here?"

Instead of answering quickly like she had expected, he looked thoughtful for a second. His lips twitched like something was on the tip of his tongue. Then he said, "I brought *Evangeline* into Charleston just over a week ago. I had supplies for the Georgia troops, and civilian goods for sale in Savannah – and to bring up here. Provisions for the hotel. Gifts."

Practically all Mahala had heard was one sentence. "You brought in military goods?" she repeated in amazement.

A quick smile touched his face, and he gave an elaborate, self-mocking bow. "You can call me the reluctant Rebel."

"Do you have time to tell me about it?"

"I'm not running off anywhere."

"Then here. You might as well help while you talk." Mahala handed Jack a corner of the sheet, hoping he didn't notice how her hands were trembling. She tried to act cool and collected, keep her voice normal as she added, "As soon as we get these hung up to dry we can go in and have a cup of coffee – if you'd like."

"I'd like that very much." He smiled at her.

Egads. "So the last I heard from you, you were living like a king in Nassau, having escaped the trap the police and Blinkwell set but still wrestling with what to do next. What tipped you in favor of the Confederacy?"

"A lot of things." Jack stretched out a sheet and reached for a pin. Seeing him do such work suddenly made Mahala want to giggle, but she bit her tongue and listened as he told her of letters from friends and family warning him about the seriousness of the suspicions in Savannah.

"And that didn't send you off in the opposite direction?"

He laughed. "Ah, you know me too well, Mahala. I admit that was my first inclination – but the selfish one," he confessed. "I had to think about the people I cared about. I don't want them or their loved ones to suffer – physically or emotionally – not when it's in my power to help them. Ultimately, this is what I have to do."

Jack paused and looked at her. She saw pain in his eyes, and some-thing else – a searching for understanding. Mahala hesitated, then touched his hand.

"I know what it cost you," she said, thinking of the little boy Jack she had recently learned about, of his struggle for acceptance and belonging. And of the man Jack, who battled constantly with conscience. "You did the right thing."

"Do you think so?" he whispered.

At this rare glimpse of vulnerability, she couldn't stop a fleeting twitch of amazement from crossing her face. "You are taking care of those left in your charge. How could you feel guilty about that?"

"No matter what I do, Mahala, I can't make everything right."

She couldn't find her voice to tell him that was life. He was too close, close enough to kiss, looking intently into her eyes. In fact, did she imag-ine it, or did he draw even a bit closer while she searched for words? She schooled her expression, afraid he would pull away as he had that time before. But she felt his hand, rough and big, curve around hers. Her heart fluttered.

Then she heard the squeak of the back door opening.

"Miss Mahley?" Maddie called.

"Yes, Maddie?" Mahala quickly pulled her hand away and turned back toward the inn.

"Will you pick me some mint while you out there? Oh, who that with you?"

Mahala cleared her throat. "It's Mr. Jack Randall. Will you pour us some coffee, please?"

"Sure thing! Mist' Jack, I think you be gone for good, sailin' out on the high seas."

"No, Miss Maddie. I will always come home."

Mahala didn't look at him. She was shaken by his manner. Quickly she hung the last sheet and went over to the herb garden to find Mad-die's mint. Jack trailed behind her with the big laundry basket, which she had forgotten, neither apologetic or ruffled. How could he act so calm, as if moments ago he hadn't been baring his heart – most uncharacteristi-cally – and inches from again trying to kiss her? She wanted to give him a good kick and get that complacent look to leave his face. She wanted to kick herself for being ready to fall into his arms mere moments after he suddenly showed up. Most of all she wanted to know which was the real Jack – the cocksure adventurer or the tender and noble man she thought she glimpsed through chinks in his armor? From one she had to guard her heart, yet to the other … to the other she could give everything.

When she served him coffee he asked how she had been. She wanted to laugh, considering her immersion into self-pity just before his arrival. But she said, "Oh, well enough. I have nothing to share that will compare with your adventures."

"Be that as it may, my sister speaks very highly of you."

"She does?" Mahala blushed.

"Did she make too much of a nuisance of herself while she was here?"

"Terrible," Mahala replied with a smile, sitting down opposite him in the parlor and stirring her coffee.

"I should have better satisfied her curiosity and maybe she wouldn't have been such a bother."

And what would you have told her? she wanted to ask. "Oh – well ... I actually enjoyed her company. Carolyn's busy with her family, and I – my – my grandfather just passed away this spring." Mahala stopped at the familiar choking sensation in her throat.

Jack looked at her a minute. "I'm sorry, Mahala. Are you all right?"

"Well, no. Not in the least." She laughed in a light, forced manner. "But I will be."

"Yes, you will," he said sincerely, "but give yourself time."

Mahala remembered that now they were both orphans, and, selfish as it was, the thought gave her some comfort. "Does it get better, then?"

Jack smiled faintly. "Only a little, and very slowly."

"Thanks for the brutal truth," Mahala said sarcastically, rolling her eyes. She took a sip of coffee to try to cover her emotions.

"I think we're always truthful with each other. That's what I like about you. No pretenses."

Again Mahala was flustered. She sat down her coffee cup and twisted it on its saucer. A change of topic would be very helpful about now. "What's it like," she asked, "running the blockade? Is it always as dangerous and dashing as they make it out to be?"

Jack shrugged. "Not always. We can slip in and out pretty safely in *South Land II*. But on the big ships, approaching port from the open seas, yeah, sometimes it's hair-raising."

He went on to tell of his most recent adventure. Mahala listened with wide eyes, reminded again of the vast difference in their lives. She laughed when he related his exchange with Officer Blake.

"Good for you," she cried. "I can't believe they were that determined to harass you. Carolyn said some people were saying you were a spy. How can people pass along that sort of harmful gossip with no proof? It's not like you've ever done anything wrong, anything but refuse to carry military cargo."

Something flickered across Jack's face that gave her pause. "What?" she demanded immediately, alarm making her heart suddenly race. "What have you done, Jack?" She lowered her voice to a whisper. "Not spying. Say it's not true."

"Of course it's not true. What do you think of me?"

"Something, though. You've done something, haven't you? Something to give the authorities cause for concern."

He stared at her, his expression hardening as he wrestled with his answer.

"Please tell me," she urged. "Please don't lie to me, Jack." *Shouldn't I know the truth about the man I love*, she thought silently, *even if that truth shocks or hurts me?*

Maddie walked by at that moment, and Jack's gaze traveled briefly to her and then back to Mahala. "It was also said by some that my ships once harbored escaping slaves, slaves in trouble."

Mahala sat there blankly. "Said?" she whispered. "You mean it's true, don't you?"

"I merely repeat gossip, Mahala, and leave you to draw your own conclusions."

But she knew him, knew his views on slavery. As she stared at him, her mouth slightly agape, a subtle change came over his features, a relaxing, a return to the laid-back manner that he so often displayed. He played with his coffee cup, leaned back in his chair. "I couldn't help thinking, about Officer Blake, that if he's so concerned about the cause being served, he ought to go enlist himself." It was clear he would not return to their former topic.

Mahala struggled to regroup her thoughts, factoring in this new information about the man sitting in front of her. Admiration fought with more nebulous emotions – indignation, fear – and gratitude that he would entrust her with something so secret, so personal. "Of course, he is rather old," she pointed out.

"Before long they might be drafting men his age."

"Drafting? If there's a draft, what will *you* do?"

Jack shook his head. "I'll cross that bridge when – and if – I come to it. Meanwhile," he said with a charming grin, "I'll enjoy my reputation as the new darling of Savannah – eliciting the gratefulness of the men and the admiration of the ladies with my swashbuckling derring-do."

Mahala rolled her eyes again. "Oh, brother!" She knew from Sylvie that Jack's family often gave freely to those in need, not charging for the supplies the women's groups used to make clothing for the troops and sending delicacies to soldiers home recovering on leave. It was largely these kindnesses that saved their reputation, not any amount of derring-do.

Jack didn't seem put off by her unladylike reaction. "You won't be so impervious to my charms when you see what I've brought you."

"You brought me something? A surprise?" she questioned, unable to disguise her eagerness.

To her dismay, he was standing up. "Yes, but you'll have to wait until tonight to get it."

"What's tonight?"

"Dinner at Forests of Green, if you'll ride out there with me."

"Carolyn invited us to dinner?" Mahala rose, too.

"No, but she will, once she sees the wagon load of goods I've brought for them. I like to generously repay my debts."

"Oh, the warning she gave you about the set-up in Savannah," Mahala recalled. "So do you owe me a debt, too?"

"Only one of the deepest admiration," Jack quipped, tweaking her nose in a most annoying manner. But now somehow she didn't mind.

Mahala took the utmost care with her toilette. She did up her hair in an elaborate braided chignon and chose a gown of light blue sprigged muslin. Silk would have been too pretentious for arriving at an unannounced visit on the seat of a wagon. Still, the dress she chose flattered her figure and set off her eyes. She pinned a small flower-trimmed hat onto her hair and put on the watch necklace Jack had given her when she'd closed up his hotel for him the season his father had been ill, but tucked it inside her bodice so Martha wouldn't see.

"What is this he's bringing you?" Martha demanded as Mahala waited for Jack.

"I don't know yet, Grandmother."

"No more gifts. If it's something useful we'll pay for it."

"You can work that out with Jack."

"Mahala, I thought you'd put hopes of this man behind you. Why are you going out to the Rousseau place with him?"

"I want to see Carolyn."

"Bah. You need a maid to go with you. You cannot go without a maid, and I can't spare Maddie."

"He's here," Mahala warned Martha eagerly, hearing footsteps at the door.

At the knock, Martha admitted the expected guest, who was clothed in a light tan frock coat with darker pin-striped brown pants. He doffed his hat and bowed regally to Martha, causing her to purse her lips. Then Jack stepped aside to allow two Palace Hotel servants bearing crates to pass to the center of the room, where they sat down their burden before departing.

"Ladies, I bear gifts."

"Hmph," Martha said. "Young man, you may as well know I do not approve. We are not your family, and for you to bring such offerings to my granddaughter is inappropriate."

"Won't you at least look inside the crates before you make up your mind?" Jack urged.

Mahala was already on her knees, her skirt spreading around her. She looked entreatingly at Martha.

"Oh, very well," said the older woman.

Mahala brushed aside old newspapers to reveal spices, tea and coffee. She gave a cry of delight. "Maddie will be so happy! And look, Grand-mother – *stacks* of Brown Windsor soap!" She laughed aloud, remembering the day she had harassed Jack for offering the fancy bath goods to his guests. "I think you've given us ammunition, too – to keep competing with The Palace," she told him.

Jack gave a nod. "Got to keep life interesting," he commented. "Look in the little boxes."

Mahala dug deeper and found needles, thread, hair pins, stationery and small office supplies – all now hard to come by.

"This is wonderful, Jack."

But Martha's face was a thundercloud. "Mr. Randall, you know we cannot accept such generosity. We are not a charity case," she told him. "I insist you name your price for these items."

"Mrs. Franklin, I mean this as a gift of friendship."

"*Name your price.*"

Jack looked from Martha to Mahala. Finally he stated an amount.

"That's far too low."

"I purchased the items. I ought to know what I'll consider a fair price," Jack retorted, losing patience.

Without another word, Martha marched into the next room and re-turned with her hotel check ledger. She wrote quickly and ripped out the check. As she handed the paper to Jack, Mahala saw that she had made the amount out for more than he had requested – but still a fair price on today's market, Mahala realized. So she held her tongue. They needed the supplies, but Martha Franklin's dignity did not come cheap.

Jack pocketed the check without looking at it. "Thank you, Ma'am," he said, bowing slightly and rather stiffly. "Should there ever be anything particular you need, you have but to request it, and I will do my best to have it delivered to you."

"I'm sure you will," Martha said tightly.

"Shall we go?" Jack asked Mahala, offering his arm.

She took it with a slight smile, expecting Martha to protest again about the need for a chaperone. But her grandmother seemed to sense that she had pushed Jack far enough. To Mahala's amazement, she said nothing. She merely watched them with a strangely knowing look as they departed.

Outside, Jack handed her up onto the wagon seat, then glanced at the sky. "We'd better set a smart pace or we might get a drenching," he observed.

Self-conscious, Mahala looked away from the curious glances they received as the horses pulled away from the inn and trotted out of town.

"Shall I go back and fetch Mrs. O'Beaty?" Jack asked teasingly, noticing her demeanor. Mrs. O'Beaty was the housekeeper at The Palace.

"Is Mrs. O'Beaty free?"

Jack roared with laughter. "So you *are* afraid for your reputation!"

"Why should I be?" Mahala retorted, her dander coming up. She gave her head a little toss. "After all, aren't you such a respected gentleman? And you shall take me straight to a friend's and straight home again."

"Of course I shall," Jack answered teasingly.

Jack's continued laughter, which Mahala found very irritating, was drowned out by a rumble of thunder. A portion of the sky was dark gray, and the wind was picking up, tossing summer's green leaves about. The breeze on Mahala's face was surprisingly cool.

"Wonderful, isn't it?" Jack continued. "I love the air just before a storm. In the mountains, or on the sea, there's that electric charge that creates just a hint of danger. It's beautiful here. I'm glad to be back in Clarkesville."

"Really?"

"Yes, I missed it. And I missed *you*."

Mahala stared at him. Finally she whispered, "Why would you say such a thing?"

"You think I don't mean it? Did you not think of *me*?"

"I – I don't know," she said. Then, in a rush of honesty: "You're not exactly the easiest man to read, Jack."

"Maybe that's true, but when I say something, you can always count on it to be the truth. I'd never lie to you. And I do think about you – God help me – all the time…" Jack's voice trailed off roughly, lost in the jingle of the harnesses and the rumble of the wheels as he urged the team ahead of the storm.

They both stared straight ahead. The moment was as charged as the air around them. Mahala was afraid to look at him. And her heart was pounding so fast she knew if she spoke her voice would give everything away. She was tired of games and distance. She only wanted this man to mean what he had just said to her, to follow it up with declarations of love and commitment. But the dream seemed so impossible, so uncertain, she feared one wrong move or word would send it skittering away.

As they turned into the Rousseau driveway, fat drops fell on Mahala's face. She brushed them away. Faster and faster they came down.

The women inside the house heard the horses galloping up the drive and came out onto the wide, white-washed porch in alarm. Jack pulled on the reins.

"Captain Randall! Mahala!" Carolyn cried. "What in the world? Is everything all right?"

"I've brought you some supplies," Jack called, while Mahala smiled and waved a greeting. "I should have sent you a message, but I admit I rather wanted to surprise you."

"Oh, it is, and the best kind!" Carolyn exclaimed over the rising wind. "What kind of supplies?"

"Farm stuff. Food. A little bit of everything."

Carolyn and Henrietta clapped their hands in delight. Then, with a groan, the sky released its burden. Mahala covered her head with her hands. Apparently without a second thought, Jack took off his hat and reached over to plop it on top of the useless confection she wore. She tugged the hat down onto her head and was preparing to climb out of the wagon when Jack yelled, "Maybe I'd better drive on around to the barn."

"Won't you come in and let the servants take over," Henrietta offered. "At least let Miss Franklin down."

But at that moment a huge clap of thunder brought the horses off their front hooves. Mahala shrieked as the wagon jerked forward, throwing her roughly back onto her bottom, and they shot around the side of the house through the yard.

"Whoa!" Jack called to the tearing team.

Mahala saw the barn ahead and pointed, holding tight to the wagon seat with the other hand. Providentially, the barn doors were propped open.

With a great whirlwind of loose straw, and much snorting and stomping, they pulled into the structure, and the team was brought to rest.

They sat there for a second, hearts racing and eyes adjusting to the dim light. Gradually Mahala's grip on the wagon seat relaxed. She glanced over at Jack.

"Well now, that was exciting, wasn't it?" he asked.

"Just a bit." She smiled.

Jack dropped down and crossed in front of the horses, patting them and speaking gently. In response they lowered their heads. Assured that they would not bolt again, he came around for Mahala. As soon as her feet touched the ground, their eyes met. Jack reached up to gently remove his hat from her head. His hair was dripping. They were both soaked. When he reached up to smooth her own hair from her face, she knew she had only a second to speak what was in her heart. Only a minute before a servant appeared, breaking the spell that now bound them together.

Past the lump of fear in her throat, she whispered, "I do. I do think about you. I did miss you."

She could say no more, for with her name on a breath, Jack wrapped his arms around her and covered her mouth with his. This was the kiss she had been waiting for all her life. This was the feeling of completeness she had been longing for. No more games, but their lips silently speaking the truth – the whole truth – to each other. One hand pressed her close. The other pushed up into her wet hair. She put her arms around his strong back and kissed him for all she was worth.

Then came the running footsteps she was dreading. With an effort that felt like pulling opposite poles of magnets apart, Mahala turned her head away. Bracing her with an arm, Jack stepped back.

They both beheld a grinning black man holding a large umbrella. "Missus send this out for ya. I'll take care of the horses," he announced.

Jack picked his hat up off the ground behind her, then took the proffered umbrella. "Thank you very much," he said dryly.

If Mahala had not been so dazed she would have laughed. As it was she took the arm Jack offered her, clinging close to him as they left the shelter of the barn for the pouring rain. Her boots squished in the mud, and the hem of her blue muslin dress quickly stained. But she didn't care. All she could think of was the man beside her.

Apparently he was having the same problem where she was concerned, for when her one foot almost slipped out from under her, he passed the arm she had been holding around her waist and turned toward her.

"Mahala," he murmured, his warm mouth descending to hers behind the partial shelter of the umbrella and a big magnolia tree. His lips trailed kisses across her damp face. She gasped and instinctively turned her mouth back up to his. His lips teased hers, their quickened breath mingling.

"You are so beautiful. I do love you. You drive me crazy, Mahala, in every way a woman should."

Spoken in ragged tones, the words were like balm upon her heart. Such joy flooded her she felt she must sparkle from head to toe. Jack loved her. At last he himself had admitted it. Moisture that had nothing to do with the rain spilled from her eyes and wet her cheeks.

"Oh, Jack." Mahala touched his curling hair and the strong line of his jaw. "I love you, too."

His eyes darkened, and he kissed her again. As he did he felt the watch chain about her neck. He delicately pulled it out and smiled approvingly. Then he encircled her hand with his on the umbrella stem, and they tip-toed and picked their way to the porch.

There Carolyn was waiting on them. "Oh, my goodness!" she exclaimed. "You're soaked clean through. Come in. Come in. I'll light a fire in the parlor. You can dry off there, Jack, and Mahala–" She broke off, staring at Mahala's face. Then she resumed, "I'll get you a towel, and you can borrow one of my dresses. Go on upstairs to my room."

As Mahala mounted the stairs, Carolyn seized Jack's hands and exclaimed, "A whole wagon load of supplies, Captain Randall! How will we ever repay you?"

"I could bring you a hundred wagon loads, Mrs. Rousseau, and still be in your debt for what you did back in Savannah," was Jack's smooth reply.

Upstairs, Mahala looked in Carolyn's mirror at her bedraggled appearance. Despite that, her cheeks were flushed and her eyes shining. She removed her useless hat and was taking the pins out of her hair when her friend entered, closing the door behind her.

"What happened?" she demanded, hands on her hips, a towel in one hand.

Mahala turned to face her, feeling that she could explode from happiness. "He loves me, Carolyn. He said he loves me!"

"I knew it! You were glowing when you came in – and you looked like you might fall if he weren't holding you up. Oh, Mahala, I'm so happy," Carolyn said, embracing her. "Ugh! Why don't you take that dress off. Here's a towel. I should have something that will fit you."

As Carolyn rummaged through her wardrobe, Mahala toweled off her hair.

"He kissed you, didn't he?"

"Mmm," Mahala murmured. She closed her eyes, remembering. She opened them when she realized Carolyn was standing before her.

"That wonderful, hm?" She held a soft purple and white checked organdy. "Try this."

"Are you sure?"

"Yes. I'll take yours to the maid to rinse out the bottom. Then I'll check on Jack. I'll try to ferret out what frame of mind he's in," Carolyn said. With a conspiratorial smile, she slipped out the door, adding as she went, "Just come down whenever you're ready."

Mahala toweled off her petticoats. They were only slightly damp as she slid Carolyn's dress over her head, admiring the many fine tucks and soft lace trim as she hooked up the bodice. She brushed and rebraided her hair and pinned it up. Her face *did* glow. She felt like an eager girl of sixteen again.

As she descended the stairs, she noticed the rain on the roof had stopped. No one was in sight, but the parlor door was partly open. Mahala approached. She stopped to listen. She heard Jack and Carolyn talking.

"She told you?" Jack was asking.

"She didn't have to. It was obvious that something had changed between the two of you the moment you walked in the door."

"Mm," Jack grunted. "Changed? I don't know. I said some things I probably shouldn't have, and now what do I do about it?"

Mahala felt like an arrow pierced her heart. She put a hand to her breast and stood just out of sight, though she caught a glimpse of Jack in his shirt sleeves, his coat drying by the fire.

"What do you mean?" Carolyn gasped.

Muttering something exasperated under his breath, Jack ran a hand through his hair. He said aloud, "I mean I'm not in a position to marry her. I can't expose her to the danger of traveling around with me, and you can well imagine how the people in Savannah would treat someone like Mahala."

Someone like Mahala.

"Mr. Randall," Carolyn's level voice spoke again. "You've always seemed to me like a man who never made decisions based on the opinions of others."

"Then you don't know me so well, Mrs. Rousseau. Everything I do in life now is influenced by the needs and desires of my family. Even if they accepted Mahala, can you truly see her living in Savannah?"

"Why not make your primary residence here?"

"And be gone all the time?" Jack was clearly growing impatient. He cast down his towel and started pacing. Mahala took a step back. "It's just not practical. I can't meet the needs and demands of a wife. Not now.

Maybe not for a long time. I've always sworn I wouldn't be roped into that. What have I gotten myself into? I've let my attraction to Mahala get the better of me."

"Please, Mr. Randall – Jack … give yourself some time to think things over, to talk with her …"

Carolyn's voice trailed off as Mahala backed away. How could she have gone from the heights of joy to the ash heap of despair in five minutes? How could she face the man who had so cruelly been the cause? She couldn't. She wouldn't.

Not really thinking past the need to get away, her mind numb with shock, she simply walked out the front door, leaving it slightly ajar. She walked straight down the steps and down the driveway, oblivious to the water dripping off the trees but holding up Carolyn's dress as she set a methodical pace for the main road. She didn't care if it took her all night. She would walk home. She didn't want to see any of them, with their money and their fine manners, revolving in their own world that would never fully embrace "someone like Mahala." The phrase echoed again and again in her mind. She might visit. She might be a friend. But marry into that world? She had deluded herself.

Fifteen minutes later, Mahala heard buggy wheels behind her. *I won't look*, she thought. She kept walking. The vehicle drew alongside her, and Carolyn's voice called out.

"Mahala! Please stop! Where do you think you are going?"

"Home." It wasn't Jack. Jack had not come for her. The fault line in her heart cracked open and cold sorrow poured in.

"And you're going to walk all the way?"

Mahala held her chin high. "I most certainly am."

"Please, just stop for a second."

Mahala obliged, turning to look at her friend.

"I know what you heard was upsetting. I want to clobber him, too. But Jack was very worried when we found out you'd gone. You must come back with me, and the two of you can talk this out like reasonable adults."

"If he was so worried, why didn't he come after me himself?"

"He thought – we both thought – I'd have better luck getting you to return."

"Well, you won't. I don't see what there is to talk about."

"Mahala, he loves you. I know he does."

"But not enough, Carolyn. Not enough." Mahala turned and started walking again.

Carolyn motioned to her driver to keep pace with Mahala. She continued. "He's independent and foolish, but I do truly believe he'll come around. He just needs time. I think he's scared, Mahala."

56

"Jack? Scared? Jack does what he wants and never thinks twice."

"I thought so, too, but did he act that way when he joined the Southern cause for his family? It may take him some soul-searching, but Mahala, I believe that with him, love always wins out."

"How long should I wait, Carolyn? I've waited six years for him to admit he loves me, only to discover it's a cheap and selfish love too ashamed to offer commitment. If he's not ready to marry me now, if he's unable by now to embrace all that I am, he never will be. If he's forced into it, he will only look at me one day with loathing. I couldn't bear that. Don't you see, Carolyn? Can't you of all people imagine – *remember* – what that feels like?"

Mahala stood in the road with tears in her eyes, staring entreatingly at Carolyn.

"Yes," said Carolyn, her eyes darkening as she recalled Dev's rejection of her early in their marriage. "I can." She opened the carriage door. "Please get in. I'll take you home."

Mahala climbed up. As she did she saw a swipe of red clay on the hem of the skirt. "Oh, Carolyn, I'm so sorry. Your dress! I'll wash it," she cried. "I'll get it clean again, white and perfect!"

"Mahala, it's all right." Seeing tears starting to flow down Mahala's face, Carolyn reached for her and wrapped her arms around her.

Mahala dissolved into her comfort as the buggy rocked forward, sobbing out her broken heart, crying aloud, "I love him so much, Carolyn! I love him so much it hurts. Why can't he just love me back?"

The street was quiet. Jack made certain of that before he picked up the first pebble. From the layout of the family quarters he was certain of the location of Mahala's bedroom. Now the curtains were drawn there, but Jack saw a lamp burning inside. Under cover of darkness, feeling like a skulking boy, he tossed the tiny rock against the window. It hit with a '*tink.*' She might not have heard that. He selected a larger pebble.

Three pebbles later, he began to wonder if his boyish analogy had been accurate. A sense of shame filled him. He only wanted to talk to her, but Mahala might interpret his nocturnal gesture in a different manner – as no more respectable than that of a master summoning a mulatto from a slave cabin. Hanging his head, Jack returned to The Palace.

Yet what else could he do? Yesterday, he had been coldly turned away by Martha Franklin. She said Mahala did not wish to see him. But Carolyn urged him to be persistent, to persevere until Mahala could express her feelings to him in person.

Being sensitive enough to imagine things from Mahala's viewpoint, he had a pretty good idea of those feelings. After months of correspondence and years of flirtation, he had showed up bearing gifts and speaking endearments – and then there had been the embrace in the barn. And in the yard. Good heaven, despite it all he wanted her in his arms again, so sweet and yielding …

But that passion and the possession that could follow came with a price. Commitment. And that was where thcy *he* – had hit a brick wall, he thought, as he mounted the stairs to his suite at the hotel.

Why?

He analyzed that question as he undressed. He knew it stemmed from the childhood trauma of losing his mother early and his father's remarriage. But lots of children went through that same trial. Why was he so scarred by it? Hadn't he seen his father's contentment in his second marriage, and made peace with both Richard and Sunny? Was he really that afraid of loving and losing?

Not fitting in in Savannah had played into the equation, magnifying his early insecurities, making him vow to be his own man, to rely on no one. With avoidance and wit he had built his defenses. Most people didn't see beyond his carefully polished façade. He knew Mahala did, and the thought of her getting in, of being as vulnerable to someone else as he knew he could be to her, was indeed daunting. But was that really the heart of the matter? Was there something darker and uglier, something that stank of pride and prejudice?

Jack didn't want to turn the light on that corner of his heart. With a sigh he sat down and poured himself a drink. Numbly he uncovered a plate of fruit and bread Mrs. O'Beaty had left on his desk. He plucked a grape off its stem.

He had said he loved her. Looking back now, Jack thought he had been just as surprised as Mahala to hear those words come out of his mouth. But did he really love her, or had it just been passion talking? *Could* he really love her, and still hesitate to commit to her?

Suddenly he realized it was just as well Mahala had refused to see him. What would he have said to her? Only things that would have sent the mixed messages of his own confusion, bringing her further pain. He knew she deserved better. He just didn't know when, or if, he would be able to give it to her.

Jack took out a piece of paper, wrote the date and began: "Dear Mahala, I am sorry for the ways I have caused you pain. I find I have blundered carelessly into an area of life for which I am ill prepared. I must return now to the coast, but I hope that when I come again to Clarkesville we will both have greater clarity of mind. Please know I do care about you, and please forgive me. Your humble servant, Jack Randall."

Placing the note in an envelope and sealing it, Jack blew out the light. He would have the correspondence delivered in the morning, before he headed back to Savannah. By the time he returned to the mountains, he would have figured out his feelings, and Mahala would then be willing to hear them.

CHAPTER FOUR

Early July, 1862
Clarkesville, Georgia

 confess I've never seen her so disheartened, Mrs. Rousseau," Martha Franklin said as she led Carolyn back to Mahala's bedroom. "*Broken*-hearted, I should say. First she stopped eating. Even Leon was alarmed. It was he who suggested Maddie's special tea. That's all she'll drink now days. The herbs in it are supposed to be soothing, but now she can hardly stomach even it! And she's taken on some sort of cold. I've never seen her so sick and listless. I *knew* better the minute that swaggering pirate came knocking on our door with his crates of goodies and his dandy manners. I told Mahala years ago he would never treat her honorably, and now this – right after her poor grandfather's passing."

Carolyn said nothing, realizing Mahala's grandmother was unaware of her own regard for Jack.

Martha paused and snatched a folded note out of the bosom of her dress. She held it out to Carolyn. "This was what sent her to bed. I finally took it away, after I caught her reading it for what must have been the hundredth time."

Standing in the hallway, Carolyn scanned the short missive in Jack's hand. "This is most regrettable," she murmured. "I will talk with her, Mrs. Franklin. Maybe I can help."

Martha knocked, and at Mahala's low reply, opened the door. She stood aside for Carolyn to enter, then closed the door behind her. Mahala was sitting up in bed, writing in what Carolyn supposed to be her journal. Carolyn's heartbeat faltered at how wan and thin her friend had grown in such a short time. There were dark smudges under her eyes. And for a Cherokee her nose and eyes were an alarming shade of red. Mahala's gaze fell immediately on the note Carolyn still held.

"I see you've read it," she commented.

Carolyn nodded.

"You cannot fail to share my conclusion now."

"And what conclusion is that?"

"That he does not love me."

"On the contrary, I firmly believe quite the opposite."

"How *can* you?" Mahala wailed, sounding for all the world like a disillusioned school girl.

"He is apologetic and admits to a struggle with his feelings," Carolyn pointed out, coming forward and sitting down on a chair next to Mahala. "If he didn't love you, he wouldn't have written the note at all. He wouldn't have come and tried to see you. He did come, didn't he?"

"Yes, but Grandmother sent him away before I knew. And then, one night he threw pebbles at my window. At first I resolved not to open it. To do so would have been to verify his low opinion of me – that I am not a lady! But then I couldn't stand it. I opened the window, but he was gone. And then – that note. No promises, no declarations. He just left, Carolyn. Just assumed I would be here waiting another year on his whims, maybe to only have my heart broken again. I can't do that. I have to put Jack Randall to rest."

"And can you do that?"

Mahala closed her eyes, and two tears squeezed out. "I must. To him I am a second class woman not worthy of a gentleman's promise." Her voice caught on a sob. "Remaining open to his future pursuit would only make me vulnerable, foolish, and even less desirable in his eyes."

"You don't know that."

Mahala pressed a handkerchief to her face. "I do, Carolyn. What could change it? What could raise my status in Jack's eyes? Nothing I have power over. I am what I am, and he is what he is."

Carolyn shook her head. "Please, Mahala, just don't do anything rash."

Mahala laughed raggedly. "What would I possibly do? Throw myself off the cliffs of Lynch Mountain?"

"That's not funny. You're not yourself, Mahala. This isn't like you to sit in bed hiding from the world." Next to her on the nightstand, she noticed a cup of half-drunk herbal tea. Picking it up and sniffing it, she made a face. It smelled awful. "And drinking this stuff."

"What does the world have to offer me?"

"The girl I know would be asking what *she* has to offer *the world*."

"I don't care anymore. I don't even want to get up in the morning to face another meaningless day."

Alarmed at the signs of depression, Carolyn stood up. "That's it," she announced. "We're going out. You need fresh air, real food and absolutely no more of this horrible tea."

"But it's the only thing that lets me sleep at night!"

"Too bad." Carolyn seized the cup, marched to the door and called for Mrs. Franklin, who appeared almost instantly. Carolyn wondered if she had been listening. She asked if Martha would have Zed hitch up the two-seater open buggy, one light enough Carolyn could drive. With a glimmer of approval, the older woman nodded. Then Carolyn turned back into the room. "Let's get you dressed."

"Thank you for your concern, Carolyn, but I have no desirc to go out," Mahala replied blandly.

"Which is exactly why you *are* going." Carolyn opened the armoire and started rifling through the dresses hanging there. When she found the tailored frock she sought, she laid it out and flung back Mahala's covers. Mahala drew back, tucking her feet in under her nightgown, but Carolyn tugged on her arm. Surprised at her own resolve, she threatened, "Don't make me call your grandmother to help me bodily move you, because I will if I have to."

Reluctantly Mahala rose and stood there, a forlorn figure with her dark hair trailing down over her white night gown, her face mutinous. Good. At least there was a stirring of emotion. Satisfied, Carolyn headed for the door, tossing over her shoulder, "I'm coming back in ten minutes, and you'd better be ready."

"Or what?"

"Or – I'll think of something. Something decidedly unpleasant. I'll be thinking of it during the ten minutes." As she closed the door, she heard the welcome sound of Mahala's laugh.

Martha stood there smiling at her. "Thank you, Mrs. Rousseau," she said. "You've been a good friend to her."

"As she has, to me." Carolyn smiled and reached out, touching Martha's hand.

Fifteen minutes later, with Mahala still looking faintly sulky, Carolyn drove them out of town in a southerly direction. Mahala didn't say much, and neither did Carolyn. But she watched the fresh air and sunshine slowly do their work. It was a hot day, but she believed more than warmth brought the color back to Mahala's cheeks.

Maddie had packed cookies and jars of lemonade. When they came to a stream, Carolyn suggested they take a break. They let the horses nibble the long grass nearby as they sat on the bank in the shade, sipping the cool drink. Carolyn was afraid Mahala's stomach would rebel, as Mahala told her it had recently at the taste of food. She was able to take in only a little, but that little seemed to revive her like the fresh air.

"Have you heard from Devereaux?" Mahala asked.

Carolyn nodded. She decided to ignore the slightly grudging tone in favor of encouraging her friend's effort to focus on something besides her own pain. "He was wounded."

"*Wounded?*"

"Only slightly, grazed on the shoulder, and had a concussion. A shell exploded next to him in some fighting at a place called Garnett's Farm."

"How alarmed you must have been!"

"I admit I was quite shaky. I knew something was wrong from the minute I saw his handwriting. But he's all right, thank God, though I still worry about him overdoing it. He went straight back to command and marching around the very next day – in the rain, no less. Dev says it seems it always rains right after a battle. Something about the changes in the air."

"Hmmm." Mahala had removed a boot and let a hot foot dangle in the creek. Carolyn looked around warily for water snakes. "So did they get to rest after that?"

"Not right away," Carolyn replied, watching Mahala take off the other shoe. She felt a little tempted to do likewise but went on with her answer. "They had to march and march – eighteen hours straight, then yet *more.* And then they had to fight again at a place called Malvern Hill. The 8th got separated from their commanders so they weren't pressed into the worst of it, but Dev said that after the assault, the whole field, the whole hill leading up to the Yankee position, was *crawling* with Confederate wounded."

"Mmm," Mahala said, this time with more feeling. A shudder passed over her. "I hope my brothers stay in camp at Loudon a long time. How can you stand it, Carolyn? Knowing Dev is exposed to that kind of danger? I'd lose my mind."

"I would, except for much prayer. It's worse now – since I feel like we have more to lose. Since it seems like we might have a chance at a real marriage. He's actually homesick, Mahala. I never thought he would need me like that."

Mahala turned to study her. "I'm happy for you," she said at last. "Truly I am. Please don't think I'm not."

"I know. It's all right. Will you just – do me a favor?"

"What's that?"

"Promise me you'll start eating and drinking regularly again."

Mahala nodded.

"I'll come by to check on you. If I see any more herbal tea, I'll throw it out the window." Her threat brought a mild smile. "And one more thing."

Carolyn brought Jack's letter out of her pocket and handed it back to Mahala. Mahala looked like she might cry again at the sight of it. "Take this. Put it away and don't look at it again, not until you and Jack have resolved things. Don't give up on him yet. If Jack is the only man who makes your heart take wing, I can honestly say no amount of waiting is too much. Time can do amazing things. I should know."

Mahala took the paper. She looked at it a long time. "I'll try," she said at last.

The day after Jack returned to Savannah he took Sylvie with him to the ship yard to view the *Fingal*, which had been blockaded in port and was in process of being converted to an ironclad. He really couldn't imagine why she had begged so hard to go. He knew ship construction and naval innovation meant nothing to her.

She pleaded lethargy and boredom. Indeed there did appear to be such a spirit hanging over the city, perhaps initiated by the fall of New Orleans and the Florida harbor of Appalachicola to the enemy back in late April. This left only the Gulf ports of Mobile and St. Marks, the latter of which was suitable only for small ships, open east of the Mississippi. The apathy extended even to the local soldiers, among whom there had been a marked increase in desertions. There was not enough fodder for the horses, and the officers were said to be cruel. Sylvie told him of the ragged tents and old uniforms as relayed to her by their brothers, who with the Savannah Cadets had just been detached by Colonel Mercer. Their orders were to aid the county provost marshal in guarding the Federal prisoners at the jail and to perform picket duty at the railroad depot.

The biggest excitement in the city appeared to be the *Atlanta*, as the one-time *Fingal* was being rechristened.

"Everybody hopes she'll scare the Yankees away," Sylvie said as they rode to the waterfront in the carriage. "That would be an even bigger morale boost than when *Kate* and *Nashville* ran their stupid blockade. I wish it had been you, Jack. Everyone would have been so impressed."

Jack chuckled. "Sorry to disappoint you, little sister, but you'll have to be content with my less than glamorous arrival from Charleston."

Sylvie clutched his arm reassuringly. "Oh, I didn't mean it that way, Jack. I *am* proud of you. So proud. Everyone is talking about all the arms and munitions you brought to our soldiers. You're a hero."

"I don't know about that."

"I do." Sylvie smiled adoringly from under her big black hat as he helped her alight from the carriage. Ribbons from her hat played in the July breeze as she tapped her way with her parasol beside him. She held his arm as they approached the dry dock, appearing impervious to the stares of the workers, just as she had to the shy, admiring gaze of Andrew Willis back at the office. But of course Jack knew she wasn't impervious. She had dressed in a pure white linen walking gown accented by black Greek key trim to elicit as much admiration as possible.

"Oh, my," she said upon sight of the unique ship in the massive, tiered hold beneath them. The blockade runner had been cut down to its main deck, widened amidship and overlaid with wood and iron. From there the casemate rose at a thirty degree angle. Sparks flew as welders secured four-inch iron plates to this portion of the ship, which would then in turn be crowned by a pilothouse. Sylvie sighed, "Poor Commodore Tattnall … to be returned to naval command here in Savannah but denied any part in such an exciting project."

"See the ram at the bow, Sylvie? They'll attach a spar there for a percussion torpedo. And they can use the bow to ram other wooden vessels … hence, the term 'ironclad ram.'"

But Sylvie wasn't listening. She was busy playing coy with a handsome nearby supervisor.

"Why would you flirt with him?" Jack asked, impatient with his sister's games. "I'd think you'd be more interested in viewing the product of the contributions of the ladies of Savannah – including yourself – than making eyes at a man you'd never give a serious thought to."

Sylvie frowned at him. "Oh, Jack, a girl's got to have a little fun. There are so few handsome men around. And to be fair, I could ask the same thing of you."

"What do you mean?"

"Have *you* been toying with the affections of someone you'd never give a serious thought to?"

The question struck him just as sharply as the bow of any ironclad ram. He turned and started walking back to the carriage.

Sylvie scurried along behind him, chiding, "So you *didn't* follow up with Mahala Franklin. I knew it! Did I just waste all my breath before you went up there telling you she's wonderful and spirited, the only match I have ever seen for you? If anyone has a right to be upset, it's me. I'm young, and sometimes silly, but I'm not stupid! Good heavens, Jack. What are you so afraid of?"

She swung around in front of him and pinned him with her eyes. It was a gaze that knew him too well. His jaw clenched. *That she'll want everything and take everything, and I swore I'd never be that vulnerable to a woman,* was his true answer, but of course he didn't speak it.

"That's enough, Sylvie. What I do with my love life is my business."

"You're a fool, Jack Randall, if you think you'll still *have* a love life after spurning a girl like Mahala."

With a huff, Sylvie climbed up into the carriage ahead of him. She didn't speak to him the whole way home.

Two weeks later, *Atlanta* steamed slowly to Pulaski within sight of the Yankees blockaders. She succeeded in scaring the Yankees enough to guarantee that they would thenceforward keep their own ironclad on patrol in the waters off Savannah. But *Atlanta's* heavy armor and ordnance increased her draft to a skulking sixteen feet, while decreasing her maneuverability and her speed. Not to mention she leaked abominably. For all intents and purposes, she was a failure.

Feeling similarly, but still too conflicted to determine a course of action, Jack returned to Charleston to ready *Evangeline* for her outward run.

The late afternoon August heat was intense inside the Clarkesville Methodist Church, even with the windows open. A bee buzzed by as Mahala attempted to prop up a particularly droopy stalk of hydrangeas in the vase in front of her. At the piano, the aging pianist completed her Saturday practice with "O For a Thousand Tongues to Sing." Today Mahala's mind dwelt on one particular verse, drawing comfort from the words:

He speaks, and listening to his voice,
New life the dead receive;
The mournful, broken hearts rejoice,
The humble poor believe.

"Mournful, broken heart" and "humble poor" certainly described her, Mahala thought. The inside of her felt like a barren winter landscape, aching from the lash of a cold wind. The weeks had passed and she had put one foot in front of the other, but there had been no letter from Jack. It appeared she had been right about him. It was humbling, hurtful. He had probably gone off to exotic ports and forgotten even the memory of their kiss, that memory that still made her shudder with yearning.

I wish I could hate him, she thought. *Anything but this longing for something I cannot have.*

"I sure hope those last until morning," the pianist commented, bringing Mahala to the realization that she had been staring at but not seeing the floral arrangement for untold minutes. The woman rose from the piano, closing her hymnal. "I'll leave the windows open overnight. Maybe that will help."

"Do you think it will be safe?"

The lady gave a shrug. They walked together toward the door. "Safer than the lot of us drooping just like those flowers in the middle of morning services."

"That's true." Mahala tried to sound like she cared.

They parted ways, the pianist heading home and Mahala going toward the square. The dust was choking, and Mahala wiped a tiny rivulet of sweat from her temple. She wished she could remove her bonnet. It felt like a shield holding in the heat.

She was almost to the hotel when the sight of a rider entering town from the opposite direction caught her attention. The bearing of the man on the dappled horse was faintly familiar. He was heading for Fraser's Store. Drawn by curiosity, Mahala kept walking. She was almost opposite the building, but across the street, when the man pulled up and swung off his horse.

He was clad in a most unusual ensemble – what looked like a dusty Confederate jacket and a floppy-brimmed hat, but combined with leather leggings – and moccasins! Long black hair clubbed back with a bit of twine hung down between the man's shoulders, she saw as he moved to tether his stallion.

Then, as if sensing her intense scrutiny, he turned. Mahala's hand flew to her heart. *Clay!* Time seemed to stop as she stared at the face – the same, yet altered – that she'd doubted she'd ever see again.

Mahala wasn't sure which one of them moved first. But the next moment Clay was sweeping her out of the path of an oncoming wagon that she hadn't even seen, over to his side of the street. Without further thought she flung her arms around his neck. He didn't hesitate to draw her close. She was surprised at his increased solidness and height, and drew back shyly. She looked into the face of a man, not a boy, broader and more sober, with high cheekbones and mobile lips. But the glint in his dark eyes was the same, and when he smiled, tentatively touching her face, she relaxed into a smile of her own.

"Ah, Mahala, I didn't dare to dream I'd receive such a welcome. You're the same. Just the same."

No, I'm not, she thought, but asked in amazement, "What are you doing here?"

"Well, it's just as it appears. I've come home."

"For good?" But before he could answer her question, a choking sound emitted from someone on the porch of the store. Clay turned to see his adoptive father standing there, shock written across his face and the broom he had been holding dropping from slackened hands.

Clay approached him and did the last thing Mahala expected. Like the prodigal son, there in the dust on the step, he went down on one knee, head bowed. Mr. Fraser just stood there staring at him like he had seen a ghost. People on the street were beginning to stop and stare, too.

"Father." Clay looked down at his feet then up into his father's eyes. "I want to say in person that I'm sorry for the pain I caused you when I left you so suddenly to go west. If you will take me back – if you will take me in – I'd like to come home."

Mahala felt tears spring to her eyes.

Mr. Franklin's shoulders were now shaking with emotion. "Oh, Son, you never left our hearts. You *are* home."

Clay rose quickly and went into a bear hug so deeply felt that Mahala turned away, sensing she was intruding on a private and personal moment. As inconclusive as her moment with her old friend had been, it needed to be enough for now. He needed time with his parents. He could seek her out later, if he wanted to.

Dazed, but with a quick stride, she walked back to the hotel, where Martha hurried out of the dining room to greet her. "Where have you been? It's time to set the tables." She pushed an apron into Mahala's hands and then paused. "What's wrong? You look like someone just hit you in the head with Maddie's biggest frying pan."

"Clay Fraser is home."

"*Home!* For good?"

"I don't know yet. I only saw him for a moment before his father came out onto the porch. It was really just coincidence that I saw him at all."

Martha looked contemplative, studying Mahala's face. "Was it?" she queried softly.

Mahala glanced at her, but Martha gave her a little shove. "Let's get to it. The guests are coming in. Maybe he'll come see you later."

"You wouldn't disapprove?"

"I can't disapprove of *anything* more than seeing you like you've been the past two months. I've been wrong about a lot of things, Mahala. I always thought Clay Fraser wasn't good enough for you, but if he can bring a smile to your face, I'll no longer stand between you."

"But he's just a friend," Mahala protested.

"We'll soon see."

So saying, Martha moved on. Mahala tied on her apron and went to work, but after the dinner rush, she couldn't remember a single thing that she had done. All she'd thought about was whether Clay would come to see her, and what he might say if he did. A hundred questions rose in her mind. Finally she told herself it would be like it had been in their letters

– sweet devotion and understanding, that was all. It would be good to have someone to talk to. If he came. Which she wanted him to. But she wouldn't be upset if he didn't. Yes, she would. She was dying of curiosity. And he had seemed so different. It was rather intriguing.

As the sky turned hazy and orange outside and the sounds of contented guests settling into their rooms filled the inn, Mahala checked her hair in the mirror of her bedroom. She put on earrings and laid out a pair of light gloves, should she need them for walking. Then she sat down on a rocking chair on the porch. She sipped a glass of tea and watched the evening traffic. Men came and went, but none with that unique appearance that had arrested her this afternoon. The sun sank slowly and, with it, her heart.

He wasn't coming.

Had he thought her hug too forward? Had he been angry that she had walked away, leaving him without saying goodbye? She had only meant to give him time with his parents. Oh. Had his parents found fault with something he had told them and turned him out, after all? Or, by not coming, did Clay mean to make a statement to her, that he was no longer enamored of her? But if that was the case, that was what she wanted. Right? Well, she did want him to desire to see her enough to come for at least one visit.

At last, disgruntled, Mahala pulled on her night gown and stretched out on her bed. She lay staring at the ceiling.

Her grandmother poked her head in, her graying hair illuminated by the oil lamp she held. "Maybe tomorrow."

"Who cares," Mahala said grumpily.

But Martha could see through her mood. "Maybe Clay Fraser is smarter than I thought." She went down the hall to bed. Soon Mahala could hear her soft snores blending with the trilling of the cicadas, long before she herself at last succumbed to sleep.

The routine of running an inn could quickly become tiring and repetitive. To help break the demanding schedule, Maddie always served a cold breakfast Sunday mornings, followed by a simple but hearty roast and yesterday's bread for lunch. Dinner consisted of leftovers. They often paid local young girls to help with serving and clean-up. Martha said she and Mahala deserved at least one day of lady-like leisure each week.

It was to this prospect that they were returning after morning worship. Mahala was as yet unsure of the nature of her feelings for Clay. Finding she could have any thoughts at this time of another man – despite the deep ache in her heart for Jack – had been rather alarming. But the service had quieted her spirit. She had been able to commit her confusion to God and now felt that she had at least enough fortitude to face the day ahead. And then Clay appeared in their path.

He was clad in a fresh white shirt with a civilian vest and pants. "Ladies," he said, removing his hat and bowing.

Martha uttered a little squeak. "What in the world type of hairdo is that?"

Mahala colored, embarrassed.

"I plan to cut it soon," Clay offered apologetically.

"That's a good thing. I'd advise doing it quickly, before you scare all the locals into thinking you're a young brave on the warpath."

Clay recovered his composure, saying firmly, "I have now seen braves on the warpath, Mrs. Franklin, and I can assure you that they are a much more alarming sight."

Before Martha could speak further, Mahala interjected in as calm a tone as possible, "Grandmother, you have not yet properly greeted Mr. Fraser."

Martha frowned at her then turned back to Clay. Mahala joined her in a small curtsy.

Martha smiled. "So the wilds didn't suit you so well, eh, Mr. Fraser?"

"No, Ma'am, they did not. And how have you fared?"

"Oh, the same as ever, though it's Mahala I'm sure you've come to see about."

Clay cast a quick glance in her direction. "I did hope she might be willing to go for a stroll with me."

"I am willing."

"What about dinner?" Martha wanted to know.

"I'm not very hungry, Grandmother. Will you ask Maddie to keep me a plate until later?"

Martha nodded. "Just don't be too long."

They walked with Martha to the hotel, and Clay opened the door for her. She cast him a glance as she passed inside. Then Clay turned to Mahala.

"Some things never change."

Mahala smiled. "You might be surprised." She realized she had almost said too much and added quickly, "At least she didn't protest our taking a walk, right? Where shall we go?"

"Is our old willow still standing?" Clay referred to their spot by the Soquee River where she had once taught him to read and write in Cherokee ... and where he had proposed to her on that fateful day, the last time she had seen him.

"Oh, yes, it's much bigger now."

Clay offered his arm with a grin. As she took it a little reluctantly, thinking of how he had not come to see her the night before, he said, "I'm sorry it took me a while to get over here. My folks had lots of questions, and we talked late into the night. I couldn't get away, though I wanted to see you."

"It's all right. I'm just glad you weren't upset with me."

"Upset with you? Why would I be?"

"Oh – I thought maybe the way I left."

"No. I knew you were trying to be considerate. You were really afraid I was upset?" Clay asked again with amazement.

Mahala tilted her head, wanting to downplay the admission. "Maybe a bit," she answered. "So, things went well with the Frasers?"

Before he could answer they were stopped by a group of church-goers who recognized Clay and welcomed him home with enthusiasm. Mahala opened and swished her fan as he talked with them, answering their many questions as courteously but as briefly as possible. Was she wrong, or was he eager to be alone with her?

"I'm sorry," he said when they were able to break free.

She smiled and shook her head. "Quite all right."

"What were we saying? Oh, yes, Mahala, it was amazing. I knew from their letters my parents weren't still angry with me, but I never had really apologized to them for the manner in which I left – and how that must have hurt them. They were all graciousness. They said they were just glad to have me back. Can you believe?"

"Yes, I can. They love you dearly," Mahala replied. "I'm sorry, but I'm afraid I'll probably have all the same questions they did. Are you on leave?"

"Not exactly."

"What do you mean?"

"I'm AWOL."

"*What?*" Mahala cried. "You're not – a deserter?"

"Not exactly."

"Well then, please explain!"

Clay gave her a hand as they descended the bank near the bridge over the Soquee. "I don't really have a regiment to desert *from*. Drew's Mounted Rifles has pretty well ceased to exist."

"What do you mean?"

"Come over here in the shade." Clay tugged her toward a stand of oak trees. He looked around with apparent satisfaction. "There's our willow. It really *has* grown. I can't believe I'm really back here." He picked up a branch and began to snap off pieces, throwing the twigs into the river and watching them slowly drift downstream.

"Clay, please – you're growing exasperating!" Mahala finally exclaimed, stomping her foot.

Clay grinned at her, looking boyish, looking like she remembered him. "I'm sorry. Well, if you're sure you want the long, sad tale ..." He paused and sighed, his face hardening into the new lines. "Back at the beginning of June, we were prepared to invade Southwest Missouri. Before we were mobilized a Yankee colonel from Kansas – Doubleday, I think – invaded our territory. He skirmished with Watie's men near the Grand River and pretty much scattered them. Anyway, Doubleday was replaced by another man named Weer, and while Weer was waiting on reinforcements – many of whom had been Opothleyahola's followers, fighting for the Union, you recall – he sent runners into the Nation to let sympathizers know he was coming. And they started joining him, Mahala! More desertions! He even told Chief Ross he was coming in case the chief wanted to show his loyalty to the U.S."

"Did he?" Mahala asked in wonder.

"Not at first. Ross called for troops, but he was only given about a hundred white men under Colonel Clarkson. Well, Weer, he started skirmishing with Stand Watie, and the Confederate Cherokees started fleeing the area. Now the tables were turned, you see. Last month Clarkson and Weer fought at Locust Grove. It was a disaster. Clarkson and his men were captured, a bunch of them killed and wounded, the wagons captured, too. Watie's men learned the enemy was coming and scattered. The few Confederate survivors who made it back to Park Hill and Tahlequah – where I was – told everyone what had happened. The men panicked. Many of them received messages from friends and family urging them to go over to the Union before it was too late. So they did. Two hundred went with our regiment's chaplain, Rev. Downing, to the other side."

"What did you do?" Mahala breathed. "Did you – think of deserting?"

"No!" Clay snapped, turning to look at her with eyes flashing. "How can you even ask me that? You know there's nothing I hate more than indecision and two-facedness in a man."

"I'm sorry. I know," Mahala said. She had to admire that, especially in view of what she had just been through with Jack.

Clay continued, more moderately, "I don't know, maybe that comes from me being abandoned as a kid during the round-up of our people – just wanting something to stick to, thinking that people should be more dependable. Kind of dumb, maybe."

Mahala tentatively touched his arm. It was lean and hard with muscles. "Not in the least," she murmured.

He sighed. "Anyway, what I did do was join the few Confederate Cherokees of Drew's regiment left guarding Chief Ross at his home in Park Hill. But I quickly discovered their sentiments were also Union. I didn't say much, just watched and listened. Weer sent a Captain Greeno to our area, and he sent a man to Park Hill to feel out the waters. Once he got a good reception Greeno came in force. He told us the Yankees had never abandoned us but had merely needed time to gather the troops necessary to repel the Confederates from the Cherokee Nation. About this same time, Ross got an order to muster with the remaining Confederate Cherokees at Cantonment Davis. He hesitated. That was all Greeno needed. He arrested Ross. By doing that he freed him of the responsibility to go. You see?"

"But didn't the soldiers get angry at his arrest?"

"No, because he was just as quickly paroled, and I learned he was preparing his family to be escorted by Greeno to protection behind Union lines. He completely turned coat. The way I saw it, I had three choices. I could go to Cantonment Davis where I heard a few loyal men were left with Captain Benge of Company K. But they weren't from my district, and who knew what *they* might decide to do next. I could try to join Stand Watie. I admire his courage, and his record is pretty good, but his men are mixed bloods, and I knew they would never trust a full-blood from Drew's band of deserters. Or I could come here. So, here I am. Done with it all. I wash my hands of it. I want no more of it. The whole thing made me sick – *sick*."

Mahala stood a moment, watching Clay's pain-twisted face as he brushed his hands together, symbolically ridding himself of all he had been through. But she knew it was not that easy. She murmured his name with sympathy, yet something held her back from trying to touch him. Instead she asked gently, "But could you not now be arrested for desertion?"

"Probably. If a provost posse wants to go to the trouble to find me."

"Surely they won't. With all the chaos that occurred, they wouldn't trouble over one private."

"My enlistment isn't officially up until October 25, but I had to come home – to figure out what to do next. To figure out a lot of things." He turned and looked at her steadily.

Mahala swallowed, and her gaze faltered. "I understand," she said. "I'm so sorry you didn't find what you were looking for in Indian Territory, Clay."

"I realize now it's because what I was looking for was here all along."

She stood silently, afraid to probe into his meaning too far.

"Are you going to marry Jack Randall, Mahala?"

Her mouth dropped open. "*What?*"

"My mother told me it was well known about town that you've corresponded with him since the beginning of the war, and that he came to see you recently. Are you engaged?"

"Well, if everything else is well known about town, I don't see how that little fact can be left in question!"

"Come on!" Clay barked, suddenly out of temper. "Just answer me!"

Tears of surprise sprang to Mahala's eyes. "No," she said. "No, we are not engaged."

Clay stepped forward and took hold of her arm, suspicion further narrowing his expressive almond eyes. "What happened? Did he trifle with you?"

Mahala pulled away from his pinching grip. "Clay, please, I really don't want to talk about it."

"He's hurt you. That blackguard! Didn't I warn you about him, years ago? You must tell me if he's harmed your reputation in any way."

"So you can do what, go after him and shoot him? Don't be silly. No, my reputation is as dull and spotless as ever. Everything's as dull as ever. Not a thing has changed since you left. I hope that comforts you, because it sure doesn't please *me*."

"You're angry with me." Clay shook his head in frustration.

"I'm angry with life. Oh, there was one big thing that happened recently, to mark the monotony of my days. My grandfather died this spring." She flung it out in a way that she knew would hurt him. She wasn't sure what had gotten her dander up. Maybe it was the way Clay took on over Jack. It felt just like they were sixteen again. Only she had nothing – not a thing – to show for all the intervening years.

Now Clay's face changed dramatically. She felt guilty as true sorrow crumpled his features. He turned away, drawing in a breath. Then he said, "Ah, Mahala, I'm so sorry to hear that. He was the best of men. I – admired him more than anyone else."

"Really?"

Clay nodded. He wiped moisture from his eyes. "He was the first – and for a long time, the only – full-blooded Cherokee man I knew. He was so wise. In my mind, he was like a symbol of our people."

Mahala stood looking at him. To hear her grandfather spoken of in such terms, in the very way she herself thought of him, opened the geyser lurking in her heart. Suddenly one sob bubbled over, then another and another. She bent at the waist, wrapping her arms around herself as all the sorrow of the past year swept over her.

Clay drew her close to him, and she did not fight him. He cradled her against his chest, rocking her back and forth, while she cried shamelessly. When she realized the words of comfort he was murmuring against her hair were spoken in Cherokee, she cried all the harder. *This* was the tender empathy she had longed for. How desperately she needed a connection to someone who was stronger than she, who always understood, and would always be there. All the memories of their childhood together and the heritage that had bonded them came rushing back full strength, and she clung to him, wishing for those carefree days when she, Patience and he had been so young and full of plans.

At last when her weeping began to quiet, Clay turned her with an arm about her waist and led her up to the willow tree. He held aside its sinewy branches so that she could enter its shade. Mahala's wobbly knees collapsed, and she sat there like a foundering colt, wiping her streaming eyes.

Clay dug in his pocket and held out a handkerchief. "Here, sweetheart," he said. "Blow."

She did not even mind the endearment. Miserably she obliged, but with a sense of gratefulness that she wasn't too embarrassed to do so in front of him. As she wiped her wet cheeks on her sleeve, Clay sat down behind her. Mahala untied and removed her bonnet, her fingers shaking. Too much emotion. The shade and her uncovered head felt much better. Clay leaned around to look at her as she tucked away the handkerchief. He smoothed back a few stray pieces of hair.

"Better?"

"Some."

When he put his arms around her and she leaned back on Clay's shoulder, she felt both relieved and guilty. Relieved because the comfort was so nice, and guilty because she wasn't sure if she should be receiving it from him. She felt suddenly shy again. They sat there in silence for some minutes.

Finally Clay said, "I've thought about this place a hundred times in my dreams – about the last time we were here. And about how I would do things differently if I had it to do over again. For one, I shouldn't have run away."

"Oh, Clay, I wish you hadn't given it a second thought," Mahala said, raising her head to look at him. "It was all me. My heart was young and wild then. I dreamed of impossible things."

"And now?"

"Now, not so much. I'm sorry, Clay."

"For what?"

"For crying." She paused, knowing she had to say the rest, but afraid to. Stalling for time, Mahala gently touched his hair. "For hurting you."

He twined his long fingers with hers and looked at her intensely. He brought her hand to his lips and softly kissed it. As had happened twice before in this same spot, a moment of panic rose in Mahala. She started to rise, but he tugged her back down.

"Are you sure you want to run away again?" Clay asked. "Be very sure."

Her eyes met his, and she thought, *Mahala, you're a fool. If you leave now it will be the last time.* The thought left her frozen with fear, the terrible fear of aloneness. So instead she leaned in. Clay met her half way. This was no sloppy boy's kiss. No, it was the possessive caress of a man who knew exactly what he wanted. Jack Randall was not the only one who knew how to be passionate.

Now why – oh, why? – did she have to think of *him* at this moment?

Mahala started to pull away, but Clay caught her chin in his hand and turned her face back. It was as if he had read her mind with that uncanny way he had.

"Do not think of him. Do not compare me to him," he said with firm, even emphasis. "There is only one man who loves you, and *I am that man.*"

They walked in silence back to the hotel. Mahala held Clay's arm, but her fingers trembled. On the porch he turned to her.

"I know you have someone else still in your head," he said, "but I don't have much time to figure out what I'm going to do. I know what I want – it's to belong. To this place, and to you. But I need you to decide, once and for all. I'll come back tomorrow, and we can talk again. And maybe I can ask you a certain question again – depending."

Mahala closed her eyes and nodded. "Fair enough," she said.

CHAPTER FIVE

Two days later, Mahala was in the kitchen garden plucking tomatoes from the vine when she heard quick, purposeful steps approaching from around the side of the inn. Carolyn came into view. Her face was flushed, and her taciturn maid, behind her, held two shopping baskets. An abrupt gesture from Carolyn halted Tania still a distance away while Carolyn marched up to Mahala. "Marched" was the only word for it. Mahala prepared herself.

Hands on her hips in a stance of un-Carolyn-like belligerency, her friend came straight to the point. "*Tell* me what I've just heard at your uncle's store is not true. *Tell* me you are not engaged to Clay Fraser."

"I can't do that, because I *am* engaged to Clay Fraser."

"Ahhh!" The unexpected screech was accompanied by closed eyes and an upturned, half-covered face. If it had been any less heartfelt, Mahala would have laughed. As it was, her stomach sank to her toes, but she gently plopped another ripe vegetable into her basket, doing her best to look unruffled. "How can you just stand there calmly picking tomatoes when you've just made the worst mistake of your life? What were you *thinking*, Mahala?"

"Let's see, what *could* I have been thinking?" Mahala returned with rising sarcasm, putting a finger to her chin. "A handsome, dependable and honorable man is in love with me – yea – has loved me for *years*, despite my fickleness, and wants to marry me. As the only heir to his family's business, he also has the means to provide for me, to set up a home right here in our town so that I would not have to leave my grandmother. What could possibly lead me to believe his is a good offer?"

"*Your heart!*"

"My heart adores and respects him."

"But does not love him."

"That is not true."

"Yes, it is, and you know it! Mahala, you must have him release you from your promise."

Mahala's face hardened. "Far be it from me to ever hurt that man again."

"Mahala! As honorable and wonderful as he might be, you know he is not the man for you. If you would just be patient …"

"I have been patient," Mahala snapped. "What would you have me do, Carolyn? Become a wasted and bitter old maid with a heart full of regret? Because that's exactly what I'd become if I keep foolishly hoping for a man who has made his unreliability evident. No. Happiness is in my grasp – a full life, love, children. My heart is ready for a haven. And Clay Fraser offers me that. I'm sorry I won't be able to run in your circles. If associating with 'Mrs. Fraser' will be beneath you, I guess I'll just have to understand. But I've given my word. It's done. And I'm glad!"

"Oh, Mahala, how could you say such things? You know that's not my motivation. You could never be beneath me."

Mahala pushed aside the leaves of the vine to uncover another ripe tomato. She discovered a worm and impatiently flicked it off. Plucking the tomato, she sighed. "I know, Carolyn. I'm sorry. I just don't want to hear this right now."

"I just have to know … are you doing this to hurt Jack? To get his attention?"

Mahala thought about that. She had already asked herself the same thing. "As satisfying as I admit that outcome might be, should he be hurt, that could only be my aim if I were prepared to renege on my agreement with Clay. And I am not."

"Yet you would take a flame for another man to the altar with you."

Mahala did not flinch at the soft but bold words. "By the time I go to the altar, I am determined to have no one but my husband on my mind."

Carolyn shook her head. "What do you mean?"

"Clay is leaving tomorrow to join the other boys from the county in Loudon. His idea. He wants to serve out his term with no blemish on his record, and he wants to do it with my brothers, to establish a family bond. So tell me that's not honorable."

"It is. In every way," Carolyn admitted. Her shoulders sank. "Oh, Mahala, I've just always been so convinced…"

"I know. You've always wanted the best for me. Well, this *is* the best. Believe it, Carolyn. Clay is my match in every way. I just didn't recognize it because it didn't begin with Fourth of July fireworks. He's my equal, socially, emotionally and mentally."

"Maybe so, but shouldn't you have been sure before you committed to him that you *could* get over Jack?"

Then I'd have to wait forever. The answer rose unbidden, but she denied it.

"I won't do again to Clay what Jack has done to me," she stated, turning away. But before she did, she knew Carolyn had read the truth in her eyes.

"Please don't do this," Carolyn said.

"It's done."

Mahala turned to walk toward the inn, ending the conversation.

"Mahala, you're going to regret this."

If she had to be cold, so be it. She had to make it clear that this matter was no longer up for discussion, or Carolyn would nag and connive forever. But as she glanced back at the door, she caught sight of her friend brushing away a tear, and her insides twisted with pain and regret.

That evening Mahala sat with head bent over the white muslin shirt she was making for Clay. Mrs. Fraser was making him a checked shirt, trousers and a kepi – a quick, more official uniform to go along with his mended jacket, so that he would be suited out like the other members of Smith's Legion.

"Are you still working on that?" Martha asked as she passed by with a stack of hotel paperwork.

"Almost finished," Mahala replied, bringing the needle up through the button hole.

Martha sat down at the table. "I just don't know about this, Mahala."

"But you said..."

"I know what I said. But you just don't seem *happy*."

"I *am* happy," Mahala insisted. Not her grandmother, too. "I may not be jumping up and down, but inside, for the first time in a long time, I feel a sense of peace. Isn't that worth a lot? And when I look at Clay's face and see how glad he is, I know it's right."

Martha sighed. "I hope so, Mahala. I surely do."

They both worked in silence a few minutes, Martha catching up on business correspondence and Mahala sewing. She had just secured the final bone button on the placket of the shirt when there was a knock on the door.

"That will be your intended," Martha said smugly, starting to gather up her things. "Now that you're engaged I guess I can't harass him anymore."

"Where are you going?" Mahala asked with a bit of alarm.

"To take my work into my bedroom. You should have a bit of time alone with him before he leaves."

"Oh. Thank you, Grandmother." The idea made her nervous. She went to open the door. "Clay!" she cried as soon as she saw him, for he stood there fully garbed in his new Confederate uniform. And he had cut his hair.

"What do you think?" he asked with a dazzling smile. "Mother just finished sewing it."

"It's very handsome. But I don't know about the hair," she reached up to touch his neck. "It was rather exciting long."

"Mmm, you almost make me wish I'd left it," he replied, pulling her close and kissing her soundly as he closed the door behind him. There was a wicked twinkle in his eye. "But I might have scared the Partisan Rangers into thinking a savage was among them."

"Oh, Clay, anybody who knew you for a minute would be divested of that notion – even my grandmother."

"She's only being nice because I'm letting her have you for a while longer. I bet her double-edged tongue will return whenever *I* do. Speaking of which, I've been thinking …"

Before he could go further, Mahala grabbed his arm and led him over to the sofa. She picked up the shirt and handed it to him.

"It's wonderful! Thank you."

"I have something else for you." Mahala handed him a small wrapped parcel. Nestled inside one of Mahala's handkerchiefs was a tintype. Clay smiled as he opened it and looked down at her likeness, and she added, "I had that made a few years ago when the traveling photographer came to town."

"Thank you."

"Actually you have my grandmother to thank. She is the one it belonged to."

"I take back everything bad I ever said about her," Clay stated quickly, causing Mahala to laugh. He laid down the photograph and drew her to him again. "I don't want to leave you. I've thought about you every day we were apart. How I tried to put you out of my mind! But at last I realized I had to try again. It was you or no one. I'm so glad I came back, Mahala. So glad."

Mahala didn't know what to say. It was she who had driven him away. And she had spent the intervening years fantasizing about Jack Randall. But it was beyond time for self-recriminations. All she could do to atone for the past was to give Clay her complete devotion from this time forward.

She nestled into his embrace, savoring the feel of his strong arms around her. It was good to feel safe and wanted, to feel treasured.

"Mahala?"

"Yes?"

"I haven't heard you say you love me."

Mahala pulled back to stare at him in surprise. Only then did she realize it was true. She had not said the words, even when accepting his proposal. Her lips parted, but it felt like something was wedged in her throat, for less than two months ago she had said those words to Jack and meant them with every fiber of her being. Was it merely a matter of will, of decision, to say them to someone else now? Yes. Love was a commitment, not a feeling.

She looked into Clay's dark eyes. "I love you."

His lids lowered briefly. "I thought I might never hear that from you. But every day I waited was worth it."

Clay lowered his mouth to hers. What began as tender quickly became more demanding. Their breath mingled. Their hearts beat faster. Mahala found it was easy to let herself respond. She knew what it was to need a man. She had been alone far too long. His hand slid down to the curve of her back, pressing her close. She lost herself in the dizzying sensation of returning Clay's kisses, aware they were slowly rotating around each other in an effort to get closer. She found herself pressed up against the plaster next to the fireplace. Her foot hit the poker, and it clattered to the brick hearth.

"Shh," she said quickly, starting to bend to pick it up. "Grandmother's in her room."

But Clay stopped her. He kissed her again, one hand bracing the side of her face. "Mahala," he whispered. "Stay with me tonight."

Her eyes widened, and her heart nearly stopped.

But she should have known Clay's intentions were honorable. "We can go get the preacher right now," he hastened to explain. "You're friends with Mrs. Burns. They wouldn't mind. They can do the ceremony this minute. We can get married before I leave."

"Not by Rev. Burns. He joined the 52nd Georgia under Charles Phillips this spring."

"Then we'll get another minister."

"B-but our families!" Mahala exclaimed.

Clay's brow drew down at her continued resistance. "They'll understand."

"Not Grandmother."

"You're twenty-four, for heaven's sake! She'll get over it."

"Oh, Clay – I can't."

"You can't? Why not?"

Misery knotted inside like a sickness, causing her to lower her gaze. "I just can't."

Clay drew back, his brows lowering. "You're going to change your mind on me."

"No, I'm not! I'm just – not ready. This is all so sudden – you showing back up, and us being engaged. I just need some time. I'm sorry," she finished meekly, hating herself.

Mahala looked down again in the face of his scrutiny, aware of how pathetic her excuses sounded after all these years and all that had passed between them. Any woman madly in love with her intended would jump at the chance to become fully his, especially before he went away to a war. As much as Mahala knew this, something in her held back. She refused to examine it, though its existence made her ashamed. All she could do was plead for a bit more of the grace that she had already claimed in abundance.

"All right," Clay said at last. "It's not really fair for me to ask you anyway – one night – and me going off to battle. Anything could happen, and you'd be left a widow. Forgive me for a weak and selfish moment."

"Please don't say that," Mahala rushed to implore him, putting a finger over his lips. "Please don't." She couldn't bear for him to take the blame for her, to shield her cowardice, her duplicity. For that was what they both knew it was. It might remain unspoken, her refusal to go to one man's bed while she still longed for another one, but she could not allow him to pretend it was his fault. Her heart squeezed at the pain in his eyes. "I just need a little more time," she whispered.

Clay nodded. "Just promise me – the day I come back you'll become my wife."

"I will."

"And you won't go back on that."

"I won't."

"Promise. Promise me."

Mahala took a calming breath, and though her insides wrenched, she stated, "I vow upon my very life I will marry you the day you come back from the war."

Clay rested his forehead upon hers, closed his eyes, and sighed. "Thank you," he breathed.

They clung together a long time, kissing lightly, whispering endearments, tender now, the passion ebbed. It was with a sense of guilt hanging as heavy as a cloak around her that Mahala let him out a half hour later. The guilt developed into dread, which sat like a rock in her stomach all night. And by the next morning, when she went to see Clay off, the dread had become a shadow of nameless fear. It was magnified even more when her grandmother told her that young William Nichols of Phillips Legion had just died in Virginia, according to a letter written to William's parents by young Alex Erwin. Mr. and Mrs. Nichols were going to fetch the body home from Brandy Station. Just that quickly, a young man could be gone forever. Here was proof that the war could and would touch them even in Habersham County. Mahala suddenly realized that she was sending into gravest danger the man who had loved her more tenderly than any other, save her grandfather. But now it was too late.

They said their proper goodbyes before Clay's weeping parents, and Mahala gave him a package to take to the Emmitt brothers. She managed to be calm until Clay mounted his dappled stallion, then the thought of losing him made panic crash through her. She ran after him, calling his name. With a pleased smile Clay bent to give her his attention, taking her hand.

"I'm sorry I didn't marry you yesterday," she said. "I'm sorry. I really do love you. I do."

"I know. And I love you. Forever."

He sealed her lips with his one last time and said, "The best is yet to be. You'll see, Mahala."

Late October, 1862
Nassau, Bahamas

"Excuse me, Captain Randall," called a clerk from the front desk of the Royal Victoria Hotel, where blockade runners always stayed while in port, as Jack prepared to brush past the tall, potted palms on his way to the stairs. He paused and turned. "You have a letter from the States, Sir."

Jack walked back to take the proffered envelope from the man's hand. He looked at the address. It was from Sylvie. "Thank you."

"Have a good night, Captain Randall."

Jack certainly hoped to. He had spent the day approving the readiness of his ship for its return to South Carolina. Her engines were fit, and her cargo packed tight into every nook and cranny. The tides and moons indicated that the first of November would be an ideal time for a run on the blockade.

Music drifted from one of the ballrooms as Jack mounted the stairs. It and the bold smile of a passing lady might have promised a grand evening's entertainment, but all he wanted was a good night's sleep for an early start. He had been plagued by one too many nights of tossing and turning lately – despite the silken sheets.

And the conclusion he had come to, for all those sleepless nights, had been startling. Revolutionary. He would marry Mahala Franklin. Once he was back in Georgia he would pay another visit to Clarkesville, where he would convince her to become his bride at hostilities' end. Running from the ties of matrimony was pointless when thoughts of the woman already pervaded his every waking moment – and many of the dreaming ones, too. It no longer mattered what her background was, or what Savannah's elite thought of her. She had captured him as fully as Sunny ever had his father, and the only way to regain any measure of control was to make her his.

Closing the door, Jack ripped open the envelope from his sister, preparing to quickly peruse the gossip and events contained within. After all, he'd see her within the week, and Sylvie would repeat everything then anyway. He already knew that Bryson and Alan had rejoined the 54th Georgia and were now near the Vernon River guarding the earthworks there. The Yankees were still expected any day. And the gossip he could do without. But suddenly he stopped. One sentence leapt off the page. He reread it, trying to make sure he understood correctly.

"You will be interested to know that our friend Miss Franklin has accepted the proposal of her childhood sweetheart, a Cherokee named Clay Fraser."

"You will be interested to know that ..."

"...accepted the proposal of her childhood sweetheart ..."

"He has joined the regiment of her adoptive brothers in Tennessee and will wed her upon his return. This confidence comes from Mrs. Rousseau, so it is indeed trustworthy. I told you so, Jack."

"I told you so, Jack ..."

November 1862
Clarkesville, Georgia

It had been a peaceful autumn in Habersham County, thought Mahala as she saddled up Unagina for an evening ride. There had been many families from the coast present in and around Clarkesville. Carolyn and her family had stayed busy with the other "summer people" – the Tattnalls, Kollocks, Alstons, Owens, Houstouns, Stiles and Warings. Occasionally Mahala crossed paths with them, and was sometimes persuaded to join Carolyn and her other friends for tea or a ride. She was often asked to tell about the area and its native people, which she did. The ladies were gracious, inquisitive. Mahala no longer minded their questions and glances. Everyone now knew Jack Randall no longer courted her, so there was no need to impress them, to try to pretend she might one day fit in with them. She was just Mahala Franklin, local innkeeper's granddaughter, and the "native" friend to Carolyn.

Last week Carolyn had gone back to Savannah. The last few months had been trying for her husband. In August, the 8th had been instrumental in taking Thoroughfare Gap, where Dev had described scrambling up a hill so thick with briars and underbrush that they had come right upon a unit of Yankees. Firing and crashing back down the hill, they'd been ordered right back up. Dev had led a skirmish line back into the tangled pass, where they had ascertained the enemy's position and driven them away, shouting bogus commands to give the Yankees the impression they possessed great numbers. He'd considered the exercise a great accomplishment, but Dev said something had happened to Dylan during that battle. Something that made him withdrawn. But he made it clear he didn't want to talk about it, and Dev was too busy to press the matter.

From Thoroughfare Gap they had marched to the old Manassas battlefield, where the two armies had again clashed at the end of August. Dev had written of the spectacular lines of gray sprinkled with waving battle flags after he had watched the attack from Chinn House Hill. Despite the visual glory of its beginning, the battle had been brutal on the 8th. A left-wheeling attack on Henry House Hill had exposed them to enfilading artillery fire. Many had lost limbs or lives, leaving most of the companies to be led in the charge by junior officers. In fact, when Colonel Towers had been carried off the field wounded by a shell fragment, Dev had been tapped to take temporary command of the regiment. Carolyn had been so proud of her husband. He had written that finally the Yankees had retreated in good order, leaving them the field, though dearly bought.

Lee had decided to cap off this victory with the move that many felt had been missing after First Manassas: a march north. In early September, he had taken his army into Maryland, which was said to be yearning for freedom from the Northern oppressor. The letters Dev and Dylan wrote home showed otherwise.

When the Confederates encountered the Union Army at Antietam Creek, the 8th was twice sent in to stabilize crumbling sections of the gray line. Their brief stints in the fray spared them from a major blood-letting, but Dev wrote that the regiment still sustained twenty percent losses of the already small number with which they had begun their march. They had also lost their third color-bearer, S.B. Barnwell of the OLI.

The men were now back in camp, sick, footsore – many barefoot – and dispirited. They were without adequate food and clothing. The officers saw that the regiment was wearing out and was badly in need of a respite. Rumors began to circulate that the 8th might be transferred to winter duty in Georgia, far away from the cold and the killing fields. Perhaps Savannah, Dev had written hopefully.

And so it was that Carolyn had hastened there to be near him, should that occur. Mahala could hardly blame her. She would miss her friend, but now at least she, too, received letters full of love and promise from afar. Clay wrote to her often from Tennessee. He had been welcomed by the regiment and embraced as family by Seth, Sam and Jacob. He had quickly found a place in White County's Company C even though he hailed from Habersham. The officers were impressed by Clay's initiative in serving out his enlistment despite the dissolution of his former regiment. This loyalty was especially meaningful to them, as they did not fully trust the men under their command, mainly uneducated, non-slaveholding farmers who displayed some Unionist sentiment. When the corporal of the Dixie Rangers died of measles, Clay, with his combat experience, was elected to fill the position.

Mahala could tell from Clay's letters that he was torn about re-enlisting. She knew his sense of honor, the promotion and the fact that the officers and her brothers urged him to stay would make him reluctant to leave the army so quickly, even while he was eager to start his new life with her. And did he also sense that the timing for that might be premature? For Mahala knew that if she strongly urged him to come home, he would. And yet she didn't. She left that decision in Clay's hands – in God's hands, she told herself.

She refused to let her mind be occupied by such weighty matters on this glorious late autumn day. The sky was jewel blue and perfectly clear, and a gentle breeze stirred the bright leaves remaining on the trees. The strange, twisted osage orange trees had dropped their bumpy yellow-green balls of pulpy fruit. Here and there nut hatches sang their cheerful presence. Sweetgum balls, nuts and dried foliage crunched underfoot, and the thickets rustled with small animals storing up winter's hoard.

Mahala found her path again led to The Highlands. She still felt the old house once occupied by Rex Clarke was so closely linked with her past. As she rode up, it looked like it guarded secrets. The Clarke family had sent a crew out a couple of months ago to clear the grounds and perform routine maintenance, but there was still a lingering air of neglect.

As she left Unagina to graze, a movement caught her attention. A very attractive orange long-haired cat darted off alongside the house. Mahala followed it. With surprise she saw its bushy tail disappear through a splintered crack in the basement kitchen door. She wondered at this oversight by the work crew. Or maybe it had been more recent damage. Mahala tried the latch. It opened! Someone had forgotten to replace the board on the inside. Hardly believing her luck, she stepped inside.

"Kitty, kitty," Mahala called.

But the feline had whisked out of sight. No doubt it stayed quite fat just mousing.

She looked around at old cooking implements covered in a thick layer of dust before mounting the stairs to the main floor. Here the musty scent was just as strong. There was still a good bit of furniture, covered now. Mahala peeked beneath some of the sheets at quality Federal-style pieces.

She gazed with admiration at the Adamesque ceiling and mantel moldings. She loved the way the evening sun warmed the front of the house. It felt like welcome, like home. She could picture herself sitting with her feet stretched out to the fire, cradling a cup of tea.

Climbing the stairs, Mahala wondered if her father had ever been here. He probably had, she realized, when he and Rex were still nominal friends, before the fight when Rex had accused Michael of holding out on him with the gold.

She investigated the bedrooms, which were sufficient in both number and size. In the master chamber, Mahala uncovered the dresser and imagined being the lady of the house getting ready to descend for dinner. *Childish*, she thought. She would never be the lady of this house, or any like it. She and Clay had already discussed taking rooms in the hotel at first, then later finding a modest cottage in town.

"Well, one can dream," she said aloud on a sigh.

"Is this your dream, then?"

Mahala was so horrified at receiving an answer in a masculine voice that she froze in terror, icy tremors running down her spine. At the same moment a figure stepped into the doorway and came into focus in the mirror. The man's appearance settled her fear but could not have been more surprising.

"Jack!" Mahala exclaimed, whirling around.

"Should I write your old nemesis and let him know you're ready to move into his house?"

"How – *er* – what are you doing here?"

"I could ask you the same thing."

"Did you follow me?"

"Certainly." Jack walked forward. He was dressed in a silk brocade vest, black pants that disappeared into riding boots, and a dark gray coat, his hair neatly combed back and curling behind his ears. As ever the picture of suave masculinity, power – and wealth. And something more. A curled, hidden tension that lurked inside now. Mahala drew back as he touched the desk she had uncovered. "So you like this, then? This piece with its straight, tapering legs and only a veneer for decoration? This house? Do you not find Federal style a bit boring and predictable? I mean, here's a window, so there must be a window. Here's a door, so there must be a door."

Mahala watched as Jack illustrated his words with weighing gestures, her brow creased in confusion. His tone was falsely easy-going, with sarcasm beneath. "No," she said. "I find the balance reassuring. Solid."

Jack turned to her and looked her in the eye. "I would have thought," he said, with an odd and rather cold emphasis, "that you would have appreciated a bit of architectural surprise."

Disturbed by his insinuation, she pretended not to understand. "Why are we talking about houses and furniture, when the real question is yet unanswered? What in the world are you doing here, in Clarkesville? I thought you were in Nassau."

"Why do you think I'm here?"

Mahala bit her lip. "You're exasperating." She moved to get past him, but to her surprise and alarm he stepped to one side to block her.

"I came," Jack said, "to see you."

Unable to meet his gaze, Mahala stared at the bright dust motes floating in the air. Her heart thudded painfully – as painful as the burden of tension in the room – and she felt hot.

"Does that disturb you, Miss Franklin?" Jack continued in that tone that had always so baited her. "And let's see, why should that be? Could it have anything to do with guilt?"

"*Guilt?* For what?" she shot back.

"I seem to recall certain words passing between us – mere weeks before your Indian sweetheart showed back up in town. Words that any lady or gentleman would consider weighty, if not binding. But maybe that had no meaning to you."

"Who are *you* to speak of binding words?" Mahala flared. "You who talk, talk, talk, but never commit? Words mean nothing when not backed up by actions. What a man *does* is everything, and in that my fiancé is without peer. And if you want to think me not a lady for feeling that way, so be it."

She again tried to march past him, her head held high, but Jack grabbed her arm and held her back. He side-stepped to come right in front of her, holding both her elbows in a vise-like grip. She could feel his anger, unfurled now. "And what of you, and your actions?" he demanded. "If actions are what you prize, why did you not marry your beau before he went off to war?"

Mahala struggled, infuriated at his incisive question, indignant at his forcefulness. "I can't think of one way this discussion or this location is appropriate. Let me go!"

"Why did you do it, Mahala?" Suddenly there was wistful agony in Jack's voice that caused her to cease struggling. He embraced her, but her back remained stiff, wary, her arms straight by her sides. "Why couldn't you just give me a little time?"

"What reason did you give me not to?" she whispered back, her heart breaking.

"I'm sorry." Jack touched the side of her face, her hair. His green eyes bored into hers. "I was a fool to assume you'd wait forever."

A small sob escaped Mahala's lips. She shook her head. "Please don't say this now," she begged, a feeling of panic rising up within her. "It's too late."

"Write to him and tell him your heart has always belonged to another."

"I can't do that."

"You can't do otherwise."

"And what kind of woman would I be then? The worst kind. Cruel and changeable. Would you want such a wife, who could so casually go back on her commitments? Would you leave me no honor?"

Jack's temper flared again. "And is there honor in marrying one man when you love another?"

"I do love Clay. I do–"

Mahala could say no more, for Jack stopped her by sealing her mouth with his. His kiss drowned out the sound and even the memory of Clay's name, challenging her to deny the bond between them. To her shame and chagrin she could not. The taste of him was the sweetest intoxication. Temporarily she sank into his arms, her lips pliable and yielding beneath his, her racing heart causing the room to spin.

Then she remembered where she was and what she was doing, and she fought to put distance between them.

His words when they came served to bolster her courage. "You've won, Mahala. I surrender. I'm prepared to put aside everything to make you my wife. Write the letter to Clay. This is what's been meant to be all along."

Mahala breathed deeply, cursing this innate attraction, trying to gain control of her pounding heart and shaking limbs. Even as she prayed for strength it came – strength and quiet assurance. She squared her shoulders and gently shook her dress into place. Her voice was unsteady but determined as she answered. "I can't do that, Jack. Because you're still making demands. You're angry with me. You think I forced you to come up here, and you don't like being forced. You think I'm playing a game, dangling Clay before you to make you capitulate. Well, it's not like that. I need a love that's given freely, not grudgingly, a love that's proud and not ashamed. With us, it's always fighting. Always unrest. But with Clay, I have peace. It's real. And it's lasting. I don't expect you to understand, but that's the way it is ... and the way it will be."

"Don't deign to judge what I understand," he said through stiff lips. At his sides, his fists clenched and unclenched.

"Then understand this: I do love you, Jack, but it's not enough to build a life on. Not like this."

Trembling, Mahala turned and walked out of the room. This time Jack didn't try to stop her. But she did hear him following her to the head of the stairs. As she descended his voice came behind her.

"You're going to regret this, Mahala."

A hand on the banister, she partly turned as she answered, "Yes. A part of me probably always will."

But the other part, the deeply rooted, sensible part, found the strength to walk out the door.

That night Mahala's pen scratched rapidly on a piece of the stationery Carolyn had given her. "Please, oh, please, come home right away. I need you now. Do not delay any longer. I know I am ready to be your wife."

She closed her eyes, remembering leaning against Unagina for a full minute that afternoon outside The Highlands, temporarily too weak with her own inner struggle to mount. Feeling like her heart was being torn out of her. But knowing what she had to do.

Mahala mailed the letter first thing the next day. She felt an inexplicable need to hurry, almost as much that she was running away from something as towards something. As she watched Mr. Erwin put the envelope into his sack, she thought, *there*. It was done. No more fighting with her conscience. No more battling between her mind and her heart. Resolution would be welcome.

But it did not come. As firmly as her mind was made up, she remained anxious, watching every new arrival who rode into town and pestering Mr. Erwin at the post office. At last the reply came.

"Oh, Mahala, if only I had received your letter a little sooner. Thinking you needed more time, and feeling no real man can with good conscience go about everyday life while our country is at war, I re-enlisted last week. If I had known you were ready, though, nothing could have stopped me from hurrying to your side…"

When she read Clay's words, Mahala hung her head in despair. Could she do nothing right? Would she always go from one debacle to another? Now, due to her indecision, their fates would hang in the balance for an untold amount of time.

During the grip of the long winter, another letter arrived. Mahala opened the envelope with shaking fingers. There was one short paragraph, neatly and firmly written.

"Mahala – you were right about everything. I have been a prideful, selfish cad most of my life. I used every excuse I could think of not to let you in. None of them matter. I now see that loving you didn't make me less. It made me more. Unfortunately this realization has come too late. May God reform me and may you forgive me. I wish you every happiness in your future life.
Your humble admirer, Jack Randall."

The words were so sincere, so un-Jack-like, that Mahala sat for stunned minutes staring at the note. Had something she had said actually gotten through to him? Now, when it was too late? Or was this just his way of backing away while trying to salvage a bit of pride?

Oh, that she had never received that letter, she thought for weeks afterwards. If he were truly thoughtful, Mahala reasoned, he might have had the integrity to maintain his silence. At least then he could have spared her the lingering agony of wondering what might have been, wondering whether it was a shared agony, or merely one of her own making. She would probably never know for sure.

CHAPTER SIX

y late January, Carolyn knew there would be no furlough for her husband. By early February a letter came confirming it. A handful of men had received leaves – those who had gone the longest without one so far – and a few even returned to Savannah, trying to gather more recruits. B was now the smallest company in the regiment. But Dev would remain in Virginia this winter. He was now the major of the 8th, having received his promotion in December. Likewise, Fred Bliss, William Shellman and Sanford Branch had also moved up the chain of command within the Oglethorpes.

Despite his new position, Dev sounded lonely. As she sat by the fire with Henrietta, Carolyn ran an index finger down the fold in his latest letter, perusing it again. In January, the men had been on half rations due to a break in the railroads – receiving only a quarter pound bacon and one pound of flour daily. No pay had been received for three months. There had been much snow and rain. Dev had written that he suspected they would soon abandon their camp to help support the security of Richmond. She wondered if they had already done so, and if so, if he had received their care package before leaving.

"Is there no good news in that letter at all?" Henrietta asked as she bent patiently over a torn petticoat hem, closing the rip with tiny stitches.

"Well, Dev and Dylan were spared from harm in the fighting at Fredericksburg last month. They're not sick, and things are now very dull. That might be trying to an army, but it's good for us, right?"

"I suppose. Though everybody knows another battle is always coming."

Carolyn flipped over the paper. "Dev does say the inactivity is reaping one good result. The men are having quite a revival. Dylan has been assisting Reverend Dunlap with the services."

"Oh, that's good. Some of those boys forgot their raising when they first got away from home."

Carolyn murmured her agreement. She folded Dev's letter back up. "I swear when this war ends I'm never going to write another letter in my life."

"Carolyn! How could you use such unladylike language?"

"I'm sorry. I'm just so disappointed and frustrated. We may as well have stayed on at Brightwell," she said. They had left her home plantation soon after Christmas, in order to be waiting in the city to welcome Dev.

"And that makes me think, Carolyn – it just seems Mr. Rousseau should have been here by now."

"Perhaps he was disturbed by the condition he found The Marshes in and stayed on a few days to do some maintenance. You know how men are," Carolyn suggested. She took her feet out of her slippers and stretched her toes out toward the warm hearth. As she did, she sighed, noticing yet another hole in her striped stocking. Another item for the mending pile.

"Maybe. But it's just not like him. He knew we were expecting him, and it should not take so long to load up a couple wagons full of furniture. I told him exactly which were the best pieces, the ones I could not do without should the Yankees land in that area and disturb the house. It seems he would have sent a message if he decided to linger and do more than what we'd agreed upon."

"Hopefully he will be here tonight."

Agreeing to turn the topic, Henrietta asked, "Any news from that wild sister of yours?"

Carolyn chuckled. "I had a letter from Eliza just this past week. She's been placed in charge of one of the wards at Chimborazo Hospital there in Richmond. She says she thinks it's because they like to keep the younger, more attractive nurses out of sight of the men, and this way she gets more desk time. Despite that, I believe she's already fallen for a handsome lieutenant from there in Virginia."

"Did she nurse him back to health?"

"I believe she did."

"How funny that your sister of all people should have such a romantic story."

Carolyn laughed and rose to put the letter away, but at that moment they heard a knock on the front door. The butler entered and presented to Henrietta a calling card upon a silver tray.

"Oh, it's Sunny and Sylvie Randall – and just in time for tea," Henrietta remarked somewhat unhappily.

Eager for news of Jack, Carolyn perked up. "Do let's receive them," she urged.

"Very well. I suppose we must, as they *are* family." Henrietta nodded to the butler. Reaching inside her sewing chest, she tucked away the petticoat she had been mending. In its place she pulled out an embroidery hoop with a picture of flowers.

Moments later the Randall women joined them, Sylvie in a hunter green and black striped silk carriage gown and her mother wearing a dark blue button dress. Carolyn knew Henrietta was thinking that only the stepmother of a blockade runner would display so many precious buttons in such a lavish manner these days. But without batting an eye at the finery,

Henrietta and Carolyn rose to properly receive the ladies and ask if they would take tea. The guests having accepted, they took seats, a maid dispatched to fetch the refreshments.

"It is fitting you should join us now," Carolyn remarked, "for we owe our tea to your Jack. How is he?"

"He's well, in Nassau," Sylvie replied.

"You might have heard of the Erlanger Loan," Sunny suggested. When Carolyn and Henrietta murmured agreement, she went on. "It's been wildly successful. European merchants are all too eager to accept the new cotton-backed bonds in exchange for merchandise. Who can blame them – receiving a rate of six pence per pound when cotton's going at twenty-four."

"So anyway," Sylvie broke in rather impatiently, "Jack has plenty of goods to bring in, but he just can't get here for all the swarms of Yankees."

The women nodded. They were all too aware of the hosts gathering at Port Royal, expected to soon move on both Charleston and Savannah. To the great alarm and fury of many Southern citizens, a Negro regiment was said to be among the Yankee horde. Five thousand Confederate re-enforcements had been hurried to the coast, with even more expected. Some said General Longstreet himself might come. The Yankees had just been checked by the strengthened battery at Genesis Point, and General Beauregard was of the opinion that if there was another attack, it would fall upon Charleston.

"Jack doesn't want to meet the fate the *Princess Royal* recently did," Sunny commented.

"Oh, was that the steamer just run aground in Charleston?" Henrietta asked.

"Yes. A whole shipment of cannons, gunpowder and marine engines for our ironclads were confiscated by the Yankees."

"What a shame," clucked Henrietta as the tea tray arrived. She stood to serve the company, asking what they would take.

"A small bit of sugar, if you have it," Sunny replied. "If not, just milk is fine."

"We do have a small stash, again thanks to your stepson, Mrs. Randall," Henrietta said, adding a lump to a tea cup and stirring. She might put up her nose at a button dress, but sugar in her tea cup was quite the necessity. "His generosity to us has been so great."

Sunny smiled at Carolyn. "Not as great as yours to him," she replied.

"I hope Jack can bring us some cloth," Sylvie put in. "We need to be able to make new suits for my brothers. And beef!" she exclaimed. "Whoever heard of paying forty cents a pound for that sad-looking stuff they are selling in the market?"

"Personally I'd like a good supply of salt set by," Sunny said. "We seem to use ours up in between Jack's runs, and of course we can't get the new allotments the state set for soldiers' widows."

"Oh, I can put you in touch with that," Henrietta said. "Mr. George Jones Kollock has a salt works in Florida. They heat the sea water to boiling and skim the impurities off the top. The quality is quite fine."

"I would love to buy some. I'll pay whatever he's asking," Sunny replied.

Henrietta passed out ginger cakes and tiny sandwiches, and they all paused to enjoy them.

Presently Sylvie said, "Jack is thinking he may have to establish a new route to Wilmington."

"Wilmington?" Carolyn echoed with dismay. "He just did move his shipping line to Charleston!"

Sylvie nodded. "Yes, but the Yankees are making even Charleston a difficult port to enter."

Carolyn ventured, "He must find that very discouraging. Already he is away from home so much, and now this. How is his frame of mind?"

Sylvie shot her an incisive glance.

Sunny delicately cleared her throat.

Sylvie answered vaguely, "He'll be all right. You know Jack. He always lands on his feet."

Carolyn smiled, but she felt disappointed. She was not settled, not settled at all, about the state of affairs between Jack and Mahala. They had known she was fishing, looking for some tidbit about Jack's loneliness that she could use to soften Mahala's heart. And Sunny did not want that. Not that it would have worked, anyway. Mahala was just as stubborn as Jack. They were both as stubborn as mules.

Now it was Sylvie's turn to do some prying. "Speaking of being away from home ... all this fuss about the Yankees hasn't scared y'all up to Clarkesville?"

Henrietta laughed. "The scare never ends. I think we will live with it until the end of the war. But actually we do plan to go to the mountains as soon as Mr. Rousseau arrives with some of our furniture from The Marshes. He thinks we will be better settled in Habersham. Not only safer, but better fed. He has plans for us to clear off even more acreage there for planting. It was awkward relying so much on Odell, last year. This way we can survive modestly on our own, without planting our coastal lands."

"It sounds like a wise plan," Sunny agreed.

Sylvie pursed her lips and gave her mother a look. "She says that, but she won't leave Savannah herself," she told them. "And I actually wouldn't mind going – just for a bit, mind you, to see how everyone is that we met up there. Miss Franklin, for instance. She was such an interesting person. Do you still hear from her much, Cousin Carolyn?"

Out of her peripheral vision, Carolyn saw Aunt Sunny nudge Sylvie with her foot. Interesting. She smiled and pretended not to notice. "All the time," she said.

"And is her wedding date set, then?"

"No," Carolyn replied, satisfied to be able to say at least that much. "It will not be until the end of the war."

"Oh. I see," Sylvie remarked thoughtfully.

Carolyn shared a brief, meaningful glance with the younger girl. For all Sylvie's youthful dramatics, she could prove a helpful ally. If Sylvie worked on Jack and Carolyn worked on Mahala, maybe they could yet bring the two star-crossed lovers together.

"Well, I think it's about time we go, don't you, Sylvie?" Sunny asked, her tone breezy but pointed. "It's been a pleasure, though, ladies."

After she saw the Randall women out, Carolyn came back into the parlor. They continued their sewing until a quiet dinner, when they partook of salted fish, rice and beans. By that time she noticed Henrietta possessed the pinched look of worry. Carolyn herself was growing concerned. Henrietta was right. Louis should be home by now.

The doorbell rang again, and the butler went to answer it. Carolyn and Henrietta looked at each other. Then, hearing the most unexpected of voices, that of Carolyn's father, they both rose, Henrietta nearly upsetting her goblet in her haste.

Lawrence appeared in the doorway, looking ever so much healthier than he had during the scarlet fever's aftermath just before the war, but nonetheless pale. Pale from something that had distressed him. Behind him was the slave who had accompanied Louis to The Marshes. The sight of the two of them nearly brought Henrietta to hysterics.

"Lawrence!" she exclaimed. "Where's Louis?"

"Father?" Carolyn ventured, a dread blossoming in her own heart.

Lawrence approached Henrietta. "Aunt Henrietta, just sit back down here for a moment," he said, directing her to her chair and pulling one out for himself.

"What is it? What's happened?" she demanded in a shrill voice.

Carolyn watched as her father took her mother-in-law's hand and looked as if he would begin to speak. But he lowered his head and licked his lips. His hesitancy caused Henrietta to cry out to the Almighty on a rising tide of fear. She knew. They both knew, before Lawrence even said:

"There's been an accident. Well, not an accident. Something more awful than words has happened."

Henrietta stood back up, trying to pull away from her nephew's grasp. "No," she shrieked. "No. Don't say it. Louis is not – is not–"

"Yes, Aunt Henrietta. While trying to remove the furniture from your house, Louis encountered two drifters who had been squatting on your land. In an altercation with them, Louis was shot. He died instantly. Your slave here saw the whole thing and ran all the way–"

Lawrence's tale was ended by a wail of agony from Henrietta. She crumpled to the floor and sat there with her face covered by both hands, a futile gesture of denial.

In shock herself, Carolyn hurried around the table to her mother-in-law's side.

With streaming eyes, Lawrence added faintly, "I've brought back his body."

Another screaming sob tore from Henrietta. Carolyn embraced her, trying to imagine her suffering. She had only to imagine it was Dev who lay dead.

Henrietta's maid came running in response to her mistress' cries. She stared with wide eyes at the tense, unfolding scene. Carolyn directed her to prepare a sleeping draught and to take it to Henrietta's room.

"I must see him," Henrietta cried.

"No, Mother, not in the street. Father will bring him in. You can see him later. Will you lie down now?"

Henrietta's only response was wracking sobs. Carolyn held her and let her cry, her anguished eyes rising to meet her father's. He looked back helplessly, and they both shed tears of sympathy and sorrow along with the grieving woman.

They sat that way at least half an hour before Henrietta began to quiet. Suddenly she said in an amazingly bland voice, "It is my fault. I have sacrificed my husband for my furniture."

"No!" Carolyn exclaimed. "You couldn't have known! How could you?"

"It is my fault," she repeated. She started to stand up, but as soon as her knees locked into place, her gaze turned glassy. Carolyn barely caught her before she fell to the floor again in a faint.

Lawrence hurried to help Carolyn with the woman's weight. He scooped her up in his arms and made for the stairs, Carolyn following.

"Oh, Father, this is beyond a nightmare," Carolyn said.

"I can't believe it myself."

"What shall we do?"

"We'll prepare the parlor to receive him and the house for mourning," Lawrence said simply. "When Aunt Henrietta comes down, it should all be done. It may be of some comfort to her that Odelle and your mother will arrive tomorrow." He paused on the landing and turned to her. "Which way to her bedroom?"

Carolyn directed him, then asked, "What of the squatters?"

"I returned to The Marshes with several slaves to find them, but they were gone – leaving no trace."

A week later, Carolyn, Henrietta, Odelle, Olivia and Lawrence sat around the dining room table, holding a family conference. A black wreath hung on the front door, and all the mirrors had been covered with crepe. Henrietta was garbed head to toe in black, and if the inconveniences and hardships of war did not cut in on formality, she would continue to observe some form of mourning for two and a half years.

Carolyn was worried about her mother-in-law. Henrietta's usual zest was gone. It was as if the life had been drained from her. She spoke little and ate even less. This was normal, others assured her. But Carolyn was alarmed at the changes.

"Henrietta and I have talked," Odelle told them, gently taking her younger sister's hand in her grasp. The skin on her own hands was paper thin and blue-veined, but Carolyn knew her grandmother's fragile appearance was not reflective of her inner strength. "She would like to return to Brightwell with me ... to stay on there indefinitely."

"We would like you to come, too, Carolyn," her father said.

Brightwell? No. That was not in her plans. She pushed down the moment of panic, forcing herself to remain calm, the better to negotiate. As much as she loved her family, Brightwell no longer felt like home, even with them there. It was time to make her own way. She knew this now as clearly as she'd ever known anything. "Thank you," she said, "but I was thinking it would be wise to honor Louis' plan."

"How so?" Olivia asked.

"By strengthening Forests of Green, in the absence of income from The Marshes."

"But, who would do this, with Louis and the boys gone?" Lawrence queried.

"I would."

Her mother gave an incredulous laugh. "But that's ridiculous, Carolyn. You know nothing about farming."

Carolyn reminded herself it was a mother's prerogative to forever see her child the way she had always been, not accounting for the changes of time and experience, especially when they had been separated from each other. "I can learn," she said. "I *will* learn. The head man up there – he knows a lot, right? What's his name?"

"Samson," Henrietta offered.

"Samson, yes."

"Is he knowledgeable, Aunt Henrietta?" Lawrence asked.

"Yes. I suppose so. Louis always trusted him to oversee everything, and of course we were away more than we were there."

"But that's not good, to have Carolyn all alone up there, a young woman unprotected," Olivia protested.

"A young *married* woman," Carolyn answered, "and I never felt safer than at Forests of Green. I have many friends among the locals. Louis had talked with us about his plans for the farm. I remember most of what he said. And I believe he had written to an older gentleman in the area, a widower, whom he thought might be willing to come live on site and act as an overseer for board and a small wage. I think his name was Mr. Conway, was it not, Mother?" Carolyn asked Henrietta.

"Yes. Mr. Zach Conway."

"Did we hear back from him?"

"Not as yet."

"Even with an overseer, if that's what you could call him, I don't like it," Lawrence insisted. "There are too many ways it could go wrong, and for what? A few rows of corn, wheat and vegetables?"

Carolyn turned to him, inwardly begging for his understanding. "If the war drags on, Father, those few rows of corn and wheat may become invaluable. Dev would not want us to be overly dependent. For that matter, neither would Louis."

"She's right," Henrietta announced, surprising everyone. "Both of them were always looking to the future. When the war is over, I have no doubt Dev will take over everything. But it may take some time. Until then, we should do all we can to take care of ourselves. I can't do this. But … I think Carolyn can."

"So do I," Odelle chimed in. "Carolyn was always a smart girl. We can't keep her sheltered forever."

Her father, however, was not yet convinced. "Do you really think this is what Devereaux would want?" he asked. "His wife up in North Georgia alone, away from her family?"

"She'd be safer there than here on the coast. Look at the attack on Fort McAllister just this week," Odelle pointed out. "Why don't you write to your husband, child, and ask his opinion?"

"That's an excellent idea, Grandmother. I'll post the letter tomorrow. But I'd like to go on up to Habersham. Someone needs to see if this Mr. Conway is available before spring planting is upon us. I think we'd all agree even a figurehead is more effective than no one in moving things along. Then, if Devereaux writes that he wishes me to go to Brightwell, I will."

Having presented her plan as confidently as possible, Carolyn stood up, wanting them all to realize there was no need for further debate. What would she say if someone asked her why she wanted this so much? Could she verbalize what was in her heart? Not yet, perhaps, for it was like a tiny green shoot, not yet unfurled. But she knew it had to do with the way she felt in Habersham – settled and at peace. And it had to do with independence, about the person she was becoming, *wanted* to become, for her sake, for Dev's sake. Someone he would admire.

"You'll need more men," Lawrence said. "Louis only kept a few slaves year round at Forests of Green. I can send for eight or ten from those at Brightwell, with your permission, Aunt Henrietta."

Henrietta's attention had drifted back into her own private world of grief. With an effort she roused herself. "Of course," she said.

"Are you all right with that, Carolyn?"

She paused at her father's question. He knew her objections to slavery, and that she had never had to directly supervise slaves. There was no doubt the idea made her uncomfortable. But what other options were there? President Lincoln's Emancipation Proclamation had just declared bondsmen in the Confederacy to be free, but as long as the outcome of the war was uncertain, as long as the slaves lived in territory not controlled by the Union ... the Rousseau slaves were not within her power to emancipate, and even if they were, there was no money to pay them.

"I can do this, Father."

Finally her father sighed, shifted back in his seat, and leaned his head to one side. "All right," he said. "Once the workers arrive you can set out for North Georgia. But if Dev doesn't approve, or if there's trouble of some sort, we'll look for you on the first stage out of there."

Carolyn gave him a faint smile. "Thank you."

The foreman at Forests of Green was a huge, very dark man with rippling muscles and white teeth. Samson. Upon first sight of him, Carolyn had mustered every bit of training not to show how intimidating she found him. Then he had smiled, and she had gone from uneasy to merely nervous. One day, when she got over her fear of him, she might actually like him. He was very intelligent and quite serious about his business – until those teeth would flash in an unexpected moment of humor. All the other slaves seemed to admire and respect him, even Tania, Carolyn's maid.

As the carriage rattled along – Samson was driving Carolyn to Mr. Conway's farm – Carolyn considered the amazing effect the foreman had upon the normally long-faced young woman. Tania's gaze followed Samson everywhere, and when his fell upon her, she actually became coy – in a calm, rather seductive manner. She was riding atop the driver's seat now instead of inside with Carolyn. Carolyn could hear the murmur of their voices. Maybe, she thought, if a romance struck up, Tania might become tolerable to have around.

Carolyn had wanted the foreman along today to meet the potential overseer. She hoped very much that the man might be at home. Everything would be so much easier if he accepted her offer. She was relying on that to happen.

The Conway place consisted of a log cabin on a small tract of land, sandwiched between the larger holdings of coastal families. It was relatively near Forests of Green. A split-rail fence lined the drive, which was rather rutted, and there was a nice creek branch gurgling off to one side. However, Carolyn was alarmed at the sight of the dwelling area. The dirt yard appeared to have not been swept clean in some time, for animal droppings and feathers dotted the ground. Chickens and dogs roamed freely. Goats with swollen udders bleated piteously from broken-down pins behind the house. A wagon with a broken wheel propped against its side sat beneath a leafless oak tree.

Samson stopped the vehicle amidst a din of dogs barking. He came around to the carriage door. "Want me to see if Mr. Conway be at home?" he asked.

Carolyn hesitated. The sight of the bedraggled dwelling should have been enough to instantly send her on her way, had she not been desperate. "No," she said, but she had hesitated too long. The dogs' barking had brought their owner to the porch of the cabin.

"Shall I drive on?" Samson inquired.

The slender man was waving, making an attempt to tuck his shirt tails in beneath the lapels of an unbuttoned vest.

Carolyn sighed. "I will speak with him."

She watched Samson approach the farmer, seemingly impervious to the canine growls surrounding him. Mr. Conway came out to the carriage with Samson, calling to his dogs to quiet, smiling crookedly at Carolyn.

"Mrs. Rousseau!" he said. "But you ain't the elder Mrs. Rousseau!"

"I am Mrs. Deveraux Rousseau. My mother-in-law is currently in residence at Brightwell Plantation in Liberty County. She is ... bereaved." As Samson opened the carriage door, Carolyn moved to step out.

"Oh! I see! Well, I'm sorry to hear that," Mr. Conway said. He held out his hand. "Mr. Zachariah Conway. Pleased to meet ya."

Gingerly Carolyn placed her gloved fingers upon his and alighted.

"Won't you come in?" Zachariah gestured toward the dark interior of his cabin. Bloodshot hazel eyes above a long beard focused on her.

Carolyn hesitated again, then motioned the servants to follow her. As she entered the dwelling, Conway said, "I know all about bereavement, Mrs. Rousseau. My wife passed just under three months ago, and I haven't been able to get back on my feet just yet. Please forgive the state of things."

"My condolences, Mr. Conway."

Was she wrong, or did the man's speech seem slightly slurred? A quick glance around served to confirm her suspicions. On the table, next to a stack of dirty dishes, sat an open bottle of whiskey. Several more empty bottles lay nearby. A faintly sour smell emanated from the entire cabin – and probably the man, too. Carolyn fought to keep her face impassive while she considered the most graceful way to extricate herself from this situation. She did not want a drunken, slovenly overseer at Forests of Green – grieving or no.

"Sit right down, Mrs. Rousseau, and your Negroes, too," Zachariah said, shooing a cat off a chair he then indicated. "Tell me what I can do for you."

Carolyn's eyes flickered over an abundance of hair lingering on the cushion before she caught Samson's gaze. The disapproval in his stony black face was unmistakable. And there was something else, too. A challenge? Remaining standing, she said, "Mr. Conway, it seems I've come at a bad time. Perhaps I should have sent ahead a note. I didn't realize you had lost your wife so – er – recently."

"Oh, no, no, it's all right. I got that letter from your father-in-law – uh, late father-in-law, but as you can imagine, I was too prostrate with grief to see fit to – I mean, to see my way clear to answer him. I'm guessing you're here because you need an overseer."

"That was my intention, but perhaps this is not the best time for you to consider such a commitment. Thank you for your time, Sir." So saying, Carolyn made her way back out of the cabin.

"Now, Mrs. Rousseau, wait just a minute," Conway said, a spark of anger in his voice. "I'm the best darn overseer you'll get in these parts. That I can guarantee. You might'n want to be so hasty." He had followed her out onto the porch. His boot caught on an uneven board, and he grabbed a post to steady himself. "Come on back in, an' I'll pour you a drink so we can talk proper."

Carolyn found herself stifling unexpected laughter. "I think you've had quite enough to drink, Mr. Conway. Good day."

Carolyn climbed into the carriage, and Samson shut the door. All laughter left her then. What was she to do now?

The following morning after breakfast, clad in a shawl and a gray wool dress to keep out the chill, Carolyn followed Samson to the corn field. She yawned, longing for her warm bed. She'd been up past midnight, pouring over Louis' section of agriculture books in the library. Before that, she had quizzed Samson about other possible overseers she might contact. He had given her a few names, but he doubted any of them would be available. And he had seemed reluctant, disapproving, though he never would have said as much. He had watched her carefully, as if trying to see beyond her face, to what was inside. This morning, when she had called him to give her a tour of the farm, he had smiled that dazzling smile.

The dew was still upon the ground and everything had that fresh, damp, earthy smell – the promise of spring – as they walked along the edge of a field. A couple of slaves with harrows were already bent over rows set about forty inches apart.

"Today we do the final tillin'," Samson said. "We dig up the weeds an' then we work in the manure. That gives the plants somethin' to grow on, makes the corn strong enough to resist pests."

"Is it time to plant tomorrow?"

"No, Ma'am, we wait a while. Soil's got to be just the right temperature. Too early an' the plant not grow. Too wet, an' the seed rot. An' we don't want no frost."

"I see. So you said it's too late to plant more rows this year?"

"Yes, Ma'am. Take lots of time to prepare new fields."

"Well, for next year Mr. Rousseau wanted us to make eight new rows, and he was quite adamant that he wanted to double the wheat crop. It's not too late for that, is it?"

Samson looked uncertain. "Guess'n we could clear part of the meadow, that what we mow for hay for the animals."

"Maybe you could put the hands I brought from the coast directly to that," Carolyn suggested.

A twitch of a smile. "Yes'm."

"What do you think of them? The workers. Will they do well?"

"Oh, they strong enough, but things be different up here. They'll have a bit to learn."

"Them and me, too. Can you keep them motivated?"

"Yes, Miz Carolyn. I think I can." Samson paused and studied her. "You still be worryin' about that old Mr. Conway not bein' up to par?"

Carolyn sighed. "A little. I was counting on his advice, and, well, someone to act as a go-between." She decided to take a chance on the big man's wisdom and understanding and just be truthful. "Frankly, Samson, I've never been in this position before, dealing with workers and making decisions about what happens on a farm. I could read all the books in the world, and there's still so much I wouldn't know. But it's important we succeed, don't you see? Not just for the family, but for all of us."

Samson nodded and grunted. "Can I tell you somethin', Miz Carolyn?" he asked.

"What's that?"

"I been farmin' all my life. I been a slave all my life. And you been a lady all your life. Seem like neither of us had to be all we can be until now. Between the two of us, I think we gots enough sense to run this farm. We don't need no overseer."

"Do you really think so?" Carolyn asked in surprise. Suddenly she realized she was asking a slave for his opinion. Henrietta would tell her that it was unwise to show her own insecurities in such a manner. But she had to trust this man. Times were changing. And only time would tell if she could.

"Yes, Ma'am. I report direct to you an' take orders straight from you. I tell you what I know, and you tell me what you know. And I think we'll get on just fine." Samson gave her one of his dazzling white smiles. "Now, I go get those rice hands started to work, if it's all right with you."

"Yes, Samson. Just come see me at the beginning and end of each work day. If you should need me, I'll be in the office going over the farm diaries and accounts."

As she watched Samson walk away, an uncomfortable sensation rose within her. They might "get on just fine," as he'd put it, but at what benefit to him? Sustenance, she had implied, but was that all?

Carolyn was only beginning to get an idea of the amount of work involved in running so small a plantation – a summer retreat, really, a farm at best – and yet already she could not imagine investing one's whole life in such a venture without any of the benefits of ownership. Without ever getting ahead. As much as it might seem like a partnership on the surface, her interaction with Samson, it was not. It was her family owning him just like they owned the land, and yes, that made her decidedly uncomfortable, whether this was the way it had always been or not.

Dignity, she thought, *I'll give him all I can.*

CHAPTER SEVEN

June 26, 1863
Near the Potomac River, Maryland

he Potomac was not as difficult to ford as the Shenandoah, the men of the 8th Georgia discovered with pleasure. At its deepest it was only about two-and-a-half feet.

Dev sat on Revere, watching the troops come across, splashing out of the water and scrambling up the bank. Spirits were so high they did not seem to mind the drizzle that had commenced shortly after their jarring two a.m. reveille. At least it was not hot as it had been the day they left their main camp at Poplar Grove. On that long, dusty march hundreds had fallen from the ranks, overcome by heat. They had crossed the Blue Ridge at Ashby's Gap and stayed a week in Berryville as the majority of the army moved north behind their cover. Leaving there on the 24th, they had found less hospitality as they traversed extreme northern Virginia, with doors and windows tightly shut and no ladies to cheer them or offer water. And now, here they were, hard as it was to believe, crossing into Maryland – part of Lee's grand invasion. It was exciting, to be sure, to turn the tables on the Yankees. Dev just hoped they would find success. Some had said they ought to be out West, helping the troops there hold Vicksburg against Ulysses S. Grant.

Company A was especially chipper today, having recovered their banner while at Berryville. It had been lost in that area the summer before, and it had been a pleasant surprise when the men had learned a local citizen had it in his keeping. Now it streamed proudly out before them, proclaiming "Our liberties we prize – our rights we will maintain."

Next came Company B. Dev felt a surge of pride as he watched the battle-seasoned veterans of the OLI.

"Whoo-whee, Major Rousseau!" yelled Hank Watson, flapping his arms like a wet chicken as he approached. "We've arrived! Now we're gonna show 'em!"

Dev smiled and saluted to him and Dylan, who looked like he was faring pretty well despite the cool, wet conditions. He had finally gotten past the urge to run for cover when a soaking was imminent, partly because the men had teased him so unmercifully about his preference for bullets over rain drops.

As Sanford Branch passed and saluted, Dev called out, "No nosebleed today, Lieutenant?"

"Not today, Sir," was the reply with a grin.

Dev had seen the young man with a handkerchief to his nose almost every day in the oppressive heat. Some believed such a blood-letting was actually helpful, but Devereaux harbored doubts. He tended to think the nosebleeds of some of the soldiers were just a sign of the extreme wear and tear to which their bodies were being exposed.

They marched about two miles beyond the river, then the order came down to halt and receive a whiskey ration. Apparently someone thought their exposure to the elements warranted a medicinal boost, or perhaps this was General Hood's way of celebrating their crossing into enemy territory.

In any case, with cheer the men set to dismantling surrounding fence rails for campfires. If the owner of the farm was in residence and had a protest to make, he did not appear to voice it. Devereaux and some of the other junior regimental officers took up lodging in a nearby barn. He was glad to find hay for Revere and the opportunity to remove his soaking hat and frock coat. He changed his shirt while Little Joe arrived to unsaddle and brush down the stallion. He heard the slave crooning to the horse, "Poor ole thing, if we turn you out to rest in the pasture after all you done been through, it wouldn't be a minute too soon." Then the black man's voice rose in a question. "Mistuh Dev, don't you reckon it be strange there not be a horse in this barn when we get here?"

"I'm guessing that has something to do with the fact that General Rhodes' division preceded us."

"Didn't Mistuh Lee say no takin' the folks' property?"

Dev came around the front of the stall and observed Little Joe carefully cleaning mud and small stones from Revere's hooves. "The soldiers aren't to plunder, true," he said, "but that doesn't mean the Quartermaster Department might not do a bit of *impressing* – as needed."

"Seem lak there a lot of needin'."

"No more than we've visited upon our own people."

"Say, that be true. Virginia's a sad lookin' place now."

Changing the subject, Devereaux asked, "How are the other valets treating you, Little Joe?"

"Oh, fine, I expect. There's not many of us left now."

"Yes, and you should have gone home with the others. There's been precious little rations these past months, and nothing I'm not capable of doing myself."

"We in the land of milk an' honey now, Mistuh Dev."

"Yes, but still on rations."

"Ain' no place I'd rather be than with you – an' Mistuh Dylan, too. There's no use for me among them women folk."

"But now Miz Carolyn is at Forests of Green all alone. I can't help thinking how much safer she'd be with you there, too."

Little Joe straightened, letting go of a back hoof, and looked at him imploringly, almost accusingly. "Mistuh Dev, promise you won't send me back there. I'll chew a piece o'rawhide before I'd rest on my laurels in the mountains while you in all this danger."

Dev laughed. "Well, it may come to that, so I might have to remind you of your words. That is, so long as you don't run off and find some Yankee housewife to take you in."

Little Joe looked truly shocked. "Now, don't say that, Mistuh Dev! You an' the family's all I ever known."

And there was the sum of it, thought Dev, for a man with any experience of the world would recognize his opportunity and do just as Devereaux had suggested. And he couldn't blame him. With a sense of sadness, Dev watched Joe with his horse. Suddenly he realized only a victory by the North could ever make a clean break of the cycle of dependency they had created in the slave system.

These thoughts were new and confusing – and smacked faintly of something almost treasonous. He was glad to be relieved of them by a touch on his arm. He turned to see his brother, looking shame-faced, water dripping off his hat.

"Is something wrong, Dylan?"

"No, Dev, I'm just a rat looking for a hole. I heard you'd established yourself in these fine quarters, so I thought I'd pay you a visit."

"Oh, good! You're just in time for a corn pone and jerky. Won't you join me on my fine couch?" Devereaux gestured to a small pile of straw where he'd spread his bed roll.

"D-do you think anyone would mind? Fraternizing with officers, y'know?"

At that moment two baritone voices from across the barn broke into the first verse of "Maryland, My Maryland."

The despot's heel is at thy door,
Maryland, my Maryland.
His torch is at thy temple door,
Maryland, my Maryland.

Dev grinned at Dylan. "Somehow I doubt it, Corporal. The bottles have clearly been uncorked."

"Indeed," Dylan murmured sourly, nonetheless sitting down with a look of satisfaction at his dry surroundings. He patted the straw into a more comfortable lump and dug inside his haversack. "The whiskey's flowing freely in camp as well. Unfortunately those who don't want their ration are giving it to those who do. I tried to get them to just pour it out, but no. They couldn't bring themselves to waste it. So instead it will waste the army. Some of the boys are very quickly getting drunk on empty stomachs. One poor fellow's falling over his own feet and cursing every officer he can think of."

"I won't ask who," Dev said wryly, sitting down as well.

Finishing up with Revere, Little Joe said, "I go see if I can find any hot coffee."

"Thanks, Joe, that would be wonderful," Dylan said with a smile.

They offered him their tin cups, and he departed, leaving the brothers to talk. As they washed down bread and meat with swigs from their canteens, Dev asked, "So how was the letter from the fair Miss Randall?"

On the day before they left Berryville, both brothers had received mail from home – Dev from Carolyn and Dylan from Sylvie – but they had not yet gotten the chance to discuss the content of the letters.

Dylan made a face, removed his kepi, and ran a hand through his hair, which was darkened by the rain. "I don't know what to make of it. She's the last person I would have expected to get a letter from."

"I suppose you have an admirer."

"Yes, but … *Sylvie Randall?* I just can't see it."

"Did she write a bunch of nonsense?"

"No, just news about the fighting on James Island in South Carolina and the capture of the ram *Atlanta*."

"The ship that was supposed to be invincible?"

Dylan tore off a piece of jerky with his teeth. "Yeah, well, so the newspapers said. Folks are furious with the commander who surrendered her – 165 men taken prisoner – but from the sound of it he had little choice. They'd run aground in Warsaw Sound and were getting hammered by a Union monitor."

"That's a shame."

Dylan nodded. "And she also said Union troops seized St. Simons down the coast and looted Christ Church and the plantations there."

Devereaux looked angry. It was hard to wait for matters to unfold here in Maryland, when their loved ones were threatened at home. But instead of dwelling upon their helplessness, Dev asked, "So are you thinking favorably of Miss Randall now?"

Dylan shrugged. "She's more intelligent than I first thought," was all he would concede. "You didn't get to tell me what Carolyn said, either. How is she?"

"Busy. They're cutting last year's wheat crop, preparing more field area for next year's, and plowing the cornfields. They're growing beans and pumpkins in among the corn crop on Mahala Franklin's suggestion, like the Indians used to do. It's supposed to keep down the pests. And she's working in the garden every day."

"Mahala Franklin?"

"No – Carolyn."

Dylan shook his head and gave a short laugh. "Amazing. She's not having any problems with the workers?"

"Nope. They are using a reward system like we did at The Marshes. She sends me details of her expenditures, and the account books look good, too. It's hard for them, though. The Confederacy's demanding one-tenth of all farm produce above what is considered for home use. Carolyn says impressment officers have fanned out over the whole state, and they aren't usually fair. Between them and deserters and drifters, they have to hide the bulk of their supplies and cure all the meat to classify it for home use."

"I never would have pictured it, Dev – not from the girl who was scared of her own shadow. Remember how terrified she was of just dancing the polka?"

Dev laughed. "Yes, I do. I'm proud of her, Dylan. We're not the only ones the war's changing."

"I hope you've let her know that."

Devereaux glanced sharply at his brother. "Of course I have. What do you take me for, a fool?" Pausing, Dev mellowed. "Yes, that's what I've been," he admitted softly. "You would have had the sense to do better, wouldn't you?"

Awareness had long ago turned to guilt where he, Carolyn and Dylan were concerned. Every time he faced battle he longed for a fully expunged conscience. He knew Dylan had forgiven him. It would just be nice to have it said.

But Dylan pretended not to have heard Dev's last words. Instead of making a direct response, he said, "I often think, Dev, that if I had known what was going to happen – with Father – I should have stayed home. I would have stayed home."

"No, Dylan, you're right where you should be."

"Maybe. I still can't believe he's gone."

"Me, either." Unspoken between them was the awful finality of it, hard to accept as news in a letter. "Things can change that quickly," Dev pointed out, meeting Dylan's eyes.

"Yeah," Dylan agreed, glancing away. Joe was arriving with two steaming mugs of coffee.

The thing between them would remain unspoken as well, for a while longer. Would it be too long? Considering the killing fields that surrounded them, Dev now found it hard to believe they would both survive the war.

July 2, 1863
Near Gettysburg, Pennsylvania

This is the worst fighting I've ever seen. Exhausted, Devereaux knelt near a tree, sliding his officer's sword behind him. They had engaged the Federals around five in the evening after what had seemed an eternity of marching and waiting in reserve on the second line of Hood's division, watching Alabamians and Texans surge through an open wood to meet the foe. Fighting spirit was at a fever pitch.

When he told the men, "It's our turn to advance," willing cheers met his pronouncement. A long wait erased nerves for battle-seasoned soldiers.

Now they passed through a farm and a field where Union artillery in a nearby peach orchard fired down the whole length of their brigade line. Within sight of a Union skirmish line they advanced at the double quick, sweeping the bluecoats back before them. Charging through another orchard and field, they entered a rocky wood and scrambled down a ravine. A line of Union muzzles sighted along the top of the fence fronting what must be the boggiest segment of Plum Run. An impossible-looking situation, even for the 8th.

Crouching next to Dylan, Dev watched as those who attempted to cross became stuck in the thigh-deep mud. Three regimental color bearers fell in quick succession while desperately trying to keep the flag aloft.

"We've got to make it to the other side," he yelled to his brother.

Dylan nodded. "But look."

Two small regiments of bluecoats plugged right into a gap in the Union line and poured lead into the struggling Confederates. Dylan shook his head at the hopelessness of the challenge.

Angered, Dev called out, "Across the ravine, 8th. No man holding back." He charged ahead, and those who had hesitated followed.

At last they crossed the ravine, but the unrelenting storm of bullets forced the enlisted men to scramble for cover. Devereaux stood just behind the fighting with the other officers, all on foot today.

"Stand up and fight fair!" the men yelled to the Yankees ensconced at the top of the rise.

But the foe, of course, was too smart to fall for such baiting.

Within seconds of each other, two lieutenants not twenty paces away crumpled to the ground, forcing Dev to take cover like the men. Why had McLaws' supporting division on their left not gone forward as soon as Hood's men began the struggle? Furious that their men were pouring out their lives in a fruitless standstill, Dev sent word behind the lines for an answer. Apparently Anderson shared his opinion, for Dev's answer was a temporary pull-back.

Soon after the 8th retreated to the edge of the woods, word came that Anderson had been shot and carried to the rear. Brigade command fell to Lieutenant Colonel Luffman of the 11th, and with the 8th's Colonel Towers also wounded, Dev learned that he would lead the regiment in the next charge.

McLaws' South Carolinians finally entered the fray, attacking the Union stronghold at Stony Hill upstream from where the 8th had already fought. Anderson's brigade had gone forward simultaneously, and now, it seemed like a horrible repeat of what had occurred the first time. Branches and dirt flew, and the small creek turned red with the blood of the fallen.

But there was a subtle difference. Dev could tell that the increased pressure to their right and left was softening the Union line.

Now, as he came even with Company B, he yelled, "Keep at it, boys! We're about to fold them!"

He caught a glimpse of Dylan loading and firing like an old pro. As his red-haired brother lunged from behind a covering tree into a crouch to get off a shot, a puff of smoke exploded from his barrel. The next instant Dylan jerked and fell backward.

Dev ran over to him. His heart lurched at the sight of blood quickly spreading from a hole in his brother's thigh. "Tie it off," he yelled. "I'll take you to the back."

Gasping in pain, Dylan rummaged in his haversack and came out with a handkerchief. Deveraux took it from him. The ends barely met in a small knot just above the wound.

"Major, the Yanks are retreating!" someone exclaimed.

Devereaux looked over his shoulder. Sure enough, the line of blue was disappearing from the wall above them – the very sight they had waited for all day. He knew what he had to do, and it was not what he wanted to do.

Dylan instantly read his expression and understood the situation. "Go! I'll make it to the rear."

Dev squeezed his arm with intensity. "Make sure you do. I'll come find you, after." Then he rose and, drawing his sword, called, "Forward, 8th Georgia!"

He did not need to say it. The battle-seasoned veterans were already surging ahead of him, jumping the stone wall with shouts of triumph, and running into the wheat field beyond.

But they did not get far. Union artillerists now had their range and bore down with a furious cannonade of shot and shell.

"Back to the wall!" Devereaux yelled.

As the men hastened to comply, Dev saw Hank Watson turn and then fly through the air like a mule had kicked him square between the shoulders. The men crouched behind the cover of the wall, staring forlornly at their beloved comrade's bloody, unmoving form.

Full of regret, Dev glanced back into the ravine and saw his brother limping in the opposite direction, leaning on his rifle like a crutch. *God, just let him make it*.

The Yankee battery was limbering up and moving off. Again he called the men to advance. This time, confronting a line of cheering infantry, they again took cover. But it had been enough time for Dev to feel Hank Watson's shoulder and ascertain that there was no pulse.

"Fire at will!" The command rang along the line of officers, few as they now were.

Union reinforcements soon appeared in the wheat field, fixed bayonets and charged. Dev knew the weary, thinned ranks stood no chance against these fresh troops. They retreated all the way back to Farmer Rose's woods, where they reformed behind some fence rows. There, fortune smiled on them, for it was *their* turn to receive reinforcements. Fortified by Semmes' and Wofford's brigades, they again scrambled into the ravine. With their increased numbers and the possession of Stony Hill, even the new brigade of Federal Army Regulars sent in could not stand against them. Dev thought he had never seen such a splendid thing as that line of brave men pushing through the wheat field and the woods and valley beyond, the broken Union ranks running before them.

But that was not to be the glorious end of it, even then. For formed up ahead along a rocky rise was another Yankee battle line. Was there always another? Must there always be more? As soon as the running bluecoats reached the shelter of that line, they fired upon the advancing Confederates. A deep-throated "hurrah!" sounded all the way down the Union ranks. Then the Yanks charged down into the valley.

Devereaux looked up and down the Confederate line. Dozens of battle flags waved under the bright July sun, but around each there were no more than fifty men – less than half of what should have been. And precious few officers.

He made a quick decision that became common consent.

"Fall back!"

Through the littered and broken wheat they again retreated, Devereaux posting pickets in mid-field. As they passed through the ravine, there was no sign of Dylan.

The men gathered, breathless and sweating, in the woods. Many eyes turned to Dev.

"Should the Yankees come back, we'll use the creek bed," he said. "Fall out in line of battle and rest, men. You have done well."

But as he looked around, a deep sadness filled him. Superior fighting could only overcome superior numbers for so long. More than half their number was indeed missing. And his brother was among them. His inquiries revealed that the wounded had been taken to Planck's farm behind the lines. Yet Dev knew he could not go there, and neither could he spare a man to go for him. Tomorrow, or even tonight, the Yankees would come again.

A bright moon slowly rose over the scene of carnage, and by unspoken truce, litter bearers moved among the wounded. Their moans and cries lifted in a continual, pathetic chorus.

Then, above the sounds of inhuman suffering, a sweet tenor voice arose from the left. Each soldier tensed, then relaxed, as an unseen Confederate sang one hymn after another. The familiar words brought back memories of church-going Sundays and families at home – and reminded the dying of their heavenly destination.

Finally, as the singer closed with "When This Cruel War is Over," thousands of soldiers from both sides cheered and applauded.

Dev lay brushing tears from his eyes, praying that his brother was at Planck farm, and being taken care of.

Dylan could hardly be angry that no one had tended his wound. After all, injured men overflowed the house and outbuildings and covered the ground. Strangely enough, it seemed many had been wounded in the upper leg today, just as he had. Dylan had no idea how seriously he was hurt, but there were many who were more grievously wounded than he – at least if one judged by the amount of blood and moaning. Of course officers received help more quickly, and he was but a lowly corporal.

Propping his leg up on a rock, he tried to focus on others to ease his own suffering. Lt. Sanford Branch had been hit in the left side of his chest, the ball having also fractured his wrist just prior to its entry. He was spitting up blood. Dylan thought the outcome did not look good – and the same for Fred Bliss. He'd heard Bliss' thigh had been shattered by a bullet. The surgeons had taken his leg off, leaving him with small chance of survival.

He closed his eyes. Opening them had been a mistake. His brain refused to comprehend the things he saw around him. The sounds were bad enough – crying, screaming, moaning, retching, cursing, death rattles. Such sounds, so inhuman, yet so profoundly human at the same time.

Dylan's worst fear was amputation.

Yea, though I walk through the valley of the shadow of death, I will fear no evil. God forgive me, but I think I'd rather die than lose my leg at the thigh. God, please spare me.

He looked down at his leg. Limping to the rear had been an arduous ordeal. No longer buoyed by the rush of combat, it had felt like every bullet was meant for him. He could hardly remember, but he must have walked a long way, blood pumping from his body with every step. His trouser leg was completely wet and sticky. He tried to pull the wool away from his flesh, but his head swam and he thought that he must be about to pass out from blood loss. Then he knew no more.

The next thing he was aware, someone was bending over him, cutting away his pants leg and wiping his wound.

"Got to get that bullet out, son," a voice said.

All he could think was, *thank God, that means they won't take my leg.* But he was too weak to speak. And when the forceps probed his wound, he blacked out again.

Hot sun beat down on him, igniting dancing sparkles of light inside his eyelids. Slowly Dylan realized what had awakened him. It was a perfect thunder of artillery from the battlefield. He had never heard such noise in all his born days. The ground shook under him. And it was only increasing.

He cracked open one eye and looked around, though the effort of raising his head made him queasy. He lay in the same spot, surrounded by other wounded. And his leg was there.

A male nurse nearby noticed his feeble effort and hurried over with a dipper of water.

"Drink," he urged, putting a hand under Dylan's head. "You've lost a lot of blood."

No kidding. "Another attack?" he managed to rasp.

"Guess so."

The orderly hurried off. Dylan would have liked more water, but there was no one to ask. His stomach rumbled. How long had it been since he had eaten? And his leg throbbed, but another glance assured him it had been properly bandaged.

Settling back, he pulled his kepi over his face and again closed his eyes. The cannonade seemed to go on forever. And then, at last, came the rattle of musketry – Lee's final assault in a desperate grab for a Northern victory. Would they succeed?

And was the 8th again in the fray?

The next day it rained. It was as if heaven was trying to cleanse the filth of death from the farmlands of Southeastern Pennsylvania. At the same time Confederate medics began loading thousands of wounded into spring-less army wagons. They were going back to Virginia. They had failed.

General Lee had wanted to use Hood's and McLaws' divisions in his July 3 assault, but being informed by Longstreet that these men had been badly torn up in the previous day's fighting, he had settled for two divisions of A.P Hill's Third Corps to accompany Pickett's. Thousands of these men had been slaughtered in a last grand charge while the 8th sparred with Union cavalry.

Now the walking wounded would follow the wagon train on foot. Considering the punishment that lay in store for him and the others traversing the muddy, rutted roads in the vehicles, Dylan envied them. But he could not bring himself to envy the critically ill, who could not be moved and who would be left to certain capture.

Just after Dylan had been placed in a wagon, he became conscious of a familiar voice somewhere down the line shouting, "Dylan Rousseau! Are you here? I'm looking for Corporal Dylan Rousseau! Has anyone seen him?"

Devereaux! His brother sounded so frantic that Dylan made every effort to broadcast his weak voice above the rain and moaning men as he called out, "I'm here, Dev! Here!"

"Dylan!"

"Devereaux!"

Minutes later the wagon shifted as a soaking figure in a major's uniform appeared in the back flap. Dev's eyes widened at the sight of the men packed in like so many sardines, then focused on him.

"Dylan, thank God! Are you going to be all right?"

116

Dylan smiled faintly. "They got the bullet out and my leg all bandaged. And now you're not the only one who's got a ride back to Virginia," he joked lamely.

"Oh, Dylan," Dev said with deep regret. He knew the suffering in the wagon would be intense. "Have you had anything to eat?"

"Not really."

Devereaux dug in his haversack and passed him some hardtack. "I wish I had better," he said. There was no way he could make it to Dylan's side, but by straining they could just touch.

Dylan took the stiff flatbread and then clasped his brother's hand for a moment.

"You hang on," Dev instructed him. "I'll see you in Virginia."

"Yeah." His heart wrenched when that familiar face disappeared from the rear of the wagon.

They pulled out around four p.m. Wagons stretched as far as the eye could see. After that point, Dylan had no further thought of food. The vehicle kept getting stuck, and the cursing driver would whip the mules until they jostled free. Dylan would bite his lip against the pain. Others were not so taciturn and screamed out in agony.

Just south of Greencastle, Union cavalry struck the column. Dylan roused from his misery when he heard the pop-pop of revolvers and rifles. The wagon stopped as the driver joined the fight. Anger flowed through him at the thought that the enemy would stoop so low. He reached for his rifle and felt for his cartridge box.

"Let me to the rear," he called.

Some of the men attempted to move. Others were incapable of doing so, many missing limbs or hands and feet. As carefully as he could, Dylan dragged himself over and around their bodies until he could see out the back of the ambulance. Down the road walking wounded were kneeling or taking cover in an attempt to hold off the raiders.

As he eased himself down from the wagon, he saw that men from some of the other vehicles were doing the same. They limped out to join the hodge-podge formation of teamsters and walking wounded and began loading and firing as rapidly as torrential rain and shattered bodies would allow.

Finally a Confederate escort unit arrived to turn the tide in their favor, but not before the Yankees had taken off 134 wagons full of prisoners.

With the help of one of the soldiers, Dylan limped back to the wagon. "What's your name, Corporal?" the sergeant asked.

"Dylan Rousseau," he answered as he collapsed, rolling under the canvas cover.

117

"You're one brave soldier."

Dylan pondered that comment with wonder as they again trundled forward. "Brave" was a word he had never thought to hear in description of himself. But it brought a small measure of satisfaction in the face of defeat, even when word circulated the following day that Vicksburg had fallen. And it remained, like a small pinpoint of light, when they again had to fight off Union cavalry near the banks of the swollen Potomac, where the pontoon bridge had been destroyed.

At last they crossed back into Virginia. They were a whipped army, but in the fiery forge of trial, Dylan had at last found dignity.

CHAPTER EIGHT

Late July, 1863
Wilmington, North Carolina

aucous laughter sounded from the adjoining gaming room as Jack spooned a bite of potato soup into his mouth. His dinner companion was Robert Lawson of the Importing and Exporting Company of South Carolina.

"Is it really so bad in Charleston harbor?" Jack half-joked as two tall young sailors, inebriated and talking in loud British accents, brushed past their table, nearly upsetting Robert's drink. Lawson grabbed it just before it toppled onto the bare hardwood floor.

"Rather uncouth company for men of old-fashioned principles, like us, eh?"

Jack just shook his head.

Faced with an onslaught of sea-faring sorts and the oft-times unsavory industries that accompanied them, many of Wilmington's respectable citizens had beat a hasty retreat inland. That left the small city, taken unawares by the wartime boom, to the control of Brigadier General Henry Chase Whiting – a handsome and well-respected but rather heavy-handed West Point grad – and his right-hand man, Colonel William Lamb. Together these two officers of port had worked to erect an extensive battery system which would give the blockade runners effective cover. Lamb had fortified Federal Point, which had been renamed Fort Fisher, with British and Brooke rifles and a flying battery. The long range of these guns had forced the blockading fleet to anchor farther out to sea.

"I don't like coming here," Jack responded, "but with the Federals hanging onto Morris Island outside Charleston, and bound and determined to take Sumter, I don't guess we have much choice."

They both knew the Yankees outside South Carolina's premiere city were now able to watch Sullivan's Island at night. When any approaching ship signaled the Confederates in the forts, Union artillerists would blanket the river with fire and send out their own ships. This made the narrow channel left open by Confederate obstructions almost impassable.

Wilmington harbor, however, possessed two entrances, well-separated by a shoal, that caused the Yankees to split their surveillance. And while

119

it lacked commission houses and banks, the town did connect with three railroad lines.

"True," Robert said, "but Wilmington's no great gift, either. I prefer New Inlet over Old, what with that shifting bar that can make things rather hairy. But I have a bad feeling both passages are going to get more challenging to run once the Yankees add more ships to the blockade here – as they're sure to do."

Jack nodded. The run in had not been bad. He had struck the coast about thirty miles up from the inlet, hugging the shore as he crept south. Having passed by the outer line of the blockade, *Evangeline* had laid low, waiting for full dark. With their steam vented underwater, their dash past the outermost Federal ship had gone undetected. Once they'd rounded Federal Point, the channel range lights had guided them into harbor. But still he preferred Charleston, where he could lodge with his mother's older sister, Ruth, and her banker husband.

"Maybe things will lighten up in Charleston. Fort Wagner did hold out against that eleven-hour bombardment and an infantry attack," Jack pointed out, unwilling to give up hope.

Robert gave perfunctory agreement and tore off a piece of bread. Briefly he studied his cravat, which he brushed lazily upon spying a small collection of crumbs in its silken folds. "I certainly hope so. This arrangement makes it much more difficult to get goods to and from home. I know that's even more the case for you. Have you thought about drawing up a contract with your governor, such as Gazaway Lamar is doing?"

"Brown knows of my loyalties."

"Maybe, but it wouldn't hurt to firm things up, would it? Get in while the getting's good. Assure him that as his most valuable shipper, you'll continue to prefer Georgia cotton and keep him stocked with supplies. I hear Savannah came awfully close to food riots this spring, before the city government borrowed all that money to sell food at cost to the citizens. Anyway, you might use your leverage to get something in return."

"Like – immunity from draft?" Jack questioned, smiling cunningly. This was indeed a question that had weighed more and more on Jack's mind. He liked the way this old gentleman thought. His advice had always been good.

"Exactly. See, me, I don't have to worry about such things, being the old man that I am. But you, however, and certain members of our crews..."

"It's a wise suggestion, Mr. Lawson. I believe I'll act on it, and right away. A letter to Mr. Governor, perhaps. Then, once I'm back in Nassau, a quiet slip into the Georgia coast on *South Land II*. But tell me–"

"Robert."

"Robert. Why did you ever take such an interest in me?"

Lawson smiled charmingly. "Why, what else could it be than that you remind me of myself at that age? You bring back happy memories of my more dashing days. I want to see you succeed."

Unaccustomed to such unconditional generosity of character, Jack shook his head. "I don't know what to say." He sat back and placed his napkin on the table.

"There's nothing *to* say. A man's got to have friends, right? And what is more gratifying than a friend that reminds you of yourself?" Lawson laughed heartily.

"I hope you don't mind me asking, but you never speak of a wife. Is there a Mrs. Lawson?" Sipping his drink, Jack watched Lawson's face for a hint of emotion.

"There is. She lives in Charleston."

"Then you are a far more successful man than I."

Robert's face shadowed. "Now what would make you assume that?"

Jack laughed, toyed with his glass. "At least you got the lady you love to marry you. The woman I want is engaged to another."

"The lady I love? Not exactly." A look of pain crossed the other man's face.

Jack felt cold, like he had trod into an area he shouldn't have. "You don't love your wife?" He couldn't stop the question.

"Love? Maybe. In a sense. But not what I once envisioned love to be."

Jack frowned. "Are you trying to tell me matrimony would erode my feelings over time?"

"No. I am not." Suddenly Lawson sat forward with a startling intensity. "We are more alike than you think. Listen to me, Jack Randall. If you truly love this woman, hold onto her. Don't give up, no matter what it takes." He paused, sighed. "When I was a lad of but twenty and two, I fell hard for a politician's beautiful daughter. She was above me, but I was handsome in those days, and had charm and wits. I was on the rise. She could have been mine – was just within my reach. But I was rough, unpolished. I did some stupid things that caused her to turn to another. I was too proud to plead for her. She married him. I told myself to accept the finality of that, which would have been sound advice except for some twists of fate. I settled for someone else. A good woman, mind you, but not my match. And selfish. I did try, Randall, but she never opened her heart to me. Five years later my sweetheart's husband died, and there I was – here I am – married – and she a widow, still."

Astonished, Jack sat silently staring at his companion, who took a hard gulp of his drink.

"I've never told all that to anyone, but it's a regret I live with every day. If I had pressed harder, she might have capitulated. If I had but waited, I'm sure she could still have been mine. I would have been better off alone than compromising for someone I did not love. Yes, I know your look. You're sure there's something I've left undone, some reservation of my heart my bride sensed. I did at first manage to put my love from my mind, and focus on my wife. It was not for lack of my trying, I assure you. There is one love my wife has, and that is herself. We live together in peace and harmony, but it is a partnership and no more. I despair of it ever becoming more. I tell you this not for your pity, but for your good. If you are sure about this woman, don't give up."

"I can't press her. To do so would only alienate her. She's already made it clear that she won't go back on her commitment to her fiancé. And Mahala means what she says."

"Is he a soldier?"

Jack nodded again. "Army of Tennessee."

"There's trouble all around Chattanooga." Lawson raised his glass, as if to toast. "Maybe fate will solve your dilemma." He laughed, a bit shrilly, as if made nervous by his own suggestion.

Jack sat back from the table.

"You're horrified. Waiting for God's lightning bolt to strike me. Oh, you can't say you haven't thought the same thing to yourself, can you? Come now."

Jack stopped himself before he could lie. He admitted, "The thought has crossed my mind. I'm hardly the self-righteous sort, but I can't let myself entertain that notion. God keep me from wishing death on any man."

Lawson nodded, sagged in his chair. "You're right, Jack. You're a better man than I. Maybe that's why you'll succeed. Don't think too badly of me. I deal with what I've chosen the best I can. But there will always be a ribbon of regret there, just underneath the surface. I try not to look at it, but there it is. You don't want that, Jack. Do all you can to win this woman you love. I hope you have a happy ending. If not, maybe your wealth will comfort you."

Pity rose in Jack, and he steeled his jaw against the emotion. "Does yours comfort you?" he asked quietly.

The unshuttered bleakness in Robert's eyes was his answer. Jack stood up, placed a hand on his companion's shoulder. "Thank you," he said, "for sharing what you did."

He would take the bud from among the thorns and keep it.

Jack settled his bill and made for the door. In his preoccupation with Lawson's advice, he wasn't watching where he was going. He bumped up against a lushly dressed quadroon woman.

"I'm sorry," With a gentle grip to the shoulders, he moved her away from him.

"No problem." As her gaze raked him, she smiled seductively.

He froze, staring down at her. His gut clenched. She uncommonly resembled Mahala. And there was no mistaking the invitation in her eyes. But the girl's flirtation did not have the desired effect. For in that moment, something crystallized in Jack's head. No other woman, and no amount of money, could substitute for what he knew to be his heart's desire. Time changed a lot. And for Mahala, he could wait forever.

For the first time in months, a sense of anticipation rose in Devereaux. Not the anxious excitement that accompanied impending battle, but the real joy of hope. He wasn't quite sure how it had happened – the moment luck had finally smiled upon them when Hood's and McLaws' divisions were being sent to bolster Bragg's army in Tennessee – but the 8th Georgia, along with Anderson's brigade, was going south. Their numbers and experience would have definitely been invaluable in Bragg's attempt to save Chattanooga from the looming threat of General Rosecrans. And the boys of the 8th who hailed from that part of the state were crushed that this was not to be their destination. But another potential emergency had developed on the South Carolina coast.

For months Federals had held the Charleston area under siege, having failed to capture Morris Island. Now, weakening under the relentless pressure, General Beauregard had at last relinquished that stronghold in favor of James Island. It was to this locale that the 8th arrived on September 16. They made camp on the bayou's bank not far from the wharves along the Ashley River. There was no shade, and there were swarms of flies. But the diet was substantially improved, and they had soap for washing and, after wells had been dug, fresh water.

As soon as camp had been established, Dev sat down beneath his tent flap and got out pen and paper. He looked out along the water, felt the salt breeze stirring his hair and shirt sleeves, and listened to the cry of a sea gull. A sense of peace filled him. He could feel in his bones that he was close to home. Memories of the old days at The Marshes made him smile. The longing was bittersweet.

Dipping the pen nib in the ink, he wrote:

> *September 18, 1863*
> *James Island, South Carolina*
> *My dearest wife, as you can see, our regiment has been trans-*
> *ferred to duty along our Southern coast. I know not how long we*
> *will remain here, but would you be able to repair to Savannah from*
> *Habersham, just in case we should be able to visit? I eagerly await*
> *your reply. I am writing to Mother, too.*
> *Your husband, Devereaux*

October 7, 1863
Savannah, Georgia

Carolyn sat on a sofa at her mother-in-law's Savannah *modiste*, waiting for Henrietta to come out of the dressing room. Having only one "good for company" mourning dress in her possession, Henrietta had decided it was time to take advantage of their visit to town and make a purchase.

At last she emerged. Carolyn tried to look encouraging, to hold in her dismay at her mother-in-law's appearance while commenting pleasantly on the gown's fit. Henrietta needed a new dress not only because she had owned only one decent gown, but because she had dropped two sizes. While her new trim waistline might be girlish, her sunken cheeks, dull hair and shadowed eyes were decidedly not.

Henrietta turned from Carolyn's approval to gaze into the mirror. "I just don't know, Carolyn," she said. "I don't care anymore what I look like, and I hate to spend the money."

Carolyn came up behind her. Gently she reminded, "Louis would not want to see his wife in rags."

Tears filled the older woman's eyes, letting Carolyn know she had hit home.

"And neither would your boys," she continued. "They may be home any day, and we must do all in our power to remind them of the value of all they are fighting for. If they see us ill-kempt and down-trodden, we will only add to their burden."

"You're right, of course," Henrietta sighed, taking Carolyn's proffered hankie and wiping her eyes. "But a hundred and eighty dollars?"

Carolyn shook her head. "I know, but they are not making much on it, Mother, by the time you consider that even the coarsest of gingham sells for seven dollars a yard. And then there are all the notions."

"Maybe I should make it myself."

"You need it now."

"All right, then, but only if you buy that muslin."

Again Carolyn shook her head. "Summer's over ... and my winter dresses are fine for North Georgia. I dress practically while I'm there."

Unhappy, Henrietta looked at her. "Then at least buy that plain straw bonnet. Yours has holes in it."

"It's sixty dollars – untrimmed!"

Henrietta took her arm and shook it. "You'll get it. You're the one who has a husband to look pretty for, and keep your skin nice for." She let go of her arm. "I have some flowers and ribbon at home."

Carolyn sighed in resignation. "Very well." She turned to the *modiste* waiting across the room. "Mrs. Rousseau will take the gown. Please box up her old dress and let her wear this one home."

"Of course, Mrs. Rousseau."

As they climbed into the vehicle moments later, with Henrietta's maid carrying the dress box, Carolyn thought her mother-in-law looked peaked. "I'll fix you some tea when we get home," she said, although they both knew they were down to a brew of dried blackberry leaves with sassafras root. "And beat in some egg yolks for strength."

Grateful but tired, Henrietta smiled and pulled her long mourning veil over her face. "Egg yolks are too precious."

As they traveled along in their open carriage, heads nodded with respect, and Carolyn noticed many more widows in black garb. She felt almost conspicuous in last year's soft blue silk organza. A sick feeling settled in the pit of her stomach. How many more widows would Savannah have before the war ended?

At home, more frustration awaited, for the kitchen maid was just returning from her own foray at the city market on Ellis Square. Instead of lying down as Carolyn prompted her, Henrietta insisted on seeing the purchases. The kitchen maid appeared nervous, and the Rousseau cook, Maum Esther, hovered near with an expression of concern.

"This is all you bought?" Henrietta questioned as she poked through the baskets. "Two dozen eggs, butter and brown sugar? No meat? How much did you spend?"

"Sixty-eight dollars, Ma'am, but I did get four bushels of sweet potatoes. They in the crate over here," the sad-looking woman responded.

Carolyn surveyed the small, twisted vegetables with a sigh. "Well, we do have the squash and pumpkins and beans I brought from Habersham."

"That's not good enough. We need meat on hand. I refuse to feed the boys a vegetable platter when they come home."

If they come home, Carolyn started to say, but held her tongue.

"I can make somethin' good without meat," Esther volunteered.

But Henrietta was not to be placated. "You'll have to go back out. Put your hat on," she insisted to the slave. "Get us some chicken. Or if there's no chicken, get a barrel of salt fish."

"But Ma'am, they cost a hundred dollars. You din' give me that much!" the girl protested.

"Then here!" Rather frantically Henrietta dug in her reticule. Carolyn saw that her hands were shaking. "Here's the money. Ten-twenty-thirty-forty-fifty-sixty-seventy-eighty. Oh, that's all I have. You see, Carolyn. I should not have bought this dress. Well, take it. Take it! And don't you dare come back without *something!*"

The flustered servant seized the money Henrietta was pressing into her hands and fairly ran out the door. Meeting Esther's gaze, Carolyn put an arm around Henrietta. She was beginning to question the wisdom of having brought the woman to the city. She was too fragile. There had been far fewer stresses in her family's care at sheltered Brightwell. And Carolyn now wondered whether they would even get to see Dev and Dylan.

"Some chamomile tea, Maum Esther," Carolyn said to the cook, who nodded her quick understanding and turned to the task as Carolyn led her mother-in-law upstairs.

Once she had the distraught widow settled on the bed with the steaming drink close by, Carolyn went to her own room. She felt weary and rattled herself. Hopelessness pressed and nudged her, like a relentless beagle crowding out her space. Everyone was always looking to her. It was good to know they considered her mature and responsible – things she had lately striven hard to become – but at times, the silent pressure built until it was almost overwhelming. Especially when she felt her shoulders were too narrow to carry the family's burdens, when she had no answers to the many questions.

This was one of those times. Carolyn removed her bonnet. She laid it on the dresser and smoothed her hair. Then, with the emotion swelling inside her, she rubbed her hands across both sides of her face, permitting herself two dry little sobs.

She heard a floor board squeak in the hall. Not another servant with another inquiry. Prepared to protect herself, with a closed door if need be, she turned. There stood her husband.

With a small, choked cry of astonishment, Carolyn flew toward him, landing hard against his chest. Dev's arms folded around her, almost as if he'd squeeze the life out of her. In response she clung to him, beginning to sob in earnest.

He cradled her face and whispered, "Shh," at the same time pulling her inside the room and closing the door with a light kick.

"Your mother – she – she needs–" Carolyn began, about to tell Dev how much Henreitta would want to know he'd arrived.

But he shook his head and said, "*I* need. *You* need," reminding her with gentle emphasis on each word that it was all right for them to come first. She would fall to pieces, a hundred tiny pieces, at his feet. The relief, the love, was so strong. Dev closed his eyes and nestled his face in her hair. He trailed kisses down her face.

"Dylan?" Carolyn gasped, afraid her brother-in-law might be right behind Dev, interrupting them.

"Coming later."

It was a dream, a splendid dream, she thought. She couldn't stop looking at him, because she needed to see him to know he was really there. But Dev had no time just for looking. He tugged the cameo off her lace collar and fumbled with the button.

Carolyn spread her fingers in Dev's dark hair, and his hat fell to the floor. Their lips met hungrily. She slipped the brass buttons through the holes in his frock coat, and it, too, was shed. Moving her toward the bed, turning as they kissed, Dev shrugged out of his suspenders. Carolyn dropped her dress and hoop to the floor and stood there in her undergarments. He unhooked her corset and brought her in close, hands and lips telling of months of longing, his voice raw with emotion murmuring love and affirmation until she forgot everything but this man, this moment, and the private world they created all to themselves.

"One night," he had said.

That was all they had. Well, they had made the most of it. Carolyn had never known such perfect union, such perfect ecstasy, was possible. Indeed, there was much her mother had never told her.

Carolyn smiled to herself in the darkness, looking over at the sleeping form of her husband beside her. Who was this man who had gazed at her with tender adoration, who had spoken of his pride in her, who had not let go of her hand even while they sat at the supper table? Gone was the cockiness based on the assurances of wealth and the shallowness of vanity. In its place was a quiet confidence, a dignity that went beyond his years. But not his experience, Carolyn thought. She shuddered just imagining the things Devereaux had seen. When he spoke of the war, a haunted look shadowed his features. And she had to send him back to all that. She had to, even now as they had truly just become one.

Over the meal that night Dev had told them that the brigade was *en route* to Chattanooga, where General Bragg held Missionary Ridge and Lookout Mountain and was attempting to siege the Yankees out of the town. Dylan, who now wore a sergeant's stripes, had not been able to stay past dinner. Like Dev, he was amazingly altered, lean and hard, sober and confident. The most pronounced change was the slight limp from his Gettysburg wound. Carolyn felt she scarcely knew him now. As a regimental officer – and one of the precious few in service since First Manassas – Dev had permission to catch up with the regiment in the morning. Seeing both sons had done Henrietta a world of good. She had cried, tears of joy, and Dev and Dylan had experienced a measure of closure in talking with her about Louis.

But for Carolyn, this leave-taking would be infinitely more painful than the first two.

She ran her hand down Dev's well-muscled back. He did not even stir. She knew he was exhausted. But she would not sleep. Each moment was too precious. She curled up tight against him, wrapping her arms around his reassuring bulk and breathing in his masculine scent. She knew that being alone again would be all the harder now. Thinking of it, hot tears ran down her face and fell against Dev's shoulder.

Amazingly, he stirred. Dev rolled over and looked at her searchingly. Seeing her tears, he wrapped an arm around her and snuggled her close. He did not need to ask what was wrong. When at last everything was right between them, it was the whole world that was wrong.

Mid-November, 1863
Habersham County, Georgia

Carolyn made it her business to know what was going on all around the farm every day. She aimed to live up to Dev's new confidence in her, and she could not send him the thorough reports she liked unless she was personally involved in the fields, stables, butler's pantry, kitchen and gardens. Plus she felt the workers had more respect for her decisions when they saw her among them, often working at the same tasks they were.

Today the last ears of corn were coming in from the stalks, and the last bit of wheat was being sown. She was at the well drawing water for the men. The bucket plunged into the depths and came up heavy and slow. As she pulled she thought, as she always did when her mind was not set upon some pressing task, of Devereaux.

She'd gotten a letter as soon as he'd reached the vicinity of Chattanooga, assuring her of his safe arrival. Soon after that another, longer missive had come, saying:

"I'm sitting now atop Lookout Point. Fourteen hundred feet below is Lookout Valley, Chattanooga, and the Tennessee River, all gloriously decked in the foliage of autumn. But no sight could ever be as beautiful to me as that of your sweet face. I said it to you last month in our too-brief meeting, but I must say it again. I'm so sorry, Carolyn, that I took so long to recognize what a treasure you are. I will never forget again. Our time together gave me fresh hope and anticipation for our life together after this war. I do not think it will be long now. Hold fast, my love. Soon we will never be separated again."

Carolyn paused, closing her eyes as she rested the bucket on the lip of the well. It would be impractical to carry the letter against her breast as some less active ladies often did, but its words were written on her heart just the same.

The most recent letter, however, had revealed that the Confederates had lost the upper hand near Chattanooga. The Federals had been able to open a supply line. Bragg wanted to turn his army east of General Grant, but this required the removal of the Union force of Major General Ambrose Burnside at Knoxville. The 8th under Longstreet was dispatched for this mission. Dev had mailed his letter just before he boarded the train.

As the fear of loss rose in Carolyn, she uttered a brief, silent prayer.

She was raising the second bucket when she heard horse hooves on the drive. She looked up to spy Mahala arriving, waving in her direction. Carolyn smiled. She continued with her task, knowing her practical friend would come join her rather than expect to be received in the house.

It had been a year since Mahala had seen Jack. Carolyn had been forced to resign herself to the fact that her friend was going to keep her word and never break her engagement to Clay Fraser. But it had been interesting to note that when she had returned from Savannah last month, Mahala had wanted to ask about Jack. Carolyn was sure of it. With such a falsely casual mien as to be comic, Mahala had danced around a direct inquiry until Carolyn had taken pity on her and revealed that yes, she had seen Jack, although briefly. He had been in the state obtaining a contract with Governor Brown.

"And did he receive it?" Mahala had asked.

"He did, yes," Carolyn had told her, "granting him and his sailors immunity from any draft. In exchange, they will ship out exclusively Georgia cotton and bring all goods not promised to the army into the state. However, it will not be as much as he would like, for the port commanders have taken over half the outward cargo of each ship. He said at least they paid well. And Jack has been able to pay his firm's investors a one hundred percent profit over their initial investment. He said a share of Randall and Ellis stock that sold for $1,000 now goes for $5,000."

"So he's as disgustingly wealthy as ever," Mahala had declared. "And probably as cocky as ever, too."

"No. I would have to say I found his manner quite altered. It was serious, purposeful – almost grave." The same manner almost all Southern men now possessed.

This information had not seemed to please Mahala. Carolyn had withheld the further fact that Jack had not asked about her.

Now, Mahala approached with a smile. "Hello! Oh, let me help you with that. Where are you taking these?" she asked upon spying Carolyn about to hook the buckets to a yoke.

"To the fields for the workers."

"Oh, I can carry one."

"All right. Thank you," Carolyn agreed. She was not feeling overly robust today. "Come for a chat?" she asked as they set out.

"Yes, just to see you. It's been over a week."

"I know. I stay as busy as you do now."

"You ought to rest up a bit. You're looking rather worn down."

"Oh, thank you," Carolyn returned sarcastically. It was a chore keeping the water from sloshing out all over her dress, even without having her hoop on. "Heard from Clay lately?"

Unexpectedly, Mahala's face fell. Carolyn thought she was going to say "no," but instead Mahala replied, "I did, in fact. The reason it took so long was that the 65th was detailed to escort the Union prisoners from the Battle of Chickamauga to Andersonville Prison. He just returned."

"That makes sense. I'm so glad Dev missed that fight while he was in South Carolina. I heard it was awful. Was Clay's regiment badly shot up?"

"No. That's rather the trouble. The officers were so afraid Colonel Moore's men would revolt they held them in reserve!"

"What?"

Mahala nodded her confirmation. "It's the same terrible story as with Drew's Mounted Rifles, Carolyn – desertions left and right. Most are simple farmers, not slaveholders, not very concerned about politics. The men just slip off home or to the Yankee lines. They don't want to fight against the Union. I just can't believe Clay is in this same position again, when he so wanted to belong to a cohesive regiment. He's a sergeant now, like your brother-in-law. And that makes him feel it's his place to try to get the men to stay."

"How awful it must be to not be able to hold his head up among the other troops."

They stopped in the cornfield and set the buckets down.

"Yes, he's really struggling with that. Such the opposite scenario from the 8th, who have such a noble record of service," Mahala said sadly. "And that's all he wanted, really. Brotherhood and faithfulness."

"What will he do?"

"Stay. What else can he do? He and my brothers will fight on to the bitter end. You stay there. Your face is red. I'll go take those men a drink."

Carolyn knew she ought to protest. It was outrageous really, allowing her guest to do her work. But she did feel so winded and weak that she mumbled her thanks and watched Mahala take a bucket and dipper over to the two men working nearby. One was driving the bang board wagon while the other was removing the ears with a hook and tossing them in. She looked around for a place to sit down, but there wasn't a good spot.

Upon Mahala's return, she said, "I've begun to think I've picked up a cold or something in Savannah. I'm tired and have no appetite, and I keep sneezing all the time. Just wait until we get to the wheat field."

Sure enough, as they approached the said area, Carolyn's nose tickled and she let loose with a loud *"achoo!"* – spilling water down the front of her skirt.

"My goodness," Mahala commented.

Samson was sowing the handfuls of kernels broadcast from an open bag looped over his neck while another slave followed at a distance, going over the seeded ground with a heavy harrow.

"Samson," Carolyn called. "Water."

The big man approached with a relieved smile. He took the dipper and said, "I thank you kindly, Miz Carolyn."

"Do you think we're getting it in early enough, Samson? Will the wheat get up far enough before the frost?" she asked a bit anxiously.

"It will have to be, Ma'am," Samson replied, passing the dipper to the man behind him.

"Will you be done today?"

"Yes, Ma'am."

"Good. We'll take a day of rest tomorrow – light chores only – and then we'll all get to shucking the corn."

"Soun' lak a good plan."

"I've been making pumpkin pies for us to enjoy when we're done. And I was thinking, whoever shucks the most can get an extra day off." Carolyn looked to the foreman for his approval, which he gave with one of his toothy smiles and a nod. Satisfied, she turned back toward the house. She confided to Mahala as they walked, "I don't like managing slaves."

Mahala said nothing. She merely appeared thoughtful.

The load was practically nonexistent now, but all the same Carolyn made for the side steps that led to the kitchen as soon as they'd taken the buckets back to the well.

Mahala's eyes opened wide. "Don't you want to go sit down inside?"

"No, let's just rest here a bit. It's cool, and there's a nice breeze."

Tania stuck her head out the door and asked, "Miz Carolyn, you wantin' for me to finish fixin' those pies?"

Carolyn took heart from the fact that the maid's voice was not overly sulky. She attributed that to the fact that last week she had given her permission for Tania and Samson to wed. They would "jump over the broom" in only a few days. "Yes," she said. "That would be wonderful. I'll be in in a minute."

Mahala sat down beside her. "How is Mrs. Burns faring these days?" Carolyn inquired. "I was so sad for her when her husband passed on in the fighting at Champion Hill outside Vicksburg."

Mahala sighed. "You know she's gone back to her family in Atlanta?"

"No, I didn't realize that."

"The church was willing for her to stay on in the parsonage, but the memories here were just too much for her to bear. I miss her so."

"I know you do. And I haven't been much help, have I?"

"It's all right. Things just aren't like they used to be."

"And might never be again," Carolyn said, and sighed. It was part sadness, and part relief for just sitting down. She took a deep breath, but Tania's stirrings in the kitchen brought to her nose the rather unappetizing scent of the pumpkins she had boiled earlier. Her stomach lurched. Carolyn held up a finger, then stumbled over to some bushes nearby. There she gave up the little bit of toast and tea she'd taken in at breakfast.

Wiping her mouth with a hankie, she tottered back to the steps on shaking legs. Mahala, who had half-risen in alarm, helped her sit down.

"I think you picked up something in Savannah, all right," Mahala said, "but not a cold."

December 1, 1863
Outside Knoxville defenses, Tennessee

Carolyn's letter could not have come at a better time. And Devereaux could not have valued it more if it had been a bag of gold.

After a heartening chase and skirmishing with Yankee cavalry and the infantry rear guard upon their approach to Knoxville, they had settled down to a siege. That situation had been altered when Tige Anderson, recovered from his Gettysburg wound, had told the brigade that in the pre-dawn of the 29th of November, they would attack the outward rifle pits of the Union stronghold at Fort Sanders. This part of their action had gone well enough, but everything after that had been a disaster.

Anderson's men were supposed to come in on the left, not against the fort itself. But the advance had gotten all out of sorts, and they had ended up in a ditch facing entrenched Yankees, following McLaws' troops into the maw of death. Once in the ditch, they had been unable to claw their way to the top, and had been exposed to galling fire before receiving the order to retreat. Losses had again been staggering. The men were angry and disgusted at such waste.

Now, they were preparing to march out again. Bragg had lost Chattanooga, opening Georgia to invasion, and Longstreet planned to withdraw his men toward Virginia. Devereaux experienced a searing hopelessness at the thought of leaving his family and home state in such a vulnerable position as he marched away. But what could he do? Not for one minute consider desertion, as he was sure some under his command were now bound to do.

His hands shook from the cold as he opened his wife's letter. Drawing his guttering candle closer, he read:

> *Dearest husband, I have received your last two letters with great appreciation. I have their precious words memorized. I am of course back in Habersham overseeing operations at Forests of Green. And I have news of the utmost importance to tell you. I would never dream now of withholding it from you even for a day, not as close as we are now, not as much danger as you are now in. You must keep yourself safe and not expose yourself to unnecessary risk. Your bravery has already been established, my dear, but your life as a father is only beginning ...*

Astonished, Devereaux laughed with blazing joy. But that emotion quickly congealed as he considered the circumstances. Carolyn alone working like a slave at Forests of Green. One baby already lost. Georgia open to the Yankee hordes. And him, leaving for Virginia for God only knew how long.

He dropped his head into his hands and wept.

December 1863
Clarkesville, Georgia

Before the year's end another letter came to Mahala, bearing important news. She knew Carolyn had worried that Clay's disappointments with his regiment would only strengthen Mahala's determination to be faithful. She hadn't said so. Mahala had merely read it in her eyes. And Mahala hadn't said so, but Carolyn had been correct.

More than ever, Clay needed something to come back to.

Now, she was relieved to discover that he had come to a place of acceptance with his situation – something she admired him for.

"During the fighting around Missionary Ridge," he had written, "our men were among the first in our sector to break and run, despite the officers' desperate urging for them to stand. I did what I could to slow the rout, but then suddenly it came to me that that was precisely all I could do. Be accountable for my own actions. The other soldiers were accountable for theirs. This was a freeing realization. What they do does not change who I am. I can stand before God and all men – for He sees the heart. So I will stay and fight, Mahala, despite my longing to be with you. I think of returning with honor with your brothers, receiving the respect of the community, and in the long years ahead, passing down stories to our children and grandchildren."

Mahala folded Clay's letter. They would have a good life, she told herself, a life to look forward to. She knew that, and she loved Clay. Why did she keep having to remind herself?

CHAPTER NINE

June 1864
Sautee Valley, Georgia

ancy Emmitt admired the fresh green leaves, clumps of blooming purple wisteria and plump livestock in the meadows as Ben drove her to Charles Williams' store and post office.

"It's hard to believe a war's on, just from looking." Nancy caught herself and reached over to touch her husband's shoulder, which she knew to be sore from helping harvest not only their wheat, but their absent sons' as well. "Of course it's not hard for you to believe. I'm sorry, Ben. How you must ache with every jostle of this wagon."

"I'm all right."

"You've done far too much for a man of your age."

"Lets me know I'm still alive," Ben said with a wry grin.

Nancy smiled and laughed. "Well, I'm glad you took a break to drive me in to mail this package," she said, patting the box on her lap. It contained baked goods and notions for all the young men in their family, Mahala's fiancé not excepted.

"I wouldn't think of letting you come alone. Need to look at some hardware anyway."

As they pulled up in front of the trading post, Ben secured the team and helped Nancy down. On the front steps she met a friend from church, whose husband was waiting nearby in a buggy.

"Oh, another care package," commented Mrs. Gaston. "And what's the latest from the boys?"

"Still trying to keep that devil Sherman up in Northwest Georgia," Nancy replied. "They just made several stands that looked to be successful – Resaca, New Hope Church, and a place called Pickett's Mill, I think it was, where our boys gave them quite a blasting."

"That's good. You're fortunate, Nancy, to have them all safe and sound. We'll keep them under the cover of our prayers. That's what it is, you know – what keeps them safe," Mrs. Gaston said, reaching out to pat Nancy's hand. Nancy nodded her agreement and appreciation. "Well, you have a good afternoon. Don't get too far from Mr. Emmitt. There are some strange sorts around today."

"Oh?" Nancy questioned, glancing about.

"Yes. Inside the trading post. A rough-looking old man asking for the whereabouts of Miss Lucy Somerston." Mrs. Gaston leaned near and lowered her voice in confidence. "He was asking about her *son*. I'm thinking he may be the father what ran off some twenty-five years ago, leaving her in a very bad way."

Nancy knew the woman of damaged virtue had been forced to live the intervening years with her parents, raising the young man on their charity, for none other would have her. But she didn't want to get into the middle of anything, so she merely bid Mrs. Gaston a polite good day. She did, however, steer clear of the rangy white-bearded stranger who was inside talking with a local old-timer. She made sure she could see Ben as she went up to mail her package.

But as she counted out her Confederate bills she heard something that made her stop in mid-payment. She swung around to give the drifter a much closer scrutiny. Forgetting to say "thank you," Nancy left the money on the counter and walked right up to the tall old man.

"Excuse me," she interrupted, "*what* did you say your name was?"

"So while Mama and Papa talked with him, Mr. Williams sent off for the sheriff, since Red Dawson was the drifter wanted for questioning in Father's murder," Mahala told Maddie, stacking an armload of dirty dishes next to the basin.

"Did he try'n' bolt?"

"No! Apparently he wasn't even aware they wanted to question him!" Mahala exclaimed. "He said he went off to California before it even happened, so they brought over poor Miss Somerston, who Mama said was not happy to see the man who'd gotten her in the family way so long ago and ruined her life. But she did admit that what he said was true. Do you know what that means, Maddie?"

"That at least the man not a liar?"

"No, silly! It means there's no way Red Dawson could have killed my father!" Mahala declared as she pushed through the kitchen door to deliver a cup of coffee and collect more dishes. That accomplished, she returned, saying as she did, "Do you realize what this means, Maddie?"

"I'm thinkin' you jus' axed me that and I had the wrong answer," Maddie replied, calmly reaching for more dishes.

136

"Now I have to figure out who did it, if it wasn't Rex Clarke and it wasn't Red Dawson."

"How you reckon on doin' that?"

"I don't know yet. But this is a huge revelation. I can't wait to tell Carolyn."

"Ain't she nigh unto havin' that baby?" Maddie inquired, lifting a soapy finger to scratch where her turban met her forehead.

"Yes, that's why I really need to check on her. They're harvesting the wheat, and I just know she's going to overdo it. I've wanted to help her out, but with Leon gone, I meet myself coming and going these days."

Back in February, the Confederacy's need for soldiers had necessitated a conscription law that drafted all white citizens between the ages of seventeen and fifty. Falling just beneath this upper limit, Leon – and his friend Abel Quitman – had been forced to join The Army of Tennessee. He had not been happy about it, but then Leon was never happy about anything. The only time Mahala had ever seen him smile was that rather stiff, fake smirk he sometimes presented when attempting to play up to wealthy guests.

At first she had felt rather sorry for him, thinking what a poor soldier he would make. But then she'd reminded herself that Leon's lack of purpose in life and the accompanying decisions could only be credited to him. He was just one of those people who'd rather be miserable and blame his lack of fortune on others.

It had been a relief to be free of his sour face, even if it meant more work for the rest of them.

But today this translated into Mahala not being able to leave the inn until around eight o'clock in the evening. Martha was not happy about Mahala going out so late, but Mahala was insistent. She promised to have one of the Rousseau slaves accompany her back into town.

At Forests of Green the door was opened by Carolyn's maid, Tania. Carolyn's hope that Tania's marriage to Samson would make the woman content had proven to be merely that – a hope. Instead, a new sense of arrogance could be detected, as if Tania tried even less to cover her resentment. It was clear to Mahala that Tania did not care for Carolyn at all, even though Carolyn was known to disapprove of holding slaves, just as her husband's brother did. She would certainly not have been responsible for encouraging Carolyn's extra rest and care during her pregnancy – which so desperately needed enforcing.

With a briefly spoken greeting, Mahala passed the long-faced maid. She found her friend in the dining room, picking at a slice of sourdough bread and a small chunk of cheese.

"Is that's what's for supper?" Mahala asked.

"Oh, hello. Come sit down. No, there's ham and snap beans and squash, if you'd like some, but this is all I could handle. I'm really glad you're here, Mahala. I've been having contractions on and off all day."

Mahala's eyes widened. "Then why didn't you call the doctor?"

Carolyn waved a dismissive hand. "Oh, nothing that regular. Just enough to be worrisome and steal my appetite. So are you hungry?"

"No, thanks. I've already eaten. I just wanted to come check on you. Are you in pain?" Mahala asked, eying her companion warily, as though she might drop a child on the floor at any moment.

"Well, I wouldn't say pain. It just takes my breath away. Like my whole body is working up to something."

"Yes – *childbirth*."

Carolyn laughed. "You're not the one who's supposed to look so scared. Here. Feel. One is starting right now."

Carolyn took Mahala's hand and placed it at the top of her very rounded stomach. It was rock hard.

"Oh, my! Carolyn, I really think we should call Dr. Mercer."

"Not yet. It could well be another day or two. I can't ask him to wait around that long. But just the same, I'd feel better if you could spend the night. Do you think you might could?"

"I – I suppose so."

"Thank you. I'll call a servant so you can send a message to your grandmother." When that was done, Carolyn asked, "So, now, any news from town?"

Mahala had almost forgotten the information she'd been so eager to share. Now she told about Nancy's visit to Sautee, and what had transpired with Red Dawson. "So I've been trying to think," she said, "if anyone else might have had motive – someone closer to home. And not just motive, but ability. I mean, someone who wouldn't blanch at the idea of murder. Or – wait, I've never considered this, but what if it was an accident?"

"Like a fight that got out of hand? But you said whoever did it took valuables from the cabin," Carolyn reminded her, distractedly placing a hand on her stomach again.

"That's true, but maybe the robbery was an afterthought to cover the killing," Mahala suggested, warming to her subject. "Maybe *Ududu* was right and Father had buried his gold somewhere, and it never *was* stolen."

But Carolyn was not really in the mood for discussion, despite her attempt at politeness. "It could still have been any number of other miners or drifters passing through the area," she said a bit impatiently, "and the robbery went wrong when Michael accosted them."

138

Mahala judged from the tightened corners of Carolyn's mouth that the most recent contraction was accompanied by a bit of discomfort. Clearly this was not the time to try to solve her father's murder. She'd have to put that aside. Her friend needed *her*, not the other way around. "Would you like to lie down?" she asked.

"I think I would. I'm sorry."

"Nothing to be sorry for," Mahala said, scooting back her chair.

She helped Carolyn from the table and up the stairs. Mahala fixed her in bed, then sat beside her to read aloud from a popular novel. She could tell Carolyn wasn't really listening, but she was still. At last, satisfied that her friend was relaxed and the contractions had eased, Mahala got up to go to bed herself.

Carolyn caught her hand. "Do you think I will be a good mother?"

Mahala smiled confidently. "Of course you will."

"I don't know. There's so much to do – without Dev. How will I find time to tend a baby, too?"

"You will."

Mahala wished she could say more, could promise support and assistance, but she, too, was overburdened right now – like all women. She patted Carolyn's hand and went to the bedroom next door. There she let down her hair and donned a borrowed nightgown. She couldn't help remembering the last time she'd been here, borrowed something of Carolyn's. The day Jack had first kissed her. Normally Mahala succeeded in not thinking about him, but whenever she did, a dull ache always rose in her chest.

Where was he? What was he doing? And why could she not forget him?

Chastising herself, she lay down and said her prayers, for Clay, fighting in the defense of Atlanta.

Listening to the soft sounds of outdoor creatures and the settling of the house for the night, she relaxed.

The next thing she knew, she jerked awake as someone stood over her, shaking her arm.

"Wh-what?" Mahala blurted, sitting up in bed.

It was Carolyn, clutching her voluminous white gown below her swollen belly. "Wake up," she said. "I think the baby's coming after all."

Startled into full alertness by those alarming words, Mahala tossed the sheet off and swung her legs over the side of the bed. "I'll go for the doctor."

"No. I want you to stay. We can send Samson. I just need you to sit with me. I'm scared."

Mahala stared at her with wide eyes. She knew better than to say it, but so was she! Her own mother had died in childbirth. "Carolyn, I have no idea what to do," she finally admitted. "Remember you're talking to an unmarried woman who's never attended a birth."

"I know. All you have to do is be here. I couldn't stand to have that awful Tania glowering down at me at such a moment. I just – need a friend."

"Shouldn't I at least boil water or something?"

But Carolyn crumpled over the side of the bed in a paroxysm of agony. "I'm not very good with pain," she whimpered as the contraction began to ease up.

Mahala took her arm. "Let's get you back to your room."

Minutes later, with shaking fingers, Mahala dressed. She ran downstairs and out to the cabin Samson shared with Tania. The nighttime dew soaked through her slippers and hose. She pounded on the door until Samson came with an uncustomary scowl.

"I need help," Mahala practically shouted at him. "Carolyn's having the baby. I need someone to go to town to fetch Dr. Mercer and Tania to boil some water and gather fresh linens – and – and – anything else! Please hurry!"

"Yes, Ma'am," Samson said, catching her sense of urgency. Neither could he miss her anxiety. Before shutting the door, he took a moment to say, "It will be all right, Miss Mahala."

Mahala had the presence of mind to bring a cloth, a glass and a pitcher of water back upstairs with her. She paused in the doorway. Carolyn, normally so composed, was weeping. Mahala remembered the day Carolyn had pulled her out of bed and made her rise above her depression. Now she would have to do the same. If she were to maintain any atmosphere of calm she would have to put her own fear aside for her friend's sake.

"Is it going to get worse?" Carolyn cried. "I don't think I can stand anymore."

"Yes, you can, and you will," Mahala replied in a firm but gentle voice. She just hoped Carolyn wouldn't realize the tone of authority was completely fake. She set the pitcher down and marched over to the cradle in the corner of the room. She started dragging it across the rug into Carolyn's line of vision, saying, "No one's trying to kill you. There's pain, but there's a purpose. You'll survive, and the pain will end, and there will be a son or daughter. Now, where's your receiving blanket?"

"In the top bureau dresser," Carolyn answered weakly, her gaze flickering to Tania, who arrived with soap, linens and water.

Mahala got out the soft knit blanket and spread it over the side of the cradle.

"Another contraction," Carolyn whispered.

Mahala sat beside her and took her hand. "I heard somewhere it helps to count through them."

In that way, they passed the next hour and a half until the doctor came. It was a relief to relinquish her place to the experienced old man, with his comfortable air of confidence. Mahala prepared to leave the room. But Carolyn again grabbed her hand, with more panic this time. Remembering their long-ago conversation about doctors, Mahala smiled.

"Wishing your sister were here now?" she joked quietly.

"Very much."

"I'll stay near."

She retired to a corner while the doctor made his assessment.

"Good work, ladies!" he exclaimed. "This baby is ready to be born!"

Comparatively, it could have been called an easy birth. But it was another good half hour of intensive effort before it seemed significant progress was made. There was no more counting. Mahala stood back and watched with an inner trembling, biting the insides of her cheeks at Carolyn's agonized cries. She had never seen such suffering. And women went through this again and again in their married lives – at least, those fortunate enough to have no fatal complications. Could this be any less fearful than the battlefield? Any less painful than the most grievous wound?

Finally the doctor said, "The head is crowning, Mrs. Rousseau. The child has dark hair. One more push."

Carolyn gritted her teeth, curled forward, and gave one last supreme effort. Her scream of pain was more chilling than a bobcat's cry. Then she fell back. Thinking Carolyn looked dead, Mahala froze in horror. Her gaze swung to the doctor, but he was busy – cleaning out the mouth and nose of a dark pink infant. He held it upside down and smacked its little bottom, and it gave forth a piercing cry of irritation.

Carolyn's eyes opened, and she strained to see the child.

Relieved, Mahala hurried to her side. "It's a boy," she told her friend, overwhelmed with unspeakable joy, so much so that tears filled her eyes.

Carolyn laughed, but then exclaimed in alarm, "Another contraction!"

"Could it be twins?" Mahala gasped at the doctor.

Doctor Mercer smiled patiently. "No, ladies, that'll just be the afterbirth."

"The what?" they both echoed.

The old gentleman turned his attention from the infant to the mother. "The sack that held the baby," he explained. "If Miss Franklin will give this child his first bath, we'll have mother and son ready to meet each other in no time."

Blushing, Mahala thought the doctor had never before encountered two such ignorant women. Dr. Mercer held up the mewling newborn and gave her an impatient look. Gingerly she came forward and took the child. He weighed next to nothing, but his fists punctuated the air like the end of so many angry exclamation points, and his face was screwed into a furious pout. She grimaced, thinking he had already formed an opinion about his treatment in this world. And she was about to add insult to injury by giving him a bath.

Testing the water that Tania poured into the basin, Mahala laid the child beside it on his blanket. Then she took a cloth and began to gently wipe away the blood and mucus. My, but he was beautiful. He looked just like Dev. She brushed the dark hair to one side. Taking him over to the cradle, she put on a nappy and wrapped him in his new blanket the way Nancy had taught her when caring for neighbors' babies. She felt both honored and excited to present Carolyn with her first child.

The weary mother, nevertheless glowing with anticipation, was now propped up on her pillows. She turned to Mahala, smiling and holding out her arms. Mahala eased the bundle into them. The faint light of dawn illuminated Carolyn's tears of joy as she surveyed her son.

"You did real well, Mrs. Rousseau," Dr. Mercer pronounced. "He's a fine boy."

"Will you call him Louis, then, as Dev wishes?" Mahala asked.

"I will name him Louis, but I don't think I can call him that. He has to be Devereaux Louis Rousseau, Jr.."

Dr. Mercer clucked forebodingly. "A man likes his wishes to be honored, even from afar."

Mahala laughed. "Dr. Mercer, I think when Major Rousseau sees the son Carolyn has given him, he will be ready to forgive her anything. And I think he'll understand. There never was a more perfect miniature, even at so young an age."

"Oh, I wish he was here. He should be here to hold his son." Carolyn's tears fell in earnest.

Dr. Mercer, clearly out of his league, made ready to go, quickly mumbling instructions and assuring them that he would come again before nightfall.

Mahala patted Carolyn's arm and followed the old gentleman to the bedroom door. "Dr. Mercer, would you mind stopping in at the hotel and telling my grandmother what has happened? Please tell her I know it will put her in a hard way, but I feel I should stay on here for a day or two to help Mrs. Rousseau."

"Of course. I'm sure she'll understand. You held up admirably for a single woman. I'd be happy to deliver your message."

Smiling her thanks, Mahala turned back into the room, confident the doctor would not mind seeing himself out. She went to sit beside Carolyn. As Tania moved about the chamber tidying up, the women admired the baby. Even Tania paused to smile down at him, no doubt thinking about her own future babies. Now that he was calm, Dev Jr. was more handsome than ever.

"Dev will be so proud," Mahala commented.

"As impossible as it seems, I think I love him now more than ever," Carolyn said. "I feel like my heart could burst from joy."

"I'm glad for you, Carolyn. Thank you for letting me be a part of this."

A half hour later, Carolyn absorbed in her first attempt to feed her newborn, Mahala dragged herself to the bed next door and collapsed. She felt the magical glow of new life in the now-quiet house, like a hush, a blessing, hovering over them. It surrounded her and buoyed her into a soft, peaceful sleep, where she dreamed of a little boy with green eyes.

Autumn 1864
Clarkesville, Georgia

News from the fronts near Atlanta and in Virginia trickled slowly to North Georgia – news so discouraging as to be difficult to believe in such a peaceful, unchanging setting. Carolyn wrote to Dev and, in July, received a response. The 8th had fought a successful battle from the trenches at Cold Harbor. Dev's letter was long, full of joy at the prospect of fatherhood and hope for the future.

"I know that whatever happens in this war, material things are fleeting. No matter how our world changes, I will be content if I just have you and Devereaux Jr. And yes, I forgive you for not calling him Louis. I'm sure my vanity will be stroked by having a namesake if he looks as much like me as you say. Talk to him about his papa and tell him how much I love him. As much as I long to be with you, I would finish this honorably – so that my son can be proud of me, can say 'my father was a brave soldier.' One day soon I'll hold him close and tell him the stories of my adventures. And he'll have many brothers and sisters. Only this time I'll be there when they're born."

By August, Carolyn learned Devereaux's regiment was fighting in the Petersburg trenches. They had to hold out there, for if Petersburg fell, so would the capital of the Confederacy.

And Atlanta was in similar danger. Mahala kept Carolyn apprised of The Army of Tennessee's fight to preserve Georgia's industrial stronghold through Clay's letters. In mid-June, Sherman had temporarily abandoned the flanking movements he had used thus far to dance around Johnston's army, attacking the Confedcrates at Kennesaw Mountain on the 27th. He was badly beaten.

"Clay says if only he'd stand up to them, they could whip him," Mahala said.

But again Sherman flanked. Union troops under Kennar Garrard secured Roswell Mill on July 5. Shortly thereafter, horrible tales about assaults on female mill workers circulated. Two hundred women and children were taken captive and shipped north as prisoners, creating a public furor, even in the North. But the Yankee army merely crossed the Chattahoochee River and proceeded down Peachtree Road. Clay wrote that one morning Confederates and Yankees swam together, and that same afternoon they fired on each other.

On July 18, the Georgia boys heard with regret that Johnston had been replaced with General Hood, who was expected to be more aggressive in his defense of the city. He attacked the enemy at Peachtree Creek and near Atlanta, but at a terrible cost. Carolyn had a letter from Sylvie Randall in Savannah saying that Josephine Habersham's two boys, Lieutenant Joseph Clay Habersham and his younger brother Willie Habersham, had died within an hour of each other. Sylvie's letter also revealed the suffering of another Savannah matron, Charlotte Branch, whose son, Sanford, had been a lieutenant in the 8th. He was now in Fort Delaware, "the Andersonville of the North," under dreadful conditions.

Closer to home, Jacob, Mahala's youngest adoptive brother, was wounded in the thigh and furloughed home to recover. Mahala went to the valley for a few days to see him. When she returned, she reported his condition to be stable, though his recovery would be slow. This was not all a bad thing, for it would keep him from danger for a while.

By July 28th, General Hooker had lost 5,000 Southern lives in a reckless assault at Ezra Church and had been pushed back to the last ditch fortifying the state capital. The men fought again on August 20th. Mahala received a letter from Clay stating that he did not believe they could hold the city. The ranks were thinned by death and disease, and the men were physically exhausted. The 65th Georgia was now the size of a small company – less than a hundred men – not a regiment. And that situation was typical throughout the army.

And then no more letters came. They knew the faltering Confederates had made one last attempt to stand at Jonesboro before the city of Atlanta was surrendered on September 2. The citizens were ordered to evacuate. The strategic rail center was in the hands of the Yankees, creating near-panic in the Liverpool banking houses, coupled as the news was with that of the fall of Mobile. The generals in Atlanta agreed to a temporary armistice. While the citizens speculated on whether the governor would make a peace with Sherman, soldiers who lived nearby were able to briefly rejoin their families.

Mahala knew better than to hope Clay and her brothers would be able to visit, for they would scarcely make it to the mountains before they were required to return. But Carolyn watched her grow more and more desperate as the days and then weeks of September passed with no word.

"I know something is wrong," Mahala said. "Clay would write. It's been too long. And if he can't, why don't Sam or Seth?"

Three days later, when Carolyn drove into town to get yarn she could use to crochet Little Dev a pair of cool weather booties, Mahala declared, "I'm going down there – to Atlanta! I'm going to find out what's happened to them."

"Don't be ridiculous," Carolyn snapped, deciding it was no time to mince words. "Do you want to be ravaged and killed by Yankees? Because that's who will greet you in Atlanta. You must get a hold of yourself. I agree, it's odd that you've heard nothing. But there have been other times letters were sporadic, other letters that have been lost. You have no choice but to stay here and wait. And you won't help anything by going crazy with worry."

Carolyn spoke more harshly than she intended. She knew the harrying effects of uncertainty better than anyone. She just didn't want Mahala to do anything foolish.

Despite this, it was a busy but fairly happy autumn for Carolyn. The slaves planned to butcher one of their two remaining hogs when the temperature fell to the right range – about forty degrees. In preparation, they had to strip the floor of the smokehouse to get the required eight pounds of salt. This meant digging up the dirt, leaching it through an ash hopper, mixing it with water, and boiling it down. The mixture of recycled salt and two pounds of molasses looked muddy and completely unappetizing, but a local farmwife who explained the whole meat process assured them that the solution would do the job. She instructed Carolyn to let the ham soak six weeks, hang it up to smoke the whole month of February, and sew it up and whitewash it the first week of March to prevent bugs. They should eat the bacon and shoulders soon after.

Meanwhile, Carolyn was busy with normal household tasks. Each day was a new adventure in her son's growth. In the mornings, she would wrap him in a blanket and take walks, showing him the delicate, dewy morning glories and the sunflowers in the garden, goldenrod stalks and changing fall leaves along the hedgerow and the pond, and the workers in the field picking the corn. Her heart would leap for joy when he vocalized in response to her words, and his smile would light up her whole day. In the afternoons, after his noontime feeding, he would nap in his cradle while Carolyn worked in the gardens or the kitchen. Sometimes they had visitors for tea or dinner, when Dev Jr. would delight and entertain his admirers. And then she would rock him to sleep at night and place him in his bed right beside hers. She would often stand over him in awe, just watching him sleep. Her love for Dev had been hard-fought and hard-won, but this love – it was the most natural and primary bond in existence.

So it was when Mahala showed up one mid-October afternoon wearing a frozen countenance, Carolyn had the absurd urge to merely turn her back, go on polishing the silver, and hope she'd go away. She didn't want to hear any more bad news. She didn't want to see any more tears. How selfish she was being, so wrapped up in new motherhood and the peace it brought! Her friend needed her, just like she had needed Mahala when Dev Jr. had been born. So she put down the silver tea pot she'd been rubbing to a high shine and turned to face Mahala in the door of the narrow butler's pantry.

"You've heard about Clay," she said as calmly as possible, bracing herself for Mahala's reaction.

"No. I've brought ... a letter for *you*."

Carolyn's heart stopped. Mahala held out an unopened envelope. Carolyn stood there staring at it, staring at not Dev's handwriting, but Dylan's. Her knees buckled.

"Carolyn!" Mahala's hand shot out to steady her. "Come sit down."

Carolyn allowed herself to be led to a bench in the hallway just opposite. She tried to take deep breaths and slow her pulse, but relentless waves of fear were crashing over her. Her hands, stained gray from the silver cleaning, were shaking so badly she dropped the letter when Mahala tried to give it to her. Mahala picked it up, and as she did, their eyes met with shared knowledge.

"Read it," Carolyn said. "Please."

ith wide eyes, Mahala looked out the train window as they approached Savannah. She had thought she might never make this journey. And now she did, though under far different circumstances than she might have hoped.

As they had traveled from Habersham County, it had become more and more apparent that Georgia was a state at war. People of all descriptions were on the move, from harried mothers with bawling children clinging to them to soldiers with glazed looks in their eyes. Everyone possessed a certain tension. Nowhere had that tension been more evident than in Mahala's companion.

As the family coach had swayed over the rutted roads leading into the hilly country cradling Hollingsworth, Bushville and Harmony Grove, Carolyn had pressed her feet to the floor as if to make them go faster. Her posture had been erect, her face a mask. Mahala knew they could never go fast enough to suit her – not even on the train they'd boarded at Athens. First, though, they had spent the night in that town at the home of her old friend Patience Blake, now Patience Sprite. Patience had been happy to receive them. Her lawyer husband had long ago joined the army, and her life consisted of taking care of their two children and whatever odd sewing jobs she could get her hands on for a bit of cash. The Sprite home was a pleasant one, situated in the old Lickskillet district of Athens. The second story windows provided a nice view of downtown, the steam company which provided telegraph lines and firefighting services, and the Oconee River. Patience and Mahala had sat up late catching up in the parlor and shaking their heads at the sound of Carolyn's feet pacing on the floor overhead.

Carolyn had dozed a little on the train the next morning, but there were still smudges under her eyes when she woke up. Mahala looked at her with pity now as the blonde woman leaned her head briefly against the side of the train opposite her.

"What condition do you think we'll find him in?" Carolyn asked. "'A bullet through the lung,' Dylan's note said. Don't men usually die from that?"

"Sometimes, but not always. He *was* well enough to travel."

"But maybe Dylan is just bringing him home to – to – say goodbye." Carolyn paused and bit her lip. "This is so awful! Could he not have been more specific? I don't know whether to be excited to see him, that maybe he'll be fine and not have to go back to that fighting, which would be so wonderful, or if he's even going to be alive when we get there!"

Mahala didn't know what to say. She knew the dark agony of uncertainty herself now, and the nameless frenzy it could produce inside a person. So she watched silently as Carolyn opened her brother-in-law's letter for the tenth time and read it again. Mahala knew well what it said:

> *Carolyn, Dev was wounded in fighting at the beginning of this month. A bullet pierced his lung and passed through his body. I am with him in Richmond. Your sister is with us and has given the best of care, but we both feel his best chance for recovery is at home. I have arranged to return with him, and Miss Calhoun is sending this note on ahead. Please hasten to meet us in Savannah, where our mother should also be arriving. Sincerely, Dylan*

Almost immediately after reading Dylan's words the first time, Carolyn had asked Mahala to accompany her to Savannah.

"I can't stand the thought of taking Tania," she had confided. "She would be so surly if I made her leave Samson. And there really is no one else. I'll need help with the baby, and he'll go with you without fussing. Please, Mahala. Please."

And so here she was, though when they'd changed trains at Union Point, she'd fought her own inward battle, knowing the other set of tracks led to Atlanta. To possible answers about Clay. And she'd also realized that she would now be unaware of any letter that might currently be bound to her in Clarkesville.

When they pulled into the Central of Georgia station with brakes screeching, steam hissing and bell clanging, Carolyn said, "Dylan won't know when we're arriving. We'll have to hire a conveyance."

Mahala looked out onto the crowded depot scene with trepidation. She gathered her things along with the baby's and followed Carolyn to the door. Carolyn was now a woman possessed with a purpose.

"Here, I'll take the baby," she said. "He might help someone take pity on me when I'm trying to hire a ride. You go get our luggage and wait by it. I'll be back with someone to help."

They had only brought one trunk, packing all their belongings in together, knowing they would be traveling alone. Mahala found it and sat on it on the bustling depot deck, watching the stream of soldiers – both well and wounded – civilians, medical personnel, and what appeared to be government officials.

True to her word, Carolyn returned shortly with a stout black man. He carried their trunk to a waiting vehicle for hire and helped them in. Carolyn gave him the address, and they were off. Mahala didn't want to guess what her friend had paid for such prompt service.

Holding Dev Jr., Mahala gazed out at the industrial complex surrounding them. A number of buildings supported the railroad operations, including an engine house with a corrugated roof and the round house with an iron roof and cast iron columns. Randall iron from the foundry of Jack's Northern family? A paved street headed off in the direction of the waterfront, which Mahala could identify by an unfamiliar smell of the dank, salty variety. A thrill of amazement filled her as she realized how close she was to actually seeing the ocean.

But the buggy moved along the sandy streets into a residential section. The houses were so big and fine. You'd never know anything was amiss, thought Mahala, except for occasional telltale signs of neglect – here an overgrown lawn and shrubbery, there peeling and flaking paint. It was clear that even Savannah's wealthiest had to put their precious remaining resources into their mouths rather than their residences.

"Let me look at him," Carolyn said suddenly. Mahala turned the infant to face her. She smoothed his hair and adjusted his bonnet with a shaking hand, then inspected his gown for stains. "He's got to look just perfect to meet his father."

"Oh, Carolyn." Mahala grabbed her friend's gloved hand and squeezed it. "Be strong."

Carolyn nodded, and her breath began to come more rapidly. "I'm just so scared, Mahala. I feel like it's going to swallow me whole."

Mahala shook her head. "In times like these we must rely on the Lord," she whispered, speaking as much to herself as to Carolyn, "and lean not on our own understanding. We may feel things are out of control, but everything is still in His hands."

"I know," Carolyn murmured, brushing away tears. "I know. But it just doesn't feel like it."

That's when it's faith, Mahala thought.

Gently jostling the infant she held, she got out of the buggy and stood at the gate of a handsome town house. It looked like the Rousseau home had been built about the same time as the other homes on the square – not much more than ten years ago – most of which were paired brick and Greek Revival in style. The driver got their trunk, and Carolyn led the way to the door, where she pulled out a wad of Confederate bills and paid the man. The door was opened by a black servant whom Carolyn recognized. "Is he here?"

"Yas'm. Major Rousseau be home." He held the door for them and stepped around to bring the trunk inside. "They all here – Mistuh Dev and Mrs. Henrietta and your mama, Mrs. Calhoun. They been waitin' on you."

As they came into the foyer, Mahala saw Carolyn's mother-in-law appear on the landing, a tall form in gray behind her. For a second, because the man possessed such an air of confidence, she thought absurdly that it was Devereaux. Then she noticed the auburn hair. Henrietta hurried down the steps and embraced Carolyn.

"Oh, my dear! You're finally here!" she cried. "Thank goodness!" She was distracted by the sight of the baby Mahala held and reached out to touch him. "Oh – so this is Dev Jr." Henrietta choked and suddenly began to weep.

Mahala looked askance at Carolyn, who met her eyes.

"It's just that he looks very like his father." Dylan came up behind his mother. His face lean and tan, the square jaw prominent. "And his father's not doing so good right now."

"Dylan! Tell me everything," Carolyn said, hugging her brother-in-law.

"He's very weak. He's been asking for you constantly. I'm glad you're here."

In response to those words, Carolyn grabbed her skirt and prepared to mount the stairs, saying, "Come, Mahala. Bring the baby."

But Dylan laid a hand on her arm. "Wait. I need to tell you – it's not just the wound. The doctors say the bullet passed through and only nicked the lung, and that the wound is closing well. Under good circumstances, he might heal. But Dev's contracted pneumonia, Carolyn. I don't think it would be good to expose an infant." Dylan cast a gentle, almost curious, glance at his new nephew.

"Pneumonia?" Carolyn's lower lip trembled. "What's being done for him?"

"He won't take morphine or opium, and we've opted not to use plasters or cupping for fear of reopening the wound, but apart from that we've done everything possible, including hot compresses and small doses of quinine. Yet he's gotten worse, not better."

"We're hoping that seeing you will help him," Henrietta said, raising her handkerchief to blot at her red-rimmed eyes.

"Then it's all the more important that he see his son," Carolyn declared, her resolution firming. "God will just have to protect us."

Mahala expected Carolyn would take Dev Jr. into her arms at that moment, but she turned and started up the stairs, so Mahala followed. She felt like an unnecessary intruder into this private family drama. At the top of the steps, Carolyn did reach for her child. She remembered Mahala's

150

needs and said, "There's an open room at the end of the hall if you'd like to freshen up. I'll call you when I need you to take the baby."

Mahala nodded.

"Thank you," Carolyn said.

Mahala smiled and patted her arm. She watched her friend go into a closed chamber. The door shut behind her.

She had washed up and refreshed herself using items from the trunk the servant brought up. She saw from the hall that the sick room door was still closed. Mahala stood there for a moment. She was about to turn and make her way downstairs when the door opened and Carolyn came out. She thrust Dev Jr. into Mahala's arms.

"Take him, change his clothes and wash him off, please," she said tersely. Her voice sounded thick.

"Carolyn, how is Dev?"

But Carolyn shook her head and looked as if she was barely holding onto her control. "I can't talk just yet." She disappeared back into her husband's room.

Mahala did as Carolyn had asked, ringing for fresh water and a basin and changing the child in the guest room. When she was done, she went downstairs, thinking she might find Henrietta or Carolyn's mother and maybe even some refreshment. Her stomach felt very empty. But the dull gloom of sickness had pervaded the whole house, and no one seemed to be around. Then she noticed a movement in the library. It was Dylan. He had his back turned to her, shoulders slumped. He braced himself on a desk that looked out on a garden. Mahala paused in the doorway, hesitating. She did not know Dylan Rousseau very well. When she heard a shuddering breath that sounded like the onset of weeping, her heart clenched. She turned to walk away, but Dev Jr. chose that moment to emit a very nice vowel sound.

Dylan turned quickly, surprise on his features as he swiped the back of a hand across his face.

"I'm sorry," Mahala blurted, still poised to go.

"No – no, do come in, Miss Franklin." Dylan came toward her, all traces of grief gone from his countenance. His eyes lit on his nephew. "He's really something, isn't he?"

Mahala smiled. "Yes. I've grown quite fond of him."

"It was good of you to come with Carolyn. But look at us! How we are treating you! Leaving you to wander about an unfamiliar house with a baby in your charge! Is there anything you need?"

"Well, maybe a glass of water …"

Dylan rang the bell pull. When a maid appeared, he said, "Bring some refreshments, please. Whatever we have."

"Really, just some water," Mahala protested, not wanting to be a nuisance on an already difficult day. "It must be almost dinner time." But the servant had already gone.

"It might be a late meal. Won't you sit down?"

Mahala did so, the baby on her lap. Dylan sat across from her on a leather sofa. Indeed the whole room smelled like leather, for it was filled with volumes and volumes of books. They regarded each other with polite, awkward smiles.

Mahala noticed a bar on Dylan's frayed collar and asked, "Are you also a major now, Mr. Rousseau?"

Dylan smiled. "No, Ma'am. Each regiment has but one major, and Devereaux is the 8th's. I am, however, now a lieutenant, silly as that seems."

"I'm sure that doesn't seem silly at all."

"If you had known what a pitiful soldier I began this war as, you might think otherwise."

"Obviously that's not the case now." After a slight pause in which Dylan bowed his head, she asked, "Didn't Major Rousseau have a body servant with him? Did he come home with you, too?"

This time the man's smile was sad. "Little Joe was a faithful friend. But he died recently of typhoid."

"Died? Oh, how awful. This war is one tragedy after another, isn't it, Lieutenant Rousseau?"

Dylan nodded. "Yes, it is."

A tray of food had arrived, some juice and ginger cakes – and roasted nuts that looked quite appealing. As Mahala sat forward to investigate, Dev Jr. pumped a chubby arm vigorously in the air.

"Would you like me to take him so you can have something?" Dylan asked.

"Oh, certainly! Thank you." *He must be eager to hold his nephew,* thought Mahala. Chastising herself for not realizing it sooner, she gently settled Dev Jr. onto Dylan's lap.

Dylan smiled down at the child and shifted him on his knee so he could better see the little face. "I don't have much experience with babies," he commented, as if to explain his awkwardness.

"He seems to like you," Mahala observed with some surprise. Dev Jr. had wrapped a hand around his uncle's finger and was busy trying to suck it. "Generally he doesn't care to go to men."

"He's awfully tiny, isn't he?"

"He's small, but he's a healthy boy."

"Yes – look how well he's holding his head up."

Pouring herself a drink, Mahala smiled at the sight of the battle-hardened soldier cradling the drooling infant. She let Dylan croon to his nephew and assist him in standing on one of Dylan's knees while she ate a ginger cake. She felt much better. Strong enough to ask: "Lieutenant Rousseau, what do you expect for your brother? Please be candid."

Dylan paused and took a deep breath. "I don't know, Miss Franklin. He sounds awful. It's hard for him to breathe, and his cough is deep. He does not have a good look about him. My only hope is that Carolyn's presence might cause him to take a turn for the better. Again, I want to apologize that your visit falls under these circumstances. If things were different–"

Mahala held up a hand. "Please don't apologize. I understand. I'm here to help in any way I can."

Dylan smiled briefly. "You are a good friend." He looked away from her, focusing on the baby and his own inward troubles. He continued, as if to himself, "It just doesn't seem right. Not now. And it halfway doesn't even seem real, either. Not Dev. Dev was always the strong one. The lucky one. I used to hate his good luck. But now, I'd do anything to see him get better. He has so much to live for."

So saying, Dylan dipped his auburn head and, in a tender and vulnerable gesture, inhaled the baby's sweet scent. Sensitive of the man's emotions, Mahala looked away.

"'Bless the Lord, O my soul: and all that is within me, bless his holy name. Bless the Lord, O my soul, and forget not all his benefits.'"

Carolyn sat quietly on the bed beside her husband as Dylan, in a chair pulled up next to Dev's other side, read aloud from the Psalms. It had been two weeks since her arrival, and no noticeable improvement had occurred. In fact, did she imagine it, or was there now a faint bluish cast to the strong hands and finely molded lips? Nothing was working, not the medicines given by the doctor, or the teas of mullein and goldenseal that Mahala had prepared.

Henrietta was so distraught by the sight of her son in his weakened condition that she only visited with him for a few minutes twice each day. Invariably, she would leave the room in tears. No one encouraged more extended contact than this, fearing his mother's hysterics would only set Devereaux back.

But during these daily Bible readings, which Dev requested – and always from Psalms – Carolyn allowed herself to hope. She saw her husband relax, his breathing slow and deepen. He would listen with eyes closed, as he was doing now, but sometimes she would find him watching her with a secret smile.

"'Who forgiveth all thine iniquities; who healeth all thy diseases;'" Dylan read in his clear preacher's voice, "'who redeemeth thy life from destruction; who crowneth thee with lovingkindness and tender mercies; who satisfieth thy mouth with good things; so that thy youth is renewed like the eagle's.'"

Carolyn's knitting needles slowed as she considered these words. They were like a promise, she thought, something Dev could grasp onto. She looked to see if he was gleaning special encouragement from today's reading.

His dark eyes were indeed on Dylan, but with an intensity of a nature she did not expect. Maybe Dev was discouraged that Dylan had to leave tomorrow. Dylan had told them that morning that he had lingered as long as he could – nay, longer than he should have, for the Oglethorpes were without officers and sore in need of him.

"'The Lord executeth righteousness and judgment for all that are oppressed,'" Dylan continued, oblivious to his brother's scrutiny.

But suddenly Dev reached out and grabbed Dylan's hand with a grip surprisingly strong.

"I'm sorry, Dylan," he said.

Dylan stared at him with a shocked expression, trying to balance the Bible in one hand.

"For what?"

"I did you both wrong," Dev said. "I was so selfish. I stepped in where I had no right."

A spasm of coughing seized him. Carolyn stared at him in amazement, then jumped into motion, bringing a glass of water to his lips. He drank, then looked at her with a faint smile.

Carolyn and Dylan sat there in embarrassed, confused silence as Dev lay back and closed his eyes, his breathing thick. He reached for Carolyn's hand.

"If I don't make it ..." Dev whispered, letting his words trail off. But his meaning was obvious as he gently placed his wife's hand upon his brother's then united them both under his own.

For a heartbeat, Carolyn's wide eyes met Dylan's, and in them she read her own reaction. Shock and anger quaked through her, and she revolted in every fiber of her being at what Devereaux was suggesting.

"No!" she cried, snatching her hand back. "No, no, no!"

And that was all she could say. She jumped off the bed and ran from the room in a storm of furious emotions, hot tears pouring from her eyes.

154

"Please stay," Dev requested when Dylan got up to follow Carolyn. Why he had that urge, or what he was going to say to her, he didn't know. Maybe he was going to assure her that he was just as taken aback at his brother's suggestion as she was. He wanted her to know he'd had no part in it. This past year, as he and Dev had grown closer and the war and God's work in his heart had changed his perspective, Dylan had finally ceased to think of Carolyn except as his sister-in-law. The days of their youthful courtship now seemed so long ago.

But at Dev's words, Dylan sat back down. "Why would you say such a thing?" he asked in an agonized voice.

"I need you to listen to me," Dev said softly.

So he sat and listened to things he did not want to hear, and he spoke his words of forgiveness and his own confession from the troubled past even as the sound of Carolyn's impassioned weeping rose from the garden below.

Carolyn lay on her side on her bed, staring into the inky darkness. She blinked her swollen eyes, but no sleep came, even though Dev Jr. slumbered in his cradle, content from his midnight feeding. Tonight not even the infant's warmth against her breast had been able to ease the solid weight of pain in her heart. For that, she needed a husband. A whole, well husband.

She got up and walked stealthily across the floor and through the door that adjoined Dev's room to hers. She had insisted on being near despite the protests of the family. She had wanted instant knowledge of the slightest change in his condition, for better or worse. But now the next room over was not close enough. Neither was waiting in case *he* might need *her*. No. *She* needed *him*.

A single oil lamp burned low on the bureau as she entered. She could hear her husband's shallow, raspy breathing. He lay facing the other way, so she walked around to that side of the bed and stood there hating him and loving him intensely in the same moment.

Without opening his eyes, Devereaux asked, "Still mad at me?"

"Still horribly mad, and hurt, and humiliated. How could you, Dev?"

His look was sad. "Because I love you both so much. And I need to fix what I messed up long ago."

Carolyn choked on a sudden sob. She lifted the sheet and climbed in beside him, lying right next to him, facing him, gently putting her arm around him. He was damp with perspiration, and she could hear the rattle of congestion in his lungs. She hated this illness – yes, that was what she hated, not Dev, never him – and she thought maybe she had not tried hard enough to love it away.

"You should not be in here like this," he whispered, even as he draped a weak arm around her in return. "You have our son to think of."

"And you – you shouldn't talk to me like you did. Didn't you listen to what Dylan was reading earlier, about God healing our diseases? If you would just try a little harder, I know you can lick this." Carolyn looked up, raising her face to his, cupping the side of his with her hand. "Please try, Dev. For our family. You must try."

She made a move to kiss him, but he turned his face away. "Please don't," he whispered.

Hearing the agony in his voice and seeing a tear run down one cheek, Carolyn thought she couldn't bear the pain. It was all so unfair. So impossible. It couldn't be happening to her. She couldn't hold back the tears, and she sobbed into his chest. She thought she felt Dev stroke her hair.

"I'm sorry," he murmured, coughing again.

She held herself stiff and apart from him so as not to jar his wound until the fit passed. Then she said, "You always win your battles, Dev. I can stand anything if you'll just get well."

"Did you ever think this may be the one I lose?"

"No. No!"

"I need to know – you'll be all right – if I'm not here. He'll take care of you. Let him take care of you, Carolyn."

"Stop it – just stop. I refuse to listen to you talk like that."

"Oh, Carolyn," Dev whispered, so softly she could barely hear him, but she thought, with a trace of humor. "You'll make a good mother."

Nothing could amuse her now. "Just hold me."

She lay in his arms for a long time after that with her hot tears flowing down her face. Would they ever run dry? She could barely hear his heart. Only the faint rattle of Dev's breathing told her he was still alive, and sleeping.

Some time during the night she dozed. She dreamed Dev was delirious, calling out her name, but she could not get to him. A dense fog separated them, and she ran through it, searching for him but never finding him.

Carolyn awoke drenched in sweat. She sat up abruptly. As dawn's faint tendrils lit Savannah with soft gray, Dev Jr. was beginning to wake and fuss in the next room. But next to her, his father did not stir. A sense of panic rose in her. How pale he looked, and how still!

"Oh, God," she prayed, bending close and placing her fingers at Dev's neck. The pulse was almost imperceptible, but she heard his faint, deeply labored breathing.

156

"Dev?" Carolyn tried gently shaking him to wakefulness, but still her husband did not rouse. "Oh, my love, please, please, wake up!"

She wrapped herself in a blanket and ran for the door, the blackness of fear engulfing her as she called out into the hall, "Dylan! Dylan, please! Call the doctor!"

CHAPTER ELEVEN

November 4, 1864
Near Charleston, South Carolina

omething told Jack not to use Maffit's Channel upon his approach to Charleston. It just didn't make sense, he thought, standing on the bridge. Blockade runners had always favored that route. Charging through the middle of the inner arch of blockaders, he would be sure to draw their fire, despite the dark night, despite their low profile. He liked to go by logic, not intuition. Intuition was women's stuff. But as they neared port, he just couldn't get a sense of peace about his normal course of running well north to landward and creeping down the coast.

"Extinguish the deck lanterns, and cover the hatches," Jack said to his first officer. "And have Mr. Birch come up."

The officer and the men within hearing range looked puzzled, but within minutes it was done and the pilot stood beside Jack and the helmsman.

"We're going to make for the North Channel," he told them. "The Yankees now expect ships in Maffit's, so we'll give them a little surprise."

Lawrence did not question him, but Jack could tell he was thinking of *Fortitude*. Jack knew it because he was, too.

"Don't worry, Birch, we'll never lose *Evangeline*," Jack said.

Running the blockade had become an increasingly dicey game, both physically and politically speaking. Early in the year, the government – which had been building more of its own ships to better transport supplies – had come up with a "New Plan" that granted them firmer control over private imports and exports. If Jack had not bowed to running arms previously, he would have been forced to acquiesce by these new laws. Luxury items were prohibited. Out-going cotton had to be approved by the government. Runners not under government contract had half of their storage space claimed by the Confederacy, regardless of previous contracts they still had to honor, with bureau agents ready to enforce the laws in each port.

Jack had quickly discovered that the government agencies did not always work well together, either. Back in February, John Billingsly of *South*

Land II had had his steamer on the Santee River loading Georgia cotton from Governor Brown via McClellanville when the War Department had demanded their share of cargo space. At first Billingsly had refused. Meanwhile, the Federals had discovered *South Land II's* presence and had been narrowly chased off by Confederate artillery. Upon learning of the incident, Jack had directed the stalwart captain to concede to the War Department. Stuffed to the gills with enough "white gold" to partially satisfy both parties, *South Land II* had at last safely escaped the Santee in June.

Fortitude had not had such good luck. In September, Jack and Dean Howell had met in Nassau. Howell had learned that the thirty-day yellow fever quarantine had just been lifted in Wilmington. He had wanted to take his cargo to that port, having more confidence in its navigation system. Jack had allowed it despite his misgivings. He knew that the presence of two Confederate commerce raiders, *Tallahassee* and *Chickamauga*, had pushed the Yankees to up the number of steamers off Wilmington. His gut instinct had been accurate. Approaching New Inlet, Howell had been fired upon by two cruisers. His propeller and rudder had been damaged, forcing him to beach *Fortitude* under a full head of steam. He had then set fire to the ship before escaping to the Confederate lines with most of his crew. The steamer and its cargo had been a total loss.

The sting of it was still all too fresh. But Jack had no intention of losing *Evangeline* – ever – or the 350 percent profit he would make on this run. His cargo was meat for the undernourished Confederate soldiers, authorized by Heyliger.

As night fell they eased at half speed between two well-spaced outer patrol boats. They set a straight course for the harbor.

That was when they all saw a flash of light and heard the whining of a shell, not toward them, but off to their right. The northernmost inner blockader was firing on a ship attempting to enter Maffit's Channel.

"Someone's bad luck is about to become our good luck," the helmsman stated.

It was true. This was the perfect distraction. The next Union gunboat in the arch could be seen pulling north to reinforce the attack. They were still a good ways out, but they could tell the bombardment was effective. The poor ship was receiving quite a pounding. One mast went down, and sparkling shell fragments illuminated the deck. While the harassed blockade runner struggled to make it to the shallow safety near Sullivan's Island, *Evangline* could pass through the North Channel unheeded.

"Looks like she just took a hit below the waterline," Birch observed, raising the spy glass. "Whew! There was another one! She's foundering."

"Give me that." Jack looked himself and said, "Oh, no."

"What?" both men asked.

"Send up a flare, the biggest, brightest flare we've got."

"What?" cried the helmsman again, and Birch yelled, "Have you lost your mind?"

"Maybe," Jack answered, "but I won't leave a friend in the lurch. That's Robert Lawson's ship, *Let Her Fly*. If we can draw off his attackers, he just might be able to make it into the shallow waters where the blockaders can't follow – or at least beach her and escape landward. Hoist the flag. Get the flare gun. Maybe if we're obnoxious enough, they'll take the bait. Then tell the chief engineer to give me all he's got."

"Yes, Sir," came the reply from all around him.

Jack was relieved to see them rise to the challenge, their honor stirred, rather than responding with anger at the risk to which he subjected them. Feet scrambled, hatches opened and steam swelled. Moments later the glare from a white flare illuminated the Stars and Bars rippling defiantly in the night air.

"I might just save your old hide," Jack murmured to himself, to Lawson, with a wry smile of memory.

The screw steamer that had turned to chase after *Let Her Fly* reversed course, leaving Lawson's first attacker to its prey. As it turned a buzz emanated from the deck of the gunboat to their left. A line of fire streaked toward them. She was still too far off to pose a threat – the shell arched into the ocean – but she'd attempt to close the distance before *Evangeline* got far enough up the channel for escape. Jack felt sure they could outrun their pursuers. He would not have alerted the Yankees to their presence otherwise, friend in danger or no. But they needed everything the chief engineer could get out of that walking beam engine.

The sleek ship trembled with her effort, sparks shooting out of her funnel.

Both blockaders were bearing on them now, the shot and shell falling within a few hundred yards, pieces of iron skimming the water. The helmsman bowed to Jack's irrepressible anxiety by allowing him to take the wheel. The excitement of the chase was everything he'd dreamed of as a boy. Displaced water spewed onto the bulwarks as they entered the channel.

Then a shell exploded in the air just overhead. A portion of the pilothouse splintered around them. With a cry the helmsman fell to the deck, and as Jack looked over he felt something hit him on the head and upper arm. But he was still thinking, still standing, so he turned his attention to the demands of the task at hand.

The enemy was falling behind.

160

Up ahead was the portion of the bay protected by the Confederate-held forts, the light on Sumter shining like a beacon.

"We're outdistancing them, Sir," a young midshipman shouted as he hurried up to the bridge. "They're slowing down, not following into the channel." The boy paused and stared at the hole in the pilothouse, then at the fallen helmsman.

"Check his pulse," Jack directed.

The sailor turned his wounded comrade over and did as requested. "Faint but steady, but he's bleeding pretty heavy from a gash in his chest. I'll go get the medical kit." As the boy stood, he exclaimed, "You're bleeding, too, Sir!"

Jack put a hand to his forehead and noticed his fingers came away red. He pulled a handkerchief out of his pocket and pressed it to the cut. "I'll be all right until we get to port. See to the helmsman."

As they entered harbor, relief surged through him. And there to the right, limping up the longer channel alongside Sullivan's Island, was *Let Her Fly*. Having a much deeper draft, the enemy had given up chasing Lawson as well. Jack was glad his friend would be able to salvage both his ship and his cargo.

Lawson must have caught sight of him at the same time, for the triple crack of a side arm from *Let Her Fly*'s deck signaled comradeship and thanks in the night.

By dawn the two blockade runners ranged along the south and east batteries and docked, battered but safe, at the North Commercial Wharf.

He was going back to Savannah, and Jack had the oddest feeling it might be for the last time. *All these hunches lately – where did they come from?* he wondered as the train steamed south.

The car was in sad shape from overuse and full of soldiers *en route* for the defense of Savannah.

"Do you really think Savannah may be attacked?" he asked an affable lieutenant with rosy cheeks and blond hair.

"If I were you I'd stay in Charleston. Nobody knows what Sherman – or his counterparts on the sea – will do. They say Governor Brown has rejected the general's offers of peace, on the advice of the president. General Hood has struck out for Alabama hoping the devil will follow, but so far, he's stayed put. Makes you wonder what comes next, eh?"

"Eh," said Jack.

"Just let him come up this way. He can bang his head on the city's defenses for a year and get nowhere."

Jack had the courtesy not to point out the discrepancy in numbers, especially minus the stalwart General Hood. *There it is again*, he thought to himself. *That same determination everyone down here began this war with. It's amazing, really, how it can still be in evidence with the Confederate Army in tatters and the Yankees on our doorstep.* Despite the element of naiveté – or whatever it was – Jack had to admire the undying spirit of the South.

He'd seen the same pluck in Robert Lawson, who had greeted him with a bear hug on the Charleston wharf.

"Come to my house. I have a bottle of Madeira in the garret that's been ripening thirty years," Lawson had said. It seemed everyone worth knowing in Charleston had a bottle of Madeira ripening in the garret. "Our close call – your heroism – puts me in the mood for a celebration. I'll call my doctor to stitch you up, and with some Madeira in you, you'll feel just fine."

Lawson's wife had for quite some time been sheltering at the resort at Summerville, some twenty miles from the city. The house had smelled musty and the dinner served by a grumpy house servant had been slim, but they had heartily toasted life and success.

Lawson had said, "As soon as we finally whip those Yankees, we'll be well set, Jack. I've been thinking I'll leave the Importing and Exporting Company. Buy my own ship. You can replace *Fortitude*. We should form a partnership. We'll be the richest men on the coast."

Jack had said he'd think about it. He had started yearning for an end to the hostilities long ago, having quickly grown tired of spending so much time in Nassau, Wilmington and Charleston, never feeling at home. That was what he wanted more than anything now: home. But he wasn't quite sure where that would be or what it would look like. And he was pretty darn sure it wouldn't be a victorious peace, not even for a war profiteer like himself.

When at last he arrived at his family's home he saw that his timing was poor, for the carriage was drawn up to the front door. Sunny and Sylvie were getting ready to go out. In fact, the door opened just as he was coming up the steps.

Jack expected the women to be surprised, but he hadn't anticipated feeling the same emotion. The ladies were in mourning garb.

"Jack!" Sylvie shrieked before flying into his arms, nearly knocking him down.

"What's wrong!?" Has something happened to Bryson or Alan?"

Sunny came and put her arms around him. "No, Jack, it's all right – at least, it's all right for us. But not for the Rousseau family."

"The Rousseaus?"

"What happened to your face?" Sylvie reached out to touch the swollen knot held together by stitches that ran down his temple, taking Jack's arm to steady herself on tiptoes. As she did he cried out in pain.

"Your arm, too?" She stepped back.

"I had a bit of excitement this last trip."

She watched his inscrutable expression and her eyes lit up. "Oh, my goodness! This is wonderful! Now you're a real war hero. No one will dare say a word against you."

Jack laughed out loud at that, glad that at least one person seemed unaltered by the world falling down around her ears. "But what of the Rousseaus?" His demeanor turned serious.

"Oh, yes. Devereaux Rousseau has died. His brother brought him home from Petersburg with a lung wound, and then the major succumbed to pneumonia. The funeral's today."

Jack's face creased as he immediately thought of Carolyn. "Oh, no," he groaned.

"In fact, we have to leave right away or we'll be late," Sunny gently put in. "I'm sorry, Jack. But we'll be back soon, and in the meantime you can eat and rest up."

"Nothing to it," Jack declared. "I'm going with you! How bad do I look?"

"Travel rumpled and like you were just attacked by thugs, but otherwise respectable," Sylvie told him.

"I need a black armband."

A servant was dispatched to fetch the item while Jack helped the women into the carriage. On the way to the Presbyterian Church, he asked for an update on his half brothers and their part in the Atlanta scenario.

"They crossed into Alabama on October 18 and went through Gadsden toward Tuscumbia," Sunny said. "That's the last we heard, anyway. Their spirits are low, Jack. The men are mostly barefoot and short on blankets and clothes for the cold weather. On some days, the boys said all they had to eat was two ears of corn per man."

Jack turned his face away in disgust. Despite his best efforts, even the members of his own family went without.

They arrived just as the service was about to begin. The church was so packed they had to stand at the back. He focused on the flag-draped coffin at the front. Even though he had not liked Devereaux Rousseau in the past, he found himself moved by the service. He now knew that the enmity between them had been because they had both been arrogant rascals thinking more of themselves than anyone else. But the war had altered everyone. To have affixed the devotion of a woman like Carolyn, Dev must have changed, too. And Jack had to admire the major's loyal years of leadership under the most galling of circumstances.

Jack's train of thought was interrupted by the movement of a dark head on the front row. There, next to the young widow in her black mourning garb. It couldn't be. What would *she* be doing here?

The dark head turned, and he saw the high cheekbones and tawny skin that confirmed his suspicion. His heart leapt. At the same moment, Jack felt his sister's eyes on his face. He looked down at her with an accusing glare. *She had known, and had not told him.* Sylvie would never own it. She gave him a pout of wounded confusion and looked back at the minister.

As they filed out of the church, he said in a low tone that only his womenfolk would hear, "I think we should not go to the graveside."

"Why?" Sunny asked. "That would be very rude, Jack. We've grown quite close to the Rousseaus. I would never slight them in that way."

He sighed and helped them into the carriage for the drive to Laurel Grove. He stared out the window.

"My goodness, Jack. I bet you never wore such a look even when facing the Yankees," Sylvie commented with a smirk.

"You enjoy my discomfort?" Jack growled at her. "I see nothing humorous in it, or nothing profitable coming from this meeting."

"What meeting?" Sunny asked.

"Then don't speak to her," Sylvie rejoined with a tinge of challenge. "If you can manage not to do so."

No one bothered to relieve Sunny's confusion as they turned into the cemetery. The place brought back memories of Richard's burial. Jack's brooding mood only deepened.

The scene at the grave did not help. The coffin was unloaded from the hearse. Devereaux's horse had been tied to the back of the vehicle, his boots reversed in the stirrups. Jack had never understood why people insisted on such heart-rending traditions. The mourners were like a black sea spreading around the hole in the earth. Weeping and sniffing could be heard from the majority. A home front honor guard stood at attention while the minister recited the well-known words of the Savior:

"'I am the resurrection, and the life: he that believeth in me, though he were dead, yet shall he live: And whosoever liveth and believeth in me shall never die.' Major Devereaux Rousseau served his country with the utmost in bravery, and he paid the dearest price. But we can take comfort in these words – that he was a man of God, whose place is now in heaven."

Henrietta Rousseau sagged sobbing against her remaining son. Dylan was so hard and thin in appearance that Jack would not have recognized him. He held his mother up, and Jack thought it was probably the strength of his arm alone that prevented her from flying completely to pieces.

Carolyn stood between Mahala and her mother. The baby had been handed off to a servant for this difficult portion of the burial. The poor blonde woman looked like a ghost, her white face in shock. It was more awful to behold than Henrietta's weeping. Mahala kept her arm around Carolyn the whole time, her blue eyes veiled.

The honor guard discharged a volley, and then two of the members systematically folded the flag that had been draped over the coffin. When they handed it to Carolyn she looked like she would faint.

"Ashes to ashes, and dust to dust," murmured the minister as the soldiers lowered the coffin into the grave. "We commit the body of Devereaux Rousseau to the ground until the final resurrection." He took a clump of sandy earth and tossed it onto the coffin.

Carolyn was expected to follow suit. Her eyes widened in denial, and a harsh sob broke from her. She turned as if to run away, but her brother-in-law saw it, and with a look of profound sympathy, reached for her arm. He whispered something in her ear. The widow took a deep sucking breath and bent down for her handful of dirt.

Next followed Henrietta and Dylan, then more distant family members. Henrietta was escorted, trembling and in tears, to the carriage. As the knot of mourners left the grave, Jack heard Carolyn say, "Give me my baby."

Mahala hurried to get the child from the slave. Dylan handed Carolyn into the family carriage and then lifted the child inside to its mother. As he did, Mahala turned and saw Jack.

Her eyes widened at the sight of him, and if it was possible for a Cherokee to look pale, she did. Holy thunder, but she was beautiful!

Sylvie hurried forward to embrace and kiss her, like Mahala was one of the Rousseau family, then she turned and did the same to Dylan. The man looked faintly surprised when Sylvie's pink lips touched his cheek. Jack remembered that she had been writing to him. Edging her daughter aside, Sunny took Dylan Rousseau's hand and murmured her condolences.

Mahala looked again at Jack. He stepped forward and removed his hat. "Miss Franklin, please convey my deepest sympathies to the Rousseau ladies."

"I will. Thank you."

"It's good of you to be here with the widow."

"I – I am helping with the child."

Jack nodded and smiled. Their eyes met again before, flustered, Mahala turned away, speaking to another mourner.

As they walked to their own conveyance, Sylvie said, "Do you not find Dylan Rousseau altered, Mother? Quite favorably, I think."

Sunny frowned at her. "He can be in no doubt of your regard for him, Sylvie. Your actions were not appropriate, even under the circumstances."

"Oh, Mother."

A moment later, as they drove away, Sunny announced, "I'm going to send some food in the morning."

"I'll take it," Sylvie volunteered, "and give it to Mahala."

"Are you sure about this, Jack?" asked Sunny, turning from the window of the family carriage as they rocked along, the autumn colors of North Georgia flashing past. Jack had sent the vehicle on ahead so that it had been waiting for them when they reached Athens. From this point they had heard that just as Jack had anticipated, General Sherman had pushed southeast from Atlanta, tearing up railroad and wreaking havoc as he went. One prong of his army had just been reported one county over from Athens. No one knew yet whether his goal would be Augusta, Macon or Savannah.

"I keep looking out the window expecting to see sharpshooters in blue. It just seems we'd be safer in Savannah, with lots of people we know, than out in the country all alone. They say Savannah's defenses will never fall."

"Saying it doesn't make it true," Jack pointed out, "as we discovered about Atlanta. Trust me, Sunny. I have good men employed at The Palace who will make sure you're safe. And we'll make it there safely, too. Sherman's wing is well to the south of us by now."

"We would have been safe in Charleston," Sylvie argued. "I still don't understand why you wouldn't let us travel with your Aunt Eugenie to Charleston, to your Aunt Ruth's house. It would be ever so much more interesting there."

"Until the Yankees arrive."

"Why would you say that?"

"Don't you think they want control over both port cities?"

"Jack, you don't seem to have much confidence in our troops," Sunny said.

"I don't. And that's why I want you well away from the coast and any other place the Yankees would want. Not Charleston with the Wises. Not Augusta. Not Brightwell with your family. Clarkesville. You'll be fine there. Besides, haven't you been harping to go there all year, Sylvie?"

"To see Miss Franklin and Mrs. Rousseau, but they're in Savannah."

"Not for long," Jack snapped. He knew he was growing impatient, but he was tired of arguing with obstinate women. If he could have convinced the rest of his relations to hie to The Palace, he would have gladly rounded them all up in his mountain retreat. His Ellis grandparents had been exceptionally challenging, determining to stay in Savannah despite both his and Eugenie's urging otherwise. But these two at least he could take charge of, and take charge he would.

"And I don't want you going to stay at Forests of Green when Mrs. Rousseau returns, either, Sunny, whether she's family or not. You two stay put at the hotel," he added grumpily.

"Or what? You'll come and spank us?" Sylvie teased.

"I might."

"Well, you can't stop us from visiting. I hope she does come back, and soon," Sylvie said. "Not that she'll be any company mourning her husband and all. I can't blame her. He was a fine-looking man. I'd be sad, too. But Mahala, she'll be back, too, and hopefully not too distraught over her missing fiancé to be any fun."

"Missing fiancé?" Jack echoed.

"Oh, I forgot you didn't want to speak of her. Sorry."

Jack could have choked his sassy little sister. Honestly, she had way too much gall for such a small body. He restrained himself and said through stiff lips with feigned politeness, "I take back my words. Now tell me what you're talking about."

"Only that when I delivered the food to the mourning family, before you insisted we pack up and leave, I inquired of Miss Franklin as to the health of her intended. She told me she had not heard from him or her adoptive brothers since a letter written in late August. She was quite concerned."

"Very concerned?"

"Very concerned. I'd say almost beside herself, but hiding it well for the sake of the Rousseaus."

"Why did you not tell me this sooner?" Jack exploded.

"You were very clear after the funeral that you did not want me–"

"Oh, never mind!"

"What are you going to do, Jack?" Sylvie asked, all innocence and sweetness again.

"Do? What *is* there to do?"

"I don't know. But you, however, are a very enterprising man ..."

November 29, 1864
Savannah, Georgia

Jack loaded the last box of records from the firm's Bay Street office into the wagon he'd borrowed from a friend and leaned on the side with a sigh. He was weary. He'd traveled long and hard the past few weeks, sleep being less than abundant. Tonight he hoped to remedy that. He had only to take these boxes to the family town house, which he had prepared to be closed up along with his Ellis grandparents' home, the valuables secured as well as possible. Then, in the morning, he would follow William and Grace to Charleston on the Charleston & Savannah Railroad, bringing only the most valuable records with him. Thankfully, he had friends along the line who had made all this possible. Everything was almost settled. He thought perhaps he might just drive by the Rousseau mansion on his way home to make sure everything was all right there, although he was sure Mahala and Carolyn would have safely returned to Clarkesville over a week ago.

He shook his head, thinking of William and Grace. If only they hadn't been so stubborn. Rather than insisting the trip would be too much for them, they should have gone with his sister and stepmother to North Georgia. Well, maybe it *would* have been too much. Only after forceful evidence had been presented that the Yankees were indeed descending on Savannah had they agreed to make the less arduous rail trip to Charleston. Jack was pretty sure they'd still find themselves in the path of an advancing Union Army. But at least for the moment they were safe. One thing at a time.

Jack latched the back of the wagon and took a moment to glance around, finding himself rather sentimental at the thought that he wouldn't see this familiar street for God knew how long. It was a cold and balmy afternoon. The Exchange steeple loomed up into the blue sky, and the river to his right gently lapped the wharf. The area was a bevy of activity, filled, as usual, with soldiers as well as civilians.

A woman on a horse coming his direction caught his eye. Even though she wore a hood over her hair, she seemed familiar. Jack narrowed his eyes. The woman's face tilted toward him. What were the chances? He dashed out into the street, calling, "Mahala!"

Startled, she pulled on the reins.

Jack caught hold of the irritated mare's harness and demanded of its rider, "What in the blazes are you still doing here?"

Mahala's surprise skittered to indignation at his tone. "Well, hello to you, too, Jack!"

168

"Mahala – I'm sorry. That wasn't very civil. But I was sure you'd be long gone to Clarkesville. Climb down here and tell me what's going on."

"Don't you ever *ask?*"

Jack sighed, wondering if she wanted to see him run over in the busy street, but with exaggerated patience he said, "Will you *please* dismount and come speak with me?"

She edged her horse to the sidewalk and climbed down. Jack took the reins and tied them to the same post to which his horse and wagon were secured. Mahala put back her hood. Only then did he see that she had very recently been crying.

He took her arm and led her to the steps in front of his office, saying in a gentler tone, "What's wrong, Mahala? Why are you still here when the Yankees are about to close in on the city?"

"It's Carolyn," Mahala said, sitting down. "She hasn't wanted to go, even when everyone began saying the army was heading here. Ever since the funeral, all she wants to do is sit in her room or go to the cemetery. Jack, she would stay there all day if I would let her, forgetting to eat or sleep or anything! Every morning, every night, I hear her crying. It's awful. There is nothing anyone can do to comfort her. Even her child sometimes fails to bring her relief."

Jack nodded sympathetically. "What of her family?" he asked.

"Gone! Of course Dylan went right after the funeral, and when he did, Mrs. Rousseau completely broke down. The Calhouns have taken her to the country, to Brightwell. Mrs. Olivia Calhoun begged us to come, too, but of course Carolyn would not. She told them she would soon go to Clarkesville with me, but of course she has not. Every day an excuse, a delay, and my grandmother needing me, no doubt worried sick!" Mahala wrung her hands.

"I know the ravages of grief well enough, but this must all be very hard on you."

Responding to the understanding in his tone, Mahala made eye contact. "Yes! If only I could have communicated with my grandmother! Every day I wonder about her, and Clay and the boys, and if she's had news of them. Jack, it's driving me crazy!"

Jack drew in the corners of his mouth, thinking of what he had to tell her but realizing now was not the time, here on the crowded street.

She went on, "And now, Carolyn has finally agreed to leave with me, so I went to the railroad office. They said the Yankees may now be ranging as far down as the branch to Augusta that goes north at Brinsonville. And that we had to have passports to leave the city! Passports!

I didn't know anything about it! So I find we are trapped, and I don't know what to do."

The last words became a sort of wail, and to Jack's intense dismay, fresh tears poured from Mahala's eyes. Uncomfortably he fished for his handkerchief – every gentleman's stalwart reaction in the face of feminine hysterics – and handed it to her. She mopped her face and added, "What you must think of me! I bet you find it amusing to see me in such a fix."

"Now why would I find it amusing?"

"I don't know. I guess because the proud and independent Mahala Franklin is now neither one."

"I don't think that at all. I think you're a strong woman who has had one too many things to bear."

The blue eyes sought his. "You do? But what should I do, Jack?"

"The Charleston and Savannah rail line is still open. But first ..." He stood up and offered his hand. "Get up, and I'll take you to the passport office."

"Must we go to Charleston?" Mahala asked with dismay, rising with his help and brushing herself off.

"The pass first, then we'll see what our options are."

"Thank you," she said, then looked puzzled. "Why are you even back in Savannah, anyway? I would have thought you would have gone to Charleston from Clarkesville."

"I – had some business to wrap up. I just got my grandparents out of the city two days ago."

"Oh."

He was glad she left it at that.

Jack handed her up into the wagon and tied her horse to the back. He had thought about Mahala constantly for the past week, and now, having her fall so providentially into his care – just like a ripe North Georgia apple would drop from the tree into his palm – his emotions were in a state of confusion. Getting a passport and tickets would be easy compared to the conversation he'd soon have to have with her. He didn't know the best way to go about it, or what her reaction would be. Dealing with women was such a tricky business, and that was well before one's own emotions got involved.

He decided to leave his charge in the waiting room while he went in to speak with the official who doled out passports, thinking the man might be more susceptible to logic and influence – and even a few discreet green-backs – than feminine tears. He was wrong. The application for the pass would be subject to the same long chain of approval as were countless others, the official told him, firmly, coldly, when Jack hinted at a bribe.

When Jack emerged in a foul mood, he regarded a scrawny older man in a frayed suit talking to Mahala, having taken a seat far too close to her for propriety. His bony knee was pressing against her skirt. Jack half expected to see drops of drool on the material at any moment.

"Are you acquainted with this lady?" Jack snapped.

The lascivious one looked up, startled. "Why – n-no."

"Then I suggest you leave her alone."

The man sat back, guffawing knowingly. "Lady?" he echoed. "Is she yours? Well, no harm done, right? I was just having a chat with her. Didn't mean anything by it. You can't expect other gentlemen not to notice such a pretty little quadroon."

Jack offered his arm to Mahala, and she stood up eagerly and took it. "Can't you tell the difference between a quadroon and a lady with Cherokee blood?" he demanded, scowling. "And even if she were a quadroon, she would be equally deserving of respect. Not that I'd expect a *gentleman* like you to know it."

"Are you questioning my honor?" the man asked, starting to rise.

"It's all right, Jack," Mahala murmured in his ear. She tugged on his arm, and he allowed himself to be turned. As he glared back over his shoulder at the ignoramus, she added, "With all that's going on now, it hardly matters."

"It matters to me." But because her hand trembled in his, he ignored the man behind him, letting the door close on the filthy name he spat out.

She ducked her head, and he helped her up into the wagon again. There was a vulnerable tilt to her proud shoulders that put things into perspective. Suddenly he realized his possessive statement had made her think of Clay. A dart of intense sadness – and yes, jealousy, even now – passed through him. He would never be resigned to the idea that she could have feelings for another man. It had to be him, if not yet, then soon. Him only in her mind.

"Did you get the passes? ... Does Carolyn need to come down with me and sign something?"

"There's going to be a bit of a delay."

"How long?" Mahala sat up straight, expectant.

Jack clicked to the horses. "That I don't know. You'll receive notification when the passports are granted."

"Do you mean *if* they are granted?"

"When," Jack said firmly. He didn't expound. There was just no way he was going to allow it to be otherwise. He would hound that office day and night and bribe any number of lesser bureaucrats necessary to make it happen. He added, "As soon as you get word, send a message to me at my family's town house."

"You mean – you'll wait for us?" she asked with amazement.

"I'll see you both safely out of town with the baby. You have my word." He glanced at her. Before she looked away, embarrassed, he saw tears fill her eyes.

"Thank you," she whispered.

She rode silently the rest of the way to Oglethorpe Square, worry pinching in her already too-thin cheeks. She was far too thin all over, and her dress was worn. He didn't like it.

"Will you stay to supper?" she asked when they arrived.

"No, thank you, but I do need to speak with you further about … another matter. Do you have a stable hand who can take care of your horse?"

"The only slaves still here are an elderly couple. I tend the horse myself. Just drive around to the carriage house, if you please."

Jack was disgruntled. Further delay. He'd have to unsaddle and brush down the mare before they could talk.

As he did so, Mahala brought food and water for the animal, which appeared upon close examination to have seen better days. That wasn't surprising. The Confederate Army had requisitioned all the fit animals in the environs, and most of the vehicles, too.

As Jack finished brushing the horse, Mahala appeared at his side. "What did you want to talk to me about?"

He straightened, his mind going back to the last time they had been alone in a similar environment. "Perhaps we should go inside."

Something in his expression caused her to step back. "Fine."

The tension in her slim body as they walked the short path to the house hinted that she sensed the gravity of his mood. He prayed no one would be around. He hadn't the patience for small talk and explanations just now. Oh, he was selfish. For Mahala would need Carolyn to lean on. But there would be no leaning there, he reminded himself. No, he was all she would have for some time, but would she turn to him, or push him away?

The house was quiet when they entered. In the parlor, Mahala sat on the sofa, inviting him with a wave of her hand to take a wing chair. He sat beside her instead. Her big blue eyes fastened on him, surprised, expectant, with a hint of fear.

"You remember when you asked me why I was back in Savannah?"

Mahala nodded.

"Well, what I told you was true, but there is more. See, I did not come here straight from Clarkesville as you may have supposed. I had to wend my way to the east of Sherman's army, just a couple days ahead of them, on my way to Augusta, and thence to here, because I spent most of last week in Atlanta."

"*Atlanta?* What were you doing there?" The question was faint, rather suspicious.

"My sister had told me you had not heard from the Emmitts – and your fiancé – since late August." Jack paused as she sat back, as if to distance herself from what he might say next. "I went and did some asking around."

"For me?" This time he could barely hear her.

"Yes, Mahala."

She cleared her throat. "And did you – find anything?"

The words stuck in Jack's throat. Staring at the print on Mahala's skirt, Jack prayed for courage. "When I got to the city, Sherman had just left." He closed his eyes at the memory of the shelled-out buildings, the still-smoking rubble. "It was mostly deserted. Many of the businesses and merchants had closed up during the summer fighting, and the wounded they could move were taken out. Almost all the remaining civilians had been forced to evacuate in mid-September. I did find some staff still on at the hospitals – a few who had been there through the whole thing – even when Sherman shelled the hospitals. I had to ask at a number of places. The wounded from the battles had so overwhelmed the city. But at least I found a doctor who remembered a – Cherokee soldier."

Mahala made a strangled sound. Her hand went to her throat.

"This – soldier – he said – had been wounded in both the leg and arm. The doctors … they amputated his leg at the knee. But the care was so poor, the city under bombardment, then evacuation. The wound became infected. The doctor said he fought for his life and spoke every day of the girl he loved, whom he planned to marry. He said in all his pain, Clay never once complained. Before the fever ranged too high, he asked one of the nurses to write a note to this girl and place it with a few of his things, to hold onto and mail when she could. A few days later …" Jack could not finish the sentence. Tears streamed down Mahala's face. How the sight wrenched his gut. "The nurse had to leave the city before she got to mail the letter. I have those things, Mahala."

Her throat worked with the effort to speak, and to keep control. She managed to ask: "My brothers?"

"Both shot dead in the same battle."

She sat staring at him in awful, complete silence, the glazed look of shock on her features. Then she closed her eyes, as if to deny the words he had just spoken. She swayed slightly. Jack thought she might be about to faint, so he reached out to clasp her elbow.

Mahala came to life, jerking her arm free and jumping to her feet. He stood, too, unsure of what to do. She held out a hand as if she would stop him from approaching.

"No," she said. "I'm – sorry–"

Then, turning, she ran out of the room.

A few days later, when Jack knocked on the door of the Rousseau town house, an elderly black man answered. Jack asked for Mahala, but it was Carolyn who came down, her black taffeta skirt rustling about her ankles. A bit of dark hair, presumably Dev's, was displayed in a brooch at her throat. Jack was alarmed at her appearance. She looked as if she could collapse at any moment, and the fine bones in her pale face stood out prominently.

"Mrs. Rousseau," Jack said, taking her hand and bowing over it. "Allow me to say in person how sorry I am about your husband."

"Thank you," she murmured. "And thank you for all you are doing on our behalf. Mahala told me about your trip to Atlanta in her interest, and the passes you are helping us procure. I'm sorry ... but she – she's having a hard time right now."

"I understand."

"Have you heard something about the passports, then?"

"No, I've heard something about the railroads."

"Oh? Would you like to sit down?"

"Thank you, no. I won't stay. I only came to say this: rail travel is no longer an option. The Yankees have taken the Central tracks, and fighting ranges along the rails to Charleston as the bluecoats try to cut that route of supply or escape. The only way out now is by buggy, if we can get over to the Carolina shore. I say we wait a bit, which we have to do anyway due to the passports. If the Confederates surrender the city, they'll make a way of escape. We will be ready to go with them."

Carolyn frowned delicately. "So – if it hadn't been for us, you could have already made your way to Charleston, to your ship there."

"Please don't trouble yourself, Mrs. Rousseau. Fighting had already begun the day before I planned to leave. If anything, it is fortunate that I was delayed and not in the midst of it. No, it was meant to be that I encountered Mahala in town. I would do nothing else but see you both to safety. You are, after all, my stepmother's niece."

She smiled very faintly. He got the impression she was trying to be responsive for his sake, but that nothing registered with much emotion at this point. He only hoped both of the women could pull together enough strength and focus for the journey ahead.

"It's imperative that we leave as soon as the passes are issued, as soon as the opportunity presents itself," Jack said. "I need you to be packed and ready at a moment's notice, day or night. Can you do that?"

Carolyn nodded, but she did not look convincing.

"Do you think you can get everything in one trunk?"

Her wide eyes swept up to his. "Oh, no. I must take my husband's things – his uniform, his sword."

"Two small trunks, then. And that reminds me ..." Jack lifted a canvas haversack from around his neck and offered it to Carolyn. She looked at him questioningly as she received it, noting a dark brownish stain on one of the bag's sides. "Clay Fraser's personal effects ... and the letter he wrote before he died. Mahala will be wanting these."

"Thank you, Captain Randall. I'll give them to her immediately."

"All right, then. I'll be going now. Only one more thing. Do you still have a closed carriage in your possession?"

"No. Only a two-seater buggy."

"I'll see what I can come up with."

As Jack walked to the door, Carolyn followed him. "Shall we take the servants with us?"

"No. We won't have room for them. And food and shelter along the way may be difficult to come by."

Carolyn protested, "But the servants – they're afraid of the Yankees."

"They'll be fine," Jack said. "They'll be free."

CHAPTER TWELVE

During the days that followed, while they waited for the Yankees, paralyzed with grief and fear, there was only one thing that gave Mahala solace. She sat on the window seat in the afternoons while everyone napped, hidden from the world, rereading Clay's short letter for the hundredth time.

Dearest Mahala, I know you are wondering why I have not written. I was wounded in the last battle for this city where I now find myself, shot through both the leg and the arm. At first I could not tell you because they had to take my leg. I did not want to think of holding you to your commitment after that happened. But I think you would have stood by me. Now, it doesn't matter because I know I am dying. I will be joining Seth and Sam, who have also recently passed on to a better place. They died quickly, Mahala, in the same battle, not suffering much. As for me, I don't want to die. I don't want to give you up just when you are finally within reach, but it seems this is how it was meant to end. I pray these words will comfort you when you are alone, that I have always loved you, and always will. Thank you for loving me.

Yours eternally, Clay Fraser

The simplicity and directness of Clay's last words to her pierced her heart afresh each time. She wished she could have been there to have comforted him in his final hours. Poor Clay. He had deserved so little of what life gave him. She could only hope that now he was happy.

Guilt swamped Mahala, and for good reason if she looked this square in its ugly face. She had not married Clay when she could have, thus providing him with a small bit of joy for all his months of sacrifice and suffering. And now, he was gone, and she was alive. And she couldn't help it, but deep down inside, she still wanted to be. She felt guilty for that, too.

What she later recalled from that time in the window seat was that Carolyn heard her heart-broken sobs. Coming to sit behind Mahala, she wrapped her arms around her and merely sat there in silence for an hour, their heads together and their hearts bound in shared misery.

After that, even though she carried the guilt with her, Mahala felt she might survive …that was, if Sherman let them. Reports from the street revealed that the commander of Savannah's forces, William J. Hardee, waited with about 10,000 poorly trained and armed men two-and-a-half miles west of the city between the Savannah and Little Ogeechee Rivers. They had flooded the rice fields in that area – very near to the Rousseau plantation. On December 10, the Yankees arrived, and by the next day, fierce bombardments shook the ground and rattled the windows.

Mahala had never heard such commotion before, and anxiety now mingled with grief. She continually sent the Rousseaus' black servant to the passport office. Each time he returned empty-handed. Surely they would have to grant their request soon. If not, the Yankees would be upon them, and speculation ran wild as to what that would mean. Sherman had left Atlanta in flames, had he not?

At sunset on the 13th, a terrific report sounded from the south. Sherman was attacking Fort McAllister on the Ogeechee River, loudly knocking on Savannah's back door. After fifteen minutes the cannonade silenced. The Union Army had been successful. Hardee would have to surrender the city or face bombardment in the streets.

For a while, no one was sure which it would be. Then Jack sent a note.

I hear Hardee will reject any demand for surrender by stating he will hold out indefinitely, but it will only be a bluff to buy time. Meanwhile the army will destroy any equipment of war they can't take with them. They will build a pontoon bridge of rice flats from the foot of Barnard near Market Dock across to Hutchinson Island, then to the South Carolina shore. I have seen to it that your passes should be ready tomorrow. Be prepared to leave at a moment's notice.

Just as Jack promised, they had the precious passports in hand the following morning. And the morning after that, a knock came on the door while they were at breakfast. Jack was admitted to the dining room. He bowed, then pulled out a chair. It was clear that he meant business, for he did not inquire as to their very questionable well-being, but instead stated:

"The pontoon bridge has been completed and will be our safest and most direct route of evacuation. The army begins the crossing today. So shall we. Can you be ready at noon?"

"Yes, of course," Mahala said. "Before."

"Good. Have your servant cook and pack up some extra food for the next day or two. With the area flooded with refugees, we can't count on hospitality along the way. I think we can find a place to stay in Hardeville tonight, but between there and Augusta is a lonely stretch of road too long to travel in one day."

Mahala's eyes opened wide at the impropriety of two now very unattached women traveling alone with a man not a close relative. Jack seemed to read her thoughts, for he said, "Under the circumstances, I think everyone will just have to overlook social *morés*. I doubt the Yankees would abide by them."

"Of course, Captain Randall," Carolyn said. "We appreciate all you are doing for us. We will be forever in your debt."

Jack didn't comment on that, stating instead, "Dress warmly. It's cold. You may want to add several layers. I'll wait in the parlor. Just call me when you're ready."

After that, everything was a bustle of activity. If she forgot the events of the last week, Mahala could almost imagine anxiety becoming excitement at the adventure before them, now that they were propelled to action and Jack would be their guide. Almost. She did not want to think too much about Jack's motivations for helping them. It didn't really matter, did it, when take his help they must? She just didn't want to examine it, or what it would be like to be thrust so closely into his company again after all this time.

It was to be more closely than imagined, Mahala discovered when she surveyed the buggy Jack brought round front a couple of hours later. As the Negro couple gathered around Carolyn, weeping and hugging her, Jack loaded their trunks onto the back of a two-bench vehicle. A ceiling ran surrey-style all the way to the front, and with this and partial sides, the back seat was almost enclosed. Mahala peeked in and was surprised to see a board nailed lengthwise down half the seat length.

Jack saw her looking and said in explanation, "I thought the baby was too big for Mrs. Rousseau to have in her arms for such a long way. She will need to lay him down, and this way he can sleep all bundled up without sliding off. You'll need to sit in front with me."

Rather than apologizing in word or expression, he turned away, as if he did not want to see her reaction. She could see his point – and Carolyn was grateful when she saw the contraption – but really, this was awkward. She didn't want to face Jack, not like this, not now, with her emotions so raw, and that looming question of why he had gone to Atlanta on her behalf. But climb up she did.

Carolyn gazed at the townhouse that held her few precious memories of married life. Mahala guessed she was wondering if she'd ever see it again. The Negro couple stood waving from the front steps, last caretakers of a family's legacy.

"Go – go." Carolyn choked on the words.

They were all silent as they drove north on Abercorn. The morning was cool and cloudy. The Bay Street area was a bevy of activity with people of all descriptions hurrying about and contingents of soldiers clogging the roads. Theirs was one of only a few buggies in sight as they inched their way across 1,000 feet of pontoon bridge with the forward echelons of Hardee's army. As their wheels left Georgia soil, a shuddering gasp of a sob came from Carolyn. Mahala glanced back to see tears pouring down her friend's pale face. She stretched a hand back over the seat and took Carolyn's. Her own eyes filled with tears as she regarded the somber ranks of ragged gray soldiers moving like a silent funeral procession from the city that was their home.

Mahala saw a few boats still on the river, puffing up and down in their last business of the Confederacy.

"What will happen to the ships?" She turned to look at Jack.

"Like those under construction at the shipyards, they will be torched so they don't fall into enemy hands."

"What a terrible shame – a terrible waste. But your boats, Jack? Are they safe?"

"I have two in Nassau. *Evangeline* is in Charleston. She'll have to go soon, too. *Fortitude* we recently lost."

"Oh. I'm sorry."

Mahala looked at him. Annoying. The scar down his temple was placed in such a way as to make him all the more rakishly handsome. She wondered what he was thinking. He had always looked out for himself first. Maybe he wasn't as noble as they were believing. Maybe when they got to Augusta he would send them on their way alone and himself hasten to Charleston to run his precious ship out of port. The idea filled her with fear. Then she chastened herself. What claim did they have on him besides Carolyn's paltry tie by marriage through her aunt? What right to expect *anything*?

Unaware of Mahala's musings, Carolyn focused on the retreating column. "It's almost all over, isn't it?"

Jack heard the sadness in Carolyn's voice. "Yes, I'm afraid so."

The horse having gone at a walk the whole day due to the congestion on the road, they arrived in Hardeeville in the early evening. The small town – founded some years ago by White William Hardee as a stop along the railroad – was overwhelmed by traffic fleeing Savannah. Mahala looked around, wondering where they would stay.

Jack went into the mercantile to inquire about lodgings. While he was gone, luck was with them. A widow with a baby about the same age as Dev Jr. stopped to speak with Carolyn. Discovering their predicament, she declared that any lodgings in town stayed full these days, but for them she would open her spare room. Jack, whom Carolyn introduced as a cousin, would have to sleep in her stable. Mahala felt rather bad about that, but Jack did not seem to mind. And Mahala was glad to have a cozy spot for the night. She and Carolyn kept warm under a quilt, and Dev Jr. only awakened once. It seemed that all night she heard the restless tramping of many feet, even in her dreams. In the morning, they had juice, toast and jam and set out with many thanks to the widow.

"Should we be worried about the Yankees?" asked Carolyn as the last vestiges of town were left behind. She glanced worriedly into the trees. In order to avoid the areas of fighting along the railroad, they were using an obscure wagon road which would join the main highway to Augusta some distance north.

"Probably not. I imagine they are moving around, all right, but some ways south of here, near the coast," Jack told them. "They'll be transferring troops down to Georgia in preparation for occupying Savannah."

"Will there be a place for us to spend the night?" Carolyn wondered.

"There will, although probably not one to your liking. Silver Bluff is along our route, but we won't reach it until we're almost to Augusta. I once heard some history about the place, and Sand Bar Ferry, just north of it, if you'd like to hear it."

Mahala watched the endless road stretching ahead of them. She had the feeling Jack was trying to distract them from boredom and their isolated surroundings. "I'd like that."

"The area along the river was long ago rumored to have silver deposits. When the explorer Hernando de Soto came, legend has it that an Indian princess welcomed him with hospitality and a string of pearls. The Spaniards were said to have believed the Indians were holding out and plundered the village, taking the princess captive. Some say it never happened – at least not at Silver Bluff – but others insist it did."

"Did they find any silver?" Carolyn asked.

"No. There was only mica along the bluffs, though they may have made off with some pearls." Jack paused a moment, then continued. "In the last century, an Irishman named George Galphin established a fur and skin trade with the local Indians. He built a brick house, one story, then later a two-story house, a grist mill and a saw mill. He let his slaves use the grist mill as their church. During the Revolution, his house was used as a fort."

180

"I've heard of Sand Bar Ferry," Carolyn said. "That's where men from Augusta used to duel."

"And South Carolina," Jack added. "Men from both sides could leave the jurisdiction of their states to settle their differences on the long sand bar there at the river."

Dev Jr. began to cry, and Carolyn picked him up. Mahala knew he was hungry. Poor Carolyn had no choice but to feed him in Jack's company. As she fumbled with the blanket to cover herself, Mahala sensed she needed to provide a distraction. So she asked, "Does anyone live south of Silver Bluff who might let us stay on their property?"

"This whole area is largely unpopulated. It's much as you see now all the way to Silverton – lakes, swamps, forests and some cotton and rice fields. I imagine the few farm owners have had their share of refugees. But I remember an abandoned cabin that we should reach before dusk. I'm hoping we can bed down there, if no one else beats us to it."

Sounds delightful, thought Mahala, longingly remembering the Rousseaus' elegant town house. She felt she had to keep Jack talking to cover the little grunting noises the baby was making as he nursed. Face pink, she asked, "Will you try to make another run on the blockade once you get back to Nassau?"

Jack shrugged. "Don't know. I have every suspicion the Yankees will march on Charleston next. I might get a load into Wilmington, but the blockade is so tight even there that ships are being lost left and right. I'm starting to think it might be time to rest on my laurels for a while."

"In Nassau," said Mahala.

"Maybe," said Jack.

They stopped every few hours for the horse to rest. At noon, they ate the corn cakes they had brought from Savannah, but Mahala's stomach still felt hungry. Occasionally she or Carolyn would walk briskly for a short stint alongside the buggy, stretching their legs. They admired the towering cypress and tupelo trees along with ash, water hickory, dogwood, saw palmettos and swamp palms. Along the blackwater tributaries that they crossed they looked for turtles and alligators. But mostly Jack made them ride in the buggy, and he kept the horse often at a trot.

"Normally I'd take another day and another night on the road to make this trip," Jack explained. "But seeing as how you ladies will be much more comfortable in Augusta, we're pressing it a bit."

Twilight was lengthening as they spotted a clearing up ahead on the right side of the road. In an overgrown yard, surrounded by abandoned fields, sat a dingy gray cabin. It appeared to only be one room. Surely this could not be the place Jack had spoken of.

But he cried with satisfaction, "There it is! And it appears no one is about!"

He stopped the horse in the yard and went to investigate. In his absence Mahala and Carolyn exchanged wide-eyed glances. They saw him knock, then disappear into the dim interior. A moment later he returned with a victorious grin.

"Aside from a few spiders, which you ladies can sweep out, the place is ours." He reached a hand up to Mahala, saying teasingly, "My lady, your castle awaits."

She smiled rather painfully. Next, Jack helped Carolyn down.

"Take in what you need. I'll bring the trunks after I get the horse settled, then I'll see about some firewood."

"Did you bring an axe?" Mahala asked in surprise.

"Strapped to the back of the buggy," Jack replied with pride.

Somehow she could not envision him playing the part of the lumberman. But that was exactly what he did, bringing in split wood and branches for tender as she hauled in water from the nearby creek for them to use for drinking and washing. She and Carolyn cleaned their faces and feet and changed their dingy stockings in between Jack's appearances.

The only furniture left in the cabin was a broken stool and an old bedstead sans mattress, so they sat on the floor before the fireplace, which was now giving off a warm orange glow and a good bit of heat, while they ate their dinner. They allowed themselves a little extra during this meal, so hunger would not keep them awake at night.

Jack seemed to find the whole experience an adventure. His mood was pleasant and joking. Mahala thought it was to keep them looking on the bright side. There was plenty that was negative in life at the moment, but the truth was, she realized, they were alive and escaping the Yankees. And before too very long they would be home in Clarkesville.

When Carolyn got up to go to the outhouse, taking their one lantern with her, Mahala and Jack sat bathed in the fire's glow, alone save Dev Jr., who snoozed on his blanket. Mahala felt the silence settle around them, pregnant with unspoken things. Now was the time to say what she'd known she'd needed to say since she first saw Jack in Savannah.

"Thank you," she murmured, not able to look at him.

"For what?"

"For going to Atlanta for me."

"You're not angry that I was that presumptuous?"

"You didn't go to be nosy or presumptuous, did you?" Mahala asked, though she knew the answer.

Jack shook his head, his arms draped around his upturned knees as he stared into the flames. "There is no worse kind of suffering than not knowing. I went because it was in my power to relieve you of at least that much."

Mahala's heart burned within her. She looked at him, and his green eyes met hers. But before more could be said, there was a thumping just outside, and Carolyn pushed the door open.

Later, Mahala lay down on her pallet – which consisted merely of one blanket – with a sense of peace. She and Carolyn were across the room from Jack, who had stretched out by the door with his pistol in easy reach. Earlier he had apologized for their lack of comfort and propriety, as if he were responsible for it.

"I think most people have more to worry about now than reputations," Carolyn had again reminded him.

It was true. Mahala was grateful merely to feel safe. She knew that with Jack guarding the door she could drift off to an uncomfortable but exhausted sleep, despite the whisper of tiny movements in the corners of the room that kept Carolyn tossing fitfully, protectively watching out for her child.

During the night Mahala heard Jack get up several times to feed the fire. Once, she met his eyes as he lay back down, and he smiled at her. She smiled back, drowsily, wondering if he slept at all or remained vigilant on their behalf.

The following day was even more exhausting than the first. Every muscle ached, and Mahala's bones felt jarred by the relentless travel. Looking at the poor horse, she feared he was about to drop, despite his sturdy size. It was cloudy and cold as they at last ferried across the Savannah River. The chill breeze off the water caused Mahala to turn up the collar of her wool coat. Her nose must be berry-red. With a pitying look, Jack said, "Almost there," and tucked the lap blanket they shared more closely around her.

Carolyn had told them she had distant cousins in Augusta. She remembered their address and gave it to Jack. While she had not seen these two maiden women in years, she believed they would willingly open their home to them – if they were in residence.

As the city came into view, Carolyn seemed to take heart. She pointed out its similarities to Savannah, with its gracious residences, churches and schools. In fact, Augusta had been laid out by James Oglethorpe in 1736 in the same forty-lot pattern he had used for Savannah. The river town situated on the fall line between the Piedmont and the Upper Coastal Plain had thrived, first on Indian trade and then on cotton and rice commerce. An early Augusta resident, George Walton, had been a signer of the Declaration of Independence.

"They built the canal here in the mid-40s," Carolyn told them. Mahala guessed she was trying to distract them all, including herself, from extreme weariness. "And of course there was the railroad, so they built the Confederate Powder Works here, too. You can see the big chimney from all around."

Mahala wondered if soon it, too, would fall into Yankee hands. The city's residents were wondering the same thing, they later discovered from Olivia Harding Calhoun's two forty-something nieces, Maybelle and Jo Harding. Mahala had been so relieved to see lights burning in the tranquil brick home Carolyn recalled from childhood visits that she had almost cried. And the plain but good-hearted sisters had welcomed them with open arms and clucks of pity. They were clearly in awe of Jack, "the blockade-running captain," and they were all too eager to offer hospitality to their young widowed cousin, whose husband had led the glorious 8th. And of course they "oohed and aahed" over the baby. Mahala did not mind that she was practically overlooked. They probably thought her some sort of hired companion or nanny. But it didn't matter, for they all had wonderfully hot baths and the anticipation of a good meal followed by feather mattresses.

Mahala put on the best of the dresses she had packed, but she felt dowdy beside the Harding sisters. They came to dinner in silk taffeta, still elegant despite being twice turned, with ribbons in their hair. They presided over the simple fare as though it was the lavish feast of pre-war days.

As they ate, they learned the city had been overwhelmed by both refugees and Confederate wounded, whom Jo and Maybelle went to nurse every day. Jo was even carrying on a flirtation with one patient. Now, Augusta was on tenterhooks as to whether Sherman would turn his avaricious eye upon them, or proceed to Charleston.

"We've thought about leaving," Maybelle said, "but where would we go? Besides, Jo's beau might pop the question any day, and at our age that's nothing to wink at."

Mahala smiled, thinking it sounded as if Maybelle considered the proposal would extend to her as well.

"I say, no need to panic," Jo declared, her silvery-gold hair glowing in the candlelight. "Panic never helped anyone. So let's pretend we're all at a nice, normal dinner, and just have a pleasant visit. Tell us, Carolyn, dear, all about your Dev."

Mahala paused with her bite in midair, wondering how her recently bereaved friend could possibly find that a "nice, normal" topic. But Carolyn smiled with pleasure and proceeded to tell of Dev's adventures with the OLI, and then as a regimental major. Her face glowed with pride. For the next half an hour, Mahala believed Carolyn actually forgot he was dead. Maybe remembering him in such a way was good for her, Mahala thought.

"Might I ask, ladies," Jack said at the first opportunity to turn the conversation, "if the railroad is still open from here to Charleston?"

"The Hamburg to Charleston? I surely believe so," said Jo. As Jack nodded, she turned her attention back to Carolyn. "Now my dear, you must tell us of your plans for the future."

As Carolyn replied, Mahala glanced at Jack. He calmly finished his dessert and didn't appear to notice. Why would he ask about the railroad to Charleston if he didn't plan to depart by it? A knot of fear formed in Mahala's stomach. She thought of the long, lonely roads between here and Clarkesville. Two young women and a baby traveling alone would never be safe. Any number of troubles might befall them. Carolyn had not seemed to have considered this. In fact, her cousins were trying to convince her to stay on for a time. She protested that Mahala must get home, and that she herself would be needed at Forests of Green, but Mahala thought she saw a flicker of uncertainty. Naturally she would be tempted by their offer. The knot tightened.

After dinner, Jack lighted them to their rooms.

Before saying goodnight, he turned to Carolyn. "It sounds as if your cousins would be pleased for us to rest here for another full day and night."

"Yes."

"That's good. The horse will need the break even more than we will. Even if the Georgia Railroad is open to Athens, I think we should go by buggy. It will be slower, but it may be safer to stay away from the tracks – and we'll need the gig once we reach Athens. ... I wouldn't count on being able to buy another horse and conveyance there."

Carolyn murmured her agreement. Mahala braced herself on the handrail, weak-kneed with relief. She was too choked up to speak. Jack *had* changed. He *was* noble. The truth of it put everything she thought she knew into a tailspin.

At the top of the stairs, Carolyn entered the room she would share with Mahala, eager to make certain Dev Jr. slept peacefully. But Jack turned to say goodnight, and doing so, saw the glisten of tears in Mahala's eyes.

"What's wrong?" Concern shone from his eyes.

185

"I – nothing–" She hastily wiped her eye with the back of one hand. A flustered laugh escaped. "It's just – I thought – when you asked about the railroad downstairs ..."

Comprehension settled over Jack's rugged features, then softened to kindness. "I would never leave you, Mahala. Don't you know that by now? I'll see you settled in Clarkesville and then come back to Augusta and Charleston by rail."

She nodded, pressing her lips together to still their trembling. My, she was a tired, emotional wreck of a woman. And it did not help a bit to have him looking at her like that.

Jack touched her arm. "Good night."

Mahala glanced at him with a faltering smile, noticing with a pinch of guilt the dark smudges under his eyes. She turned before she could further embarrass herself and closed the door behind her.

Inside, Carolyn looked up from the mattress her cousins had provided for the baby. "You were worried he would leave us, weren't you?"

"Yes."

"The war has changed us all, Mahala. Give Jack credit where it's due."

"You *are* his stepmother's niece."

"Bah. That's nothing. Have you thought of the danger he risked, a man of draftable age in civilian clothes, traveling through countryside swarming with two armies when he went to Atlanta for you? Did you ask him what lengths he went to to avoid capture? I did. Sherman's soldiers don't hesitate to hang civilian men as guerrillas. They took civilians hostage to exchange for their own captured troops. I wasn't Jack's motivation for what he did then, or for this. *You* are the woman he loves."

Mahala turned away and began unbuttoning her dress, her rigid back stating resistance, but her mind racing at what Carolyn had said.

But Carolyn would not be quiet. "I know you're hurting because of your brothers and Clay, but don't make the mistake of holding Jack at arm's length for too long, Mahala. He's waited a long time."

Mahala whirled around. "*He's* waited!? You're forgetting all those long, lonely years I pined for *him*! And Clay ... Clay was my *fiancé*, Carolyn. I just found out two weeks ago that he's dead. Would you have me forget him so soon?"

"Don't be silly, Mahala. It's not forgetting him to acknowledge your feelings for Jack."

"Isn't it? Would *you* be ready now to toss Dev's memory aside?"

Carolyn's face hardened. "You can't compare your engagement to Clay to the way I felt about Dev. Don't look at me like that. You know it's true. Dev was the love of my life, and deep inside, I know you know

Jack is yours. Just don't let guilt or pride keep you from being able to admit it."

Under a stone gray sky on December 20, Jack, Carolyn and Mahala set out to traverse the length of Columbia County on White Oak Road, a route that took them past silent stands of pine forest and wide, wind-swept cotton fields. They crossed the occasional creek and changed roads, following the sign pointing towards Washington.

The ladies were so tired by the time they reached Aonia that they discussed staying there, but Jack convinced them the eight extra miles to Washington would be worth traveling. The larger town had long been a busy junction for mail and stagecoach routes, further enhanced by a spur of the Georgia Railroad in the last decade. As they entered the city limits, Mahala was surprised to see white-columned mansions, churches, a theatre, an 1817 Federal red brick courthouse which had been a pattern for many of the state's early brick court buildings, and a branch of the Georgia State Bank. Jack told them there was also a prominent female seminary.

"I would never have expected all this in the middle of nowhere," Mahala commented, taken with the quaint charm of the place.

"Well, much the same for Clarkesville, right?" Jack pointed out.

She nodded. "True. In fact, this has a bit of the feel of home."

"I've heard there's a mineral springs just outside town," Carolyn said. "I know some people who used to go there. There's a hotel at the springs. Shall we stay at it?"

"Only if the ones in town are full."

Mahala sagged with relief as Jack stopped the buggy before a three-story inn near the square. Golden lights glowed in some of the windows, and pungent smoke curled from the building's double chimneys. They waited while Jack went inside to check for accommodations, anxiously noting the number of people on the porch.

But he returned with a grin, holding a room key up between thumb and forefinger. "We're in luck!" he cried. "There's an ostler who will restore our horse to life, and potato soup and bread for our dinner."

As Jack handed her down, Mahala found she had to cling to his arm for a moment. When he glanced at her in surprise, she flushed and murmured, "Sorry. My leg's half asleep." Giving the offending limb a shake, she moved as quickly as possible up to the porch.

It was so late Mahala and Carolyn did not take the time to change clothes or brush the dust from their hair. They washed their faces in the narrow and sparse but private bedroom and went down to the dining room. There, beside a crackling fire, they partook of the hearty soup. Dev Jr. liked it, too, once his mother mashed up the potato chunks. He sat with rosy cheeks in a high chair, kicking his plump legs and rounding his mouth into an 'O' in constant demand of his next bite. His jolly mood infected them all, despite their heavy eyelids and aching limbs.

When they were done, Carolyn stood up and gathered her child. "Well, I'm going on to bed," she declared. "That is, if I can get this little fellow to quiet down."

Mahala smiled and rose, Jack sliding out her chair.

Jack said, "I know it's late, but perhaps your legs could do with a stretch, Mahala?"

She hesitated, immediately torn.

"Just a short one?"

The combination of plea in Jack's tone – an unusual sound, indeed – and the memory of Carolyn's words spoken in Augusta made up her mind. "All right," she agreed.

They bid Carolyn good night at the stairs. Jack held the door for Mahala and then offered his arm with a flourish and a gallant smile that made her feel like she was the highest born of ladies. But his deference also made her uneasy. She kept waiting for it to end and the sharp-tongued, imperious Jack to return. Oh, the barbed wit had still been in occasional evidence during the past week, but always directed at their circumstances instead of at his companions.

"There's a puzzled furrow on your forehead," Jack commented. "What are you thinking of?"

Mahala blushed. "Oh, I – I was thinking it's rather strange that we haven't argued – like we used to," she admitted, looking down at the street.

"Perhaps the things that once separated us no longer matter."

Mahala glanced at him, but Jack was looking at the clock on the tower of the courthouse. "It's later than I thought," he murmured. "Are you too cold?"

"No, I'm fine."

It was true that a damp chill had settled over the town. Their breath became a fog before them. But in her wool paletot and bonnet, with warmth emanating from Jack's solid frame next to her, she had hardly noticed the temperature.

"All right, then. Maybe if we walk a bit we won't be bothered by leg cramps during the night. By the way, you ladies are holding up admirably."

"Everything we are enduring is for our own safety, so we can hardly complain. You, however …"

188

Jack shrugged. "It's no matter." He turned to her. "Did you really think me such a blackguard as to leave you in Augusta?"

"I – I thought we had no right to expect otherwise."

"Didn't you?" His green eyes searched hers until she dropped her gaze. "Well, I hope your opinion of me has altered at least a little bit."

Embarrassed, Mahala nodded.

"And that reminds me, I've been waiting for a good time to express my condolences on Clay Fraser and the Emmitts. I'm sorry about them, Mahala."

"Are you really?" she couldn't help asking, something inside her pushing her to speak what should have remained unsaid. "About Clay?"

Jack frowned. "You always knew I didn't want to see you married to him, so if you're asking if I regret you are no longer committed, it would be stupid of me to pretend that. I've had a long time to think about why you turned to him, Mahala, and while I've never accepted it – I'm human, after all – I did start to think that perhaps he had some traits I was lacking."

Mahala's lips parted. This was an astounding admission for a man like Jack. But before she could speak he continued.

"I was stubborn and proud. It took being forced to make choices about this war and losing you for me to see that. *God* let me see it. Now I know it can't be about what other people think. It can't be about me. It has to be about love."

"That's good, Jack," Mahala said quickly, wanting to belittle the implications behind his words. She wasn't ready to hear them. There was too much pain, too much risk. She turned and tried to walk away.

But he wasn't about to let her go that easily. "Mahala, listen. I would never wish death on any man. Especially that sort of death."

Mahala's lip trembled, and he saw it. Instead of growing angry, amazingly, Jack's tone tendered. "Knowing he suffered so much, alone, makes it all the harder for you, doesn't it?"

"Y-yes."

Jack patted her arm. "You did all that you could, Mahala."

"No, I didn't!" She stopped and covered her mouth, surprised at herself for admitting this in his presence. Guilt made her sick inside. Here she was again, ready to throw herself into Jack's arms, and him the very reason she had cheated Clay of love.

A glance at the man beside her betrayed something it would have been better if she had not seen it at that moment: hope. He was actually hopeful, guessing that the weakness she admitted was because of him. How dare he? And how dare *she* begin to welcome such a look? Anger rose in her

189

chest, a protective barrier that blocked him out. It was as if Clay's ghost had appeared there between them.

Her back straightened. "Please take me back to the hotel."

"Very well," he agreed, disappointment edging his quiet tone.

Jack turned and escorted her back. Sensing the stiffness of her body, he was silent, but obviously in deep thought. He took her up to her room, but before she could say goodnight and escape to its privacy, he caught her arm.

"Is it so hard to forgive yourself, Mahala? And me, for not being able to stop loving you?"

Jack's honest words pierced Mahala's heart. Overwhelmed with emotions, she strangled on a rising sob and turned away.

CHAPTER THIRTEEN

riday, December 23rd was cold and rainy, and the Old Federal Highway north of Athens, already well-churned this season, quickly became slippery for horse and buggy.

Their route from Washington had taken them through Lexington to Athens, where they had enjoyed shelter at the home of Patience Sprite. They had remained in the university town an extra day to rest, and of course Patience had hostessed them with as much generosity as her meager larder allowed. She had in fact begged them to stay on, but Mahala had explained how long they had already been away with no communication with Martha.

"I understand," Patience had said to her in a private moment. "And Mahala, Captain Randall seems quite favorably altered … not that he didn't have plentiful charms before." She had smirked. "It's clear that he's very devoted to you. I guess the two of you will come to an understanding soon?"

"I would hardly assume *that*," Mahala had said stiffly. "It's silly to think the payment for his helping me will be a wedding."

Now well away from Athens, she glanced over at him, wondering.

Did *he* assume that? Did he even want such a thing now? And why was she even thinking along such a line? She was not ready for that, just not ready. But his words from the night in Washington bored themselves into her head like bees, impossible to ignore.

Caught staring when Jack turned his gaze upon her, she blushed hotly, as if he could read her thoughts.

"What?" he asked with a suspicious laugh. "Are you wishing ill on me because I wanted to press on past Harmony Grove?"

Glad he had misunderstood, Mahala smiled and shook her head. The town with its nearby wool factory might have offered better accommodation than the small communities ahead, but she didn't mind. "Every mile brings us closer to home."

"I know, but it does appear the rain is picking up. You're getting wet. Perhaps we should stop and let me pry that board in the back seat loose so that you can sit beside Mrs. Rousseau."

"Are you satisfied that I've submitted to being forced to sit here beside you long enough?"

"Ouch! Now, Mahala, that was quite unworthy."

He was teasing, a sparkle in his eye, but Carolyn didn't see it, and from behind them she said, "Yes, it was. Jack is only trying to be considerate, Mahala. I think it's a good idea. Dev Jr. is not going to sleep for a while anyway."

Jack winked at Mahala.

"Really, it's all right," Mahala protested. "Don't bother with it, Jack."

"Look – a creek. A perfect spot to stop."

Mahala sighed in defeat as Jack slowed the horse. He eased the stallion down a gentle embankment. Once they were beside the swollen waters, Jack let him drink. He helped the ladies down and went to fetch the axe to use as a lever.

While Jack was absorbed in prying out the nails of the baby's make-shift crib and Carolyn was digging in the hamper Patience had sent for a hard biscuit Dev Jr. could teethe on, Mahala wandered a few feet downstream, pulling her scarf over her bonnet. Here under the trees the effect of the rain was somewhat diminished. Sounding happy, the water gurgled over small stones, and Mahala's boots sunk in last autumn's damp leaves. The creek took a turn. She followed it, then stopped, for too late she saw a small encampment near a sand bar. A man was lying under a tarp rolled out from a tree branch and staked with sharp sticks while another man attempted to feed a tiny blaze within a circle of rocks. A string of a few small fish hung nearby, and in the trees just beyond, two bony horses were tied. Both men appeared to be wearing a hodge-podge of Confederate and civilian apparel. And they both saw her at the same time.

The middle-aged fisherman's eyes widened, and lips within a full dark beard turned up in a smile. "Well, lookee here, James. A beautiful wood sprite's done come upon us!"

The other one sat up, saying, "Hey, where did you come from, sweetie?"

Mahala started to back away, wary and apologetic. "I – I'm sorry. I didn't know anyone was here. My friends and I – we just stopped a minute by the road. We'll be going on now."

"Well, don't run off, honey." The man by the fire was rising, still half-coiled, as if he were prepared to chase her. "Are you hungry? Gimme a minute and I'll fry you some fish."

"N-no, thank you," Mahala tossed over her shoulder.

As fast as she could walk without breaking into a run, she hurried back toward the buggy. Jack looked up as she came near, her eyes wide and leaves blowing up around her swishing skirt like a small tornado.

"We've got to go – now," she hissed.

She saw that his lips formed a question, but before he could speak it his eyes went over her shoulder and beheld her pursuer. Still holding the axe, Jack immediately stepped forward, motioning the women into the buggy with a flick of his other hand.

The lean deserter – or whoever he was – slowed when he saw Jack.

"Is there a problem?" Jack asked.

"No problem. This little lady here just stumbled into our camp site so I thought I'd come over and say howdy. Where are you folks headed?"

Jack hesitated for an almost imperceptible moment. "Athens."

The man was still coming closer, his gait now meant to suggest languor. Jack wasn't fooled. By contrast, he stood with muscles tensed, watching each move of this new potential enemy.

"Well, then, if you're coming from the north I guess you've no news of the fighting," said the ex-Confederate, as his friend also wandered into view.

"No. Sorry. Just taking a moment to water our horse. We'll be going now."

Jack moved to take the horse's bridle to back him from the creek. But the dark-haired soldier's hand snaked out and connected with the leather first. The indignant stallion snorted, and Jack said, "Take your hand off my animal."

In the buggy, Carolyn and Mahala sat ramrod straight and unmoving.

With a falsely friendly pat to the horse's head, the stranger said, "No need to get antsy. I was just admiring a nice piece of horse flesh. You wouldn't consider a trade, would you?"

The other man standing at the edge of the trees laughed loudly in a harsh, mirthless manner.

"No trade." Jack led the horse back and, tracing the lines with one hand, backed up to the buggy, placing the axe inside and hopping up in one fluid motion. Mahala noticed he never took his eyes from the deserters.

"Hey, where's your uniform, anyway?" one of the men called mockingly after them as Jack urged the rig up onto the road. "Don't you want to serve the Confederacy? Don't you want to help out two poor old soldiers? You could really help us out!"

They were laughing as the horse trotted south, back the way they had come. Jack's jaw was set. Mahala and Carolyn rode in frozen silence. Even Dev Jr. seemed to sense their tension and sat gnawing his fingers and drooling.

When they were well out of sight of the bridge, Jack glanced behind them. "See anyone, Mahala?"

She took a long look. "No." Then she added in a small voice, "I'm sorry, Jack."

"It's not your fault."

"I should have stayed with you."

Carolyn's faint voice came from behind them. "Will we really have to go all the way back to Harmony Grove?"

"No. Just up ahead was the road we passed that led toward Grove Level. Remember? We can take it to another route that will lead back into this highway at Bushville. It will be well out of our way, but worth it under the circumstances, I think."

Mahala agreed. The looks in the eyes of those men had told her exactly what they would have done to the three of them if they'd had the chance. She shuddered. "Do you think they were deserters?"

"Probably. ... War sifts out the best and worst of the human race, no matter what army they belong to."

After that, Jack was silent so long Mahala began to wonder about him. Finally she leaned forward and asked, "Are you all right?"

"No, I'm not," he replied grumpily. "I'm thinking of a hundred ways I could have handled that situation better. I should have been more forceful with them."

"They never did anything that cued you to act other than you did."

"I still don't have a good feeling about it. I don't think we should stay in Bushville tonight. The more distance we put between ourselves and those drifters, the better."

"You don't think they'd actually follow us?" Carolyn asked.

But Jack just shook his head uncertainly.

At last they passed through Bushville. The longer road had cost them precious time. They stopped only for a brief rest – a bite to eat and a drink from the public well. Then they were on their way again, though dark clouds hovered low and the rain fell with more persistence. The red clay road over the rolling hills of the Piedmont quickly became treacherous. The horse's hooves slid and slipped, and Jack had to constantly prod the animal forward. Soon it became apparent that if they wanted the poor beast to take them all the way to Clarkesville they would have to stop and continue the journey the next day.

The tiny community of Hudson nearby did not offer up any ready accommodation but just north of it, when Mahala was beginning to fear they would have to sleep out in the open, they came across a small farm. It appeared to be abandoned – not an unusual case. With men away at the war, the women and children often found lodging with relatives in larger cities. But Jack was loath to break into the tiny clapboard house.

"It just goes against my grain," he said, peering dismally in the window. "Would you ladies be mortified at staying in the barn?"

"We'll be fine," they both said, although they knew this meant no cozy fire and no privacy.

They found the building devoid of livestock. Jack checked every corner to assure that no traveler or wild creature had prior claim on the shelter. He pronounced it sound, with a solid back wall and a wide single door in the front which could be left open a crack as a lookout.

They unhitched the horse and placed him in a stall near the buggy. As Jack cared for the animal, Carolyn spread a blanket for Dev Jr. to roll around on, and Mahala attempted to put together a cold supper. This they ate with little conversation. Mahala sensed they were all silently straining toward home, thinking the quicker they went to sleep the quicker they could travel in the morning. They now had but to travel through Homer and Hollingsworth, home of the White family. She'd heard that back in October, local men had lain in ambush in the pass to hold off raiding Union cavalry. They'd called the skirmish "The Battle of Narrows." The climb up the Chattahoochee Ridge was a challenging feat indeed. But they could be home in another day or two.

The possibility greatly cheered Mahala. She thought with longing of her grandmother's arms, and the tender relief with which Martha would welcome her. And there would have to be a visit to Ben, Nancy and Jacob, to tell them about Seth and Sam. While Mahala dreaded that, shared grief might bring a sense of closure, too.

Dark came early. Mahala spread her blanket near Carolyn in the back of the barn, while Jack took a spot near the front door.

Holding Dev Jr. close, Carolyn murmured bleakly, "Tomorrow is Christmas Eve."

No one said anything. There was nothing to say. Within minutes Carolyn's breathing told Mahala she was asleep. In the last dim light from outside she could still see Jack lying across the way. He had shed his greatcoat, which had gotten soaked through as he'd driven, and he was now covered by the thinnest of their blankets, having given the women the warmer quilts. After a few minutes Mahala heard a sound that she finally realized were his teeth chattering.

Her heart wrenched inside her as pity – and something else – swept over her. Against the strong sense of propriety instilled in her by Nancy and Martha, Mahala got up and tiptoed across the barn. Reaching Jack's side, she knelt beside him and draped half of her quilt over his shaking shoulders. He started when she did, looking back at her in amazement – about to protest – but she stopped that and his turning over by a firm hand on his shoulder. Mahala lay down behind him, facing him, her face hot at her boldness but the first sense of peace in her heart. She thought of the story of Ruth in the Bible, lying at the feet of her kinsman-redeemer. She knew all that her action implied, and he seemed to understand, for he did not turn over. But he did reach for her hand and held it, pulling her arm atop him, as she fell asleep, comforted by his nearness.

Something pulled Mahala from sleep. Someone was touching her hair. Stroking it. It felt nice. She opened her eyes slowly to the faint gray of an overcast dawn and looked up into Jack's face. His expression could be described as nothing but adoring, and her reaction was a smile that said every unpremeditated thing in her heart. She couldn't help it, couldn't hide it. She loved him.

He whispered her name with what sounded like amazement and lowered his mouth to hers. Her lips parted in welcome beneath his. The kiss seemed the most natural thing in the world. Her heart raced as heat infused her being head to toe. Her arms wrapped around him as again and again their lips met. Jack's solid weight pressed into her, and his hand moved down her body, possessively pulling her closer.

I am yours, she thought. *I always have been.*

"Jack," she whispered as he kissed her ear and throat, the stubble of a day and night's growth of beard rasping against her tender skin. Every sense was heightened, hands and lips telling of long-suppressed desire.

She sought to wrap herself around him, driven to communicate her love. As they rolled to one side, a stray fowl roosting in the trees decided it was time to herald the new day. They hardly heeded it, so intense was their passion, but providence further intervened. The baby heard the rooster and awakened with his own irritable and hungry wail.

This jerked Mahala back to awareness. She put a hand on Jack's chest and tried to still her quickened breathing before Carolyn came to alertness. He tried to kiss her again. She put her hand on his mouth. He started to kiss her fingers, but suddenly he tensed. She saw his gaze focus on a point behind her, beyond the cracked-open door, out in the yard. In a matter of seconds, before she could realize what was happening, he grabbed for his pistol and rolled up into a squat. He motioned her to stay back as he slowly straightened, peering out. As she cautiously rose behind the cover of the barn door, she could see in the opposite direction, could see what he could not yet. The flash of a gray jacket.

"Jack!" she screamed as at the same moment the report of a rifle shattered the early morning stillness. Without a conscious thought, Mahala flung herself in Jack's direction. Something kicked her shoulder, hard. The small cloud of gun powder from the deserter's muzzle loader registered in her brain in a haze of shock as she collapsed into Jack's arms.

196

Jack called her name, but she couldn't quite focus on his face. Before the fuzzy darkness claimed her the crack of Jack's pistol mingled with the roaring in her ears.

Carolyn screamed Mahala's name and ran up just as the man who had shot Mahala fell dead in the yard, a bullet through his brain. The other assailant bounded off through the trees. Jack relinquished the woman he loved to her best friend's arms and ran after him. He had to make sure this villain would do them no more harm.

Jack never got off a second shot, however. The accomplice had a horse tied nearby. He mounted it and galloped away at a break-neck pace, mud flying from the animal's hooves.

Jack ran back to where Mahala lay unconscious, a red stain of blood spreading quickly from the entry wound just below her right collar bone. Carolyn was sobbing hysterically. Jack began unhooking Mahala's bodice. That stopped Carolyn's tears.

"Do you have an extra petticoat?" he demanded.

"W-what?"

Over the tearful cries of Dev Jr. he repeated himself. "An extra petticoat! Are you wearing one?"

"Yes."

"Tear a strip from it, quick."

Thankfully Carolyn obeyed without hesitation. She lifted her wool skirt and took firm hold of the ruffled hem of the white undergarment beneath. There was a loud ripping sound. Jack wadded up the piece of material she gave him and held it over the bullet hole. Immediately it turned red.

He was trying not to let rising panic rob him of his senses. Clear thinking and quick action could mean the difference in whether Mahala lived or died. And he wasn't about to let her die for trying to save him.

"Keep tearing more strips," Jack directed. He put pressure on the wound while Carolyn did as he told her. "Give me one really long one."

Carolyn stood and unbuttoned her now ragged petticoat and shimmied out of it so that she could finish shredding it.

Then Jack said, "Help me gently lift her. We need to see if the bullet passed through."

He repressed a curse when he saw it hadn't. While he held Mahala as stable as possible, he instructed Carolyn in passing the longest piece of fabric around Mahala's chest just beneath her dress. They then tied a bit of padding in place above the wound.

"Get your child ready to go while I hitch up the horse. We need to get her to a doctor as fast as possible."

Minutes later, he laid Mahala across the back seat with her upper body cradled in Carolyn's arms.

"Hold her tight and keep pressure on the wound."

"But what about Dev Jr.?"

"I'll have to hold him."

Carolyn looked further distressed, but she did not argue. Jack sat the baby on his lap and held him with one arm. The child was squalling in furious protest of his neglect and harassment. They rode out of the farm yard at full speed, leaving the Confederate deserter lying dead in the rain.

All the way to Homer Carolyn kept crying out, "She won't stop bleeding! She just keeps bleeding everywhere, Jack!" And he drove the poor horse to a furious run despite the muddy road, swallowing down the bile of fear the whole time and praying, *Please, God, let her live. Don't take her from me now.*

Finally they passed Grady's Hotel, Homer Presbyterian and some houses. There was a handsome new Greek Revival courthouse built with mud bricks from the Hudson River. Surely there would be a doctor's office. But Jack did not see one.

A shop keeper just opening his mercantile for the day stopped in horrified surprise at the sight of the buggy barreling into town, the wounded woman in the back seat.

Jack yelled at him, "We need a doctor! Where's the nearest doctor's office?"

The man pointed to a narrow two-story building just down the street. Jack pulled the heaving stallion to a stop in front of it and ran to bang on the door. No response. He shifted Dev Jr.'s weight to his other hip. The baby howled in response. There was no shingle hung, but he knocked again, louder, rattling the window panes.

"I need a doctor!"

People were beginning to stick their heads out of homes and businesses to see what the ruckus was about. Finally a tall, middle-aged woman, dark-haired with silver at the temple, eased open the door. She was still wearing her nightgown and wrapper. She stared round-eyed at the screaming infant Jack was holding.

"Are you the doctor's wife?" Jack demanded, barely restraining himself from barging in past her.

"I am Dr. Parker's wife, but my husband is away at the war."

"You mean there's no doctor here?"

The woman shook her head. "We had many doctors here in the county, but most who weren't already working as surgeons in the army were of an age to be taken in the draft. If you would like, I can give you directions to one of our retired physicians' residences—"

"A woman has been shot. She'll bleed to death if I keep hauling her around. How far is it?"

"Shot?" Mrs. Parker echoed indignantly. Jack realized she had thought Dev Jr. was the cause of the errand. The woman looked beyond him to Carolyn sitting in the buggy holding Mahala's still, pale, blood-stained body. Her face firmed with resolve. "If you will trust a woman, I can help you."

"She's wounded just below the collar bone. You know what to do?" Jack asked, uncertainty making his tone harsh.

"Yes. I swear it."

She spoke so calmly, and he felt the precious minutes ticking away so relentlessly, that he decided to believe her. He shoved Dev Jr. toward the unsuspecting woman and ran back to the buggy. Carolyn helped him take Mahala into his arms. As he did, she stirred slightly and moaned. Carolyn climbed down and followed them into the office, taking her baby from Mrs. Parker, who shut the door behind them.

It was still dark inside, no lamps having yet been lit.

"Where do I put her?" Jack asked.

Mrs. Parker gestured to their left. He followed her through a waiting room and an exam room into what had been the surgery. There Jack laid Mahala on the table.

"My husband took his best instruments with him to the army, but he left a set that had been his father's. Did the bullet come out the back?"

"No."

She nodded and went to a cabinet on the wall, getting out an old black satchel. The room was well-illuminated by two windows, but Mrs. Parker lit some lamps and fetched water, a basin and a bottle of whiskey.

Jack pulled away Mahala's sticky dress to see that – just as Carolyn had said – the last of the bandages was sopping with blood. He had to wonder if the bullet had at least nicked an artery.

"Is this your wife, Sir?" asked Mrs. Parker as she approached the table.

"Not yet."

"Then does the lady want to assist me?" she inquired, gesturing to Carolyn, who hovered wide-eyed in the doorway with a still-sobbing Dev Jr.

"No," Jack said. "She will tend to her infant while I assist you."

With a muffled sob of fear, Carolyn left the room. She must have found a place in the waiting room to feed the baby, for the nerve-wracking crying finally ceased. Mrs. Parker was quietly but deftly cleaning each instrument with the alcohol.

Jack took a deep breath. "Have you really done this before?" he asked the statuesque woman beside him.

"I have watched my husband at work many times, and even assisted him, but I have never done surgery without him," she confessed, laying out the instruments in a neat row. "But I assure you, this is not beyond my skill, and my hand is steady, which is more than I can say for the retired physician in town."

"I guess I have to trust you."

Mrs. Parker poured alcohol on a clean cloth and liberally swabbed Mahala's wound. Mahala jerked but did not wake up. "It's a mercy she's out. Let's hope she stays that way – for I don't have any ether." She picked up a small pair of forceps. "Now, you keep dabbing with this cloth so I can see to find the bullet. Here we go."

Mahala swam back to consciousness. Despite the throbbing pain in her shoulder, she felt there was something she had to do. It was that unexplained sense of urgency that made her open her eyes.

A hand seized hers and a face came into view, the green eyes focusing intently on her above an unfamiliar growth of beard.

"Hello, my Benedick," she whispered with a smile as a memory from the Rousseaus' Shakespeare ball, before the war, came into focus in her groggy mind.

Jack laughed. "Hello, my Beatrice," he said. Then he did something Mahala had never thought to see him do. He dropped his head and started crying. Mahala wanted to reach out and smooth his thick brown hair to comfort him, but she was too weak.

"Jack, it's all right," she murmured instead.

He heard her and, wiping his eyes, looked up. "I think it will be now."

"Was it that bad?"

"You lost a lot of blood. You could have died, Mahala." Jack's features turned momentarily stern. "What were you thinking, anyway? Jumping in front of me like that?"

"Didn't think. Just did it." She licked her parched lips. "Thirsty."

"Of course!" Jack jumped up and poured water from a nearby pitcher into a glass. Very gently he helped her raise her head. She winced but drank deeply and then lay back, satisfied.

"Where am I?"

"At the home of a Mrs. Parker, wife of a doctor here in Homer. They live above the office where we took out your bullet."

"We?"

Jack smiled, a bit smugly, she thought. "Mrs. Parker and I. Dr. Parker is away to the war."

Mahala raised her eyebrows. "Oh, great. So now I really owe you."

The smug smile firmed into a positive smirk. "Everything."

She smiled back, then frowned. "Droggy – groggy."

"That would be the medicine Mrs. Parker gave you to help with the pain. Don't you remember taking it?"

"Mmm," Mahala murmured and hoped he understood her answer was 'no.' Suddenly her eyes, which had been sliding closed, popped open. "It's Christmas," she added with sudden clarity.

"Yes, it is, and you should sleep the rest of it away," Jack told her, taking her hand again between both of his. He leaned forward so that she could more easily focus on him. "But before you do, I want you to know that I promise every one after this one is going to be far better. We have a lot to talk about when you feel stronger."

Mahala nodded, trying to remain alert for his sake, but feeling herself drift away despite herself. Before she retreated into the inky neverland of sleep, she murmured that pressing thing she knew she had really wanted to say aloud.

"I love you, Jack Randall."

She didn't see his smile, but she knew it was there.

"Where's Jack?" Mahala asked Carolyn two days later when she woke up from her nap.

Carolyn had brought broth, and she sat it down on the bedside table. "He went out for a bit."

"Out? Where?"

"How should I know? He hardly tells me his every whim. He'll be back soon. And don't give him a hard time. This is the first time he's left the house."

Mahala raised her left hand to her limp, tangled hair. "Ugh. I don't want him to see me like this. Will you help me wash my hair?"

Carolyn put her hands on her hips. "You're not well enough for that."

"Well, let's at least brush it and put some powder in it or something."

"Two steps from death's door and already your vanity reasserts itself," Carolyn teased. "I will help you, but after that you must eat all that broth."

"Yes, my bossy friend."

Mahala felt much better with her hair combed and braided and a little gloss on her cracked lips. She was ready to lean on the pillows while Carolyn fed her the soup.

"Really, I can do it myself," she commented a little grumpily.

"Not yet."

"Are we to leave here soon?"

"Jack and Mrs. Parker agree you should stay here a while. Mrs. Parker has said we are welcome to remain until you can stand the jostling on the road. She's a very nice person."

"But my grandmother!" Mahala protested.

Carolyn paused with the spoon in the air. "Didn't Jack tell you?" she asked. "The day after you were shot he sent a note in the mail to Clarkesville telling Mrs. Franklin what had happened but that you would make a recovery. He explained everything."

"Oh. Maybe he did. I can't remember much before this morning."

Carolyn smiled. "I'm just so relieved you're getting well, Mahala. You really scared me. And actually, that made me realize all that I do have left to live for myself."

Mahala smiled back and took her hand. "Good."

At that moment there was a brief knock on the door. When the women called "come in," Jack entered, looking every bit his old dashing self, clean-shaven and dressed in fresh clothes.

"You look like an Indian princess with those braids," he declared on sight of her, coming to her side and kissing her hand.

"If you think you're going to make me mad, you're not," Mahala retorted.

"Ah, the sparkle is back in the eyes."

"Where have you been?"

"And the edge on the tongue."

Carolyn collected the tray and got out of the way so that Jack could sit down on the side of the bed. "I'll leave you two to your romantic sparring," she said. "It's good to have you both back to your old selves."

With a smirk, she passed from the room.

"Not quite back to our old selves," Jack observed, "because I was a fool before and I'll never be one again – at least not where you're concerned. Nothing, and I mean nothing, can come between us again."

He leaned forward to kiss Mahala's lips. It was a sweet and tender gesture, and brief, but thorough nonetheless. "That's better," he said as they parted.

"You'd have me always silent and submissive?"

"If it's in that fashion, most definitely!"

Mahala blushed. "Now as to where you went …" she prompted, more gently this time.

"Oh, yes. Well, it seems there were a number of questions about the dead deserter we left in the farmyard. I had to have a visit with the sheriff."

Mahala's eyes widened. "You're not in trouble, Jack?"

"Thanks to you, I have proof that I acted in our defense," he stated with a gleam of satisfaction.

"Well, you're very welcome. Happy to be of service."

Jack laughed and tugged her braid.

"I'm glad I didn't know you when you were a boy. I don't think I would have liked you very much."

"You didn't like me when we did first meet."

No point arguing about that. Mahala went back to the subject at hand. "So there's still a sheriff around here?" she asked with some wonder.

"Yes, though he's very rheumatic."

Mahala giggled. Then she put her hand over her mouth. She hadn't heard herself make such a sound in months. Or was it years? Immediately she sobered.

"It's all right, you know," Jack said, sensing her mood. "You don't have to feel guilty for being happy. At least, I hope you're happy."

She sighed. "I am – it's just – I guess it will take some time to feel like I deserve it."

A quick smile creased the corners of Jack's mouth. "You do. And so … I confess the sheriff's office was not my only errand." Jack shifted and dug in his coat pocket. To her surprise, he laid a tiny box on the covers over her lap.

"What's this? A late Christmas present?"

Jack actually looked sheepish. "Sort of."

"You shouldn't have! I don't have anything for …" Her voice trailed away in shock, for she had sprung the latch and found herself gazing at a sparkling ruby and diamond ring.

"You do have something for me, I hope," Jack said. "An answer. Listen to me, Mahala. I have to go to Clarkesville now to check in on my stepmother and sister. From there I'll get a fast horse to ride to Athens. I must get to Charleston to get *Evangeline* safely to Nassau. Then, I promise, I'll come straight back. Before I go, please tell me–"

But Mahala cut him off. "No!" she wailed, tears springing to her eyes. "You can't go! What if something happens? It would kill me, Jack – it would! How will you even get back into the coast?"

"I'll find a way. I promise. But before I go, I want to know that you'll be mine."

"No," she said again, covering her ears and squeezing her eyes closed. She had heard this all before, and look how it had ended. If the same thing happened with Jack, the true love of her heart, she simply could not go on.

But Jack took her hands and gently pried them away, careful not to jostle her. He kissed her face and the tears that eased out of her eyes. "Mahala, I know you're scared, but please, trust me. Haven't I always returned?"

"Let someone else go," she sobbed.

"There is no one else. All I ask is that you wait a little while. Wear this ring as a sign of my promise to you, of our engagement, and then, I'll never leave you again. I'd marry you now if you were well. But I'm getting ahead of myself. I would hardly want you to accuse me of being assuming again."

Mahala's crying ceased as she watched Jack get off the bed and kneel beside it, holding one of her hands in his own.

"Will you, Mahala Franklin, do me the honor of becoming my wife?"

She closed her eyes, unable to believe the scene before her, the words just spoken. But when she reopened them, he was still there, kneeling before her and waiting expectantly. She had listened to her head long enough. It was time to obey her heart.

"Yes, Jack, yes, I will!" she cried, despite herself, her fears, and the uncertainty of tomorrow.

Jack grinned, looking happier than she had ever seen him. "Then put on this ring."

"Yes, Sir."

Jack took it out of the box and slid it onto her finger. "My Michaela," he said. "My beautiful Cherokee bride…"

Jack had only been gone a day, and Mahala felt melancholy as dark as the gray winter sky outside pressing in on her. She sat in her bedroom at Mrs. Parker's with a book, but it didn't hold her attention. She looked at the beautiful ruby and diamond ring on her finger and felt a little better. Jack's commitment was real. Their long struggle against their emotions was over. Now nothing could stand in their way … except the danger of the enemy on the high seas.

No. She wouldn't think about that. She'd go crazy thinking and waiting, waiting and thinking. If only she could go home. Argh. This blasted wound.

She heard carriage wheels outside but didn't bother to get up. Mrs. Parker had lots of company. In her husband's absence, all her friends called upon her both socially and to inquire from her considerable store of medical knowledge.

But then, a few minutes later, someone knocked on her own bedroom door.

"Come in," Mahala called.

In walked her grandmother. Mahala was so delighted and surprised that she forgot her bandaged shoulder and flew into the older woman's welcoming arms.

"What's this I hear, you troublesome girl! You're gone forever, with no word, enemy armies marching all around between us, and then I get a note from that blackguard Jack Randall telling me you've been *shot* and are staying at some woman's house here in Homer!"

"Oh, Grandmother, you musn't call him a blackguard anymore. He brought Carolyn and me to safety – well, except for the deserter who did shoot me. And – don't be angry – but he's asked me to marry him, and I've agreed."

"Silly girl," Martha said, holding Mahala's face between her hands. Tears formed in Martha's eyes. "No, I can't call you a girl, can I? For you're a woman grown and soon to be married. No, I'm not angry. Captain Randall told me everything. I met him on the road here, and he told me of your engagement. I'm just so relieved you are all right."

Mahala relaxed into another embrace. "You don't disapprove, then?"

"Disapprove? After gallivanting across the state with you the only decent thing for the man to do is to marry you."

Mahala laughed.

"I only disliked him because I was sure he'd break your heart. But if he'll take care of you, if he'll return your love … then I'm happy for you. And you deserve happiness, Mahala. You've had more than your share of heartache. I'm so sorry about Clay and your brothers. And sorry I wasn't there to be a comfort to you."

Mahala nodded, but she thought, *but Jack was there. And that was just how it was meant to be.* She pulled back as something dawned on her. "You actually left the hotel!"

"Yes, but not entirely untended. That is, I left it under Leon's care."

"*Leon?*"

Martha nodded. Her face looked troubled. Mahala encouraged her to sit in the other chair in the room. When they were both settled by the fire and Martha had drawn off her bonnet, Mahala said, "Do tell me."

"Well, he's home with a medical discharge. He, too, was wounded in the fighting and actually had to have his arm amputated. I wasn't going to have him come back to work, but he was very aggressive about doing so. He kept telling me he can still help at the hotel and that he must have a job or he's useless. He rather frightened me, he was so insistent. He seemed, well, almost unbalanced. There's an anger in him I haven't seen since his youth. But then, when I needed to come here, having him return to duty seemed the obvious answer ..."

"Of course," Mahala agreed, but she felt concerned about what her grandmother had said. The old Leon had been difficult enough to deal with. Living with a man in the throes of bitterness and self-pity – emotions he had already possessed, but which would now be many times magnified – seemed a recipe for misery. But she put on a smile. "I'm glad you came. And don't worry. We have to remember the future is no longer bleak. When I marry Jack, many things will change for the better. Knowing that should make Leon a little less imperious. And maybe, in the meantime, he will find his peace."

CHAPTER FOURTEEN

April 9, 1865
Near Appomattox Courthouse, Virginia

he men of the 8th Georgia had known something was wrong some days ago, when they were ordered to pull out of the trenches they had occupied for so long and withdraw west, through Richmond. Weeping citizens had lined the streets. It was then they had learned that Lee had been dealt a serious blow south of the James River.

They had marched on empty, burning stomachs for several days, speculating about joining up with Joe Johnston's army. At Farmville two days prior their regiment had been ordered to charge to protect the army's rear. Of course they had gone into action as gallantly and effectively as ever. Then, more marching. Dylan had been told the hungry men would be fed at Appomattox Courthouse. After that, he expected they would receive orders. Though dazed with hunger and weariness, many still believed they could still tear victory from the talons of defeat.

These were the die-hards, those who refused to give up. Great numbers of others had slunk away in the night to the enemy's camp, seeking a course of action that would best ensure a quicker reunion with their loved ones at home. With the enemy occupying their towns, the ideal of fighting to defend hearth and home had vanished. Many now simply thought of preservation. But these, the stalwart, tattered remains of a once-grand army, would soldier on to the bitter end.

Dylan had never thought he would be among them – he, and not Dev. Yet here he was. And he had forgotten so many things – how it felt to be clean and full, to sleep through the whole night without being jarred awake by a bugle, to think beyond survival. He'd seen death so much that, though he'd never welcome it, he'd almost even forgotten how to fear it. But he had learned many things, too – mostly about himself. Not much rattled him anymore. He had the respect of the men. He had honor. And for now that had to be enough.

As they marched Dylan heard a cheer swelling among the ranks and turned to see none other than Robert E. Lee mounted on Traveler. In his dress uniform, he galloped toward the front – toward where they'd been hearing sporadic fire. Dylan frowned, unable to shake a feeling of foreboding.

Orders came down to fall out. Some of the men got hold of parched corn and sat crunching on it. Dylan was no longer hungry. He reclined on a bank to rest. Like his men, he was on foot. For a while he'd had a horse captured from the Yankees, but it had been shot out from under him. Now his boots, too, like his men's, were in tatters, and there were blisters on his feet.

Dylan looked around, and his heart sank as it always did when he surveyed what was left of their army. Most of the soldiers were barefoot, their blackened and swollen feet wrapped in rags. They were emaciated. Their tattered gray uniforms blended hauntingly with the color of their skin. For weeks they'd been reduced to foraging for roots and berries. Sometimes men lost their sanity over hunger. Even now, the most stalwart often wore the blank expression of the starved and sleep-deprived, the hopeless. They were an army of phantoms.

Suddenly he caught sight of Colonel Towers. He was talking to John Reed, captain of Company I, and from his demeanor Dylan could tell he was weeping. A moment later, Dylan's shocked gaze shifted to a Federal officer galloping by, carrying a white flag. Realization was dawning on all the men as it dawned on Dylan.

"Surrender."

The word spread like a wildfire, followed swiftly by a rising sound: that of thousands of men weeping, sobbing and wailing. Dylan had never heard or imagined such a sound in all his life. But he felt its reverberations in his own soul. It was over. All the bloodshed. All the suffering. They had lost.

But it wasn't over, he realized, even then. It was merely the beginning of a new era, a new type of suffering for the South. Nothing would ever be the same again.

Four days later, they were the last of Lee's divisions to stack their arms and receive their paroles. The 8th Georgia Regiment ceased to exist. Lieutenant Colonel Magruder hid the regimental flag on his person and wore it back to Rome. And Dylan started the journey back to Brightwell, where he knew he would find his mother ... and his brother's widow.

When Mahala told Carolyn the news of the surrender, Carolyn stood frozen in her faded work dress for a full minute, staring blankly in disbelief. Her son sat at her feet, tracking the slow course of a caterpillar across the porch of Forests of Green.

Finally she said, "Then he died for nothing."

Scooping up Dev Jr. just before he could squish the insect between his chubby fingers, she turned and went into the house.

Mahala stood there holding Gina's reins, having just ridden out from Clarkesville to relay the news. She had also meant to tell Carolyn that President Lincoln had been shot and had died. She stared at the closed front door, knowing Carolyn had not meant to be rude. She was in shock, and needed time alone for the awful truth to find its place of acceptance in her brain. Mahala knew her well enough to be pitying instead of slighted. She merely remounted and rode back toward home.

Along the way, she noted that a "for sale" sign had been placed at the driveway of The Highlands. How she wished they had the money to buy the old place. But that was a foolish dream. For the same ill fortune that had forced the Clarke family to let it go now plagued the Franklins. Through the winter and early spring, their hotel had still been full of refugees from the coast, but most of the guests had paid in now-worthless Confederate bills, or in jewelry, which might one day be traded at a profit, but no time soon. The market was too bad. The hotel was showing the wear and tear of several years of heavy use without proper maintenance. There was simply no money or manpower for replacement of frayed and broken furnishings and peeling paint. The limited assets they had possessed had quickly dwindled in an effort to keep their guests fed. And now, with word of the surrender, Mahala had little doubt the people would soon begin to leave. Once they felt the area clear enough of Yankees to travel, they would return home and salvage what they could of their lives.

Despite her engagement and the future abundance it promised, the situation at The Franklin Hotel bothered Mahala. She didn't want it said that Jack Randall's money would rescue her family and their business from bankruptcy. She was sure people would think it, sure Sunny Randall already was.

As soon as Mahala had gotten settled at home back in January, Sunny and Sylvie had called upon her. Smelling of faint floral perfume, Sunny had embraced and kissed her and spoken perfect, polished words congratulating Mahala on her engagement. Now that the ring was on Mahala's finger, not an ill word would pass Mrs. Randall's lips. But Mahala doubted Sunny would ever seek out or approve of her society.

Sylvie, however, was quite another matter. Eager to plan the wedding, the young woman visited frequently, although Mahala insisted it must be put off until Jack's return. No one knew when that would be. No one had heard from him. As winter turned to spring, Mahala's uneasiness and impatience grew. She had loved Clay, and had worried over him during his absence. But not like this. Oh, not like this.

Sometimes, when anxiety would swell to choking, heart-stopping proportions, Mahala would stop in the midst of what she was doing, clutch the ruby and diamond ring in her palm, and say a prayer for the safe return of the man she loved. That would help just enough for her to be able to continue about her tasks.

Mahala could have predicted the reaction her engagement had upon Sunny and Sylvie. Not so where Leon was concerned. The disdain her father's cousin had long exhibited toward her had thawed to friendliness. He actually seemed happy for her. This was so contrary to his personality that Mahala kept her guard up. He wanted something, she knew it. It didn't take long to find out what.

One afternoon as she was watering the kitchen garden his lopsided shadow loomed across her.

"I've been thinking, Mahala," he said, after a few preliminary comments about the weather and the plants, "that maybe you could speak to your grandmother about the future."

"What about the future?"

"Well, I imagine once your fiancé returns you won't be around here much. You'll probably take a long honeymoon, spend some time in Savannah–" he laughed, a stiff, unnatural sound, as if he were about to choke on the forced geniality – "and even when you do come back, I reckon you'll buy a house of your own. And of course, he does own The Palace Hotel."

"That's the one fact we know. To assume anything beyond that – even his return – is a bit premature."

Leon frowned. "Well, assuming he will come home safely, don't you think it would be wise to prepare Aunt Martha for some changes? Talk to her about what the future might hold? Who will help her run the hotel when you're gone?"

"If all you say does happen, we can hire more help."

That was not the response Leon was looking for. "Who knows this place better than I do? I should be guaranteed a future here! And yet you speak of hiring help."

Mahala stood up straight, her watering can empty. She looked her cousin in the eye. "I did not mean to imply anything about your future here. You've served the hotel well for many years. I'm sure my grandmother will take that into account when she makes her decisions. Those decisions will be hers, not mine. If you have ideas about your future here, it is she with whom you should speak."

So saying, Mahala walked past Leon into the hotel. She felt his anger like a separate entity, eating into her back.

That night, as Mahala headed to bed, she heard the voices of her cousin and grandmother in the office. She was too tired to be tempted to eavesdrop. But before she could drift off to sleep, snug under her quilt, Martha knocked and slipped into her room.

Placing a hand on her shoulder, the older woman murmured, "Mahala, you should know that Leon has asked me to pass the hotel to him in my will in the event that you wed Jack Randall. He said you'll want for nothing as Jack's wife, whereas he has nothing, and has earned his place here. Even though he spoke the truth, I have refused."

Mahala turned over and stared at Martha's face.

"I cannot bring myself to leave to him what I always intended for you," she continued. "Somehow, I don't trust him. You are my flesh and blood, and you also have labored beside me when my children have pursued their own lives. This hotel is your rightful inheritance – and it's precious little when set beside Randall's vast wealth. I won't have you going to him empty-handed. A woman should always have something to call her own."

"Oh, grandmother," Mahala sighed, feeling gratitude, and something else – fear – well up inside her. "Leon was very angry."

Martha nodded. She sighed. "Yes. Very. I think he would have left – and that would have been a good thing – but perhaps foolishly I took pity on him. He's like a bad taste in my mouth, but I could not be so harsh as to just – well, spit him out. In honor of his loyal years of service and our family tie I *did* guarantee him the management of the place, so long as he continued to do a good job."

Leon would have seen the gesture as little more than a bone being thrown to a dog. "Was he too angry to accept your offer?" she asked hopefully.

"I believe he's staying for now. I've never known a man to evoke such pity and such mistrust at the same time."

"He is a mystery," Mahala agreed, "and unfortunately, one we cannot be easily rid of."

The next Thursday, May 4, Mahala stood in her bedroom, staring down at a stunning emerald brooch which rested in the palm of her hand. She placed it back into its velvet bag and headed for the kitchen. There the back door was open to the bright coolness of a mountain spring early morning, and the air hung with the tang of woodsmoke from Maddie's hearth fire and the tempting scent of fresh biscuits which she was removing from a pan.

"Looky there – bottoms nigh unto burnt!" declared the old woman as she turned the bread over for inspection.

"Maddie, I want you to take this," Mahala stated. She held out the little pouch.

Maddie turned to look at her. With a frown, she dumped the brooch onto her gnarled hand. Its brilliance in no way altered her expression. She might as well have been looking at a lump of coal. "What you 'xpecting me to do with it?"

"I know you probably can't find a buyer now, but keep it. In a few months, maybe, you can pawn it for a decent amount of greenbacks. It's the best thing I have to pay you with."

"Pay me?"

"Yes, pay you. You're free, remember?"

Maddie began to chuckle. "Oh, yes. I lak to forget. Nothin's changed so it don't seem real."

"Do you want things to change? Do you want to – leave?"

"Good grief, honey, no. Where'd I go at my age? But I think I keep dis. It will be my freedom brooch. Every time I see it, I remember, I'm free." With a smile Maddie pinned the piece of jewelry on her old work dress. "How it look?"

Mahala laughed. "Stunning."

She reached for the biscuits and put them on waiting plates, beside the grits and gravy Maddie had already ladled out. As she did, she bit into a biscuit herself. She was long accustomed to sneaking her own meals in between serving everyone else's.

Mahala was in the dining room handing blueberry preserves to an elderly man from Beaufort when an adolescent boy burst through the front door. He yelled, "The Yankees are coming! Yankee cavalry!"

A young woman known to have a delicate constitution was standing just behind him. She promptly fainted. Mahala's eyes swung to Leon's. He hurried over to the prostrate patroness.

"Are you sure?" Mahala demanded of the boy. She had to speak above the rising swell of panicked voices in the half-filled room. They were all saying, "Yankees! In Clarkesville! What can they want?"

"Yes'm. A worker from The Palace done seen them comin' up the road from Hollingsworth. He rode out ahead of them. Excuse me – I have to spread the word."

So saying, the news bearer dashed out the door. People were beginning to run from the room. Martha had come out of their private quarters. Mahala hurried over to her and asked, "What should we do?"

The lady at her feet took that minute to partially revive. But spying Leon bent over her, she passed out again.

"Give her to me," Martha said. "I have some smelling salts. Leon, go get a gun. Mahala, hide our silver and jewelry. The compost heap out back will be the quickest place to dig."

Mahala was looking at Leon as her grandmother spoke. Something unexpected – was it alarm? – flashed across his face. She frowned in confusion, but she didn't have time to analyze it. She did as her grandmother bid her, taking a sheet and wrapping their most valuable possessions inside it. Hands shaking, she removed Jack's ring and hung it on the watch chain around her neck, then tucked the necklace inside her bodice.

Mahala ran to the stable for a shovel and took it to the compost heap. She used it to toss aside yesterday's scraps, then she began to dig right under where they had lain. Her grandmother was correct. The ground here was soft, and her efforts could be easily concealed. She was able to create a fairly large, deep hole in a fraction of the time it would have taken elsewhere.

On her last shovelful, something round and hard flew through the air with the lumps of red clay. Mahala bent over and picked it up. She brushed the dirt aside and held up the object to examine it. Despite its clay-coated and tarnished appearance, it seemed to be silver. A piece of jewelry? Part of a serving set?

On impulse, Mahala stuck the object in her apron pocket and lowered the knotted sheet into the hole. She hurried to refill the cavity and liberally scatter scraps over the top. Then, with the shovel wiped clean and stashed back in the barn, she went inside to wash all evidence of clay from around her fingernails, her heart beating a tattoo rhythm all the time.

Maybe the Yankees would just pass through.

The inn was quiet. The guests had retreated to their rooms behind locked doors. Leon sat on the front porch with a revolver in his pocket and his tattered Confederate kepi defiantly on his head. Mahala and Martha peered out the window as the front of a two-by-two column of mounted, blue-clad soldiers trotted into what almost appeared to be a deserted town. At the sight of the Union troops, Martha reached for Mahala's hand.

The soldiers halted around the courthouse and dismounted, leaving a few men to guard the horses. They split into several groups and headed for various points around the square. Mahala realized what they were seeking.

"Breakfast. They're coming to the inns for breakfast."

"And hopefully that's all," Martha whispered in response.

A lieutenant – Mahala knew that was his rank from her memory of Dylan Rousseau's uniform – led one group of men onto their front porch. He slapped his gloves into the palm of one hand and addressed Leon, who remained sitting by the front door.

"Are you the owner of this establishment?"

"I am."

Martha and Mahala exchanged glances.

"My men need refreshment. You will see that your staff provides us with breakfast."

"Hell will freeze over before I serve a bluecoat anything except a belly full of lead."

A brown-bearded, stocky man to the lieutenant's right leapt forward and grabbed Leon by the throat. At the same moment, Martha sprang into action. She opened the door and said as naturally as if she were greeting a bunch of church ladies calling for tea, "Gentlemen, do come in. *I* am the owner of this hotel. Please forgive my nephew. You'll understand the recent hostilities … have unsettled his mind." She cast a meaningful glance at Leon's empty sleeve.

Mahala had never admired her grandmother's smooth control more. She didn't know whether to quake at the idea of Yankees entering the inn or laugh at the sight of Leon dangling like a scrawny chicken in his enemy's gauntleted grasp.

Giving Martha a silent once-over, the lieutenant nodded curtly to the soldier who had Leon by the gullet. "That'll do, Sergeant Wilson."

Wilson obliged, but Mahala heard him growl in Leon's ear, "Disrespect the lieutenant again, and I'll shoot your other arm off."

The door opened wide to admit the flow of soldiers, revealing a Leon red-faced with repressed fury and hatred. At last, an adversary he despised more than Mahala. The men grinned at the sight of her standing just inside the foyer. The lieutenant paused in the door of the dining room and surveyed tables still set with half-eaten plates of food. He smiled as if amused. Then he turned to her.

"Think we could get this cleaned up, and some fresh food out to my men?"

Mahala pressed her lips together and gave a nod. She set about the task, and her grandmother joined her.

"Just try to act as though everything is normal," Martha whispered to her as they passed in the kitchen.

But that was impossible. As she moved among the tables of men clad in blue uniforms that stank of horse, dust and sweat, feeling their eyes on her, she thought of Clay, Devereaux, Sam and Seth, and she felt nauseous. These men were probably among the same ones who had fought against her brothers and Clay this time last year. And now here she was setting Maddie's biscuits and gravy before them.

The officer in charge, she had to admit, was well-mannered. The men ate and talked in moderated tones while he was present. But as soon as he stepped out back, presumably to use the facilities – and hopefully not to do any snooping around, Mahala thought with a shudder – the soldiers instantly became more demanding.

"We're still hungry," one of them declared. "Bring more food."

"I'm sorry, that's all we have," Martha replied calmly. "You have already consumed all the breakfast intended for our guests."

"We'll just see about that," another man said. He jumped up and barged into the kitchen. Mahala froze when she heard Maddie cry out in indignation. The soldier reappeared in the dining room, holding up the emerald brooch clasped in his hand. "Looky here, Sergeant. What's a piece of jewelry like this doing on a slave?"

"Ex-slave," Mahala spoke up. "Or had you forgotten you've been fighting to free them? I gave her that brooch. Give it back!" She started forward, forgetting in her anger to be afraid, but a hand reached out and grabbed her skirt. She was pulled backward onto the lap of a leering private.

"You're a pretty thing," he said into her face as she struggled to rise. "What are you, Indian?"

"Get your hands off my granddaughter!" Martha demanded, as Leon appeared in the doorway to see what the ruckus was about.

The sergeant was paying no attention to the soldier's attempts to grope Mahala. His eyes were on the glittering brooch. "Perhaps there's more where that came from," he said. "Perhaps we should search the rooms of the rich refugees upstairs and find out."

There were cheers of approval. Mahala fought to free herself from the octopus-like clutches of her captor, whose hot, sour breath panted across her face and neck. Then she heard a click behind her. Both she and the soldier froze as Leon's voice said, "Let her go."

It was clear that Leon needed no further excuse to avenge his insult with injury. Instant obedience met his demand. Trembling with indignation, Mahala scrambled to her feet and hurried toward the kitchen, wanting only to be out of sight of the soldiers. But she collided squarely into the chest of the polished Yankee lieutenant, who set her away from him almost gently, regarded her, and then took in the boisterous scene in the dining room.

"*Atten-tion!*"

As the sharp command rang out, every man in blue leapt to his feet and held a ramrod posture. The lieutenant walked out among them.

"Regardless of what you may hear of other commands, or what grievances you think you need to repay upon these people, *my* men will act with discipline and honor. There will be no manhandling, no mayhem, no stealing of civilian property. Is that understood?"

Of course complete silence was his answer. Mahala ventured forward a step. Timidly she said, "Lieutenant? One of your men took a brooch from our servant. Will you please have him return it?"

The officer's eyes fell upon the offender, guiltily clutching the piece of jewelry under the barrel of Leon's revolver. "He will do so immediately and with grave apologies, Ma'am."

"Thank you," Mahala replied as the brooch was placed in her hand.

"Take that gun from that man," the lieutenant brusquely told his men. "And tie his hands – er, hand. Tie him to something!"

The soldiers were all too eager to oblige. Not wanting to witness Leon's further indignity, Mahala hurried into the kitchen, to Maddie's waiting arms.

"You all right, Miss Mahaley?"

"Yes, Maddie. Thank God that lieutenant is a gentleman, or I don't know what would have happened," Mahala whispered.

"Seem to me Mist' Leon woulda blown that man's brains out."

"Yes, maybe." Mahala still had trouble believing her cousin had come to her rescue. "But he would have probably been killed himself for doing it. And there might have been more violence if those men had gone upstairs. The Lord protected us just now. Here, do you want to put your brooch back on?"

Maddie chuckled as they heard the soldiers receive orders to convene at the courthouse. The sound of marching boots filled the hotel. Mahala sagged with relief as Maddie said, "I think for now I just put it in a safe place." She turned as her husband appeared in the back door and embraced her.

"You o.k., Maddie?"

"Yes, Zed."

"I thought I needed to watch that Yankeeman while he in the back yard. Turn out I needed to be here with you."

"Oh, that reminds me," Mahala said aloud and put her hand in her apron pocket. A shiver of fear passed over her as she realized she had forgotten the round object she had dug up. If it had fallen out while that soldier tried to hold her, the Yankees would have known she'd buried their valuables in the back yard, and the decent lieutenant might not have been able to stand in the way of his men's greedy determination.

Martha entered, saying, "They're gone. They're all on the square." She hugged Mahala. "That was a close call. Zed, can you please go help release Leon? The lieutenant told us to keep him tied until they rode away. What's this?" She paused as she saw the tarnished object Mahala held out to her.

216

"I'm hoping you might know. I found it while I was digging in the compost heap."

"It looks like the front part of a pocket watch," Martha commented, turning it over. Her face paled as her thumb ran over a tiny curved protrusion. "Your father's watch had a special latch just like this."

Silence reigned over the little assembly as all of them focused on the unearthed piece of the past.

"But who would have put it in the compost heap?" asked Mahala.

Martha's eyes rose to meet hers. "Someone close to him," she whispered. "Close to *us*."

Mahala's mind struggled to take in the implications of this discovery, accepting and rejecting possibilities as quick as lightning. "Are – are there initials still there?"

Martha held out the item. "Not visible now, but maybe if I cleaned it with silver cleaner ..."

At that moment Zed and Leon appeared in the doorway. Leon looked more furious than ever. "I hope you're all happy," he declared. "I sure stuck my neck out for you – and almost got it wrung. And I could have been killed standing up for *you*, Mahala. Maybe now you'll both realize what you owe me – what you've always owed me!"

"I think you owe *us*, Leon. An explanation," Martha said.

Mahala's gaze swung between the two as her mind scurried to catch up. She stepped aside so that her cousin could see the object Martha held. She thought she detected a flash of recognition – and panic – before the well-trained façade returned to place. Then she wondered if she had been so eager to see it that she had imagined it.

"You know what this is, don't you, Leon?" Martha asked, her voice shaking a little. Mahala saw that her hand on the work table trembled, too.

"A lid? An – instrument of some sort?" he guessed aloud. "How should I know? It looks like it was just dug out of the earth!"

"It was. In the compost heap. Here. Hold it. Examine it. And tell me what you think it is." Martha shoved the object into his face. Leon did appear unsettled then. Mahala thought they could have cut the tension in the room with a knife.

"It looks ... like a pocket watch cover," Leon said finally.

"Where have you seen one with a latch like that before?"

"Uh – not for some time."

"Not since Michael's."

"What are you saying?"

"Do you think this could be Michael's?"

"What? No! What are you implying? You think someone killed him and buried this in the compost heap?"

Mahala's stomach lurched at the words spoken aloud. It was ludicrous, truly ludicrous. Her grandmother was getting ahead of herself. The stress of the day had unhinged her.

"It was the part with his initials," Martha said, her voice no longer calm. "The part that couldn't be sold, couldn't be seen."

"Grandmother, please," Mahala said, taking Martha's arm.

"Get me the silver cleaner, Maddie!"

As the black woman ran off to do her bidding, Leon exploded, "All I've done for you, and this is what I get? Questions? Accusations? Have you lost your mind? I was almost killed for you today, and you think I could have killed your son, your precious son?"

"She didn't say that, Leon," Mahala cut in. There was no way, absolutely no way, that Leon's thin, bird-like face had been the last sight her father had ever seen.

"No, but that's what she means, what she's thinking behind that proper little face. I could never be good enough, could I? But all *you* had to do – all you ever had to do–" he turned a gaze full of hate on Mahala – "was be his daughter."

Leon whirled and stalked off.

"Grandmother," Mahala said, shaken by the family drama unexpectedly unfolding, "this really could be anyone's."

"In *our* compost heap?"

"You should sit down."

"You should call the sheriff. Now."

"Grandmother … *Leon*?"

"I'm not crazy! I know it in my gut. I saw it in his eyes. Think about it, Mahala. It all makes sense. Give me that," Martha cried as Maddie appeared with a small gray-smudged tub of the special cleaner. She grabbed a cloth, dipped it in the solution, laid the lid down on the work table, and began rubbing. Her motions were gentle but quick, her expression like a woman possessed. Mahala felt sick to her stomach, wondering if Martha could be right, if the bare truth were about to be revealed at long last, with the initials, as the grime of the years was rubbed away. She exchanged glances with Maddie and Zed.

"It's been over twenty-five years," Mahala said. "Nothing is going to show up."

"Even if it doesn't, I know what I know," Martha responded. "And the sheriff should question Leon."

"She's right," Maddie declared. "It sure look suspicious."

Mahala sighed, not wanting to believe it – not wanting to think that they could all have been so blind. Leon had certainly seemed genuinely offended by their suspicion. But then, he would be a consummate actor, wouldn't he – if he *were* guilty? He would have been acting for decades.

"All right," she agreed. "As soon as the Yankees are clear of the area Zed can go for the sheriff."

Fifteen minutes later, the metal disc was still dingy, but they watched Martha's finger trace the faintest of outlines, of the double hump of an "M." Martha sat down and began to weep.

"Oh, Michael, Michael," she cried. "It's been under our noses for all these years."

"This still doesn't prove it was Leon," Mahala said quietly. She placed a gentle hand on her grandmother's shoulder. "You have to admit it's very circumstantial evidence. Someone could argue my father himself lost the lid."

"Why are you defending him?" Martha exclaimed, shrugging her hand away.

"I'm not – I'm just trying to look at it logically, as the law officers will. I know Leon wanted the hotel to be left to him, but enough to kill my father?"

"You have no idea how much he detested the idea of Michael's marriage to your mother. I never told you this, but he felt it was responsible for his break-up with the judge's daughter. She was very high in her own opinion, above marrying into a family mixed with Cherokees," Martha said. Her eyes swung to Mahala's. "And if his envy and hate were really that strong, you could be in danger, too, Mahala."

Mahala shook her head. "He'll know he's showed his hand. There's no way you'd leave him the hotel now. But why, if he killed Michael, did he not … try to kill me all these years?" The words were hard to get out. "Removing me would have almost ensured he'd inherit."

"I don't know the answer to that. Maybe he has a spark of humanity and would stop before killing a young woman. More likely, he thought he'd find another way around you. Oh, Mahala, I can't stop shaking. I can't believe after all these years, we might have an answer."

But when Zed arrived with the sheriff, they knew from the faces of the men that something was wrong.

"He's gone," the sheriff told them. "A few personal items and a valise are missing, and one of the horses from the livery. I will conduct a search, but whether it was guilt or anger that sent him packing, I doubt we'll ever see Leon Franklin again."

That night Mahala sat on her bed with the oil lamp turned up high. It had been a physically and emotionally exhausting day. Just after dinner, the sheriff had stopped in to report that no one about town seemed to have noticed Leon riding out. The presence of Yankee cavalry had been the ideal distraction from his flight.

Martha was beside herself with anger and self-recrimination. She had gone to bed with one of Maddie's toddies, but Mahala knew that her own mind was too overwhelmed to settle into sleep's numbness, even with herbal intervention. Questions had battered themselves back and forth inside her head all day, chief among them the mystery of where her father could have hidden his gold ... assuming all this was true. That must have plagued Leon like salt on a wound. If he had found gold in the cabin the night he killed his cousin, he would have absconded with it. And if he had found a clue years later in the strong box – that time she had found its contents strewn on her bedroom floor, when Leon must have made an excuse to his customers to dash off to her room and go through the box – the same thing would have held true.

Now, she held the box in her lap. She didn't harbor much hope that she could now solve the mystery where Leon, over the course of many years, had failed, but she opened the latch. Henry had always told her he figured $5,750 in gold was unaccounted for. She carefully went over the receipts in Michael's faded handwriting. They seemed to verify her grandfather's figure.

Then, for the hundredth time, she reread the note Michael had left: "'Receipts from the Dahlonega mint, stamp mill and Aurarian bank, with payments shown to Rex Clarke, Clarkesville, whose signature shall bear witness along with these papers that one-fourth proceeds were delivered to him. Should the spring of our friendship dry up and hope for future partnership be buried, honesty will at least be proved and my assets found to be in order.'"

Mahala frowned. She had always agreed with Henry: the style of the letter was strange. Stiff. But if her father had been trying to tell them something, realizing his partnership had gone sour and wanting to leave a record to his family in case he came to an untimely end, what was it? If there was some sort of secret code, where was the key?

Mahala noted heavy blotches on certain words. She looked more closely. Yes! Some were much darker than the rest, as though her father had gone over them twice. "Clarke," "spring," and "buried."

Her heart began to beat rapidly. She told herself she was on a wild goose chase. But she felt around under the bed for her slippers and shoved her feet into them. She didn't want to disturb her grandmother, but there was someone else who might be able to answer her questions.

Mahala knew she'd find Zed still in the barn, bedding down the horses. She saw his lantern swinging at the far end and ran toward him.

"Miss Mahaley! What's the matter now?" he asked, his grizzled old face concerned in the yellow light.

"I need you to think back, Zed, think way, way back, to the last time you saw my father – the last visit he made to town."

Zed scratched his head and rolled his eyes back. "That be a long time ago, Miss Mahaley. Eighteen and thirty-eight, I guess."

"Yes. About this time of year. He came to town, and grandmother always said how upset she later was that their last meeting went so badly. Grandfather told him he would not recognize my mother – or me – as part of the family. Father bought the farm from Simon Grant on that trip to town. Do you remember if he went anywhere else?"

"Not as I can reckon. He did stay at The Habersham House after his daddy done hurt him so bad."

"Did you happen to notice, that last time you saw him, if Leon left *our* hotel about the same time Father went back to the valley?"

"Naw, Miss Mahaley, Mist' Leon stayed with his family then jus' lak he always done. He never did miss any time at work, though. If he followed yo' daddy home that night I don't know about it."

"And – the time before that? Did Father make any special visits to anyone when he was here?"

Zed sighed. "Miss Mahaley, I jus' don't know. What do it matter?"

"Maybe a great deal," Mahala said impatiently. "Please, Zed. Try to think."

"Well, there was one time Mr. Michael come in from the valley when Mist' Charles and Miz Martha was gone to Athens. That sorry old Leon had run of the place. He was stayin' here while they was gone, just lak Mist' Rex Clarke wuz. Mist' Clarke was rentin' out rooms while his house was bein' built."

"Oh," said Mahala with some disappointment. "Mr. Clarke was living *here*."

"Yes, but they did ride out to The Highlands, that I remember. Mist' Clarke wanted to show it to yo' daddy. He always was one for braggin'. I saddled up yo' grandaddy's horse fo' yo' daddy to ride. I remember 'cuz I wondered why he'd go anywheres with that no account Mist' Clarke."

Mahala's eyes widened. "They went to The Highlands? You're sure?"

"Yep. An' there was somethin' funny. Mist' Michael, he went somewheres else, too, in the dead of night. I heard him ride out real late like. I figured he wuz just upset."

Mahala grabbed Zed's arm. "And you never asked him where?" she gasped.

"Well, no, Miss Mahaley, that weren't my business now, was it?"

"Thank you, Zed," Mahala said, and kissed the wrinkled cheek.

Morning could not come fast enough.

CHAPTER FIFTEEN

he didn't want to tell anyone in case she was wrong, in case they would laugh at her and insist she abandon her flights of fancy. But it was worth checking out, wasn't it? Where was the harm in that? Mahala reasoned to herself as she urged Unagina up Tallulah Road at dawn.

It was going to be a beautiful day. The wildflowers and the fresh leaves on the trees were opening to the spring sun, and birds tweetered from branches overhanging the road. Everything around her vibrated with new life. She felt it in her bones, in her very marrow, that it was time for her new life to begin, too. But first, how appropriate it would be if she could finally solve the mystery of the past.

When she turned into The Highlands drive, she almost stopped. She had to look twice to make sure the "For Sale" sign was really gone. Had someone purchased the property, or had the Clarkes changed their minds about selling?

All the more reason to hurry. No telling when someone might take up residence.

Well, and there was also the fact that her grandmother would be worked up into a high shine when she found Mahala's note – "Had an errand to run up toward Carolyn's place. Be back soon. Mahala." – and realized she wouldn't be around to help with the breakfast rush. Some things just couldn't wait any more. She would have had a fit herself if she'd had to serve all those people biscuits and gravy while her future hung in the balance.

The house came into view, and it seemed the past rushed at Mahala full speed. She could almost imagine her father riding up this very drive with Rex Clarke, scaffolding surrounding the façade and hammers ringing. Michael hadn't liked banks, and they had been scarce enough anyway in 1838. His father had rejected him. Folks knew he kept a load of cash and gold at his cabin. For his family's safety, and the preservation of his earnings, he had to find a place to stash it – at least temporarily. He would bury it. And what better place, what least expected location, than right under his suspicious and demanding partner's nose?

It was a leap, but Mahala liked to think if anyone could figure out her father's mind, it was his daughter. Even though she had never met him. The notion made her feel she had made a connection beyond the decades, beyond the grave.

Her notion might be shattered in a matter of minutes.

She rode past the house right up to the little sloping roof of the spring house on the creek branch. "Clarke," "spring," and "buried." There were no natural springs anywhere nearby. She knew the outbuildings here pre-dated the house. It was worth a quick dig.

Mahala entered the tiny building, ducking to avoid hitting her head. The smell of damp earth filled her nose. If she were burying treasure, would she pick a corner or right in the middle?

The ground was softest near the paved trough where the tricklet of water ran through. Mahala positioned her shovel next to it, put her foot on it, and pushed down hard.

Jack closed his eyes briefly, trying to clear his vision. He just hadn't been able to bring himself to stop for the night, not when home was so close.

He smiled. He now knew where that was. It lay just up ahead, in the little town nestled in the Georgia foothills – at Mahala's side.

He urged his stallion on at a quicker pace, trying to picture their re-union. He wouldn't be early enough to wake her, but maybe she would just be emerging from the family quarters into the hotel, and she'd almost walk past him before she realized he was there. Or she might be already serving a guest breakfast. She'd look up, and those amazing blue eyes would open wide with joy and wonder. Knowing her, she'd drop whatever was in her hand all over the floor. Coffee. Jam. Gravy.

Jack laughed aloud. He'd be hard pressed not to kiss her on the spot.

And after that, after he had whisked her away some place private and hugged and kissed her almost to his heart's content, he would take her to The Palace, and they would dine with his stepmother and sister. He would see them all sitting down together over breakfast like a real family, and they would discuss the future.

Oh, what a bright future. Jack had all kinds of plans, and every one of them involved lavishing love and money on his new bride.

The town was stirring as Jack rode into Clarkesville. Shops were open-ing, a blacksmith's anvil rang, and people gathered on the hotel porches, taking in the mountain air with their coffee. He tethered his mount in front of The Franklin and took the steps in two long strides. Inside the foyer, he paused, looking around, his heart beating like a drum.

He was here. Really here. Where was she?

The door to the family quarters was closed. Mahala was not serving the early morning guests. But Martha was. She looked up and saw him, and an expression of what appeared to be concern melted into relief – and, low and behold – could it be? – joy. She rushed over to him. Jack took her hand, instantly alerted to her returning frown of distress.

"Captain Randall, I never thought I'd say this, but it's a real relief to see you."

"What's wrong?" Jack demanded. "Is it Mahala? Where is she?"

"Well, that's just it. I'm not quite sure *where* she is – or what she's up to."

Drawing him into the family parlor, Martha gave account of the amazing happenings of the day before – the Yankee troops, the discovery of the pocket watch lid, and Leon's disappearance on the heels of their accusations.

"This morning, Mahala left me this note. Yesterday she kept talking about her father's missing gold. Whatever she's doing, it probably has to do with that. But I'm worried about her. There have been too many trouble makers about lately for her to just strike off on her own like this."

Jack took the slip of paper Martha handed him. He read it and frowned. "'Up toward Carolyn's place,'" he murmured. Then: "I think I may have an idea where she is. Try not to worry, Mrs. Franklin. Everything will be fine. With any luck I'll have her back in time for lunch."

"I hope so, Captain Randall. And – I *am* glad to see you. Mahala will be, too. We've been – quite concerned for your safety."

Jack smiled. "Thank you," he said, knowing what the words cost the redoubtable widow.

Lifting his hat in a temporary farewell, he returned to the street and, not very happily, to the saddle.

Mahala surveyed the mess she had made, sighed, and paused to rub her aching shoulders. She had dug a whole strip along the trough with no sign of her father's buried gold. The only spot left undisturbed near where the water ran was right next to the wall. Wearily she shifted to that area and started digging again – much more slowly than before. She was having to use her left arm now, for her right ached at the spot of her old wound. She had healed well, but that arm was just a bit weaker than it had been.

By now she was wondering if she was going to have to dig up the whole spring house. But how deep should she dig? And was it all a waste of time? She was starting to feel very foolish.

Mahala thought she sensed a movement outside. She turned, telling herself it was probably just shadows cast by the new leaves swaying in the breeze. But she jumped as a solid form scampered into the springhouse.

"Oh!" Mahala cried, relieved that it was only the big orange cat she had seen on her last visit. "You scared me. Are you still here?"

The cat rubbed against her legs.

"Did something startle you?" She paused to go to the door and peer about. She saw nothing unusual.

The cat sat down and curled its tail about itself, watching her with luminous unblinking eyes. Wiping a trickle of sweat from her forehead, she jumped on top of the shovel again, forcing it down deep, deep.

Clunk.

Was it her imagination, or did she meet with solid resistance? Just a rock, no doubt.

But a little more quickly Mahala cast away the earth and dug again. Again the shovel pressed something solid. She used it to scrape side to side in the bottom of the pit. There was indeed something firm – and even!

Gasping, Mahala knelt, heedless of the red clay on her dress. Using the shovel and her hands, she cleared the dirt away until the top of a small chest came into view. Heart hammering, she dug some more along one side until she could free it. She lifted it upwards. It was heavy.

At last she sat back, the chest on the ground beside her. There was no lock. But then, if there had been, Michael would have put the key in the strong box, wouldn't he?

"Is this it, Father?" she asked aloud.

With shaking hands, feeling as if she were in a dream, she reached out and lifted the lid. She peered inside. Before her were a variety of canvas sacks. Mahala looked in each, hardly daring to breathe. Cash, gold bars and gold coins. A treasure. *Her* treasure.

Time seemed to stop with her heart.

Suddenly a large, lopsided shadow fell over her. Mahala looked up, the laughter of discovery freezing on her lips.

"I would think that a moment like this was meant to be shared with family," Leon said.

"Leon – I – I – thought–"

He laughed. "You thought I had run far, far away. Well, not yet, and lucky for me. Here I was, hiding in the old Clarke place, trying to decide where to go, and I look out and see none but my dear cousin. It's fate, don't you see? I searched the cabin from top to bottom that night, and I've looked everywhere I could think of since. I always knew it was hidden *somewhere*. And here on the eve of my untimely flight, you lead me right to it. Now, I have financing for the journey ahead. Thank you, dear cousin." Leon swept her a mocking bow.

"You – you did kill him, then," Mahala said in a strangled voice.

"I guess there's no harm in admitting it now. I'll soon be far away with Michael's gold. And you – well, you will be tied up here in the spring house – or dead. I haven't decided which yet."

Mahala leapt to her feet. Her only weapon was a shovel, but if she took him in a rush she could knock him down.

But as her hand tightened on the handle, Leon reached into his pocket. He pulled out a revolver – the same one he had used the day before to save her – and aimed it at her. Up to that point she had half believed he was bluffing. "Uh-uh-uh," he said, waving the barrel. "Drop it."

Mahala's wide eyes fixed on the small black hole. She knew all too well the power Leon now held over her. She let the shovel fall to the ground, causing the orange cat to scamper out of the building. As Leon's gaze darted after it, Mahala made an instinctive move, tensing to run, too, but her cousin immediately snapped his attention back to her, the arm that held the revolver firming.

"Don't move!"

She tried to reason with him. "I know you. You wouldn't really try to kill me."

Leon grinned, more of an evil grimace. "Wouldn't I?"

"All these years – you must have had many opportunities. And yet you didn't."

"No, not many opportunities. Before the war, you were guarded very closely by your dear grandmother. And that Fraser boy. And one does have to be subtle. I did try a couple of times to dispatch you, though, when occasion presented itself. A loose horse shoe and a snake here … a bit of special powder in your tea when you were oh-so-sad over your dear fiancé there … *but someone always interfered*!" The last words were shouted, making her quake all the way through to her bones. She had known Leon detested her for her mixed blood and her place at the hotel, but she'd never dreamed he would consider physically harming her.

Mahala's mind reeled, going back over what she had thought were merely coincidences so long ago. On the day she had visited the minister's wife and her horse had thrown a shoe after being frightened by a black snake, Zed had been blamed for not keeping the animal up to par.

"But if you placed the snake, you must have been–"

"Right ahead of you, yes," Leon finished for her, looking proud of himself. "Minutes after I loosened the shoes on the horse while you were visiting. Best case scenario, she would have thrown you. But you managed to evade that and Rex Clarke's attempted rape as well! That stupid friend of yours had to show up, just as she did to start hovering over your diet when all you would drink was Maddie's tea. You didn't wonder why I was so willing to bring you your tea, dear Mahala? If only you'd taken just a little more. I should have been less gradual, less careful."

Tears sprang to Mahala's eyes that someone would hate her that much. "You didn't – you couldn't ... but you're my cousin," she finished through numb lips.

"So was your father." Leon paused, his eyes darkening. "Of course, when I went to see him I only intended to talk him out of staying in the valley. I just wanted him to take his Indian squaw somewhere far, far away – maybe west – so the taint of it wouldn't ruin my own chances. Miss Sylvia and I – I know she would have married me – if only your father's mixed marriage wasn't right under her nose. I – loved her. She was my one chance to be happy. And your father – your stupid, stubborn father – he wouldn't listen!"

Rage flashed in Leon's eyes, and his lips parted in a snarl. He started toward her, the gun held out, backing her across the spring house. But as they went, Mahala thought she heard something that Leon didn't – horse hooves.

He was yelling, "He made me so mad! I wanted to beat him to a pulp! He always thought he was better – that he could do whatever he wanted to and let everyone else go to the devil. It was bad enough he turned up his nose at what he could have had – his own hotel and a respected place in town – but he had to drag me down with him, take away my one chance at happiness, I who already had *nothing*! "

"You got into a fight," Mahala said breathlessly, hands in the air. "Everyone will understand. It was an accident. All you have to do is tell the sheriff that. But if you kill me, Leon – if you kill me, you'll be a hunted man all your days!"

Leon stopped, his lip drawn back to show his yellowed teeth. A lank strand of graying hair fell across his sweat-beaded forehead. Momentarily the revolver in his hand trembled. Then an evil smile spread across his face.

"But it wasn't an accident," he said slowly, as if relishing each word. "I hated him. I knew exactly what I was doing. And I was glad when I killed him."

His last word was punctuated by a distinctive metallic click. At the same moment, like the bullet entering the chamber, the reality of the pure evil in front of her dropped into Mahala's mind. Evil that had maliciously ripped the fabric of her very life before she had even been born. A sheet of white-hot anger surged through her, anger that gave no heed to danger. With a growl of fury, she launched herself toward her father's killer, instinctively curling herself into a powerful lunge at his middrift, below the trajectory of the revolver. As she hit him, the weapon discharged above her with a deafening report. The revolver flew from Leon's hand as Mahala landed on top of him, punching, hitting, clawing and screaming in rage.

Leon fought back with surprising skill for a one-armed man, kicking, wrapping his legs around her to get leverage, and scratching her face.

"Mahala!" she heard a voice yell.

But the fact that someone else was there did not fully register until a large form appeared in the doorway and sprang toward the two bodies grappling in the dirt. She was lifted off her cousin. When Leon tried to rise to meet his new opponent, a solid fist connected squarely with his clay-streaked face, and he fell senseless to the ground only feet away from the chest containing Michael's gold.

Breathing heavily, Mahala turned wondering eyes upon her savior. Jack stood there staring back. With a cry she flung herself into his arms. She was enveloped in a mighty embrace and sobbed hysterically against his chest.

"He killed my father," she cried. "Leon killed–"

"I know."

"He – he loosened Gina's shoes and put a snake in the road the day Carolyn saved me from Rex."

"What? What! Slow down!" Jack pulled her head back so she could face him.

But Mahala was too overwhelmed to obey. "And when you left me before I was engaged to Clay and I was so sad, he said he was poisoning my tea. I was so sick. But Carolyn saved me again and made me go back to eating!"

"Oh, dear Lord, Mahala." He pressed her head again against his chest and held her tightly. "If what you say is true, it wasn't just Carolyn who saved you, but God." His breath came fast, and his fingers bit into her back as she could tell anger took the upper hand. "I want to finish him off myself, right now."

Mahala could never let him consider such a crime, not even for a minute. She wrapped her arms all the way around him, shaking her head. "Jack, remember what you just said. About God saving me. And He did it again today. This time He sent *you*. I'm fine. Even though … he could have killed me! He really could have killed me!" The reality of it caused her to start shaking again.

"I don't think so."

The dead pan way he said it hinted of repressed humor and was enough to cut off Mahala's tears. She drew back to look at him with indignation. Sure enough, he was pressing his lips into a flat line that not-so-nobly resisted a curve.

"I almost died and you stand there *laughing* about it!" Mahala cried.

"I'm sorry, but please remind me to never get into a fist fight with you."

Mahala released her breath in a half-laugh. She could not be mad at him. His was the face she had been longing to see for five months, and he was actually here. She was overwhelmed with confused emotions. Her chin wobbled. "He had a gun," she pointed out petulantly.

"I know." He glanced around, and seeing the weapon lying on the ground, bent to pick it up. He tucked it into his own gun belt. He looked at her and swiped her cheek with his thumb. It came away red with her smeared blood. "Come here," he said, and he crushed her to him again. She trembled in his arms.

"Thank God you're all right, Mahala. Can I never find you just waiting peacefully at home?" he asked in a voice rough with emotion.

"Remember, there's no such thing as a Cherokee princess," Mahala quipped, before Jack sealed her lips with his.

Leon hung upside down across Mahala's mare. He began to revive as they were tying him in place. Protesting vehemently, he attempted to right himself by using his one arm.

"Let me up!" he cried. "Let me up!"

Jack, who was securing the sacks of gold in the saddlebags of his stallion, looked up from his efforts. "Shut up."

Leon continued to thrash about. "You can't take me this way all the way to Clarkesville!"

"Watch me."

"I'll pass out. I'll die of all the blood to my head!"

Mahala watched wide-eyed as Jack drew his pistol and walked calmly around the horse. Leon saw him coming and reared back in wild fear, sniveling and putting up a hand.

"Jack!" Mahala exclaimed.

But her intended merely brought the butt of the revolver down hard on Leon's temple, and the guilty man again sagged senseless.

"Just because I made a joke about your superior fighting skills doesn't mean I don't understand your feelings," Jack told her, walking away from his captive. "I have no pity for that man. He took your father away, he tried to kill you, and I'll see him tried and hanged for it."

Tears filled Mahala's eyes. "This *has* been a big ordeal. I still can't believe everything that's happened."

Jack came and put an arm around her. "You're not alone anymore. I love you, Mahala."

"Oh, Jack, I love *you* – so much!" she exclaimed, nestling closer.

He kissed the tears that spilled out of her eyes and held her until she again mastered her emotions.

"How did you get here, anyway?" she asked finally.

"Galveston," Jack told her, moving away to buckle his saddlebags. "The last port open before the Confederacy fell. And you don't even want to know the adventures I've endured between there and here."

"Oh, yes, I do," Mahala declared, brightening.

Jack laughed and affectionately tipped her nose. "One day, maybe. When you're bored and languid. You've had enough adventure for this week. The first thing to do is to deliver this murdering scum to jail and you to the bathtub. I might find you appealing looking like the pirate wench of my dreams, but I doubt my sister and stepmother would share my feelings."

She glared at him. "I might need a little recovery time before my next battle, if you don't mind."

He grinned. "Fair enough. Well, it's a long way, but I'm afraid we'll need to walk most of it. This horse passed his prime at the Alabama border, and the gold we put in his saddlebags is more of a load than I was."

"That's all right," Mahala said, joy suddenly swelling within her. She took Unagina's reins and reached for Jack's hand. She gave it a tug, and they started away from the house. "I have you with me, and we have a lot to talk about. The first thing being, do you realize I'm a rich woman now, Jack? You don't have to take a penniless bride!"

"Sweetheart, I would take you any way I could get you."

Mahala laughed and blushed. Then, in a sudden reversal of emotion, she moaned and hung her head.

"What is it?"

"Oh, Jack, I wish – I wish …"

"Yes?"

"It seems ungrateful to wish for anything more, but if only I had found father's money a little sooner." Mahala paused and looked back over her shoulder. She stared longingly at the stately Federal home framed among the trees.

"That? That is what you would buy with all that gold?" Jack asked.

"Yes."

"You'd just better hope the new owners don't hear about you digging that money out of their springhouse. They might have legal claim to it. After all, it *was* on their property."

"But it's my father's – and so it's mine, mine and Grandmother's!"

"Can you prove that?"

"I – I don't know." Mahala's voice dropped in volume as she realized things might not be as neat and simple as she had assumed. She grabbed Jack's arm. "Jack, you've got to keep it a secret – where we found the gold. You won't tell anyone, will you?"

"You would ask me to be dishonest?" Jack asked with mock indignation, placing a hand on his chest.

"Well, no, just – quiet."

"You don't think the truth will eventually come out? Truth has a way of doing that, you know."

"Why are you being difficult about this?" Mahala demanded. "Did you not just claim to understand my feelings? Don't you realize how important this is?"

Jack appeared to think a few minutes, contemplatively rubbing his shadowed jaw. "Well," he said at length, "if it came to it, I guess you could always bribe the land owner."

"So you won't keep my secret!" Mahala wailed, confused and dismayed by Jack's strange behavior. Just when she thought he was going to be reasonable! How could she marry such a man?

"I don't know. It's just that I can think of so many *fascinating* forms of payment."

Mahala stopped in the road and stared at him, mouth agape. A slow grin spread over Jack's face. He reached inside his coat, pulled out a key, and waved it tantalizingly in front of her. She spluttered in disbelief.

"Not – not *you*!" she cried.

"I've had my eye on that property for some time. A certain young lady of my acquaintance likes plain and simple houses for some reason, and I thought that maybe if I possessed one, it might be an added attraction."

"Oh, Jack!" Mahala exclaimed, throwing herself into his arms. She half wanted to clobber him, but her joy took the upper hand. He swung her in an arc, her feet leaving the ground. "But how–?" she questioned, pulling back to stare at the key.

"Does it really matter? You're to have the house of your dreams."

"I'm to have the man of my dreams, exasperating blackguard that he is, and *that's* all that matters."

June 1865

The time for wheat harvest had come in Northeast Georgia. It had been a dry season, so the crop stood stunted in the field. Its color had changed early from dark green to tan and then to golden brown. Carolyn watched Samson pluck a single head of wheat, rub it between his hands and blow the chaff away. The sun haloed his curly head in a moment of crystalline clarity. Slowly, thoughtfully, he chewed a bit of the grain while Carolyn and the assembled workers all waited breathlessly. At last he nodded. The kernels had cracked and softened. They all knew the most strenuous work of the year was upon them – immediately. To wait any longer would risk the wheat drying to the point that it would shatter and waste when cut.

"I don't have ready cash to pay you all," Carolyn told the field hands her husband's family had owned – now slaves no longer. "But I will. I swear I will. Mr. Dylan will be home soon. And getting in this wheat will help ensure that we all have food to eat this winter."

There were murmurs among the men, and Tania's face seemed longer than normal. They were free, all of them. They could go at any time. But she had no choice but to beg them to stay. Ultimately, it all rested with Samson. He was the undisputed leader.

The big man made a slow growling sound of thought, like a machine cranking up. Then he said, "We be at it bright and early, Miz Carolyn."

"Thank you," she sighed, smiling gratefully at all the familiar black faces. "Thank you all."

Her fate truly rested in their hands. She had known when she came back from Savannah that she would be alone here with the workers. But now, knowing Devereaux was gone for good, so much hung in the balance. Dylan would come, that was for sure. There was no way the family could continue to plant rice on the coast with the slave system in ruins, even though that fact did far more to relieve Carolyn than grieve her. But when he came, he brought almost no experience. His youthful days had been spent on the rice plantation, not an upland farm, before he turned to the ministry. And then there was the further question of how he would respond to his brother's widow. Would he even want her to stay? How *could* she? She knew Dylan had been just as shocked by Dev's suggestion that he take care of her as Carolyn had been. That meant that during the years fighting away from home, by his brother's side, he'd finally been able to put romantic thoughts of her from his mind.

Those pre-war days now felt like someone else's life, Carolyn thought that night as she gave Dev Jr. his bath. His antics convinced her it would not be long before she could add running around after him to her list of daily chores. She couldn't believe he was almost a year old. As she rocked him to sleep, she smoothed his dark hair and traced the line of his jaw. He was so like his father, who had only gotten to see him once. Just before he died.

After the child fell asleep, she went up to the attic and climbed the stairs to the widow's walk of the queenly Greek Revival-style house. She stood looking over Habersham County, bathed in silvery moonlight, and wondered, *Why am I doing this? Why does it even matter?*

But she knew the answer: the rosy-cheeked little boy now slumbering in his crib was the reason. A semblance of order, of normalcy, must be maintained at all costs, even with the world falling down in pieces around them. What little could be preserved must be. And it might be within her meager power to preserve this particular corner of the world for her son – Dev's son.

Even so, even despite her great love for the child, the emptiness of his father's loss still almost ate her alive most days. At first, she had not even wanted to wake each morning. It had been all she could do to lift her head; the weight of grief was so crushing. The only thing that made her go on was Dev Jr.. And eventually, others who cared, like Mahala, had broken through the fog of her depression.

That did not mean she was whole. She was one of the walking wounded. The peace of the mountains had begun to effect a very slow healing, but even here, where she and Dev had spent limited time together, she lived with his ghost. She met him in the barn, where he had ridden out on Revere. She met him in the garden, where he had proposed to her. And tonight she brushed against him on the widow's walk, in the memory of Donati's comet and their first kiss.

Carolyn shivered despite the warm night. How could a man be dead who still lived so strongly in her mind?

Oh, Devereaux, I miss you, she thought. *God, please help me endure this.*

She had better go to bed. Tomorrow was a big day.

The next morning, Tuesday, June 13, she found out how big.

In the warm June sun, Samson and the next strongest man swung cradles, instruments with four wooden fingers attached to a scythe, across the base of the ripened wheat. The fingers caught the falling stalks and allowed them to be laid on the ground in neat piles. Other workers came behind, grasping a bunch of sheaves and tying them into bundles with several stalks of wheat twisted together. A dozen or so sheaves would be leaned against each other, heads up, in shocks.

Carolyn knew the process well, but with a baby who was just ready to walk under foot, her place was in the house, helping cook for the workers, and taking water to them out in the field. This Carolyn did in mid-afternoon with Tania's help. Tania carried two buckets and Carolyn one, with Dev Jr. on the other hip.

Tania didn't seem to want to speak with her. Carolyn thought the maid must believe her a selfish taskmaster, goading men into harvesting wheat when they should be seeking their fortunes elsewhere. Her suspicions weren't entirely unfounded. She had observed Tania whispering intently to her husband Samson on more than one occasion recently, and what little Carolyn had overheard indicated that the black woman was eager to leave Forests of Green.

They had almost reached the field via the narrow dirt lane when Carolyn became aware the ground was vibrating beneath them. She turned in alarm and beheld the last sight she expected to see: a column of soldiers in blue trotting toward them on powerful steeds. Carolyn cried a warning to Tania, and they both moved to one side of the path, setting down their load.

As they drew even with the women, the man in front – apparently the officer in command – held up his hand, and all the soldiers behind him halted.

"Ma'am, are you Mrs. Rousseau?" he inquired.

Trembling with shock, Carolyn drew her son close to her breast. "I am. And who are you?"

"Neigh," Dev Jr. said with delight, reaching out a plump hand. Carolyn pushed it down.

The officer smiled, dismounted and introduced himself. Carolyn didn't even hear his name, so intent was she on holding Dev back from the nostrils of the invader's stallion.

"What is your business here?" she did manage to ask in a voice that was husky with fear.

His eyes swept her with the interest a man gives an attractive woman. But his reply, when it came, was another question, very business-like. "Do these people work for you?"

"Yes. They work on this estate."

"They were your slaves?"

"My husband's."

"Mmm-hmm. I see." The officer waved a hand, and his second-in-command trotted toward the workers in the field, who had ceased laboring and were staring in their direction. Carolyn also noticed something else. There were two wagons behind the column, filled with black faces, some of which she recognized as being from the neighboring Kollock and Owens estates. Her alarm escalated.

"What are you doing? This is private property. What right do you have to even be here?"

"What right do you have to force free men into labor?"

"I'm not forcing them!" Carolyn cried. "I – I'm going to pay them, as soon as I have money. And I've told them so!"

Instead of responding to her declaration, the Yankee turned toward Tania, whose moon-like brown eyes drifted up to meet his. Carolyn was astonished that the woman was capable of looking so innocent. "And are you here by your own decision?" he asked her.

Tania released the rope on the bucket she had been holding and stood up straighter. "No, Suh," she replied. "I told my husban' we oughta go, but she convince him otherwise."

Carolyn's mouth dropped open. "This is ludicrous! How could I – a woman alone with a baby – force grown men to stay?"

"Jus' lak that," Tania murmured, though she refused to look at Carolyn.

"Come with me. Let's have another talk with that husband of yours," the officer directed Tania. He glanced back at Carolyn. "And you, Ma'am, are not to interfere. The days of the slave-holding aristocracy are over. Thousands of white men died so that these blacks could be free."

Carolyn stood there frozen in mute horror as the Yankee officers conversed with the workers. Tania placed a hand on her husband's shoulder and gestured emphatically. Never had Carolyn felt so alone and powerless. A few minutes later, the blacks left cradles and sheaves lying in the field and followed the soldiers toward the waiting wagons.

"Samson!" Carolyn cried as he passed. "Samson, please!"

The big man cast a look in her direction. "I'm sorry, Miz Carolyn. You be all right."

"How? How will I be all right?"

But there was no reply. No one else spoke to her. Why would they? The "Yankee man" had made their decision clear and easy. The ex-slaves fanned off into their residences. Within minutes, they returned with bundles of their personal possessions and climbed into the vehicles beside the other blacks. All the while Carolyn stood rooted to the spot in shock. The leader gave a command, and the horses started forward. She watched until the cavalrymen and the wagons disappeared, leaving only a trail of dust, and her, standing there listening to the chirping of the crickets, clutching her squirming son.

"Neigh," said Dev again. "Bye-bye."

He and Carolyn were all alone on a two hundred acre upland farm.

She could go into town – or to a neighboring estate – and throw herself on the mercy of friends. Mahala would take her in and would in fact be angry if she later found out Carolyn *hadn't* gone to her. But Mahala and Martha already had their hands full.

236

She could pack up and buy a stage ticket south, and make her way to Brightwell. That made the most sense. Her family was there, and Henrietta. It was also most likely the first place Dylan would have gone upon returning from the battlefields of Virginia. That was what she should do, but not what she wanted to do – to arrive defeated, admitting she was helpless on her own. Admitting that without black workers, or a husband, or a family, she could do nothing. She had been weak and uncertain of herself for too many years. She'd fought too hard the last two to change that, trying to earn Dev's respect. And she wasn't going to go back on it now.

Carolyn raised her chin and marched down the lane to the field. Setting Dev Jr. down, she surveyed the scene. There was no way she could muster the strength to swing the cradle, but there were a number of fallen stacks of grain not yet bound. This at least she could do. She could finish stacking the sheaves. If she decided to close up the house and go into town, it would be time by then to bring the wheat into the barn. She could hire someone to do that, and to return to thresh it in August. Well, she'd have to get a loan for that.

Her mind working feverishly, Carolyn seized several strands of wheat and twisted them, then tied them around a sheaf. Then she did it again, and again, though the rough grain chafed her hands. Poor Dev Jr. was getting filthy, and she had to keep going after him, saying, "Come back, Devie. Stay near Mama."

At last he'd had enough and began to cry, lamenting his hungry stomach. Carolyn straightened and looked at the sky. She had almost finished what the workers had left, and there was no threat of rain. She pulled the last near-dozen sheaves together and with aching arms picked up her little boy.

They made their way to the kitchen door. The silence inside the house seemed to mock her. A shiver of fear passed through her. All those soldiers knew she was alone here. What if some of them returned to prey upon her?

Carolyn forced herself to put the possibility out of her mind and concentrated on warming some porridge for Dev Jr. She wasn't hungry herself, but the child ate ravenously, and then she sat on the settle by the side kitchen door to nurse him a bit. She stared into the falling shadows, emotionally drained and numb with fatigue.

Finally she realized the baby had fallen asleep. She would not wake him to wash his dirty legs and change his gown. The idea of doing so was more than she could contemplate just now. Carolyn placed the boy in his crib and fell across her own bed. She lay there staring at the ceiling, listening to the soft creakings of the house and remembering how enchanted the place had seemed on her very first visit here, a roomy retreat not so elegant as The Marshes but twice as welcoming. Then, it had been bustling with life. Now there were only echoes of the past.

Suddenly she sat up. Her heart thundered. Yes. Horse hooves. Fearing there would not be time to defend herself if she wasted time going to the window and ascertaining who it was, she reached into the top dresser drawer and pulled out the derringer she kept there, slipping two bullets into the chamber. Carolyn descended to the main floor, sidling up to the narrow windows beside the front door. She took a steadying breath. Over the rushing of blood through her veins and the pounding in her chest, she could barely hear the steps coming up the front porch. A man's booted, heavy steps. She prepared herself with prayer to meet what might come next. *Lord, be with me.* Then Carolyn turned to peek out the window.

End of Book Three

Denise Weimer

·

I n the fourth and final installment of The Georgia Gold Series, the Randalls and Rousseaus rebuild their lives following The War Between the States. Becoming the bride of former blockade runner Jack Randall is doubly challenging for a half-Cherokee girl from the mountains, but Mahala Franklin is determined to not only make a place in old Savannah ... but bring redemption to the Randall name as well as the city's shattered society. Her unique plan enlists the help of Jack's half-sister Sylvie and cousin Ella Beth, both of whom learn that, like Mahala and Jack, love can be found in the most unlikely places.

Meanwhile, battle-hardered Dylan Rousseau returns to the family farm in Habersham County, where his inner wounds threaten to crack him open as surely as the drought-baked earth he must learn to subdue. And somehow he must find a way past his brother's memory into the heart of Mahala's best friend Carolyn, the woman he has always loved. Weaving between them comes the secret promise - or the deadly lure? - of lost Confederate gold. Will it divide them forever and devour a family legacy, or will they emerge from the furnace of afflictions as *Bright as Gold*?

ABOUT THE AUTHOR

Denise Weimer

N ative Georgia resident Denise Weimer earned her journalism degree with a minor in history from Asbury University. Her magazine articles about Northeast Georgia have appeared in numerous regional publications. She is a wife and mother, a life-long historian, and for many years directed a mid-1800s dance group, The 1860s Civilian Society of Georgia. Her first two books in The Georgia Gold Series, *Sautee Shadows* and *The Gray Divide*, were released in 2013.

The First Book in the Georgia Gold Series:

Sautee Shadows by Denise Weimer
ISBN: 978-1-933251-66-0
Trade Soft Cover, 256 pages
Price: $15.95
April 2013

Sautee Shadows: Book One of the Georgia Gold Series is the sweeping saga of four families whose lives intertwine through romance, adventure and mystery — linking antebellum Georgia's coast and mountains during the economic expansion of the 1830s.

"A novel as intriguing in its history as it is beautiful in its descriptions. Sautee Shadows will bring to life an era of travesty and dreams and leave the reader wanting more."

—Roseanna White, author of *Ring of Secrets* and *Love Finds You in Annapolis, Maryland*

"Sautee Shadows is a rich work of history and heart, showcasing the author's love of a time and place often overlooked in history. Step into the pages of this story and you won't want to step out, nor will you have to as this is a four book series. A wonderful offering from a new novelist!"

—Laura Frantz, author of *The Frontiersman's Daughter, Courting Morrow Little, The Colonel's Lady,* and *Love's Reckoning*

"A riveting interpersonal drama and romance set in 1830s Georgia. Enticing reading all the way through, Sautee Shadows is a strong addition to historical fiction collections, recommended."

—James A. Cox, Editor-in-Chief, Midwest Reviews

The Second Book in the Georgia Gold Series:

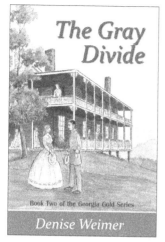

The Gray Divide by Denise Weimer
ISBN 978-0-9881897-2-0
Trade Soft Cover, 256 pages
Price: $15.95
September 2013

In **The Gray Divide: Book Two of the Georgia Gold Series**, sibling rivalry, romance and an unsolved murder threaten relationships. Hidden loyalties are exposed and the lives of four families and a nation endangered as Georgia seeks to become its own republic, only to be plunged into civil war.

Conflicting attractions continue between half-Cherokee hotel owner Mahala Franklin and arrogant ship builder and rival Jack Randall. Awkward coastal socialite Carolyn Calhoun must choose between two very different men, rice planter Devereaux Rousseau and his minister brother Dylan. Can she even be sure of the love of the one she chooses, or will she merely be a prize?

"An exciting historical novel, its roots in the forced emigration of southeastern tribes and the story expanding into mystery as the Union divides."
–Paul Yarbrough for Southern Literary Review, author of *Mississippi Cotton*

"Chocked full of history, with dialogue true to the time, characters that intrigue and beguile, and what promises to be an adventurous and exciting journey, this is certain to be an interesting, entertaining series."
— Christy Tillery French, Midwest Reviews

"Reminds me of the works of one of my favorite Southern authors, Eugenia Price."
— Brenda Knight Graham, author of *Her Name Was Rebekah* and *On Wings of Songs*

CPSIA information can be obtained
at www.ICGtesting.com
Printed in the USA
FFHW02n1921190918
48490244-52357FF

9 780988 189744